Hale County

By Chad R Martin

ISBN-13: 978-1-944583-38-5

Contact:

Email: chadmartin39@gmail.com

Published by Chad R Martin

Dedications

Dedicated with love, to my family, to my friends, and to all those who have a dream and chase it. To my children I say this: never be afraid to be who you are. Never fear your dreams, nor let failure hold you back. Be you and embrace it. Dad loves you, always.

To Wraith and Psycho; this story started in a tiny building, in a squared circle, and with trust that you would let me tell the stories and origins of these characters. This wouldn't have been possible without your friendship, trust, & love. RIP Psycho.

And to Mrs Kathy Schexnayder, this book never gets completed without you pushing me every time I saw you at the Tobie.

Contents

Book 1: The Asylum 7

Prologue..8

Chapter 1 12

Chapter 2 31

Chapter 3 48

Chapter 4 70

Chapter 5 88

Chapter 6 105

Chapter 7 129

Chapter 8 145

Chapter 9 153

Chapter 10 169

Book 2: Awakenings..203

Chapter 11 204

Chapter 12 223

Chapter 13 237

Chapter 14 254

Chapter 15 280

CHAPTER 16 294

Book 3: Oncoming Storm..314

CHAPTER 17 315

CHAPTER 18 341

CHAPTER 19 359

CHAPTER 20 372

CHAPTER 21 397

CHAPTER 22 423

CHAPTER 23 443

CHAPTER 24... 459

CHAPTER 25... 486

EPILOGUE 513

    About the Author 520

Book 1: The Asylum

'We are each our own devil, and we make this world our hell'-
Oscar Wilde

Prologue

A brilliant flash of light lit up the small iron fenced cemetery, followed by a loud clap of thunder. Large drops of rain began pelting the century old headstones. The wrought-iron fencing leaned heavily in places; the soggy earth no longer able to support the cumbersome weight of the iron barrier after a half century of neglect. It was the oldest cemetery in Hale County. As the rain began falling harder, it was no doubt the last place anyone wanted to be, especially Sheriff Jake Hooks.

The tall, imposing Sheriff wore an irritated expression as he shined the large Mag flashlight on the unmarked grave his deputies were digging up. He was a throwback to a different era of lawmen, straight out of the Old West. His manner was rugged and non-amused, and while the local Indian Medicine Man called him an "old soul", the truth was that Jake was just perennially pissed off. If his gruff demeanor wasn't enough to warn the unaccustomed to his dangerous disposition, the fresh scar that jaggedly ran from beneath his cowboy hat certainly was. It started at the corner of his left eye, ran over the bridge of his nose, down the opposite cheek just above his lip before disappearing under his jawline. It was enough to give even the stoutest of men pause and avert their gaze.

Jake cared little for what people thought of him. Hell, he wasn't even that old. But life didn't count years, it counted mileage, and he had plenty of that in spades. When it came to his job, there was no one with more tenacity. Even as he watched his men digging into the earth, the Sherriff knew he wasn't going to like what they found.

The grave was fresh, and he knew no one had been buried in that graveyard in the last twenty years. An unknown caller had phoned in the tip; another mystery in a county that needed no more mysteries. His gaze hardened as he watched his men dig deeper into the muddy earth, the thunder and lightning reflecting the mood in his eyes.

The rain bounced uncaringly off of the Sheriff's cowboy hat. It was only the three of them out there, searching for any clue as to who had dug the grave. He put his deputies to digging as he lorded over them, suspicious eyes attuned to his surroundings. Jake doubted they would find much, especially in this god-awful monsoon. Still, it gave them something to do other than irritate him with questions he couldn't possibly have an answer to...yet. He had no doubt he would find the culprit. His mother used to say he was "part blood hound, part Cherokee" and that he could "tree a coon better than any hunting dog". *Probably some damn high school kids playing a prank, videoing us and going to upload it on that damn YouTube,* he thought angrily. If that was the case, they would regret it.

His face hardened even more, if that was possible. It wasn't that Jake Hooks was an ugly man, quite the contrary according to most of the women in Hale County. It was more his sour disposition than the scar that rubbed people the wrong way. He didn't care. Hale County was his, and you didn't cross Sheriff Jake Hooks...everyone knew that. At least, they should. His county was going to shit, and not by coincidence.

He heard the loud thud of a shovel hitting something solid, bringing him out of his train of thought. As he turned his gaze to the noise, a beam of light blinded his vision then was quickly removed. The Sheriff gazed into the face of the trepid deputy holding the offending flashlight. Jake didn't blink. "Well?" he asked irritated.

"Um, it looks like a coffin, sir."

Sure enough, just about three feet under the surface, Jake could make out something made of wood. The deputy seemed to shrink under the Sheriff's withering stare. "Get it out." *Why wouldn't there be a coffin, you damn fool, you're in a cemetery.* Yet that was the point. There shouldn't be any new coffins here.

Jake motioned for the other deputy to come over and help. The steady rainfall made the object hard to grasp and even harder to lift. Finally, the deputies managed to hoist a six-foot-long makeshift wooden casket out of the hole. It was covered in mud, grass, and rain. The newness of the casket was obvious as the wood still had its light sheen as opposed to the grayish aged wood one would expect to find in an old cemetery.

The thunder and lightning increased in intensity as the rain pounded the earth harder almost in outrage of the casket being removed from its place of rest. The skinny deputy with the offensive light looked up at the Sheriff in hesitation. They were fidgety, more-so than usual, and Jake knew why. Ulterior motives, everyone in Hale County had them and his deputies were no different.

Jake stared steadily back, unflinching. "Open it."

The deputy with the flashlight climbed his way out of the gravesite, leaving the other deputy to remain in the freshly excavated hole. "Y-y-yessir," the flashlight deputy said as he kneeled over the wooden casket.

Uncertain, but doing as they were told, the deputies used crowbars to pry off the lid of the fairly new looking casket. The deputies flinched back as a putrid odor rushed over them. Almost as fast as the lightning that was raging in the skies around them, Jake whipped his .44 Magnum from his holster.

The muzzle of the gun flashed in the storm, quickly followed by a deafening report that was almost masked by the thunder. The bullet slammed into the face of the larger deputy that was still in the hole, exploding from the back of his head and spraying the simple marker and mud with his brains.

The flashlight deputy had the temerity to look surprised before his face became a blank mask, all timidity gone. Jake didn't hesitate. His finger expertly squeezed the trigger of the massive handgun. The deputy made no expression as the bullet tore into his chest. The force was so great it lifted him slightly off his feet and flung him into the grave where he landed atop the corpse of the other deputy.

If he had any regrets Jake didn't show it as he holstered his gun, nor did he look to see if anyone else had seen or heard him. It was Hale County. They were alone. If someone had heard the shots well then so be it, everything was going to Hell anyway. The time for self-restraint was over.

Jake knelt by the casket to get a better look, his knees sinking into the rain-soaked mud. He pointed his flashlight inside, ignoring the odor. The only emotion on his face was the set of his jaw and the tightening around his eyes. "I'll be damned."

Chapter 1

The road was winding and narrow, twisting through a wild and overgrown forest. The gravel of the unkempt road spun out from beneath the speeding sheriff's old Grayish Dodge Truck as the siren echoed hauntingly off the thick greenery of the Tennessee hills. Mud and grime caked the lower chassis in the sparingly washed vehicle. The sheriff wasn't known for his cleanliness nor his friendliness for that matter. He had a mean streak and didn't hide it. The cowboy hat he wore on his shaggy dark hair hid the tell-tale lines on his forehead as did the dark shades that covered the crow's feet around his eyes. The scruffy growth on his face couldn't quite be called a beard which added to his sour appearance.

His boot mashed the pedal clean to the floor sending the truck into overdrive. The hemi roared as the truck made an angry lurch forward, the engine growling in protest. The sheriff's lips curved into a slight smirk as he closed in on the champagne-colored Crown Victoria. It took a lot to get him excited about anything anymore. This was one of those things.

The Crown Vic wasn't slowing down so the sheriff decided the driver might need some incentive. With a casualness that most people use to breathe the sheriff nudged the cars bumper with the iron cage attached to the front of his truck. One warning, that's all he would give. The driver of the car must have sensed that as well because he immediately pulled to the side of the narrow road leaving half of the car on the pavement while the rest was nesting in the grass.

The sheriff parked directly behind the Crown Vic and thoughtfully rubbed a hand across the stiff stubble on his face before stepping from the truck. The driver of the freshly polished car, a tall well-dressed black man, stepped from the vehicle visibly angry. The large muscular sheriff never hesitated as he walked towards the furious man that was shouting at him.

"What the hell, man?! You know how much this paint job cost me?" The man appeared well cultured, even handsome. Right then though he just looked pissed. "Give a cracker a badge and they think they can do anything."

"License and registration," the sheriff said, never breaking stride.

The angry man walked towards the sheriff, not intimidated in the least. "I got your registration right here," he said defiantly, flipping the sheriff off.

That stopped the sheriff. His smirk turned dark. He took off his shades, dark eyes glaring into those of the brown skinned man before him. The sheriff's hand suddenly snapped down towards his hip. In the blink of an eye, he whipped the .44 Magnum from its holster training the barrel on the startled man who reflexively went for his own gun only to realize he didn't have one.

"Oh, I see! Po-po gotta pull a gun on a black man!"

"Well, that's just racist," the sheriff sneered mockingly.

"I still don't see how your old ass draws that heavy piece of iron so quickly," the man said, his expression softening into a hearty grin.

The sheriff smiled back and just as quickly re-holstered the pistol. "Feels weird without one on your hip doesn't it Marcus?"

"It really does, Jake. But hey, it was time I traded one uniform in for another. Mayor has a much nicer ring to it than deputy...and the pay's better."

"You haven't won re-election yet."

"Give it time, give it time. The election is almost upon us, my friend. Just a few more weeks. I'll win them back over."

"Of all the towns in all the country it WOULD be ours that has elections on Halloween."

"What can I say, you backwoods white folk are superstitious as hell. How have you been brother?" Marcus said, pulling the sheriff in for a quick hug.

"I'm good. Just out patrolling" Jake replied with a smile as he released the hug.

"Uh huh," Marcus responded slyly, "I know what you're patrolling."

Jake gave a slight chuckle. "Yeah, well, that's the least I can do for the son-of-a-bitch."

"Ole Chief Malone is going to catch you banging his wife one day then all hell is going to break loose."

"After what they did to Cutty..." Jake frowned, letting his voice trail off.

Marcus clasped him on the shoulder, "I know brother, I know. Those crooked city cops think they can do anything."

"With Grey running the board of Aldermen, they can. That's why we are all counting on you amigo."

"Amigo? Do I look Mexican to you?" he laughed at Jake's predictable term of endearment. Marcus' jovial attitude turned serious. "I can't fire Malone because of Grey's control. People are scared, Jake. That whole mess with the Donaldson's..." The Mayoral candidate could only shake his head sadly. "Any leads?"

Jake kicked the loose gravel in frustration. "None. They are just gone. Nothing was packed, both cars still in the garage. It's like they vanished off the face of the damn earth. Malone has been no help at all."

"Been a lot of that going around."

The sheriff could only nod his head in agreement. The tension in Hale County was palpable. The fear was so bad that people only spoke of it behind closed doors. A rumbling broke the silence. Both men looked up past the canopy of tree limbs into the grey skies.

"We haven't had sunshine in a week. It's depressing" Marcus said as he moved towards the back of his car. "And speaking of depressing. Man, seriously, I just got this paint job."

Jake bent down and rubbed his hand over the small black mark where his grill had tapped the bumper. "It'll buff out. Take it to my cousin, tell him to put it on the county tab."

"The county is broke."

"Even better, I never really liked the bastard anyway" Jake replied with a half-grin.

"Do you like *anybody*?" Marcus laughed sarcastically.

"I like you...Amigo." He put his shades back on and walked back to his truck. "Mayor vs Mayor," the Sheriff said wryly, shaking his head. "Come over for a beer sometime. You haven't been around in a while," he said over his shoulder.

"You got it. And Jake..."

The sheriff stopped and turned back to his friend.

"...be careful man. Malone is bad news."

"Careful? Yeah, that's not me" Jake said with a chuckle and hopped in his patrol truck.

Marcus watched him speed off as the rumbling overhead grew louder.

Hale County.

Trouble.

It didn't take a smart man to see something bad was coming. Everyone knew it, everyone except Jake Hooks. The sheriff didn't have a superstitious bone in his body. The man only knew what was right in front of him. He was reckless to the point of stupidity. It was one of the reasons Marcus quit the department though he would never tell his friend that. That recklessness was also the reason Jake was perfect for the job. But even Jake wasn't invincible. Sheriffs in Hale County didn't have a long tenure and Jake was well past his shelf life.

Drops of rain speckled the car. Marcus ran to the driver's seat and strapped himself in. Change was coming. Whether good or bad was anyone's guess. One thing was for certain, fall was almost over and bitter days were on their way with his best friend right in the middle of it. Marcus peered down the now empty highway. "Be careful brother."

A dilapidated computer sat on an old Formica kitchen table.

A pale hand reached out and hit the power button on the old box shaped monitor, which blared to life with a tired whine. The long, narrow fingers drifted across the keyboard, typing an address into the URL. The old computer processors commenced their search and began loading the page, which seemed to take forever due to the outdated software. The hands, however, hovered over the keyboard with patience until the page finally loaded.

The web page blared to life with some eerie X-Files type music playing annoyingly in the background. The page was a jumbled mess of pictures from just about every myth known to man. Bigfoot, vampires, UFO's, ghosts; they were plastered all over the site in a way that could only make sense to a schizophrenic. The page header explained it all very simplistically with its bold, in your face, header that seemed to jump out of the screen in an electric blue glowing old English font.

The Dark Truth

Conspiracy theories revealed!

The ghostly hand grasped the mouse and moved the cursor over the link that read "Web Streams." A drop-down menu gave a listing of all the web streams that were archived. The mysterious hand clicked on the latest link. After a few moments of loading, and without any preamble, the screen was filled with the image of a scrawny, long bearded man with piercing blue eyes that shined as brightly as the wild look that flashed from them.

The man was disheveled and unkempt. If there was ever a picture of insanity, William Tyler was most certainly it. His age was hard to tell because of his state of uncleanliness, as well as the bandana he wore that covered his mouth and nose like an old timey bank robber. William wore a mask before the pandemic made it common place. Only his eyes, which looked sunken and bloodshot, gave any indication of what he might look like underneath his disguise. William wore an old toboggan that stretched over his ears, hiding much of his head. He could have been 25 or 35, maybe even 45. But whatever his age, William looked unhealthy. His hands shook visibly and out of sync with the nervous twitching of his head. But if any of that bothered William, it didn't show as the weird man peered into the camera.

William began to speak. Whatever preconception his image seemed to convey, the passion and intelligence in his voice spoke of something else entirely. When William finally spoke it was with a quick broken rhythm, as if at any moment he would be out of time and desperately needed to say what was on his mind.

"I'm just going to jump right into it. William Tyler here, insanity and Transformer virus survivor, local expert on strange and forbidden lore, the kind that seems to permeate our poor county, man. I keep my identity concealed because if they knew who I was they would throw me back into that Hell I finally escaped from. Ain't nobody sending me back there, man, nobody. I tell you up front that I've had psychological issues but I ain't crazy, I ain't crazy at all. They messed with my brain, man. I don't hide from my past like so many others in Hale County. I wear it on my sleeves proudly, my fellow truthers. The only way to the promised land is through the darkness, and I plan on leading the charge through the chaos! There have been many topics covered on this website from werewolves to UFO's but there is one subject that has been taboo."

A large thud echoed from somewhere behind William. He turned to listen, head cocked at a strange, unnatural angle. When he was convinced that nothing was going to come out of nowhere and attack him, he continued. William took a slow, steadying breath.

"The subject I want to talk about is our own Hale County, and that illegal mental institute that hides way back in those dark haunted hills, man. You see, there are evil forces at play people, creeping in the background, unseen by the few good people left in this county. Real shit, not that hokey made-up garbage you see on those specials of the week, man." His eyes darted all about the room he was in, once again in expectation of something waiting to get him. His hands kept fidgeting around his chin as if they moved of their own accord. When William finally spoke, his voice and manner seemed to change dramatically. There was an anxiety he could no longer hide, the tempo of his speech increasing.

"That's right my friends; I'm talking about the thing we are all afraid to speak out against; that vile evil that resides in the form of science! Except, it's not science. It's Frankenstein butchery! The horrific experiments of Dippel, Aldini, Brukhonenko, Mengele, and so many others are NOTHING to what happens up there! I know! I've seen it first-hand!"

Tears glistened in William's eyes as his passion overwhelmed him. He stuttered for more words, fought to control himself. His voice came out in a whisper. His eyes grew distant.

"What they did to me..."

A large thud, much larger and far closer than the one before, startled William. Genuine fear washed through him. He turned to the camera in a hurry, half-standing as he did. He leaned in closely, voice suddenly becoming clear and purposeful.

"They are everywhere, the eyes and ears of the darkness that resides in Hale County..." William gave a quick look around as an even louder, more emphatic sound echoed through his room. He stared once more into the camera. "Oh shit. Gotta hide. I'll continue this later if I can." He squinted at something off screen, his posture becoming statuesque as he strained to hear what he imagined was out there. He suddenly turned back to the screen "Protect yourselves."

William reached towards his own computer and the feed went dead. The ghostly hand stretched out its boney fingers and did the same.

"Stop!" a deep baritone voice commanded loudly.

Steven James ducked into an alley, even in the cool October air, his hair drenched with sweat which was plastered to his head. His clothes, a dark green hoodie and khaki pants, looked as if they hadn't been washed in weeks. That was the least of his concerns. He ran down the narrow alley in a panic, tripping over various debris in an effort to get away from his pursuers. Steven could see the opening of the alley looming closer. He could see the grass and daylight on the other side.

Small town alleys weren't like their big city counterparts. These were simply tiny walkways unintentionally made because someone didn't want to extend their property another five feet and join another tiny row of small businesses. Kids walking home from school used it frequently as a pass through from the Shell gas station on the one side to the four-screen family-owned Tobie Theater on the other. To Steven, it was his opportunity to escape.

He managed a quick look over his shoulder. His red, tear-stained eyes grew wide at what they saw…two very large sheriff deputies entering the alley behind him, looking very pissed. Steven felt a bit of renewed hope as his feet hit the grass and he raced out of the alley, the shouts of the angry deputies calling out after him. He couldn't afford to be caught again.

Archibald Brubaker was a mountain of a man. He had a promising football career until he broke the jaw of an assistant coach who tried to make him run sprints for being late to practice. Two years after getting kicked off the University football team for disciplinary reasons, the former defensive tackle landed on the sheriff's department. No one but the Sheriff dared to call him by his first name, everyone just called him Bru; and Bru hated to run.

His partner, another large beefy man named Rodney Hankins, was two steps ahead of him and exited the alley first. Bru could see they were losing ground to the tiny dope head they were pursuing. The punk was heading towards a creek. If he made it to the other side before them then they would lose him. There was good money in catching these guys. It was THE reason they hadn't called for backup. That thought spurred him on.

Steven saw the creek before him. This was his chance at escape, the only one he would get. Unlike those muscle-bound jerks chasing him, Steven was light on his feet and the creek had to only be about eight feet across. He could clear it and not break stride. The deputies would have to slow down to get across. That would give him a huge lead. After that, he could get lost in the jumble of houses, schools, and trees that made up the small community of Hale.

He gave one final look back as he neared the creek, almost as a snub to the living mountains that pursued him, then he leapt. There was a moment of sheer exhilaration and freedom in his flight across the creek. For a brief second, the world around him slowed, then suddenly seemed to fast-forward as he crashed in a loud splash in the half empty creek. The shock of the cold late fall water caused Steven to momentarily pause from its bitter bite. He recovered quickly but not nearly fast enough.

Bru saw the punk crash into the creek and begin to frantically drag himself out on the other side. Rodney didn't hesitate and jumped into the muddy water.

Steven felt a large hand grab his hoodie and swung wildly, connecting solidly with Rodney's chin.

The deputy only stared at him with cool amusement.

Steven turned to flee and caught a crushing fist to the face from Bru. The only thing that kept him upright was the massive paw of the deputy that had just hit him. Steven was sure his face was destroyed completely as the copper taste of blood filled his mouth; his lungs were stinging from the chase as they drank in the chilly air.

Rodney searched the dope-head roughly, pulling out a few small bags of marijuana that were ready to sell as well as a wad of twenties that were secured with a rubber band. "Payday," he said as he smiled at Bru, flashing the wad of twenties at his partner.

"Please, please," Steven pleaded through broken teeth and a crushed nose, "no jail...no jail."

Bru pulled the junkie in close, menace filling the large man's voice. The last thing Steven heard before unconsciousness took him were Bru's foreboding words.

"Jail? You'll wish that's where you were going."

Then, blackness took him.

Hale County Mental Institute sat way back in the deep wooded hills of Hale County Tennessee. It was haunted, if you believed the local legends. It had been a prison back in the early part of the twentieth century. But much like everything else in the county, its distance from a main highway, as well as its location in the steep hills, made it a liability. So, the state government decided on a new prison three counties over where the interstate ran through, leaving a bunch of people jobless.

A couple of decades later, it was turned into a mental institute for the criminally insane; although criminals weren't the only ones treated there. The government called it a mental institute, the county called it the asylum, and the inmates...they called it Hell. Rumors of all kinds, from the silly to the frightening, became associated with the place in the past few years. But whether any of them were true or not, the very appearance of the asylum was enough to ignite a primal reaction from even the bravest souls.

Amanda Richardson wasn't a believer in superstition, fantasy, or fairy tales. She was a hard-nosed investigative reporter that dug into the most controversial, and sometimes dangerous, stories with unbridled tenacity. The truth was her religion. Yet even Amanda, long dark hair pulled back into a tight bun, gave a start as the long drive opened up into the parking lot of the mental institute.

The walls were tall, made of a dark grey stone that had been worn and mildewed from decades of weather damage. There were guards stationed in the guard towers, as if it were still a functioning prison. She hadn't realized the asylum, even one for the criminally insane, had that kind of protection. She was glad to see the front of the institution contained an office area, obviously a much more recent addition. She parked her car in the nearest available space and gathered her things: tape recorder, notebook, pen, .38.

She paused before putting the gun in her bag. Perhaps it wasn't wise to take it into the building, not that she was expecting something to happen in there. Finally, giving a sigh, she tucked it into the glove box. Amanda didn't like leaving it behind. She had been in some rough places over the years, and it had come in handy. Although she never actually used it, it was enough just for it to be seen, especially when some cocky low-life, who thought she was some dainty female, pegged her for easy prey. One look at her gun and none ever dared to actually try and find out.

Amanda gave the glove box one last look then stepped out of her car, locking it up tight. She stepped into the nippy wind and pulled her coat tighter. She headed for the office building, her high heels clicking on the pavement with each step, echoing off the old stone walls. She understood the reason for the rumors. She glanced up at the ominous walls one last time, reached for the door handle automatically and paused against her will, transfixed by this place.

Get a hold of yourself, Amanda, she chastised herself silently, *you're a professional.* Still, she couldn't quite shake the unease that the asylum seemed to cast upon her. Her hand slowly released the handle and went to the bag she carried on her shoulder but stopped halfway there, remembering she had left her gun in the car. *Dammit.*

Her attention was drawn to the tree line that surrounded the entire property. Someone was watching her. Amanda couldn't see them, but she was sure they were. Her gut was hardly ever wrong. She gave the area a quick glance then took a deep breath.

Nothing.

Something.

This time there was no pause. She quickly grabbed the door handle and entered the asylum, determined not to look back.

The eyes that watched her from the forest edge were blood red, mesmerized, and curious by the dark-haired lady. As they watched her disappear into the asylum, the eyes were full of something else...hunger. Sweat poured down the dirty, bearded face of the impossibly large man, his long stringy hair dangling like moss over a tattered orange jumpsuit.

A meaty, grime covered hand reached down, without looking, eyes still fixated on the door the reporter had just disappeared through and latched on to the lifeless mass lying in the damp leaves beside it. Giving an inhuman grunt, the large man gave a quick, powerful tug, moving further into the forest.

A groggy human moan came from the form he was dragging. Without looking, the man gave one giant powerful swing that connected with a sickening thud. Then...silence. He continued his purposeful lumber deeper into the forest as a trail of blood soaked the earth behind him.

Hale County Community College was small, even for a junior college. It was, however, the closest one for a hundred miles. Kids from all over the northern part of the state attended it, at least the kids who couldn't afford to go anywhere else. The college itself was old, just like the rest of the county, but the teaching curriculum was one of the best in the state. That distinction did little to help the enrollment grow as the rest of Hale County's reputation tended to disparage a greater portion of potential students from visiting the campus.

"Papers are due Monday! I'll be in my office til 3!"

The halls crowded with students rushing from their classrooms, ready to get the weekend started. In their midst, a thin, dark haired man was jostling papers into a leather satchel as he walked along the hall. He seemed barely into his thirties, horned rim glasses perched precariously on the end of his nose. He gave a nod to a few students as he passed and was soon standing in front of an office door. The title on the placard read: Professor Jason Locke, History Department, Office 319.

Jason shook his head as he fished his office keys from his pocket with a half-hearted chuckle. Six months after he first saw it and it still made him laugh. He never considered himself a professor. His background was archeology, although he rarely went on any digs. *I'm a historian more than anything,* he thought dejectedly, *yet they only want to learn about bones. I'm not a damn paleontologist. What the hell is wrong with kids wanting to know their history...any history?*

Working at the junior college in Hale County required teaching more than one subject and left little time for excursions. He preferred human history; it was one of the reasons he took the job. The nearby Cherokee Reservation was a gold mine of artifacts, but he had yet been able to get out there. Jason stepped into the office, locking the door behind him. He cursed himself for the thousandth time for not accepting those offers from Yale, Harvard, hell, even Tennessee State would have made more sense. Still, he had to admit this area intrigued him.

The whole mystery of Hale County pulled at its innermost curiosity. Very little was known about the area, even by local standards. The locals, rather than the elders, were very tight lipped. It was almost as if talking about the past would call forth some dark plague. Superstition and folklore were very much the foundation for the way urban development had avoided Hale County. Alternate roadways were created to steer well around that part of the country. That was what intrigued Jason. He needed to know all he could about his new home.

Jason sighed as he slung the satchel onto a shelf. *I'm my own worst enemy.*

The office was small, bordering on claustrophobic. There was just enough room for a desk, his chair and a couple of chairs on the opposite side. A trip to the Lowes in Nashville provided him with enough shelving to house his book collection, which reached the ceiling of the tiny room. He was promised a much bigger space once the renovation on the new wing was done. In the meantime, his office kept piling up with clutter. Organized chaos is what his wife had called it.

His stomach grumbled. The coffee he had for breakfast wasn't going to sustain him. He needed food. A greasy burger from Homer's Hamburger Haven would hit the spot. Jason usually ate fairly healthy, his wife saw to that. But she was out of town, so it was time to indulge. He would simply call in his order and by the time he got across town to Homer's, it would be ready. Now, all he had to do was find his menu.

Jason began shuffling through the papers on his desk until a small brown package caught his attention. He picked it up, and examined it carefully, a leery look upon his face. He gave the little box a light shake. Whatever was inside was solid. There were no markings of any kind on the package, just his name typed in a typical Arial font. He took a letter opener from his desk and expertly cut the package open, revealing a plain white 6x6 box.

His neck began to tingle, a small feeling of foreboding creeping through him. Jason suddenly didn't want to open the box. How had it gotten there? Who was it from? *His office had been locked, hadn't it?* He quickly put the unopened box back on the desk.

You're being ridiculous, he chastised himself silently. While he knew that his reaction was unfounded, there was still that sense of dread. *Why?*

Jason shook off the feeling and picked the box back up. His fingers hovered over the lid for a moment, breathing becoming labored.

"Ridiculous," he said out loud to break the awful silence of the office.

Fingers grasping the lid with a firm grip, he took a deep, steadying breath. His breathing became more shallow with each little movement of the lid. Why was this affecting him so much? Where was this sudden dread coming from? Jason shook his head, the lid was almost clear of the main body of the box. His eyes narrowed in anticipation...

RING! RING! RING!

Jason jumped at the sudden noise. The box slipped out of his grasp, bounced off the desk, and fell underneath it.

"Damnit..." he swore, trying to calm himself.

The phone kept ringing insistently.

He tried to see where the box landed as he groped blindly for his cell phone. Where could it have fallen?

There.

Jason tapped the answer button on his phone, never taking his eyes off the box as he knelt down behind the desk.

"Hello?" he asked, breathing heavily as his hands reached out for the box.

Got it.

He sat the box on the desk, sliding into his chair as he did so, listening to the voice on the other end of the call.

"Oh, hey honey. No, I'm fine…you just startled me." *That was an understatement,* he thought to himself, eyes glued once more to the box.

Slowly and intently, he began to take the lid off again, only half hearing the conversation.

"No, no, I wasn't expecting anyone else. I meant that the phone startled me. You know me, buried in my work. How's Rome?" Usually, her playful attempts at jealousy were cute, but this box from an unknown sender had him curious.

With one simple jerk, the lid came free. The furrow in his brow deepened at the sight of the object. It was a small pouch made of deer skin tied off with a worn leather string. A shiver of trepidation shook through his fingers as he began carefully untying the pouch string. His eyes went wide, an expression of disbelief and panic flooded over him.

BAM, BAM, BAM, BAM!!

The pouch slipped from his grasp and fell to the desk once more with a heavy thud, the loud knock on his door startling him once again.

"What the hell??"

The knock rattled the door once more.

Jason realized his wife was speaking to him.

"What? Oh no, sorry hon. I have an emergency, student conference. Call you later."

His eyes went to the object that spilled out of the pouch and was now rolling across his desk. It came to rest beside his mouse pad. He was transfixed by the sight of it.

The rapping at the door continued.

Jason reluctantly pushed himself away from his desk. He opened the door, a familiar face staring concernedly back at him.

The young man, who was clean cut save for the shoulder length hair and the heavy metal T-shirt, gave Jason a measuring look. "Are you ok, Prof?"

Jason glanced at his desk then back to the young man in his doorway. "Yeah, yeah JC, I'm fine." He left the door open and went back to his desk, casually sliding some papers over the object. "What can I do for you, Mr. Michaels?"

"Mr. Michaels?" JC asked quizzically, "Are you feeling okay?"

Jason gave a quick laugh. "Sorry about that. Crazy day. What's going on?"

"Heading out to get some lunch, want anything?"

Any hunger Jason felt earlier was gone. He glanced down at his desk, the object of his sudden loss of appetite hiding under those papers. "No thank you, I'm fine."

"Alright Prof." JC began backing out of the door, closing it in the process.

A thought occurred to Jason. He had to tear his gaze away from the desk and back to JC. "How did the auditions go?"

"It probably sucked," JC said with a shrug. "Ashlyn is coming over later to find out with me. They are supposed to post the cast list sometime this afternoon. I'll probably end up getting an ensemble part."

Jason looked at his young friend. "All roles are important."

"So says the man over the entire History department."

"Touché."

"Later Prof."

JC shut the door, leaving Jason alone in the room once more. He reached for the papers and removed them from covering the object. It had his attention, mesmerizingly so. He took a steadying breath, reached across the desk and pulled the object towards him using the paper it had landed on. Jason examined it disbelievingly.

It was just slightly smaller than a billiard ball, made of granite, mostly covered in a red swirling pattern. Almost, that is, with the exception of the snow-white owl on one side and the brownish cougar on the opposite. The images were slightly faded and weather worn but there was no mistaking them for what they were. His heartbeat faster.

"Impossible."

Chapter 2

The office was cozy, almost familial, with soft natural colors and inviting furniture. Various books on psychology lined the shelves complementing the degrees and certificates that adorned the walls. It was made to put patients at ease. At that moment Amanda Richardson felt as comfortable as she could ever remember being. It was that feeling that put her on edge. She straightened her posture and forced herself to focus.

"Can I get you anything to drink, Miss Richardson?" The low baritone voice was fluid, intelligent and calming. There was no doubt in her mind that it was the voice of a man who was accustomed to being in control and supremely assured of himself.

As she studied the man sitting before her in the high-backed leather chair, hands steepled just below his chin, dark eyes boring into hers, Amanda was reminded of something her first mentor had warned her about: *It's not the wolf you have to worry about, he is what he is. It's the lamb that lulls you to sleep.*

Dr. Evan Michaels fit that description, the wolf in sheep's clothing. His eyes were kind yet powerful. His voice was steady, thoughtful. He was almost gorgeous, she had to admit that; his deep dark eyes matching his dark, perfect hair. His body was lean and controlled, a living statue. His smile. Well, she had seen or met very few men that could match the magnetism of his smile.

"Miss Richardson?"

The sound of her name snapped her back to the moment. *Damn,* she thought, irritated with herself for her lapse in control. She could feel the blood rushing to her cheeks.

"I'm sorry," she said, a little too quickly, "I'm fine."

"Are you sure?"

Stop looking at me like that, she thought, fighting to regain her composure. *I've interviewed heads of state!* She took a silent breath.

"I'm fine, really. Long drive."

"Alright, then what can I do for you?"

It was her turn to make him feel uncomfortable. Subtlety wasn't the way to handle this, so she dove in headfirst. "What is really going on here at this so-called institute?"

He smiled slightly, his outward calm never wavering. "Miss Richardson, the only reason I consented to do this interview was because you assured me that you were interested in doing research on psychological effects of the human mind."

"There have been numerous reports of illegal experiments, patients going missing...unexplained deaths." She let that last part linger in the air.

"I suppose those same reports claim we are also recreating Frankenstein's monster, hiding bigfoot, and doing autopsies on aliens?"

She glared at him. "Are you?"

Evan dropped his hands, his expression turning thoughtful. "Amanda Richardson, investigative reporter for KETV out of Nashville. Winner of the Casey Award for Meritorious Journalism, Heywood Broun Award, 2011 IRE Award winner, etc. etc.."

Amanda felt her composure slip just a fraction as Evan listed her accomplishments.

"I wonder," he continued smoothly, "is this to be your Pulitzer story? The one that gets you the one prize that's avoided you?"

"I'm after the truth."

"The truth? Miss Richardson, you've come all the way from Nashville to chase ghost stories and sensationalism, neither of which I have time for. Is this what's become of your career?"

Ouch! That stung. But Amanda was determined to not let it phase her, which she assumed was the doctor's strategy. "So, you're saying the accusations are false," she stated pointedly. "You're not experimenting with unethical practices and procedures?"

"What I am saying, Amanda, is that you are dealing in fairy tales and hysteria when there are real medical issues at hand that REAL people are attempting to deal with on a daily basis. THAT is what we treat in this institution."

She wasn't sure if it was the personal use of her name or the passion that exuded from him, but Amanda backed off of the sensationalism. Maybe Evan was just who he said he was; then again, maybe not. He was good but so was she. She smiled a slight smile, her own little weapon. "So you have no problems giving me the full tour?"

Evan didn't hesitate. "None at all," he said happily, his own disarming smile on full display.

There was a brief knock on his door.

"Come in."

A young nurse, dressed in scrubs, long blonde hair pinned up, stepped into the office holding a chart. Amanda thought the young lady could have been a model, she even walked with purpose towards Evan's desk as if to show the intruding female reporter that this walkway belonged to her and her alone. The nurse handed the chart to him, which he briefly perused. Evan signed it quickly and handed the chart back.

"Sam, have Miss Terry hold all my calls." He gave a knowing look to Amanda, rising from his chair. The reporter followed his lead. "I'll be giving a tour of the facility for the next hour or so."

"Certainly, Dr. Michaels," the young nurse confirmed and smiled.

Evan motioned for Amanda to follow him from the office. As the door shut behind them, Sam's smile melted. Her eyes drilled into Amanda's back with pure malice.

William hugged his legs close to his chest, eyes clinched tightly shut. He tried to concentrate on breathing, but it was difficult. The small wooden box he was in pressed in on all sides. He felt it was constricting him, but there, in that tiny space, he was safe. He pulled his skull cap down further over his ears and cinched his scarf tighter. Even his eyes were hidden behind a pair of dark sunglasses.

He had barely gotten out of his secret cabin. There had been no time to finish the new podcast, the one where he would tell the world about the asylum, about the research and the vile things that really go on while no suspects a thing. So close, he was so close to telling the true story when the found his secret place. Secret. No one should have known how to find it much less that it belonged to William. How had they found him? No one knew his secret place, not even his family, if you considered two cousins three times removed family. His parents were long dead, leaving the burden of raising a special child to grandparents who were far beyond their years of being able to rise to such a task. The cabin had been left to him by his grandfather when he passed away a few years ago. That was before William's supposed psychotic break. William had moved back in when he was 'cured.'

No one knew about his hide out. He had made sure of that. He stroked his mask covered chin absently at the thought. Maybe he had been mistaken. *Squirrels,* he thought hopefully, *maybe it was squirrels.* That thought seemed to comfort him. Squirrels were pesky creatures, everyone knew that. They were always chewing into power lines and climbing onto things and into attics. *Had to be squirrels.*

William let his body tension ease. He still believed the danger to be real, especially with everything he knew. They didn't want him talking. Once the secret was out then things would HAVE to change. Maybe the army would come in and close down the county and the asylum. Then they would all see. William Tyler would be a hero! They would apologize for how they treated him; maybe even throw him a parade. He loved parades.

A small ache was building in his legs. He slowly stretched them out as much as he could in the small space he was in, massaging the muscles as gently and quietly as possible.

"William?"

His head perked up, all movement stopped. He listened, afraid to breathe. Was it the squirrels? *Don't be silly! Squirrels don't talk,* he chastised himself silently. But if it wasn't squirrels, then who could it be?

"William," the unseen voice asked again, this time with an obvious note of concern.

"Reverend Gillian?"

"Yes, my boy."

He was at the church! How was that possible? He didn't remember coming to the church. Things were spinning out of his control. He needed his medicine. *You left it on the desk when you ran from the squirrels,* his inner voice mocking him once more.

"Are you okay, William?"

William couldn't see the Reverend, but he heard him just fine. He had gone too long without his meds. The panic attack would happen soon. *Or had it already happened? Was it happening again??* He had to get out of there. His hand found the latch to the confessional. William emerged to see the elderly Reverend staring at him but he paid the man no mind and headed quickly for the front door. He had to get out of there now. Every movement was forced, determined.

The Reverend followed him, brow furrowed in worry. Although tall and lanky, some might say skeletal, with receding thin wisps of silver hair, tinged with the tell-tell glint of ginger, the Reverend had deep dark commanding eyes. "I can help you."

William's breathing was coming out in short gasps, eyes blinking rapidly as little beads of sweat began dotting his forehead.

"No one can save me," he stammered wildly, pushing the church doors open.

"From what?" Reverend Gillian pleaded.

William stopped, finally turning to face the Reverend, eyes wild and darting behind the dark sunglasses, "from the squirrels."

The Reverend could only watch, speechless, as William buried his hands in his coat pockets and disappeared out the door. Reverend Gillian stood at the doorstep, watching William dart awkwardly into the brush, his chalk white face an expressionless mask.

William stopped before fleeing into the woods, cocking his head to the side in a nervous twitch, once again listening for something that wasn't there. He seemed to remember something...

...that's it!

The Reverend.

William turned back to the church as if seeing it clearly for the first time. The paint was faded and cracked leaving the wood grayish with mildewed flecks caked on the sides of it. The windows, those that remained, were broken and jagged. Weeds had overtaken the church grounds while vines snaked up the sides of the building. At the top, the old iron cross leaned heavily to one side. The old, rotted supports barely able to support its weight. In the doorway, standing like a marble statue, was Reverend Gillian.

The old man stood motionless in the doorway, dark eyes peering straight into Williams, rooting the delusional man in place. A slight smile, devoid of happiness, twitched the corner of the Reverends mouth.

William began shaking, his body ravaged by an onslaught of sudden chills and cold electricity.

The door to the church suddenly slammed shut with a loud bang, sending paint chips flying from the old frame.

William found his feet...and ran...

"We treat many kinds of disorders," Evan explained as he guided Amanda on her tour of the mental institute. "The first wing I showed you is basically for outpatients with simple neurosis and phobias. Most of them just need to speak to someone with a nonjudgmental ear but with more frequency than a weekly one hour visit to a shrink who only cares about billing hours."

They had arrived at a set of locked double doors. He pushed a button. The door buzzed and he held the door open for her, motioning the intrepid reporter through.

"This wing, however, houses those patients who need extensive therapy."

Amanda recognized a noticeable difference when they stepped onto the ward. There was a walled-in office with very thick glass as soon as they entered. She could see a dozen or more monitors on the far wall, each one recording the various hallways on that wing. An orderly sat beneath them, checking off something on a notepad as he inspected each one.

The nurse in charge of the ward was nothing like the nurses from the outpatient wing. She was very stern looking. If a bulldog could take human form, it would have been that woman. The name on the nurse's lanyard was Alice. She certainly didn't look like an Alice to Amanda. Amanda doubted anything got past her. The nurse acknowledged Dr. Michaels with a simple nod of her head and continued writing in her charts. Amanda could sense the gloom.

Evan took her down a hallway and stopped at a door. He motioned for Amanda to look through the window. She was curious, stepping up to the window to see what the Doctor wanted to impress her with. The room was predictably bare, save for a small bed and a chair that was placed in a corner. The lady that sat in that chair was slightly overweight, her hair in disarray from the lack of grooming. But what struck Amanda most was the vacant expression on the woman's face.

"This young lady suffers from clinical depression, brought on by the death of her mother. She hardly sleeps. Most times she is just like you see her now. Then there are times when all she does is cry. The problem is that patients like this can be just as harmful to themselves as to others."

Amanda couldn't look away from the woman, noticing a small scar on her temple, "How sad. Can you help her?"

"We are trying. Emotion focused therapy, interpersonal therapy; nothing has worked so far. Everyone handles depression differently. There are so many triggers and types of depression that it makes narrowing the root cause very difficult." He stepped up to the window, gazing at the young lady in the chair, "We WILL help her."

It was Evan's passionate determination when he said that that drew her attention. She looked at the man standing beside her, close enough she could almost count the individual stubble on his chin. "You sound convinced," she said earnestly.

Evan continued looking at the young woman, eyes never wavering. "It's my job, my life, to help these people."

Amanda opened her mouth to respond when a commotion at the end of the hall drew her attention. Two incredibly large sheriff's deputies were dragging a very disheveled and uncooperative man into the corridor, dried blood on his face. The man's eyes were wild, like a caged animal from her grandfather's farm. He tried to struggle against the grip of the deputies, but Amanda could tell it was a futile attempt: the men were far too strong. But while they could control him physically, the man's mouth was another issue.

"Please man," he screamed shrilly, "I ain't supposed to be here! Take me to jail, man!"

Amanda glanced at Evan, an unhappy expression darkening his face. The look made her flinch, silencing any protest she may have had.

"Excuse me," he told her, voice deep with anger yet trying to remain professional.

She watched him walk down the hallway, a lion ready to pounce. Experiencing his charm in his office had led her to believe that he was a politician, a salesman, able to make friends with the devil himself. Only now, seeing him like this, she knew he was much more. Evan was a man of power, a genius with charm. The type of man that achieved whatever goals he set before him. There were plenty of men like that throughout history; Alexander the Great, Julius Caesar, Ghandi, Theodore Roosevelt...Adolph Hitler.

Every step Evan took radiated that power, commanded attention. How had she not seen it earlier? *Because,* she quickly concluded, *he didn't want me to.* Amanda became acutely aware that there was far more to this man than she realized.

The struggling man grew silent and still as Evan approached. The deputies stood straighter, almost at attention. Evan came to a stop, back to Amanda, and began speaking to the deputies. Although she couldn't hear what was being said, the doctor's posture made it clear that there was little room for discussion.

The blonde nurse from his office, Sam, she thought Evan had called her, was suddenly at his side, handing the doctor a clipboard. Evan hastily jotted something on the clipboard, handing it back to the nurse as he spoke to the deputies again. Evans body seemed to unwind as he turned away and walked back towards Amanda.

The look on the bloody man's face became one of pure horror. He began shaking, unwilling or unable to utter a word as the deputies hauled him down the hallway.

"Sorry you had to witness that," Evan said apologetically as he reached her.

Amanda greeted him with a questioning look. "He was terrified."

"Addicts normally are when they find out they are about to be detoxed," his calm demeanor neatly back in place.

"Why did the deputies bring him here instead of jail?"

"Family request," he said with a smile, putting his arm around her shoulder and guiding her away. "Come on, there's more to see."

Amanda let him lead her on, but she couldn't help but glance back down the hallway at the deputies dragging the man away. He wasn't fighting against them anymore, instead he was looking directly in her eyes. A chill went up her spine. The last time she had seen such a look was when her father gave up his fight with cancer. It was a look that only the dying shared.

The deputies took the man through another set of double doors. When Amanda turned back to Evan, the doctor was smiling down at her as he led her deeper into the asylum.

Daniel Lane sat at his desk reading charts by a single lamp. The balding middle-aged man preferred the lower light and less flamboyant office style. It allowed him to focus. He always felt that being comfortable provided him the mindset he needed to diagnose problems. Working at Hale County Institute was a huge challenge, something he enjoyed. Sure, he could go to work at more prominent institutions, but this is where he felt he could do the most good.

Besides, he told himself honestly, *Evan needs me.*

His wife chastised him regularly for the blind loyalty he showed to Evan. She tried every way imaginable to get him to move away from Hale County. Their children were grown and had lives of their own so nothing was tying them down anymore. It frustrated her to no end that he refused to even test the waters elsewhere. But Daniel was nothing if not loyal. Not only that, but he honestly loved his work. He might disagree with Evan on his practices and philosophies sometimes but that was the nature of psychology. After the tragedy his friend had experienced, he could afford Evan his little eccentricities; just so long as it didn't cross ethical boundaries.

A knock on the door interrupted his reading. He looked up to see Samantha standing there, face drawn up in agitation. *A pretty girl if not for her sour attitude,* he thought as she approached the desk. She didn't like Daniel, not since the day she tried to charm her way out of her duties. He had simply called her on it, something she was certainly not used to. Since then, Sam made no pretense of her dislike for the doctor. Why Evan tolerated her, he couldn't begin to understand.

"Evan...um, Dr. Michaels, wanted me to give you this, Dr. Lane" she said as she handed him a folder.

Daniel, not missing Samantha's Freudian slip, took the file. *Perhaps I understand why he keeps her around after all.* He knew his friend was lonely but certainly he could do better. Or perhaps that was all she was to Evan, a need that had to be filled. The nurse was beautiful to be sure but she certainly wouldn't be able to stimulate Evan mentally the way... He shook his head internally. *No,* he thought determinedly, I can't think of her now. *Not now.* There had to be other options. He glanced down at the file, putting that train of thought out of his mind. Daniel felt eyes studying him. He looked up to see Sam standing there, unmoving.

"You may leave now," he said matter-of-factly.

Sam's cheeks flushed briefly, a nasty scowl blemishing her otherwise flawless features. She rolled her eyes, turned haughtily, and marched out of the office. Apparently, she wasn't used to being summarily dismissed.

Daniel chuckled out loud as she disappeared from sight. With an amused shake of his head, he opened the folder and began reading. His amusement turned to one of outrage. *He can't do this,* Daniel fumed silently. He scanned the last few pages, not needing to read them thoroughly to know he didn't like where it was going.

"He has lost his mind!" he whispered aloud, anger filling his voice. Daniel slammed the folder shut and rushed from the office.

Daddy?

A pair of bloodshot eyes flickered in the darkness.

Wake up, daddy.

The eyes flickered once more then shot open.

That's good, daddy.

The voice was all around him, in every fiber of his being...so was the rage. He felt the familiar coolness of the steel around his wrists; heard the clanking of the chains that secured him to the stone walls. The sound angered him. He shook them harder, the sounds of metal hitting concrete echoing through the dark place he was in.

Stop, daddy.

He fought harder, hatred building with each movement. He hated this place. He hated his chains. He wanted out. The thrashing intensified, the metal clamps digging into his wrists in the pitch black of the room.

Daddy stop!

Her voice! It was her! He immediately stopped fighting the chains, eyes trying to focus in the dark, ears perked to hear her voice. It seemed an eternity, but then there it was once again, calming him with its presence.

They can't know your awake, daddy, the disembodied voice whispered, *save your strength. We will be together soon.*

The hatred was stirring within him, but her voice calmed him even while the raw emotion burned inside. His eyes squeezed tightly together then slowly opened. In the darkness a faint pale light stirred. As it got closer his heart raced.

"Katie," he growled desperately.

Who was this Katie? His shattered mind struggled to understand.

The ghost like face of a young girl began to manifest before him. It was fuzzy and unclear, but he KNEW it was here. *I'm here, daddy. We will be together soon.*

He closed his eyes, letting the hate consume him.

The young girl's specter drifted closer, her form glowing with an ethereal blue light that cast eerie shadows against the stone walls. Her pale face was a perfect oval, framed by long dark hair that seemed to float as if suspended in water. Her eyes, unnaturally large and completely black, fixed on him with an intensity that would have terrified anyone else.

"Yes, daddy," she whispered, her voice echoing as if from the bottom of a well. "I'm here."

The chains rattled as he strained toward her, his massive frame taut with desperation. Blood trickled from his wrists where the metal had cut into his flesh, but he felt no pain—only the burning need to reach his daughter.

"They're coming, daddy," Katie said, her head tilting at an impossible angle. "They bring another one. Like you. Like us."

His breathing quickened, chest heaving beneath the tattered remains of his jumpsuit. Memories flickered through his broken mind—fragmented images of white coats, needles, and pain. So much pain. The rage built again, a living thing inside him that clawed and scraped, demanding release.

"Kill," he growled, the word rumbling from deep in his chest.

Katie's ghostly form drifted closer until she was inches from his face. Her small hand reached out, hovering just above his scarred cheek without touching.

"Not yet," she whispered. "Wait. Patient. Like the doctor taught you."

The doctor. The name burned in his mind, bringing with it a fresh wave of hatred that threatened to consume him. Dr. Michaels. The man who had strapped him to tables, who had put things in his head, who had taken Katie from him.

"Soon," Katie promised, her form beginning to fade. "When the lights go out. When the doors open. Then you can come find me."

As her image dissolved into the darkness, he slumped against the wall, his massive body suddenly drained. The rage still burned, but it was banked now, a smoldering coal waiting for the right moment to ignite.

Somewhere in the darkness, water dripped steadily onto stone. The rhythmic sound became his heartbeat, his focus. He would wait. He would be patient.

For Katie.

A bulb was hanging from a makeshift light in the middle of a damp, mildewed room. The slight sway of the light cast eerie shadows on the surrounding walls. An old large metal chair sat ominously in the middle of the room. Hold down straps hung from the arm and feet rests. A rustic cart with varied medical instruments, all of which were sharpened, was tucked away in a corner.

The iron door to the room opened noisily. Bru and Rodney drug Steven into the room and slammed him into the chair. He had been changed into scrubs at some point but couldn't remember when or how. Steven felt a strap clamp around his leg. His eyes came alive with fear. He tried to leap from the chair but was shoved roughly back into it.

"Let me go you bastards!" he screamed at the men, lunging one more time for freedom.

Bru hit Steven square between the eyes, sending the smaller man into semi-unconsciousness. The fight drained out of him, the two big men clamped his arms and legs firmly into place with the straps.

Samantha stepped into the room carrying a silver tray, which looked out of place with the archaic equipment. She sat the tray, which was filled with vials, syringes, swabs, gauze, and a gagging device, on top of the cart.

Steven tried to regain his bearings. He tried to mumble a protest, but Rodney stuffed a gag ball in his mouth, securing the strap firmly around his head. Tears began streaming from his eyes as he fought against his restraints.

The two deputies stepped back out of the way as Samantha shined a pen light into his eyes and took his pulse. She took a small towel and dabbed it against his forehead, cleaning the dirt and sweat from his brow. Steven felt his body begin to relax as Sam smiled comfortingly. He closed his eyes and tried to breathe. When he opened them again, he saw Samantha standing by the cart.

The nurse was holding a vial, filled with discolored fluid, up to the light. Sam took a large syringe off the cart and jabbed it into the vial, filling the needle with the cloudy liquid. Steven's eyes filled with terror as she squirted some of it into the air. She took a step towards him, her calming smile becoming sinister.

"The doctor will be with you shortly," she stated devilishly as she plunged the needle into his neck.

All Steven could do was scream.

Chapter 3

'Let thy light shine, then, in dark places'- Edgar Cayce

William turned on his computer, righting his web camera as he waited for it to boot up. Glass of water in hand, he lifted his scarf enough so that he could down his medicine. He was exhausted. Returning to his hideout unseen had been a challenge. All the sneaking, moving inch by inch, making sure that no one so much as caught a glimpse of him, not even the squirrels...or the Reverend, had been a draining experience. But being careful was more important than being comfortable. Even when he made it safely back to the cabin he sat hidden in the trees and watched just to be sure no one was there waiting for him to return. Several hours later he felt it was safe to go in again. He needed a new plan. A contingency plan the movies called it. If they got him, no one would ever know the truth.

The Reverend. What was the deal with him? *Not human, no, couldn't be. Did he follow me home??* William began to breathe heavily, almost hyperventilating. Calm. He had to be calm.

The computer was ready. He made sure the bandanna was wrapped tightly around his face, then slipped on the oversized toboggan. William pulled himself upright in the chair as best he could, staring into the camera, uncaring that he looked like a wild man, and hit the record button. The bottle of pills lay tipped over beside the keyboard, lid haphazardly tossed aside. The truth was more important than his personal grooming.

"They thought they were going to get me, coming to my house and all, but they don't think the way I do, people!" William's medicine still hadn't kicked in fully. He was erratic, voice full of paranoia. "I'm like ten steps ahead of them! Twenty even! Not even the squirrels know!"

William's eyes flickered off camera at nothing in particular, his mind wandering madly. When he spoke again it was soft and distant. "You see, the doctors at the asylum, they have all kinds of methods for 'curing you' as they say. But they're not curing you." Tears flowed from his eyes, lost in memory. "They are making you a monster."

A scratching noise snapped him back to the moment. He gazed sternly into the camera, eyes shifting from sorrow to anger. "They give you these experimental drugs that haven't even been tested on animals, man! They strap you to these mechanical chairs and attach all sorts of things to your body! They stick these long needles in your temple! Makes you see things, say things…do things."

William paused, eyes once more losing their focus. "And if that don't work, they got scary ways, terrifying ways, of making you change, man. They leave things for you, terrible dark things." Another thought seemed to occur to him. He looked back into the camera. "The Reverend, beware the Reverend…he works for them…he must…"

He stopped the recording. He shook his head slightly. The medicine was beginning to take hold. He felt the rational part of his mind rise above the schizophrenic portion. There were so many things he had to say, and time was running out. William was going to tell his story, no matter what that meant. He began to furiously reconfigure his computer, building a loop so that he could feed various videos on a timed broadcast. They may get him, but his voice would be heard.

Dr. Michaels walked Amanda to her car. The intrepid reporter shot a look around the area, suddenly remembering the fact that someone had been watching her earlier. Or perhaps she was just being cynical. It was no doubt the ominous surroundings that had put her on guard. Now she was back to her car, her tour through the mental institute complete, she felt more alert. There was something about the place, walking through those corridors, watching the almost rehearsed movements of care givers and patients alike that seemed too neat. It was as if Amanda was the center of her own secret movie with everyone in on it but her. Other than one little incident, everything about the place seemed perfectly normal. Everything, that is, but the doctor who was walking beside her. She had set up the meeting with the intent of breaking a story yet all she left with was respect for the facility and the passion of the doctor who oversaw it.

Amanda clicked the automatic door locks from her remote as they approached the car. To her surprise, Evan opened her door for her. Oddly, she didn't feel the cool air like she had earlier. She had to wonder if that had something to do with Evan and the tingling he ignited within her. She looked at him quizzically.

"What?" He asked with that disarming smile of his.

"I may have misjudged you," she said, smiling herself.

"May have?" he teased.

"Well, you DID sugar coat the tour," she said, only half-kidding. It was a huge facility. They hadn't covered half of it. Of course, she knew his time was precious. Amanda was actually surprised he had taken that much time out of his schedule. "But I do believe you genuinely care about helping people."

"Fair enough. Do I get to ask a question now?"

"Okay."

"Have dinner with me?"

Amanda hadn't been sure of what question he was going to ask but that certainly wasn't the one she expected. Taken aback, she didn't know how to respond.

"I'm committed," she finally said.

Evan smiled. "You're committed," he agreed, "to your job." He took her left hand, his fingers encircling where a wedding band should be. Warmth spread through Amanda's body at his touch. "And you live out of your car," he said with a chuckle.

She glanced around the interior, littered with fast food containers and empty coffee cups. "Very good," she said, impressed, "what's my favorite food?"

"I'm not that good," he laughed, "but I would love to find out."

"Why would you go to dinner with me? I'm trying to dig up dirt on your hospital," she said with a smile.

"Then this would be the perfect opportunity."

Amanda was about to respond when someone shouted out across the parking lot.

"Dr. Michaels! A word, please!"

They turned to see Dr. Lane stalking towards them, the expression on his face was beyond angry.

"Now, I KNOW what his favorite food is," Evan told her slyly.

Amanda couldn't help but smile. She reached into her glove box and pulled out a card. "If you're serious about dinner," she said as she handed Evan the card.

"I'll call you later," he grinned as she put the key in the ignition. He closed the door for her. Amanda cranked the car and was pulling away just as the other doctor made it to Evan.

She was about to turn out of the drive but couldn't resist a look back. In her rearview mirror she could see the two men having a very heated discussion. The older doctor handed Evan a folder and was stabbing angrily at it with his finger, shaking his head no. Evan slammed the folder into the other doctor's chest and stalked off to the asylum without so much as a backwards glance.

The look on the older man's face was one of shock, mingled with fear. The man was standing there, dumbfounded. Amanda herself was transfixed by the scene. Dr. Lane looked her way. For just a moment, the two locked disbelieving stares. Dr. Lane lowered his head in disappointment and walked back to the building, leaving Amanda to wonder what could have caused such a confrontation. One thing was certain, dinner would be very interesting.

"Mr. Winkler, I'm just trying to figure out how it got into my office. The door was locked," Jason said for the third time into the phone. It had been a blur since lunch, since the discovery of the package. He had to cancel his remaining classes for the day. Whoever had left the package for him had somehow managed to sneak it into his office unawares. "Yes, I'm sure. I had to unlock the door to get in."

Jason was exasperated as he scoured the box the pouch was delivered in for any clue as to who might have sent it. It didn't help matters that the head janitor didn't have an answer either. Not many people had a key to his office. It had disturbed him so much that he took a long lunch break to calm himself as well as to see if anyone would enter the office again while he was away.

Jason had set the package on the corner of the desk at a forty-five-degree angle, not daring to touch the old round stone, he couldn't. He locked his office up securely and went for lunch, hoping beyond hope that the episode was merely his imagination running wild for lack of food. But as he sat in the car, his lunch uneaten, Jason couldn't shake the feeling that someone, somehow, *knew*.

The impossible fact that it was now sitting in his office twisted his stomach in knots. No one knew about it, at all. Certainly no one in Hale County knew of its existence or even its significance and why it couldn't be the actual Cherokee marble he remembered all those years ago.

A Cherokee Marble, and an old one at that. Most people never knew they existed, that Cherokee Marbles were a sport dating back to 800 A.D. This specific one was ancient and unique. No two were ever the same. Jason had only seen that particular marble one other time, supposedly for the last time. Yet there it sat on the desk in his office. But how? No one could have known...

Jason had spent the next few hours in anticipation, anxious to see if someone had gone back into his office and left him any more surprises, or perhaps they had taken it back. When he had unlocked the door and entered his office it was readily apparent that someone had indeed been there. The package was now lying across the room on a shelf filled with his archaeology books. Only three people had keys. One of them couldn't have done it, the other, well, it was farfetched, but he had to call and find out. The resulting argument wasn't getting him anywhere.

"No," he gritted out into the phone, willing a patience he didn't possess at that moment, "the only other people who have a key are you and Dean Robinson, and he's out of town. I even left for lunch a little bit ago and came back. The door was still locked but the box had been moved from where I purposefully left it!" If he wasn't convinced the janitor didn't have a sense of humor he'd have believed he was pulling a prank on him. As it was, Jason fully believed the grumpy caretaker.

"No, I haven't been drinking! Look, Mr. Winkler, if you would ask your staff if they have seen anyone near my office I would appreciate it." He grimaced as the janitor mumbled out a litany of swear words before finally agreeing to do it. Before Jason could bite out a 'thank you' the phone went dead. The last time he made the janitor angry his office trash wasn't taken out for a month.

He gave the packaging one more going over. Someone had to see something. He crushed the brown box and tossed it in the trash, immediately turning his focus to the old granite marble that had been inside. It just wasn't possible.

Jason sat there for the next two hours staring at the artifact, studying every crease in it. He hadn't wanted to touch it at first but there was no getting around it. He was afraid that if he did then it was confirmation that it actually existed. There were too many memories attached to it. Memories he was afraid to access. More to the point, if he did allow those memories to take hold, he was terrified of what that would mean. Finally, he could stand it no more. Carefully, he reached out and lifted the worn marble off the desk.

The large granite orb was smooth, carefully crafted to perfection hundreds of years before the first Anglo settlers ever arrived in the New World. There was a light film of aged dirt across its surface. He took a handkerchief from his desk drawer and began lightly polishing one of the symbols until the white owl became clearer. It was only a few moments before the entire image shone through. Seeing an exposed figure, Jason began to polish in earnest. In moments the Cherokee Marble was free of the dirt, the granite looking as smooth as the day it was so carefully created, now exposing the cougar just as clearly.

Jason was mesmerized by its brilliance, just as he had been all those years ago when he first saw it. He had found it by accident in a dig in Northern Georgia. He remembered the day so vividly. It was the day he met Rachel. A smile played on his lips at the memory.

That smile evaporated at the thought of a darker memory; the memory of why he never expected to see it again. This time when he took the rag to the marble he did so with hesitancy. He wrapped his finger in the rag, licking the rag enough to dampen it. He turned the marble around until he found exactly what he knew he would find, the one imperfection in an otherwise pristine artifact, a small pin sized hole directly above the eye of the cougar. There was an overwhelming feeling of nausea mixed with fear.

"It's not possible." But even as he said it, he knew it was. He pressed his finger to the granite surface wiping at the image of the cougar. Jason's hands fell away from the orb, dropping it back into the deer skin pouch he had pulled it from. He glanced at the dirty white rag. There, amongst the greyish brown stain was a small red smudge. Blood.

His nightmares had come true.

Impossible, he thought again and again, as if constantly repeating it to himself would make it not real.

The room became a memory, his vision saw only a dark, fog intensive winter morning. He remembered the marble sinking beneath the frigid waters, how the white image of the owl seemed to glisten at him for a brief moment before quickly vanishing from sight. How many times had he held it in his hands? How many times had he stared at those images, knew their meaning, felt their weight? Jason grabbed the trash can and vomited violently, the Cherokee Orb lying there accusingly.

Laurel Rose Manor sat on a hill overlooking the sprawling countryside. The tall, three-story French Acadian style house struck a majestic pose as the afternoon sun began its descent. Beams of sunlight swept over the front of the house, bathing it in bright fall colors. A small red Chevrolet Cavalier made its way up the long winding drive.

Behind the house, sitting in a rustic lawn chair by the expansive pool, JC Michaels waited on his visitor. He took a sip of his beer, peering at the last of the hummingbirds that had yet to fly south. In the summer there were almost twenty feeders in the meditation area off to the side of the pool but now as fall was quickly fading there were only two, just enough to feed those stragglers who were late to leave for the warmer Mexico climate. JC had put out the feeders when he came across an old one stored in his mother's belongings. This was his tribute to her. At their peak there would be over a hundred or so hummingbirds. Now, however, fall was here, and they were almost all gone until spring. When he needed some internal peace, he would come out and watch them.

A shadow loomed over him.

Ashlyn was beautiful. Her dark chestnut hair and light blue eyes lent an air of electricity to her already magnetic smile. Her light sweater hugged her perfect form. She was one of those girls who didn't have to work at being beautiful, she just was. When she spoke? Well, that was the closest thing JC could ever imagine to hearing angels sing. He saw in her what he wanted most out of life; normalcy. She accepted him without question, through all his faults. A huge silly grin spread across his face as he rose to meet her. He took her in his arms, their lips meeting softly.

"How was your day?" he asked after they broke the kiss.

Ashlyn sighed as she put her purse and laptop on the lawn table beside his chair, her smile never wavering, "I've been running all day it seems." She noticed the beer on the table and raised her eyebrows questioningly.

"Oh," he laughed, "Trey came over earlier, brought some beer. He said I was a wuss if I didn't have at least one."

"And what was the verdict?"

JC picked up the warm beer that was still almost completely full. "I'm a wuss." He tossed the beer into a small wastebasket as they both laughed. "Have you seen the cast list yet?"

"Nope, I told you we would look at it together and so we are," she said as she teasingly patted her laptop.

"You never go anywhere without that thing," he laughed.

"Inspiration can strike at any moment."

"Are you ever going to let me read it?"

Ashlyn covered the laptop playfully. "When I'm done, which should be soon," She leaned over, giving him a kiss, "you will be the first to read it."

"Very nice," a coy smile on his face, "is there a part for me in there?"

She bit her lip playfully, almost seductively so and said, "If you are very nice."

JC leaned towards her, matching her smile. "I'm always nice."

Her face instinctively moved closer to his. "Not always."

"Mostly."

Their lips met again; a long slow kiss between two people who were content in the moment. Everything ceased to exist but them. When they finally broke the kiss, Ashlyn smiled and opened the laptop.

"It's dead," she said apologetically.

JC rose from his chair and took her by the hand. "Come on, we'll use the one in the study."

In the few months she had been dating JC and coming to his house she had only seen probably half of it, and never the study. The study belonged to his dad. JC hated talking about his dad. Not that he didn't love him, but being the son of the director of Hale County Mental Institute carried its baggage. Especially with all the rumors and gossip that surrounded the place.

A huge black cherry desk sat against the far wall. The walls were lined with bookshelves, which were loaded with books of all kinds. Most of the volumes were psychology and science related. The walls were bare of any family photos. The two murals that hung on the wall behind the desk were the only decorations.

JC guided Ashlyn to the high-backed leather chair behind the desk. As he was signing on to the computer, she found herself staring at the sole picture that was framed on the desk. The resemblance to her boyfriend was amazing. Father and son were peering back at her, smiling as they posed by a lake. His dad held up a tiny one while the six-year-old JC was holding a catfish nearly as big as he was.

"Is this your dad?" she asked.

He pursed his lips disdainfully, not taking his eyes off the computer screen. "That's him."

She looked at JC, studying his face. "I don't think I've ever met him."

"He's my dad, we live in the same house, and I'VE hardly met him," he said sarcastically. He felt a touch on his hand. JC glanced down to see Ashlyn smiling sympathetically at him. "It's okay— and you are signed on."

"Alright mister, let's find out who is playing what."

JC rolled his eyes, a gesture she didn't miss. She took him by the hand. "You had a great audition. It doesn't matter who they cast you as."

"That's easy for you to say. You always get the lead."

"Not always," she said sheepishly.

"Just watch," he joked again, "I'll be playing a tree."

"You have to be positive."

"I'm positive I'll be playing a tree."

Ashlyn playfully punched him in the arm.

JC gave her a knowing look but softened it with a smile. Her positivity was yet another reason he liked her. Never had he met someone with such a great outlook. Sometimes he wondered if this were real or if he were like one of those patients at his dad's hospital, living in a fantasy world that didn't exist. If that was the case, then he already knew which world he preferred.

Ashlyn typed in the url address to the school's theater department. In mere moments the information lit up the screen. They scanned the page until their eyes focused on the cast list, a look of disbelief on both of their faces.

JC quickly turned off the computer, his skin drained of color. Without a word he marched out of the study. Ashlyn watched him go, a look of total shock on her face. She glanced once more at the darkened screen and chased out after him.

Steven was drenched in sweat, his head lolled to the side. Some of the droplets smacked off the concrete floor sending liquid echoes through the room. Barely lucid, he hardly noticed anything at all— except fear. That, he knew well. Whatever drug they had given him made him feel disassociated with his body. He KNEW he should be afraid, felt the fear all around him, but he was strangely apart from it.

Another needle buried into his arm. Within seconds he could feel the liquid that was pumped into him from this latest assault. It was burning him from the inside out. Steven let loose with a painful roar, snapping him out of his stupor. He tried to lunge forward but a massive hand landed heavily on his chest and forced him back into the seat. "Get your hands off of me you big ass gorilla," he hissed through clinched teeth.

Bru, all three hundred pounds of him, drew back a fist.

"Now, now, Bru. Let's not break him yet," Samantha said from somewhere behind the large brute. The big man stepped out of the way allowing Steven to see her writing on a clipboard. The nurse had that same half smile, half sneer she wore earlier. "Can you tell me your name?"

"Piss on you," he spat angrily. Every vein in his body felt like it was on fire.

Samantha stared at him right in the eyes, the half sneer becoming a fully nasty one. "Bru," was all she said.

Suddenly, the massive hand latched around Steven's throat like a vice. His own hands and feet were still strapped to the chair he was in. The crushing pressure on his throat choked off any screams he might have had. He was going to die.

"I think that's enough," she said calmly.

The hand was swiftly and thankfully gone. Steven gasped for air, gagging at the same time. The lights in the room seemed to dance before him like a disco ball. He felt his neck bruising from the inside.

"You're lucky I got to ya' first," Bru growled in his deep voice, soiled breath forcing an involuntary cough from Steven. As he coughed he turned slightly to see an enormous bald black man standing off to the side in an orderly outfit. He was even bigger than Bru, if that was possible. He could make out the name 'Tony' on the ID badge as light reflected off of it. Steven gulped as softly as possible, trying to mask his fear, but it was just too much. He felt his body begin to shiver.

"Let's start over, shall we," Samantha said so politely that for a moment it was as if nothing had happened. "Name?"

"Steven...its Steven," he sobbed, tears mixing with his sweat.

Samantha jotted something on the clipboard, a self-satisfied smirk replacing the sneer. Her frequent mood switch scared him more than anything the brute could do to him. Even her tone was different when she said, "it's going to be okay Steven, we are here to help you." It was so nice that hope flared within him. Perhaps he had misjudged her. The drugs, he was having a reaction to the drugs, that's what was happening.

"Thank you," he sobbed again, "thank you."

At those words, her smile vanished as if being washed away by acid. The pure malice in her voice when she spoke chilled him to his core.

"You're welcome."

Mag wheels hummed against the black top as the Dodge truck dipped around the bend in the road. Calloused fingers tapped lazily on the steering wheel as an old Hank Jr song blared over the radio. Jake hardly heard the lyrics as his thoughts were busy going over the Donaldson's disappearance along with a rash of other disappearances and murders that had begun to plague his county.

He wasn't getting any help from the city cops no matter how much Marcus ordered them to share information so Jake felt no guilt at all in not reciprocating. Still, nothing made sense. There were no patterns or connections, just randomized violence. Of course, the townspeople all had theories as to the cause: big city thugs coming down to prey on their county. And while there was always a straggler or two that would find their way into Hale County there was no influx of big city trouble. No, this was deeper than that. It was as if there was a full moon 24/7 tugging at the minds of everyone in the county.

Jake scoffed at the thought, *horse shit*. But whatever was going on, he was determined to get to the bottom of it. The Donaldson's were just the latest in a long line of increasing misery and mystery to hit their community. The Sheriff hated unsolved mysteries. He knew there was always an answer, a solution, some piece of evidence that would lead to breaking any case. *You're stubborn to the point of obsession*, the voice whispered through his thoughts.

"Dammit, not now…" Jake growled under his breath. Suddenly, he slammed on his brakes, the large truck slightly fish-tailing but righting itself before coming to a dead stop. The Sheriff glanced in his rearview mirror.

Dale's Bait & Tackle store sat just around the bend. The parking lot was more of a big dusty space with pressed gravel and dirt with a dual sided gas pump straight out of the fifties. The store was tiny, known more for its breakfast and lunch that old man Peasley prepared every day than for the goods he sold. Catering to the hunters and fishermen, it was bait and breakfast. You picked up your sausage biscuit, your bait, a little bit of gas and you were set.

The Sheriff made a habit of stopping by and grabbing lunch there a couple times a week as there wasn't a lot of traffic on the weekdays and the old man had to get lonely since his wife passed on a couple years back. Old man Peasley would sit and whittle all day on that little bench by the front door until a customer would show up. He would help the customer, talk awhile, and when the customer left he was right back to his bench and whittling. If some lucky customer caught him at the right time said customer would be leaving with a free custom creation Peasley had just finished. Jake himself has several of the old man's carvings on his mantle in his office.

As Jake peered in the rearview mirror he wondered where the old man was. The bench was empty. Peasley's truck was parked beside the building as always. *He's probably taking a piss*, Jake thought to himself. *Maybe all these disappearances are getting to me.* Still, something seemed off.

He put the truck in reverse, whipped around in the middle of the road, and pulled into the parking lot. Switching the truck off, the Sheriff scanned the scene slowly, taking in every detail. It all seemed perfectly normal with the exception of the absent proprietor. The ice machine was thumping along in its odd cadence, kept together with duct tape and zip ties.

Opposite the bench by the door, as if standing guard, was Ole Chief the ancient wooden carved Native that had been gifted to Peasley five decades earlier, the day he took over the store from his father. Peasley's family had ties with the local tribes that went back almost 200 years with a mutual respect that you didn't dare try to tarnish with bigotry. Those who felt that particular rule didn't apply to them found out real quick how wrong they were. Mr. Peasley may have aged but his ability to suddenly sling Lil Amos into action, the sawed-off shotgun under the register, was quick to squash any hostility.

Jake stepped from the truck. As he shut the door, he took off his sunglasses and pitched them through the open driver's window and onto the seat. He took a step towards the door and stopped, casting his steely eyes once more around the scene. *Normal*, he thought skeptically. Intuition was sounding the alarm in his head, and Jake learned a long time ago not to ignore it.

Jake approached the store cautiously, his hand hovering near his holstered pistol. As he neared the entrance, a faint metallic odor caught his attention. His eyes narrowed as he recognized the scent - blood.

Heart rate quickening, Jake drew his weapon and pushed open the creaky screen door. The interior was dim, lit only by the afternoon sun filtering through dusty windows. Shelves of fishing tackle and outdoor supplies were tossed about at odd angles casting weird shadows across the floor. Merchandise was scattered everywhere, as if a tornado had formed inside the shop and completely sent everything flying in every direction.

"Mr. Peasley?" Jake called out, sweeping his gun from side to side as he moved deeper into the store. No response.

He made his way behind the counter, eyes scanning for any sign of the old shopkeeper. That's when he saw it - a dark smear on the linoleum floor, leading towards the back room. Jake's jaw clenched as he followed the trail.

The storeroom door was ajar.

From outside the front door the sound of tires on gravel skidding to a stop caught his attention. The sheriff was about to continue trailing the blood through the door when a familiar voice called out to him from the front door. "Sheriff, you in there?" a deep baritone voice called out.

Jake stood up and waved the figure over. It was Dan Roundtree, a Cherokee elder that oversaw a 400-acre plot of land with several different native families that called it home. The families were from different tribes, Cherokee, Chickasaw, Muskogee and Apalachee to name a few, all practicing their respective beliefs in peace. The unofficial name of the land was the Rez, but they all just called it home. It was to Dan's family that the Peasley's had deeded the land to all those years earlier, a close familial tie that still existed to that day. Dan was of medium height, squarely built with broad shoulders. His black hair peppered with grey, eyes a deep dark brown that most people would swear could see into your soul. Jake considered him a friend, and one of the few people he could trust unequivocally.

Dan's expression darkened as he took in the scene, his eyes lingering on the blood trail. "What happened here, Jake?"

"Not sure yet" Jake replied grimly. "Mr. Peasley's missing. You see anything unusual on your way in?"

Dan shook his head. "Nothing out of the ordinary. I did smell what I thought was blood. But something feels...off." He paused, seeming to listen to some unheard whisper. "There's darkness here, Jake. An old evil stirring."

Jake fought the urge to roll his eyes. He respected Dan but had little patience for superstition. "Let's focus on finding Mr. Peasley. What brought you out here?"

Dan was taking in the surroundings as he answered, "Tommy Two Feet."

The sheriff looked at Dan quizzically, "Stan's kid? The kid who can't walk and chew gum at the same time?"

Dan nodded solemnly head swiveling to and fro, "the same. He just started working here last week. He brings in the fish on Tuesdays for Elmer, cleans them and gets them ready for the fish plates the next day. I pick him up in the afternoon and drop him off at home."

Jake didn't miss the look on Dan's face. The kid would have been here when whatever happened went down. The sheriff nodded in understanding and began to make his way towards the back-room door. "Good thing you did. Stay here while I clear the back."

Weapon raised; Jake slowly pushed open the back door. The metallic scent of blood grew stronger. The back was in as much disarray as the front part of the store. A small ray of sunlight pierced the darkness from the far door leading outback. As his eyes adjusted to the dimness, he saw a pair of legs sprawled on the floor behind a stack of boxes, the trail of blood leading right to that area.

Jake's heart sank as he recognized Mr. Peasley's worn boots. He moved quickly around the boxes, gun still at the ready. The old shopkeeper lay motionless on the floor, a deep gash across his throat and chest, his clothing ripped to shreds. His eyes stared blankly at the ceiling.

"Dammit," Jake muttered, kneeling to check for a pulse he knew wouldn't be there.

He heard Dan's footsteps approaching behind him. "Stay back, Dan," he called out. "It's not good."

Jake stood and turned to block Dan's view, but the Cherokee elder had already seen enough. His face was grim as he met Jake's eyes.

"This is dark magic, Jake," Dan said quietly. "I can feel it."

Jake sighed, beginning to holster his weapon but deciding against it as he pointed to the back door. "Let's not jump to conclusions. We need to find Tommy and figure out what happened here."

Both men slowly made their way to the back door, being as silent as the wrecked storeroom would allow. They stopped by the barely closed door, the sheriff giving his friend a readied look then bolted out the back door…

…and into the bright sunlight.

All was quiet and the men took in their surroundings. If not for the carnage inside the store you would have sworn it was just another peaceful day. Perhaps, too peaceful. "Look," Dan pointed at the ground as he knelt, "more blood."

"Tommy," Jake stated matter-of-factly, eyes darting around the area, grip tightening on the butt of his pistol.

Dan followed the trail to the tree line that wasn't more than twenty yards away. It was there that the trail seemed to vanish. "The trail is gone," he told Jake in bewilderment.

The sheriff returned the look of doubt, "no way that trail disappears with that amount of blood…" He was about to finish that statement when his eyes locked onto more evidence. Dan stood up from the ground when Jake had just abruptly stopped talking, his eyes following the line of sight of the sheriff's.

There, at almost eye level on the tree before them, was a huge smudge of blood on a thick branch of the oak tree. The blood seemed to move up the barrel of the tree to the next branch, getting thicker and thicker.

"Sweet Dayunsi…" Dan exclaimed, taking a stuttering step backwards, almost falling over.

"Fuck me…" Jake swore under his breath, as his eyes settled on the most horrible thing he had ever witnessed. There, fifteen feet into the tree, Tommy Two Feet had a death grip on the tree with both arms and legs wrapped around the trunk. His back was ripped to shreds, all the way to the bone, blood covering every inch of the poor boy. It was the face though that would haunt both men. Tommy's face was contorted into a mixture of unimaginable fear and pain simultaneously, a face that wanted to scream in agony but never would again.

The clouds were massing ominously along the horizon, casting a heavy, brooding pall over the sprawling grounds of Laurel Rose Manor. JC observed Sammy, his spirited two-year-old Chocolate Lab, joyfully paddling in the tranquil waters of the front pond. A solitary, towering tree stood sentinel halfway between the pond and the grand old house. Its gnarled limbs, bearing the wisdom of over a century, played host to a merry troupe of squirrels, their tiny forms darting and leaping with playful exuberance.

Everything should have felt perfect. JC was in college, excelling with impressive grades, and blessed with the companionship of an extraordinary girlfriend. Yet, as he gazed from the upper balcony, a turbulent storm of emotions swirled within him.

Ashlyn gently slid her hand into his, her touch warm and reassuring. "What's wrong?" she asked softly.

JC let his chin drop to his chest in a gesture of defeat. "Come on, Ash. The lead? Seriously? There were so many guys better than me."

"No, there weren't," she countered firmly.

"There were a couple, and you know it," he insisted.

"So, you're mad because you got the lead instead of being a tree? That's a new one," she remarked with playful sarcasm, her voice lilting with a charm that only Ashlyn could muster.

"It's not that," he replied, a hint of frustration lacing his words.

"Oh," she continued teasingly, "so you don't want to act opposite of me?"

"You know better." JC began to smile, though it wavered as he paused, grappling with how to articulate his feelings. "It's just..." his voice dwindled into silence. He turned to face her, seeking solace in the depth of her eyes. "I don't think I earned it. I..."

Ashlyn placed a gentle finger on his lips, silencing him with a tender gesture. She was curious about the roots of this sudden self-doubt but sensed that now was not the moment to probe. Instead, she leaned in, bestowing a soft, quick kiss. "You did. Now let's go celebrate. Dinner and a movie?"

"You're amazing," he said, his smile returning with genuine warmth.

"I know," she whispered joyfully, their lips meeting once more as dusk descended gently upon the manor. Neither of them noticed the sinister shadow that slipped stealthily from behind the ancient tree, its gaze fixed on the young lovers with a dark, vengeful hatred.

Chapter 4

"Damn," Daniel Lane swore under his breath. He discarded file after file that had been sitting in an unused drawer of his desk for almost twenty years. He was on his knees, digging in the bottom drawer. Each file he grabbed he gave a quick once over then tossed aside like garbage. He cursed himself for his lack of organization in his early years. These were files that had been kept under lock and key then were promptly forgotten in the ensuing decades.

How had he not seen this coming? Was he so blinded by loyalty that he never paid attention? Or was the truth that he simply didn't want to know? Evan was headed down a dangerous road. Why did Evan send him that report? Did he think he would get Daniel's support on this? Sure, there had been some experimenting with different techniques and drug combinations over the course of the years; that's science. But this? This was a road Daniel didn't want to travel.

His confrontation with Evan in the parking lot left him sick. Not because they had argued over the course of twenty years that's inevitable. No, it was the look in his eyes; the determination to do whatever it took at whatever the cost. It was in that moment that tiny crack in Evan's iron façade, that Daniel realized the truth behind his friend's drive. "I will not allow this to happen again," Evan had shouted at him as he shoved the folder into his chest and walked away.

Daniel had assumed that over the span of years since the tragedy that had befallen Evan and his family that he had coped and moved on. Evan went through the mourning period then slowly pulled himself out of it, raising his son by himself and taking pride in that accomplishment. It was obvious now that Evan had never coped but buried his hurt in obsession.

A file heading caught his eye. He pulled the file with trepidation. Taking a deep breath, he opened the file, scanning the pages. His brow furrowed in concern the more he read. The intimate details of what happened came back as a rush. He could see the events playing out before him as he read. It was like stepping back in time.

"Find what you were looking for?"

Daniel snapped his head up, startled by the unexpected sound of Evan's voice. Evan stood in the doorway, body loose and relaxed. Daniel slid into his chair, sitting the file down shakily on the desk. "I will not help you do this."

Evan sat in the chair opposite Daniel, his face one of exhaustion. He let all pretenses fall away as he picked up the file that Daniel had been reading, but didn't look at it. Instead, he looked into the eyes of the elder doctor. "What is our job, my friend?"

Daniel answered automatically, "to help people, to..."

"...cure them," Evan finished for him.

Dr. Lane glanced at the file Evan was holding and pointed, "not like this."

Evan straightened in his chair, leaning towards Daniel pleadingly. "This PC world we live in has handcuffed science in socio-sensitive handholding. They don't push to find cures, they are happy where they are, just keeping things in check. We can be like Wundt or Freud, leading the way instead of being mired in texts and outdated theorems!"

Daniel felt for his friend, he honestly did. He got out of his chair and walked around the desk until he was standing beside Evan, looking down at him. "The Milgram Experiment and the Stanford Prison Experiment both prove the dangers of willfully forcing yourself into the human mind."

"Don't you see," Evan stated agitatedly, "they both worked to a degree! They didn't go far enough. The results were right there! The Pineal Gland is the frontier that holds the cure. Look at the pandemic, the number of suicides and mental instability has become astronomical, all because the studies have lost focus and meaning, afraid that someone's feelings will get hurt. Science has become lax. We must push it further!" He softened his voice as he looked hopefully up at his mentor. "Who's to say that's wrong?"

"Morality does," Daniel said kindly, putting a comforting hand on Evan's shoulder.

Evan stared at the file, eyes losing focus. When he spoke it was the voice of a man who was lost. "The mentally wasted have no concept of morality, or reality for that matter!" A heaviness settled upon Evan as his gaze seemed to drift to the past. "You don't understand, Daniel."

Daniel tapped the name on the file. "Would she?" He gave Evan a sympathetic pat on the shoulder and left the office.

Evan stared at the name on the file, tears burning his eyes. It read: Miranda Michaels.

Jason Locke walked slowly across the all but abandoned campus parking lot. There were few cars parked sporadically across the small campus. A couple of students shouted out to him, but he couldn't hear them. His mind was solely on the object in his hand. He had spent the afternoon making calls, trying to get some information on how this was even possible. Even if someone had somehow managed to find the marble, how would they know where to send it and whom it belonged to? Every call he made came up empty.

He stepped off the curb, attention solely on the ancient artifact, and almost got hit by a car. Only the car horn and his stumbling backwards kept him from almost getting crushed. He hit the ground hard, breath rushing from his chest, the marble falling out of his hand. The ground was cool against his body. Air slowly filled his lungs. *That was close,* he thought shakily. That's when he noticed the prized marble was gone.

Jason pushed himself up on all fours, desperately searching all around him. It was dark, and the few lights that were on barely shed enough light to see anything clearly. He took the phone from his pocket and used the light to see as his free hand brushed the grass. He couldn't lose it now. There were so many questions that needed answers. Just as he thought that he felt the cool sphere brush his fingers and quickly closed his hand around it. Jason didn't have to see the marble to know that was it. He had handled it many times as a young boy. He stood slowly, putting the Cherokee Marble into its pouch then tucked it safely in his pocket and released a breath he wasn't aware he had been holding.

That's when he saw it.

He wasn't sure at first if he had or not. It was dark, what light there was had to be playing tricks on him. The black figure stood about twenty feet from him, slightly to the left of the science building. *It was a shadow,* he told himself unconvincingly, *nothing more.*

Then it moved.

Jason's body locked up, rooted to the ground by the fear that was running through him. At the same time his scientific mind was trying to discern who or what it was. The figure appeared to be around five feet tall, but it was hard to tell. It stayed in the shadow. It was darker than the shadow. Whatever the thing was, one thing was certain, it was moving towards him. Jason dared to glance around him, wanting to call for help, but no one was in sight.

There, not forty feet away, sat his car. The shadow thing was closer to him than he was to the car.

He had to get to it.

It was safety.

The struggle to get on his feet was somewhat like trying to lift an elephant. The fight or flight response warred with itself, his body betraying him as it listened to the fear in his mind.

The shadow inched closer.

Jason couldn't move. He felt a frigid cold grasp his heart.

The shadow was only a few feet from him except, he noticed, it wasn't a shadow at all. It was a black mist. A black mist that was malevolent. It radiated from the dark cloud as clear as any spoken word—and it wanted Jason.

He felt the marble crushing into his palm as he gripped it vice-like. He wanted to scream, but the only sound he could make was a muttered guttural moan. It reached a misty tendril towards him.

A beam of light swept across Jason. He immediately felt the coldness leave him. Jason snapped his head around to see where it had come from. A car had passed through the parking lot, raking him and the cloud with its bright beams. When Jason turned back to the cloud, it was gone. Jason felt his legs underneath him once more. He pushed himself off the ground and ran to his car while fishing in his pocket for his keys. He refused to look behind him.

Once at the car, the key easily slipped into the lock. Jason wrenched the door open and leapt inside, hitting the automatic door locks as he did. He thrust the key into the ignition and brought the car to life, turning on the bright beams of his headlights. The black mist was nowhere in sight.

Jason let out an audible sigh, almost hyperventilating as the surreal nature of what he just experienced flooded through him. He felt a sharp pain in his hand, which had a death grip on the marble. It hadn't pierced the skin, but it did leave an indentation. He held the object up to the dome light, eyes trying to fathom its existence.

"What can it mean?" he whispered loudly.

"Fate," a gravelly voice replied.

Jason's eyes widened in surprise as a black gloved hand reached out from behind him, grabbing his chin and pulling his head back against the head rest. He couldn't see his attacker. A sharp sting pierced his neck. Jason struggled briefly before slumping over in the passenger's seat, the marble falling from his hand once again.

The damp air stank with mildew and body odor. Although the room was cool, the man chained in its dark center was drenched with sweat. He was dressed in a dirty orange jumpsuit, long dark hair plastered to his head. His rotund face was masked by a thick beard. The man's overweight physique hid enormous strength, which was one of the reasons he had been chained. But the most chilling aspect was the chained man's slate grey eyes, which seemed to gaze unblinkingly at the floor.

They were eyes that served as a gateway between the outside world and the evil that lurked within him. He was once known as Ronald Williams by those that had grown up with him in Missouri. A dumpy kid that everyone, even the nerds, had picked on. There wasn't one person in the town of Kennett that liked Ronald, including his parents.

From his earliest memories he had been beaten and treated as an outcast by his own family. Through all of the beatings, the bullies, the hate that was cast at him, Ronald never cried, never showed one emotion. Love was not something he ever experienced, not until the day he discovered his passion.

He was at a babysitter's house. The old lady usually kept ten to twelve kids at any given time. Ronald was usually the first one dropped off and the last to be picked up. He had no friends, generally spending his time exploring the large yard, using the one tool he had to escape his misery: imagination. The older children bullied Ronald on a daily basis. If he told on them then the old lady would have hit him with a switch and yelled at him for not being tougher. Every day Ronald grew more and more bitter.

The old lady had cats and kittens everywhere, earning her the derisive name cat lady. Ronald would often carry around a couple of the kittens, their soft purring seemed to have a relaxing effect on him. He had two favorites, Leo, an orange tabby, and Minx, a jet-black cat with green eyes. It was that fateful day while carrying around Leo and Minx, just after another beating by the bullies, that Ronald found the well under the house. What happened then was euphoric; a moment of clarity that he knew instinctively was his purpose in life.

Curious as the kittens he held in his hands, Ronald pulled the wooden planks off the top of the sealed well. Without thought he dropped both kittens into the well, listening to their desperate mewings as they hit the water far below. Their death cries played a symphony to his ears. For the first time in his life, Ronald knew joy—and power. The torture of animals became a source of enjoyment.

It started out simply enough. He would find a stray cat or dog, neither really mattered to him, and then he would find unique ways to kill them, the more horrific the better. His imagination was focused on how to inflict the most pain on the poor creatures before they died.

Then one day he found something he enjoyed more.

He remembered his first kill with the clarity and excitement that most people remembered their first kiss. He remembered them all; every detail etched into his memory: the feel of his mother's throat collapsing in on itself beneath his hands; his alcoholic father drowning in a bottle of liquor that Ronald kept pouring into his drunken, bloated body.

Ronald had never shown emotion, but the image of the whiskey bottle lodged halfway down his father's throat, mouth stretched impossibly wide, was almost enough to make him laugh. But Ronald didn't laugh. He didn't feel remorse. It had been the first real joy he had ever experienced in his life. Joy, a real emotion that jolted through his synapses like the perfect drug, pulsated its reach within his broken mind. Like any addict, he wanted more.

The FBI profilers that caught him had done so by sheer luck; and not until after Ronald had claimed his twelfth victim. It wasn't that he had gotten sloppy, Ronald simply didn't care. He would kill until he couldn't anymore. There was no art to it. He killed in whatever manner brought him the greatest pleasure. Men and women alike became his victims, but not children; never them. Adults deserved what they got.

When the FBI found him, he was sitting amongst the mangled corpses of an elderly couple, their bodies broken and twisted in almost impossible angles. Ronald was rocking back and forth, a strange noise rasping from his throat. One of the FBI agents vomited at the sight. As they were putting the cuffs on him they noticed something else. On his chest he had carved a word with the elderly lady's severed hand: Psycho.

Five years had passed. He was sent to Hale County Mental Institute and forgotten. It could have been anywhere in the world and he wouldn't have known the difference. Ronald simply knew that this new place was special. Here, things were different. He had a friend, his first. His friend didn't call him by his old name, only by Psycho. For his friend, Psycho would do anything. Because his friend let him do what he loved.

He heard the chains clink, felt the shackles around his wrists fall to the floor. It was time. Psycho didn't look back. He walked to the end of his cell disappearing into the shadows.

Tonight, he would kill. Again.

William sat staring into the camera, his mind trying to organize the thoughts he wanted to say. He noticed something with the camera and grabbed it, unplugging the wires from the computer and then plugging them back in another port, his frustration mounting.

"...hate this damn thing," he muttered through the bandana as he readjusted it yet again. Finally, when he was satisfied it was working, he began recording.

"Don't have time to go into a long broadcast right now. They have been following me. They appear everywhere. Gotta go get supplies, man."

William took off his shirt revealing various painful looking scars. As he did he knocked a portion of his bandana from his face sending him in a frantic fit to get it back in position. He reached past the computer, grabbed another shirt, and pulled it over his wiry frame.

"They've got so many people on their payroll," he said once the shirt was on, staring back into the camera. "People you least expect: police officers, lawyers, teachers...Mr. Wallace the ice cream man his truck just keeps circling and circling...they are everywhere people!"

William's mood changed suddenly into a sad state of depression, tears welling in his eyes. "Even your parents could be on their side, man, waiting till you're weak, preying on your love!"

The tears were streaming as he suddenly grabbed the camera, forcing his bandana enclosed face to cover the entire frame. "They will use your entire family to destroy you, to make you a slave, damnit!"

Just as suddenly, William calmed down, voice becoming distant, eyes staring into nothing. "But of course, if that doesn't work. They have their monsters." He stared back into the camera, eyes full of determination, "You don't believe me. No one believes me. I'll get the proof...tonight."

William switched off the live feed. He grabbed a backpack sitting beside the desk and flung it over his shoulder. If no one wanted to believe him then it was up to him to force them to. He turned off the light and was about to leave the room when his computer came back on. The screen blanked out then flashed once more.

Fear stopped him where he stood as he read the screen: We know where you are.

William dropped to his knees. They really were coming.

JC tousled his hair as he looked in the mirror, wearing it in that messy jelled look. He sprayed on some cologne and took a long look in the mirror, a slow smile spreading across his face. *You did it,* he thought happily, *you got the lead.*

There had been a lot of hard work involved, mostly thanks to Ashlyn being such a taskmaster. He laughed at that thought and shook his head wryly. She really did believe in him. "Those other guys just show up and expect that their looks and minimal talent will get them whatever part they want. But it's the hard work and dedication that's going to win you that roll," she had told him with conviction. She was right—as usual.

"JC, I'm home!" JC winced, quickly losing his smile. He had hoped to be gone well before his father got home. No such luck. His dad would force him to talk to him, which would end up turning into an argument. It always did. JC couldn't remember the last time they had gotten along, or how it happened that they had become enemies. There had been happier times, but he couldn't remember when.

As he walked into the kitchen, he saw his father was pouring whiskey, Dewar's to be exact, into a shot glass. JC frowned at the sight, leaning back against the wall. "Hitting it a little early, aren't you?"

Evan killed the liquid, grimacing as the liquor burned down his throat. "Rough day at work." He put down the shot glass and immediately began filling a glass of wine, pointing to a sack on the table as he did so. "Brought Chinese."

"No thanks."

"You've eaten?"

"No, Ashlyn and I are going out."

"Ashlyn?" Evan asked with a hint of surprise in his voice.

JC sighed audibly, growing perturbed by the conversation, pushed himself off the wall, "I've been dating her for three months, dad."

Evans eyes narrowed in thought. *Three months? Where the hell have I been?* He thought resignedly, already knowing the answer. "I didn't know that."

"Why would you," JC asked as he made his way across the kitchen to where his jacket was resting on a chair, "You're never here." He shrugged on his jacket and snatched his keys from the tabletop, making his way to the door.

Evan grabbed JC lightly by the arm as he walked past. "Son..."

JC wrenched his arm free and kept on walking. "Don't wait up," he called back over his shoulder as he marched out the door.

Evan just let him go, a look of distress on his face. What had happened between them? It was like this all the time. Sure he worked a lot, but because of that JC didn't have to and could focus on his school. Evan downed the glass of wine and pulled out his cell phone. He walked into the foyer, peering through the glass in the front door as he dialed. He watched the taillights of JC's new truck streak down the drive. He had tried buying the boy's affections, which he knew through his years of study and from knowing his son's independent personality, that it was a mistake. After a moment, someone on the other end of the line picked up.

"It's time," he said, his voice low and dark, as he watched his son's truck disappear into the distance. Evan snatched his keys from the counter and walked out the door. At the entrance he paused. There, at the top of the stairs, he could almost see her. He closed his eyes, trying to see an image that burned vivid in his memory. *Miranda, I'm losing him.*

Jake poured himself another glass of bourbon.

He held the cool glass against his temple as he leaned back in his leather desk chair, eyes closed as if trying to will away the insanity of the world. The sheriff had made all the calls to family and kin of Mr. Peasley and Tommy Two Feet. He had listened to the whaling cries of grief-stricken children and parents alike, shamed because he had no words of comfort nor any leads to follow. He knew his friend Dan felt the loss just as heavily, more-so even, than he did. Now those loved ones had to pick up the pieces with little to no explanation as to why.

The bourbon burned deep as the memories of all the people he lost over the last few years came intruding in his alcohol-infused stupor as usual. Cutty, Dean, Peasely, his parents...the list kept growing.

Jake reached down and pulled the jewelry box from his drawer and set it on his desk. Although the small jewelry box was nearly weightless it was all he could do to lift it, the voice in his head fighting him, begging him, not to do this to himself anymore. The mental weight is what he feared. It was the one thing that could defeat him.

The fingers of his right hand twitched as he reached for it as if knowing what it was doing was wrong but could not fight the power that commanded it. His hand closed around the slightly cool surface of the box forcing a weary sigh to escape his lips.

How much longer could Jake do this to himself?

People saw him as a rock, unbreakable, dependable, tougher than a two-dollar steak. Yet the outside was only a façade, an eggshell that was barely containing his agony. Agony? No, his hell. For that's what this was…hell.

This was the person he hid from everyone. The weakness would consume him if he let it. It wasn't that he didn't understand what he was doing to himself, he did, he just couldn't control it.

He opened the box.

They stared at him tauntingly, daring him to forget, chastising him for remembering. They shone brightly in the dim light of his office, a pair of matching earrings. Light danced from the semi-precious stones entrancing him further.

That memory. That single memory that splintered into a cascade of memories threatening to drown him in regret. There was the irony. He didn't regret it at all. He welcomed the pain because it was a reminder, a reminder of her.

His mind fluttered to the night she had sat in that very office, giggling in that way she had, always keeping him off balance with her easy with and knowing charm. She was the counterbalance to his stoic exterior. Her beauty wasn't perfect, but it was perfect to him.

Sitting back in his chair, closing his eyes, he saw her as she was that night, laughing and flirting…wanting him to kiss her. He had hesitated. Jake had never been bad with women but there was something about her that always kept him guessing.

She reached a hand up and took one earring out and then the other, smiling tauntingly as she did so. They laughed some more and talked well into the night. The night waned into morning and she finally announced she had to leave.

Jake didn't want her to go but walked her to his office door. She turned and stared directly into his eyes. "Are you ever going to kiss me," she asked voice full of want laced with a knowing smile.

Their lips met.

Jake was trapped at that moment.

The couch in his office, where he had spent many a night alone, became their bed. It wasn't hurried, forced, or animalistic. The love making was slow, a dance that swayed easily from one motion to the next.

Jake opened his eyes. The memory transposed over the cold, unused office furniture. The thunder from the storm outside mimicked the roiling emotions that continued to swirl within.

The affair was brief.

When she left part of him left with her. No one had ever had that power over him. Not before. Not since.

Whatever else he had screwed up in his life that was the worst because it was the one thing he had no control over. She had possessed him like a ghostly lover, caressed his soul with hers, blanketing his heart with promises of hope. Then she was gone.

He brought the earrings to his lips as lightning flashed through the window. He kissed the cold gems lightly and put them back into their box.

She had left without them, promising to come back for them.

Like so many others it was a promise left unfulfilled. Jake found the case at his mother's and stored the only memento he had of her within. He would let no other woman close to him. Period.

Jake gently put them back into their case and shut them back in his desk. He turned and stared out into the storm, lightening reflecting in his eyes, thunder matching the beating of his heart.

It would be another night that her ghost refused to let him rest.

WAKE UP!!

His eyes snapped open. He lunged forward, only to be slammed back against the wall by the massive chains that secured him. Again and again, he strained against the binds that held him so tightly.

Stop daddy, save your strength.

He stopped, body going rigid, eyes taking in everything around him. He searched the darkness for her, for Katie. Rational thought was beyond him, but her; she was his voice, his anchor.

I'm here, daddy.

He followed the sound of her voice. There, in the dark only a few feet away, he saw her. Her smile was perfect, lips dark as cherries. Her eyes were doe-like. His little girl. He wanted to reach out to her, to speak to her—to comfort her as she had him. But he had no voice. He didn't even know who he was. But he knew her. The chains clanged loudly as he fought against them.

No, daddy, you have to stop, she's coming!

He stopped moving instantly. The yellow haired lady was coming. He didn't like her. She was always stabbing him with things, putting medicines into him. The medicines burned. They made his thoughts fuzzy, made him forget. He no longer knew his own name. He had forgotten everything, except his little girl. Nothing they could do could make him forget her. He felt the rage boiling within him at the thought. He would kill them all for what they had done.

But not now, daddy. Not now.

He looked longingly at his daughter once more. She was right, now wasn't the time. But there WOULD be a time. Of that, he was certain.

He heard the lock on the door being released, followed by the slow creak of the door opening. Light poured into the room. He had to squint against the brightness of it. A hazy figure appeared in the doorway. And although he couldn't see the figure fully, he knew who it was. The yellow lady.

The yellow lady walked up to him. How he wanted to rip her throat out. She grabbed his long dirty blonde hair with one hand, wrenching his head back. With the other hand she jabbed a long needle into the side of his neck. An animalistic growl escaped his throat as she released him and stepped back. He could already feel the medicine burning through him, clouding his mind.

Fight it, daddy!

Daddy? Who is daddy? His muddled mind wondered as sleep tried to claim him.

The yellow lady spoke, her voice clear and sharp in his head. "It's almost time, Wraith. Give in and relax. We're going to help you."

Yes, he thought insanely, *help me.* He wanted to hurt people, to destroy everything. He felt the uncontrollable rage rising to the surface. Saliva oozed from his mouth as he set his jaw angrily.

Please daddy, don't listen.

My name is Wraith, he growled in his mind, *I will kill them all.*

Samantha smiled her devilish smile at the familiar look of obedience on Wraith's face. She walked to the corner where Katie was huddled and picked the doll up, studying the porcelain face. The word "Hate" was scribbled in blood on the dolls head. On the floor where Sam had picked up the doll was a logging chain with other doll heads attached to it. The doll heads were in various mangle states. Some had nails buried in the skulls, eyes missing on others, but on all of them were words etched in blood: love, death, anger. She tossed it back in the corner where it landed roughly on the chains, marring the doll's face.

She wasn't sure why Evan insisted on keeping the ugly things. He just told her it was useful. Whatever Evan wanted was all that mattered to her. He trusted her with all of this. Not even his so-called best friend, Dr. Lane, knew about these experiments. Evan loved her, she was sure of it. She turned her back to the dirty nut job chained to the wall and walked out of the room.

Wraith was unaware of it all, the only thing he had on his mind— was death.

Chapter 5

The darkness moved, shadow to shadow, snaking through the unseen places as silent as non-existence. Yet exist it did. There was purpose to its movements, a sentience born of the lasting night, fueled by a consuming hunger. That hunger craved to be satiated on the agony of the dying. But not just any sort of death would do. No, this particular darkness only fed on the fear and anguish that resulted from terror, horror.

You could run from it, but there was no hiding. The darkness always came. When it hunted there was no escape, and the hunt was coming more and more regularly. It hadn't hunted so freely in over 2000 years. After so long a time its appetite was ravenous. Still, it couldn't feed wantonly, no matter how much it desired to do so. It was still bound, but not for much longer.

It wafted, house to house, searching for the right morsel. Families, unaware of the danger, went about their routines; supper, baths, movies, reading, video games, all wrapped up in their insufferable human regularities.

The misty form slipped through the cracked window into the kitchen, which was lit only by the small light in the refrigerator door. The sounds of a football game were overlapped with the sounds of a man shouting his disappointment. "Damn, Vols!! What the hell?!?! No coaching! No recruiting! I could coach the damn team!!"

The thing followed the disgruntled voice, finding its owner reclined in an old worn chair in the living room. The overweight plumber, greasy orange Vols hat sliding precariously on his round head, an almost empty Bud Light in one hand and a Vape mod in the other, was red-faced as he shouted at the television screen.

Murphy Bowles was a huge Tennessee Vols fan, his love of the team surpassing his love for his wife in recent years. He kept the bills paid, gave her spending money, she left him alone. All-in-all it was a great life as far as he was concerned. His only child spent most of his time on some popular video game jumping out of buses and shooting other cartoon type characters. Murphy didn't understand it and didn't want to. Apparently, that game was the latest craze. As long as it kept Nate off the street he didn't care, and it kept him from bothering his dad except for when he needed money for the stupid game skins. Again, better that than those new drugs all the kids were getting into. "Damn drugs," the drunken man slurred as he watched the sorry excuse for football unfolding on his television screen, "kids will do anything these days."

The mist swirled beneath Murphy's seat unawares, the temperature dropping second by second as the alcohol fueled body heat kept him from noticing. The lights flickered, giving the drunk man pause, but only for a second before he once again turned his anger towards the images running across the screen. "What are you doing!?!?" he yelled, hurling a half-empty bottle at the wall. Little wafts of dark vapor floated off the entity, entering the nasal cavity of the drunk and unawares man, heightening his rage as the main portion of the wispy creature snaked its way up the stairs.

The darkness made its way to the top of the landing, pausing as two distinct sounds filtered from opposite sides of the dim hallway, the only light seeping in from the bottoms of the respective doorways. The room further up on the right was filled with digital sounds of gunfire mixed with Nate's yelling commands to his teammates as they immersed themselves into the pixel-filled dominion where they unwittingly slaved their minds, the loud mixture of hard rock music only adding to the increasing intensity in the air. Another piece of the shadow broke away from the creature, weaving its way under the door, the worked up and frustrated teenager inside never noticing as it wrapped around the cord that connected the headphones to the controller, moving up to its target and entering the angry teen with each sharp intake of breath.

From the left doorway drifted the sounds of slow depressing, life has sucked me dry, country music. The dark mist crept into the bathroom, dimly lit by candlelight. An almost empty bottle of wine set haphazardly on the edge of the bathtub as a middle-aged woman soaked herself in the steaming hot water, humming along to the tune. The mist allowed parts of itself to intermingle with the steam which the drunk woman unknowingly inhaled.

Moments later, a thunderous explosion erupted through the house, startling the mother out of her wine-induced bliss. She stumbled from the tub, almost slipping on the wet tile floor, dawned her robe and headed quickly downstairs. The site before her was chaos. Murphy was standing in the middle of the living room, the television scattered in pieces. There was a hole in the wall where her idiot husband and ripped it off studs in anger. Parts of the television had been tossed into her china cabinet, with pieces of the expensive dinnerware damaged beyond repair.

"Are you out of your fucking mind?!?!" She yelled with an anger she never before possessed, picking up a lamp and hurling it at her husband.

The lamp smashed into Murphy's face, crushing his nose and sending a cascade of blood everywhere. The crazed man let out a guttural roar of pain and fury. In mere seconds he had leaped across the room, grabbed his wife by the throat and tossed her halfway up the stairs. The force of the landing broke three of her ribs instantly, knocking the wind from her, but only for a second.

She could see her husband's angry intent as he began climbing the stairs after her, blood gushing from the mangled spot his nose used to be.

She clambered up the stairs, not with fear but with intent. *How dare that son-of-a-bitch touch me like that* she raged. She pulled herself to her feet and staggered down the hallway, trying to get to her room. The door to her son's room opened as she passed, the wide-eyed teenager taking in the scene.

"Mom…" he began as she passed then stopped at the site of his dad's mangled face lurching after her. Nate stepped into the hallway to plead with his father, but the angry man shoved the teen back into the room, his body slamming against the footboard of his bed. It was enough time to allow his mother to reach the nightstand.

She opened the drawer, pulled out a .38 revolver and swung around to face her husband…just in time to catch a large angry fist to her face, completely crushing her orbital socket, sending shattered bone into her brain. The dazed and confused woman hit the floor, barely registering the large man standing over her, reigning down one deadly blow after the next. The last sound she heard was a sustained ringing in her eyes, guiding her into eternity.

Murphy's hands were soaked in her blood, his sole focus on the utter destruction of the monster who had broken his face. There was no wife, no person, no love who he had sworn to cherish and protect. Rage was his fuel. Suddenly the angry man let out a yelp and then another as something sharp drove into his body.

Nate was slashing and thrusting a knife repeatedly into his father, the image of his dead mother fueling his own rage. Slash. Stab. Thrust. Slash. Thrust. Stab.

Pop…

That was the only sound Nate heard before being lifted from the bed and dropped in the floor by the bullet that slammed into his head. The teenager didn't even have time to register what happened before joining his mother in the void. Wafts of smoke, unobserved, drifted from the mother and son.

Murphy stood in the center of the room breathing deeply in hatred as the mist left his body, all three pieces rejoining the whole as it contemplated the carnage it had wrought from its shadowy perch in the corner of the room. The rage seeped from the bloody man with ragged breaths, as if awakening from a terrible nightmare, only this nightmare lingered. Realization set in as the fog of the creature's influence lifted, the bodies of his beloved family lying awkwardly around him.

"No...no, no, no, no, no..." he whimpered, noticing the gun in his hand. It was unconceivable to him, the brutality, the act, the finality. The rock music drifted to him from his son's room.

"Click. Click. Pull."

Murphy placed the gun under his jaw and did just that, following his family into the darkness.

The creature was pleased. After all these centuries humans were still...just human.

Jason was slumped over in his seat, head resting on the console that separated the driver's side from the passenger's side. A low moan escaped his lips as he slowly began to regain consciousness. The first thing he was aware of was the crippling pain in his head, a severe migraine that made him feel as if his brain was about to explode. He pushed himself into a sitting position, resting against the headrest as he tried to fight through the pain.

Suddenly he remembered the hand that had grabbed him in the darkness. He whipped around; fearful the intruder was still in his car preparing to attack him again. But there was no one there. There was no evidence of any kind that someone HAD been there. Nothing, that is, but the massive headache he now suffered and the soreness in his neck from where he had been stuck with that needle. *Why? What were they after?*

Jason glanced quickly at his clinched fist, suddenly remembering the marble. It was gone. He frantically searched the car; under the seats, the mats, anywhere it could have fallen. Nothing. Whoever attacked him had taken it, that he was sure of. None of it made any sense. The marble, the attack—the black mist. A chill crawled through him at the thought of that.

The supernatural was not something Jason believed in, not in the slightest. He was always about science and facts. Things like spirits and ghosts were just something the masses told themselves so they could feel better about dying. While the black cloud had freaked him out somewhat, there had to be an explanation. But that was a secondary problem, at the moment his focus was on that marble, who had sent it, and who had just as abruptly absconded with it. *More and more questions*, he thought tiredly. He realized there was also another question, where the hell was he?

Looking out of his car it was apparent he was no longer on campus. As a matter of fact, he was no longer in Hale at all. He turned on his headlights and stepped out of his car. It was pitch black all around him. He looked up and couldn't even see the moon or stars. The glow of his headlights revealed that the trees formed a canopy over the small two-lane road.

Up ahead he could tell that the road forked. He also noticed a sign leading up the road that veered to the right. He walked towards it, no longer afraid of something happening. *If whoever attacked me had wanted me dead, I wouldn't have woken up in the first place,* he thought rationally.

As he got closer, he noticed the sign was made of stone. It was rather large, probably six foot wide and four feet tall. It read: Hale County Mental Institute. *Hale County Mental Institute?* He had, of course, heard the urban legends about the place. It was another one of those fascinating reasons he had taken the teaching job in Hale County. The land around here was full of mystery.

"And now I'm caught up in one," he said loudly, as much to break the creepy silence of the night. For now, that he thought about it, there was no noise at all; no animals, birds, insects, nothing.

Jason walked back to his car, mind full of questions and a severe migraine. As he neared his car, the flashing lights of a police car lit up the highway, the siren echoed off the cavernous trees. It wasn't a car but rather a truck. The police truck pulled up right behind him. When the door opened, he read Hale County Sheriff on the side.

A large man stepped from the truck, his cowboy boots clapping off the pavement. He wore blue jeans and a beige short sleeve uniform shirt whose sleeves couldn't contain the muscled arms that wore it. The straw cowboy hat made it difficult for Jason to see his face until the man was right up on him. When he got close enough that Jason COULD see his face, he instantly wished he hadn't. The man didn't look like he had ever smiled in his life. The two-day growth of hair on his face added even more fierceness to an otherwise scornful expression. Jason read the name on the badge: Sheriff Jake Hooks.

"Is there a problem officer?" he asked as the sheriff came to a stop in front of him.

"You tell me, professor," came the no-nonsense reply. If Clint Eastwood had an evil alter ego, then this man was surely it.

"Do I, uh, know you?" Jason asked.

"Nope, but I know you."

"How do…"

"My county. I know everybody," Jake said roughly, cutting Jason off. "So," the sheriff asked expectantly.

"Oh, I was just out driving and uh, I got sick, so I pulled over." Jason didn't know why he felt the need to lie, but he did. Certainly, it would have been easier to tell the sheriff what had happened to him. But if Jason didn't believe in the supernatural, he was almost certain the sheriff would commit him to that institution up the road right here on the spot. So he lied. It was all he could do until he found out what was going on.

"Driving where?"

Damn, the sheriff wasn't an idiot. "Um, uh, over to uh, Riley…they uh, have a great little seafood restaurant. You should try it." Thankfully he had heard some of his students talk about the restaurant. Jason grabbed his stomach as he leaned slightly against the car.

"Sobriety test in order?"

The steely gaze was locked onto the professor. This was not the moment for chicanery, especially with the mood the sheriff was obviously in. The time for lies was past. "No sir, to be honest I'm not sure what's going on. I felt bad. Pulled over and I guess I passed out for a bit. But I can assure you I have had nothing to drink. You're free to check."

The sheriff studied the professor for a moment, nodded once seemingly having made up his mind, then walked back to his patrol car. He was about to enter when he spoke to Jason once more. "Hope you get to feeling better."

Jason breathed a sigh of relief. "Thanks officer."

"And professor?"

"Yeah?"

"Riley is in Marion County, about twenty minutes on the other side of Hale. Just so you know." The sheriff didn't wait for a response. He simply got in his car, turned off the flashing lights, and sped off back to town.

Jason realized the sheriff knew he was lying. He looked back at the Hale County Mental Institute sign then noticed his hands. They were shaking. *Oh no, not again.*

A shoe went flying across the room, crashing with a loud thud against the far wall. "Damn bugs," Amanda hissed as she went to collect her shoe and make sure the offending insect was properly squashed. This was not how she had planned to spend her evening. Evan had called a couple hours earlier apologizing but saying that he was going to have to cancel their dinner arrangement. Something had come up at the institute.

She assured him it was okay and ordered a pizza. The plus side was that she could begin to sort her information out. The tour of the asylum had been fascinating. Still, her instincts told her that something else was going on. Well, her instincts and the mystery informant that had initially caused her producer to give her the assignment. Some assignment. All she had to show for it was having been stood up by the hot doctor who ran the institution.

Amanda smacked another roach as she dialed her producer. Phil was going to pay for this. If this was supposed to have been the nice hotel, she could only imagine what the bad hotels were like. WHACK! Another roach down.

The voice who picked up on the other end sounded groggy, as if he had been awoken from a deep sleep. Well, that was fine with Amanda seeing as how she doubted sleep was in her future with all the roaches scouring about.

"You said your sources were reliable. I drove all the way down here to break a story that would get me to New York and all I'm doing is battling bionic roaches in a two-bit motel!!"

She sighed angrily and opened her laptop as she listened to her producer explain to her that the best journalist had to endure the biggest hardships to get the best stories. That's what separates the good reporters from the great ones.

"Well, I'm telling you that place was anything but creepy. The outside was fairly foreboding, but once inside it was like any other place. The doctor who runs it looks like a model." Her thoughts temporarily flashed to Evan as she listened to her producer. It occurred to her that she was disappointed the date fell through.

"Of course I didn't give him my number," she started to lie. "Well, maybe I did. But just so I could grill him more, see if he really is hiding anything."

She keyed in the password to her Windows screen and brought up the search bar. "I'm looking it up now," she said as she typed an address in the URL. *At least the Wi-Fi works in this dump,* she thought sarcastically as the webpage quickly loaded.

'The Dark Truth' flashed across the top of the screen. Amanda furrowed her brow as she tried to decipher the chaotic page. Finally, she located the webstream listing and tabbed to the latest entry. The figure that appeared on the screen wasn't precisely what she was expecting as William's disheveled and covered image filled the video.

"Okay, now here's a weird looking character," she said into the phone, "Are you watching this?" Amanda listened intently as William rambled on about the people that were after him and the asylum in particular. But what really got her attention was when William took off his shirt and accidentally moved part of his mask.

There.

Right there.

There was a small scar on his temple, just like the comatose woman in the institute. She paused the feed and tried to zoom in. She cursed loudly, her computer not having the ability to cooperate.

"Sorry, not you Phil," she said quickly. "I think I've found something. The scar on that man's temple, I saw another one exactly like it on one of Dr. Michael's patients today. Can you get one of your contacts to run the IP address? I need to find this guy."

Amanda studied the image. As crazy as she figured this William person to be, she found, in her experience, that the truth is seldom laced with sanity. "Come on Phil, this is important…and you owe me. I'll call you back, Phil, send that address to my phone when you get it" she said distantly, abruptly hanging up on her boss. He wouldn't hold it against her. Phil knew that's just the way she was.

She opened her little black book, but it wasn't a book for potential dates. Her book contained numbers to sources, work acquaintances, and certain dubious types that could find people when most couldn't. Amanda found the number she was looking for and dialed. She needed to find William and knew just the person who could do it. She couldn't wait on Phil. She hated to call this favor in but this could be the break she had been searching for.

As she waited for her source to pick up, she couldn't help but wonder what William's story was. Evan's charm had almost derailed her. Amanda wasn't accustomed to that. But now her bloodhound mentality was back on track. There was a connection here and she meant to find it.

"Let's see what we can learn about you Mr. Tyler," she was fully focused now, "and where I can find you." She tucked her notes and SD cards in a black metal box and locked it. Amanda listened for the tell-tale sound of the phone being answered as she stored the box away. "Hey. Yeah, I need a small favor."

The Tobie Theater was a small family-owned movie house that was as much a part of the history of Hale County as anything else. There were no big movie theaters such as the Malco's or the Carmike's, in Hale. Just ask anyone in Hale though, and they would tell you that the Tobie was their theater of choice. Whenever anyone walked through those doors they were immediately made to feel like family. It was never a surprise to find the small community of Hale packed into the little four screen theater whenever a new movie was released.

Kevin Snyder, a friendly musician that sported a perennially shaved head had inherited the place when his grandmother had passed a few years earlier. He wasn't one to let everyone else do the work and him reap the rewards; just the opposite in fact. Fridays and Saturdays would find him at the ticket booth greeting customers and when they left, he always asked how they enjoyed their experience.

Therefore, it was no surprise at all to JC when Kevin stopped him and Ashlyn as they were exiting the theater.

"Well, what did you think?" Kevin asked, sincerely curious.

"I have to say I was pleasantly surprised," JC said with a satisfied smile.

Ashlyn hooked her arm in his. "It was a fight to get him in here to see it."

Kevin gave a brief laugh then leaned in conspiringly, "We are having a sneak peek for the new Star Wars movie in a couple of months. Here are a couple of tickets."

"Wow, thanks man. We appreciate it!" they both said enthusiastically.

"You kids have a good night," he said with a wave goodbye.

"You too," JC replied with a wave of his own.

They walked arm and arm up the sidewalk, enjoying the evening.

"Well?" Ashlyn finally asked, breaking the silence.

"Okay," JC said grudgingly, "you were right. Not bad at all."

"For a chick flick," Ashlyn finished jokingly as they moved further up the sidewalk into the darkened part of the parking lot.

"For a chick flick," JC confirmed, smiling. He was always smiling around her. He had been so depressed and unhappy for so long that he didn't know such feelings could exist. But Ashlyn had shown him they could.

"So, you're feeling better?"

JC stopped, slipping his arms around her waist and pulling her in close. "I know how I could feel a LOT better," he said slyly.

"Oh really," she teased, moving closer to him, "and what's that?"

Their eyes locked. Nothing existed in the universe at that moment but them. JC slipped a gentle hand under her chin, tilting her face to his. He leaned in, feeling the electricity of the kiss before they ever made contact.

"Y'all wanna buy something?"

The sharp, uneducated drub of a voice stole the moment from them. JC looked around to see where it had come from only to notice a man, dressed in dirty jeans and a hoodie, stepping from the shadows.

"Come on, Ash," JC said, taking her by the hand, pulling her away from the dirty man.

The thug was persistent. He followed the two young lovers, hassling them. When neither one would respond, the thug grabbed JC by the shoulder and spun him around. "Just a dime-bag, man. Help a brother out."

"I'm not your brother, now get lost," JC shot back at him.

The thug buried a fist into JC's gut, sending him to the ground. Ashlyn yelped in surprise as JC hit the hard concrete. As he started to get up, a glint of silver caught his attention. The thug was standing beside Ashlyn, the pointy end of a vicious looking knife less than an inch from her throat.

"Gimme your wallet Romeo, or I gut the girl," the thug said with a nasty toothless grin.

JC looked from the thug to his petrified girlfriend. "Alright, alright, just calm down."

"The wallet..." the thug managed to get out before a large boot came out of nowhere, connecting with the back of his skull, sending the would-be robber to the ground beside JC. The thug tried to recover quickly from the unseen attack only to catch a gloved fist to the eye as he got to his feet. The thug felt his eye socket explode from the blow, sending him crashing to the pavement once again.

JC rushed to Ashlyn's side, turning to see the imposing form of Sheriff Jake Hooks scowling like death at the thug.

"Get the girl home," he said in that low commanding voice.

"Yes sir," JC said shakily, taking Ashlyn by the arm and hurrying her off to his car.

Jake reached down and snatched the thug by the hood, tired and pissed off and maybe slightly inebriated after the day he had. The sheriff snatched the man up in one motion, slammed him against a random car then spun the pusher around to face him. The thug's eye was crushed and bloody, but that wasn't a second thought to Jake who roughly drug the piece of garbage to his patrol car. Jake lifted the man up again, once more slamming him into the car, growling into the scared hood's face.

"No one sells drugs in my county."

The sheriff brought a powerful knee into the beaten man's stomach. As the thug lay on the ground, puking and gasping for air, Jake stood over him. Hell had come to Hale County.

Steven was mumbling incoherently, his entire body covered in sweat. An IV was inserted into his arm, dripping saline at a steady pace. His mumbling seemed to be in sync with the beeping of the heart monitor. He could see the needle in his arm; the sensors for the heart monitor were taped to his chest.

He knew he shouldn't be there. He knew he should scream for help. Surely someone would hear him and come to investigate. Yet Steven couldn't do any of those things. Just as he thought about them, his mind began wandering, pulling up spontaneous memories. He remembered his sixth birthday. His mom and dad were happy and laughing, sharing a beautiful summer day outdoors with their son and the neighborhood kids. That was years before his drug use would destroy his family. His parents divorced. His mother spiraled into depression and eventually took her own life. Steven began to cry. He didn't want to, but the memory was too strong, and the tears came uncontrollably.

The now familiar creak of the steel door opening drew his attention. Every time that door opened, bad things happened. "Please," he sobbed, defeated, "please, no more. I won't, I won't…never…please…"

A handsome man in a white lab coat sat down beside him. Steven remembered him from the hallway when he was first brought in. The man took a chart off of a nearby cart and proceeded to scan through it. When he was done, the man smiled down at him. For the first time since he arrived, Steven felt relief.

"It's going to be okay, Steven," the doctor said kindly. "I am Doctor Michaels."

Steven looked around to see if the evil nurse or the large hulking man were standing nearby. When he was satisfied, they weren't, he whispered to Evan in a pleading voice. "Help me, please."

Evan patted his arm and smiled again. "I'm going to my young friend."

"Nurse…bad…" Steven managed to stutter.

Evan smiled as he tilted Steven's head up, shining a pen light into the man's eyes. He made a note on the chart then took Steven's pulse. Seeming satisfied, Evan made another notation in the chart.

"Sam tends to be overzealous, but she means well," Evan said with a sigh. "Now listen to me, we are going to get you better."

"Not sick," Steven stammered, eyes still red and swollen from the tears.

"Steven, you're a drug addict. And the first step to getting better is for you to recognize that." Evan looked in Steven's eyes, into his soul. "Do you deny it?"

He wanted to; more than anything he wanted to. But even as he went to shake his head yes, his body was nodding no. "I'm an addict," he whimpered.

"Good, that's a great first step, I didn't want to have to call the nurse back in," Evan joked.

Steven's eyes filled with horror at that thought, but Evan gave him a comforting pat on the shoulder.

"We are going to cure you, young man, cravings and all." The confidence in Evan's voice gave Steven hope.

"You are? How?" he asked, daring to believe.

Evan's eyes became thoughtful and focused. "By going deep into your brain and operating on your insular cortex. It has long been thought to control addiction. We are going to find out."

Panic began to consume Steven once again, "But isn't that dangerous?"

Evan stood up patting Steven on the shoulder once more, "Oh yes, but then again, so is addiction." As Evan moved out of the way, Samantha stepped into view, a very large needle in hand that matched the sinister smile on her face.

Chapter 6

The dark road out of Hale County was intimidating, inundated
with sharp winding curves and steep hills. Trees hugged the roads,
leaving little room for error, and created a canvas over the
highway so thick in places that not even sunlight could penetrate
it. The highway had few shoulders. More people lost their lives in
car accidents in Hale County than in any other county in
Tennessee.

All of that mattered little to Jake Hooks. He took the hairpin
curves at breakneck speeds, his squad car, with its flashing L.e.d.
lights, looked like a laser beam zipping through the night. Jake
wasn't a thrill seeker, he just had things to do, especially tonight.

The embattled sheriff had a bad habit of doing the opposite of
what was required of a man in his position. Politically correct, he
was not. Jake's father had taught him early on that there were two
kinds of men in life: those who took action and those who
cowered from it. Jake Hooks was no coward.

His family was poor so an education after high school had been
out of the question. Jake's dad was an alcoholic, a condition most
of the men from Hale seemed to suffer from. The man was useless
as a father and husband, although Jake learned a valuable lesson
from him: the world was tough, and to make it you had to be
tougher. Jake spent his youth fighting for everything he had,
especially respect from the other kids. It was soon well known
that getting into a fight with Jake Hooks was like fighting a bear;
you just didn't do it. It was that toughness that landed him a job
with the Sheriff's Department.

Sheriff Willard Cutty had mentored Jake, seeing it as his duty to groom someone to take over Hale County and the darkness that came with it. Jake, like everyone in Hale County, grew up with the stories of the cursed county in which they lived. People disappeared without a trace, crops died for no apparent reason, healthy people suddenly dropped dead, and then there was the biggest blight on Hale County, that damn asylum. Sure, it brought in jobs, kept people employed, but it also brought an element to the county that the already plagued area didn't need, the criminally insane.

Cutty had explained to Jake that Hale County was alone, abandoned by the rest of the state and its political machine. It was a small county that had no real value, which is why it was selected as a backwater dumping spot for prisoners the state wanted to disappear. The only law was the Sheriff's office. The city police department was so small they only had an eight-person force, a force led by that damn corrupt Malone. The Sheriff's department was continuously bumping heads with the city police. It made keeping the peace more difficult.

"Sometimes we have to do what's necessary for the greater good," Cutty had told him late one night. They had busted a small-time drug ring on a remote farm, catching the dealers by surprise in a small barn at the back of the property. The joke of a legal system would just release them back on the street. Cutty had long suspected, and reliable sources had confirmed, Mayor Grey and his handpicked judges of accepting bribes to keep those operations running.

Cutty and Jake had beaten the three drug dealers into unconsciousness. The old sheriff had Jake take the few thousand dollars they had found to the car while Cutty collected the drugs. When Jake had returned from placing the money in the patrol car, the barn was ablaze with the drug dealers inside. Jake tried to run in and save them but Cutty blocked his way. "What are you doing?" he had yelled at his mentor.

"What's necessary, these guys are stone cold killers, poisoning the youth of our county. Malone and his ilk get their cut and let it happen. No more," the grizzled old man told him, escorting the shocked deputy away from the burning barn. Cutty split the money with Jake who at first refused. "We can't exactly turn in money from this when we can't let anyone know we were here," he rationalized to Jake as they sped away from the scene, "Mayor Grey will have us thrown away in that asylum forever. Take the money and put it to good use. Get your ass out of here one day. This place is evil."

Jake hid that money in his attic, and to that day he hadn't touched it. Nor had he touched any of the money that he and Cutty continued to take off the dealers, pimps, and thieves. Jake knew what they were doing was necessary, but he didn't have to like it. And he certainly wasn't about to profit from it. The strangest part was Cutty's faith in him to never say a word. Honestly, who could he tell? The whole county was overrun with corrupt, self-serving bastards. Cutty had warned him of the dark nature of their home. Jake overlooked it as the ravings of an old superstitious backwoods' upbringing.

But Cutty's view of the evil of Hale County proved accurate two years later when he was stabbed to death as he left his office one stormy night, left bleeding by a storm drain, belly split open so wide his guts were hanging out. Cutty's killer was never caught. Jake was named the new Sheriff following the tragedy.

Shortly thereafter the pale skinned Mayor Grey paid him a visit. "Sorry for your loss, Sherriff Hooks," the old weasel of a man said, voice as smooth as a snake's, "I hope you prove far wiser than your predecessor." There it was. The mayor had all but admitted to having Cutty killed. If he thought that would intimidate Jake, then he was wrong.

That was when he had realized that Cutty had been right, that the system didn't apply to Hale County as it did to others. Here, they were on their own. Jake Hooks vowed to do whatever was necessary to make sure Hale survived, no matter the cost to his own soul. Just hours earlier that point was beaten home to him once again as yet another friend and a young boy were brutally murdered in a nonsensical way that baffled description. The sheriff had reached his limit.

The patrol car came to a stop at the same fork in the road where Jake had encountered Jason Locke a couple of hours earlier. The high beams of the headlights reflected off the stone Hale County Mental Institute sign. Jake got out of the car and opened the back door. Inside, lying half-unconscious on the seat, was the thug he had prevented from robbing the Michaels kid. Jake snagged the man by his hood, dragging him out of the patrol car and dumping him roughly, face first, on the cold pavement. Jake put a boot on the back of the man's neck as he undid the handcuffs.

Jake rolled the man over and leaned him against the back tire, then suddenly slapped the thug hard across the face. "Get up," the sheriff growled.

The thug's eyes shot open at the sting of the slap. It took him a moment to realize he was on the pavement, and another moment to realize the sheriff had un-cuffed him. A barrage of profane words came to the thug, but looking into the face of the Sheriff convinced him that now wasn't the time. *Still,* he thought as he touched his shattered eye, *I owe the bastard.*

Jake grabbed the handcuffs and placed them in the patrol car, turning his back to the thug. He took a slow, measured breath— waiting. He didn't have to wait long. Jake heard the click of heel on pavement. With a sudden move that seemed much too quick for a man of Jake's size to make, the sheriff spun to the side, the thug leaping past him headfirst into the open door, hitting his head on the inside frame. Jake slammed the door on the thug's head, causing an instant concussion and temporarily blinding him. He pulled the man up by his throat and shoved him against the car, jamming his .44 halfway into the thug's mouth.

"Well, you're about a dumb piece of shit, aren't you," Jake stated coldly, cocking the hammer on the gun.

The thug's one good eye filled with tears of fear as he peed all over himself. Jake searched the man. He found four small sandwich bags of marijuana, a lighter, and a couple of hundred dollars in his billfold. Jake took the drugs, and the money then tossed the empty wallet towards the left fork of the road.

"Small time little prick. That road will take you to Davis County. If you ever step in MY County again, they will never find the body. Understand?"

The drug dealer nodded as best he could with the gun shoved down his throat. Satisfied, Jake took the gun out of his mouth and shoved the man towards the road. Jake didn't say another word. He simply got in his car and headed back to Hale; certain the thug would never visit his town again.

The beaten man laid on the ground for a few minutes, trying to collect his composure, hurting in every part of his body. He hauled himself off the pavement, dazed and confused by the assault of the Sheriff, and began staggering down the lightless road. Thunder rumbled somewhere in the distance. Just his luck to get his ass kicked and get caught in a storm. In the dark, he didn't realize that he had taken the right fork instead of the left; and what awaited him there was far worse than anything the Sheriff could ever do.

The steaming hot water rolled off his body, turning his skin a bright red. It was hotter than he normally took a shower but at the moment the overly hot water didn't faze him. His only concern was stopping the involuntary twitching of his hands. He concentrated on calming them as best he could.

Jason hadn't had an episode in years. In fact, it had been such a long time since the last one that he had forgotten ever having had the problem. His shaking hands were a stark reminder that the past wasn't that far removed after all.

I should have called Rachel, he thought absently, watching the twitching of his hands. He knew she would have cut her trip short and rushed right home to care for him. He wasn't an invalid, and he certainly wasn't going to make his wife abandon her friends and her trip because of him. Besides, there were much larger problems; and he wanted her nowhere near this.

Jason kept replaying the events over and over in his mind; the marble, the black mist, the person who had him drugged and stole the marble. He reached up to feel the sore spot on his neck where the needle had pierced his skin. The whole thing felt like a nightmare; except it wasn't a nightmare at all. Someone had dredged up his past and was now toying with him.

He let his mind drift as the hot water cascaded over the back of his neck, easing some of the tension that had knotted there. *No one knows of my past nor of the significance of that marble and why it is not possible for that to be the original,* he thought, eyes closed in contemplation as the steam built around him. *But if it was a forgery then someone went through a hell of a lot of trouble. How could they know its significance? And the personalized inscription? NO one knows about that! The black mist? Easy, I was hungry, hadn't eaten all day. I hit my head when I fell. But who the hell drugged me?*

Each question seemed to be answered with two more. And the last question was the one that plagued him the most. Whoever it was didn't want him dead or they would have killed when they had the opportunity. Blackmail? He lived comfortably but he wasn't rich by any means. Too many questions.

Jason turned off the water and toweled himself dry. He needed sleep. But first he had to eat. He dug through the refrigerator and found enough lunch meat to make a quick sandwich. He dug the wheat bread out of the pantry. He threw together some ham, turkey, a little cheese, some spicy mustard, topped off by a couple of pickles and bam: an awesome sandwich.

Lightning flashed outside his window followed quickly by thunder. He poured himself a glass of sweet tea and sat down at the kitchen table with his sandwich. Jason ate mindlessly as the rain began falling heavily outside. Exhaustion and hunger had overcome his fear. Eating and sleeping were all he could think of. He would worry about the rest tomorrow.

Finishing his sandwich, Jason took his plate and empty tea glass to the sink. Without warning, a bright flash, followed almost simultaneously with a deafening clap of thunder, hit right outside his kitchen window, shaking the house violently and plunging it into darkness. Jason felt his way out of the kitchen. Lightning illuminated the house with chaotic flashes of brilliance, casting deep shadows all around him.

Jason took a step into the hallway when he heard the clattering of something tiny, like little claws, running through the ceiling.

Squirrels! Squirrels? Where did that come from? He shook his head quickly to push aside that train of thought.

Another step took him fully into the hallway as he listened closely to the clicking sound. He felt a slight tingle and turned to gaze into the darkness, the lightning casting even more oddly angled shadows.

There, at the end of the hall. That was no shadow. Jason froze in fear, hair standing on end, chills extending head to foot. It was no shadow at all, darker than the dark. The black mist flowed toward him. As the lightning and thunder pounded through the downpour, no one heard Jason Locke's screams as he darted into his basement.

Ashlyn's family was part of the disappearing middle-class America. They weren't rich, but neither were they poor. Ashlyn's mom and dad worked hard to provide their daughter with anything she needed. It might not have been the best, but she never went without. Their house was a reflection of that lifestyle. A far cry from the mansion where JC and his father lived, the Taylor's small brick home in the older section of town was still very nice. And more than that, it actually FELT like a home.

Mr. Taylor had taken the news of their near mugging with extreme calm, nothing much seemed to bother man. Her mom, however, had been a different matter. Mrs. Taylor fawned and pawed over her daughter until Mr. Taylor threatened to send her to her room. Ashlyn's dad had been joking when he said it but it served its purpose. Soon they were all laughing. Mrs. Taylor sent them out to the front porch to watch the storm roll in while she made them some hot chocolate.

JC was envious of the Taylors. He longed for the family that they were. Mrs. Taylor brought the hot chocolate and homemade chocolate chip cookies and set it on the small wrought iron table between them. JC thanked her. He hadn't realized he was staring until Ashlyn called him on it.

"You got a thing for my mom?" She said laughingly.

"Huh?" JC said, the question shaking him from his revelry.

"Are you crushing on my mom?"

JC turned bright red. "Of course not. Only…"

Ash took his hand as he turned serious, "What is it?"

It took him a moment to get the words out. "Your family. They are amazing. I wish sometimes that I knew what that was like; I wish I knew what my mom had been like."

"Your dad never told you?"

JC scoffed at that. "He refuses to speak about her at all. He has barely acknowledged she even existed."

"I'm sorry," Ashlyn said sincerely, stroking the back of his hand.

JC smiled at her, pulling her in close. There was nothing to ruin their kiss this time. When they broke apart, he smiled at her, "Your mom IS kinda hot."

Ashlyn laughed as she punched him playfully. He was about to kiss her again when a long black Cadillac pulled into the driveway, blocking his car in. The driver, dressed in a black suit, got out of the car and opened the rear passenger door.

A tall slender man in a charcoal suit stepped out of the car, his skin a pale white. His angular features, the way he carried himself, gave him an air of aristocracy. He moved with purpose, as if every motion was planned. The look in his crystal blue eyes was that of a predator. And when he spoke, it was the voice of the Prince of Lies, smooth and flattering.

"Good evening," he spoke with a thin, welcoming smile, "how is my goddaughter?" He gave Ashlyn a kiss on the cheek.

"Hi, Uncle Grey," Ashlyn said as she gave him a hug.

The tall man turned his attention to JC, extending a boney hand, "And you, Mr. Michaels, a pleasure to meet you."

"Mr. Mayor," JC said as he accepted the handshake.

"I'm an admirer of your father's work. Please give him my regards."

"Yes sir, I will," JC said, puzzled to know that the Mayor had any interest in his father.

The mayor turned back to Ashlyn. "I heard you two had quite the run in tonight. Are you okay?"

"Yes sir, we were lucky the Sheriff was there," Ashlyn said thankfully.

"Yes, lucky indeed."

Something in the way he said it sent a chill up JC's spine. There was no love loss there apparently. The Alderman's dangerous glint in his eyes at the mention of the Sheriff.

"Well," the Grey finally said, "I'll leave you two kids alone. I just need a word with your father."

"He's in the living room, make yourself at home."

The wretched pale man gave them a curt nod of his head and entered the house. JC watched him disappear then turned back to Ashlyn. What he saw on her face was like a blow to his stomach. She was terrified.

"Ash," he said, putting his hands on her face, forcing her to look at him, "what's wrong?"

It took her a moment to answer, but when she was finally able her voice came out in a whisper, full of anxiety, "The Mayor...he's evil."

JC looked fixedly into her eyes, "What do you mean?"

Ashlyn pulled him in close, arms vice-like around his waist. Her voice came out in a broken hush. "He hurt me."

JC felt a dark pit open up beneath him, threatening to swallow him whole. He held Ashlyn tight. When he looked up he could see through the glass door, right into the living room. The mayor was glaring at him, expressionless accept for the gleam in his eye. JC's first impression of him had been correct; he was the devil.

Amanda could barely see the front of her car as she drove blindly through the sudden thunderstorm. It came on quickly and without warning. It aggravated her. Her day had kept getting worse since the moment she drove off the asylum parking lot earlier in the day. But to her credit she was persistent; and that persistence usually paid off with a big story.

"Nail this story, Amanda, and it's off to New York," she said out loud, trying to keep herself motivated that driving in this storm was the right thing to do. Her contact had traced William's whereabouts to an old home right outside of Hale. There was little doubt in her mind that the man was crazy. The fact that he had admitted to the world that he had been a patient there was evidence enough. But it was that same craziness that could give her valuable insight into anything suspicious going on at the mental institute.

All she had to do was get the strange man to talk to her, which, considering the website he ran, didn't seem to be an issue. The issue was her popping in on him unannounced. From all the measures he took in rerouting his server data, she was certain William thought he was safe; and from the normal person he would be. Her source, however, was a computer hacker.

Amanda's biggest worry was how William would react to her showing up at his supposed safe haven rather suddenly. Well, she would have to worry about that when she got there. Phil wasn't happy either, although he knew better than to talk her out of it. Amanda did what Amanda wanted to do, and that was the end of it. It's also what made her successful.

As she drove on through the rain, she let her mind drift to Evan. It was the first time since he cancelled on her that she let herself think of him. She had no time for men. They could only slow down her success. In her mind there was always time to fall in love and have a family; that time just wasn't now. Changing diapers and cooking supper every night while washing clothes and cleaning house, was nowhere on her to do list.

So why was she thinking about Evan? *Because he's cute,* she thought wryly. Yet, it was more than that. His charm was undeniable. He was smart, funny, and passionate. Passion, now that was something she hadn't had in life in quite some time. She felt a tingle at the thought of him taking her in his arms and bringing some much-needed passion into her life. Amanda shook her head, trying to clear the direction her thoughts were taking.

Her phone began chirping at her annoyingly. She picked it up and looked at the name: Evan Michaels. A small smile appeared at the corner of her mouth as she hit the answer button. As she glanced back up a shadow darted in front of her car.

Amanda swerved hard to avoid hitting whatever had darted in front of her car. The tires lost traction on the rain-slicked road, sending the vehicle into a wild spin. She frantically tried to regain control as the world whirled around her in a blur of darkness and flashing lightning.

With a sickening crunch of metal, the car slammed into something solid, bringing it to an abrupt halt. Amanda's head smacked against the steering wheel, dazing her, along with a heavy pressure on her chest. For several long moments, she sat there stunned, her ears ringing. Slowly, she became aware of the hissing sound of rain on the roof and the tinny voice coming from her phone, which had fallen to the floor.

"Hello? Amanda? Are you there? What happened?"

With shaking hands, she retrieved the phone. "E-Evan? I...I think I crashed." Her voice sounded distant and strange to her own ears.

"Are you hurt? Where are you?" Evan's voice was filled with concern.

Amanda gingerly touched her forehead, wincing at the tender lump forming there. "I...I, there's...water," with shocking realization she realized the 'water' was sticky. "Blood...b...blood..."

"Stay put. I'm coming to get you. I've got to call 9-1-1. Hang on. I'll call you right back," Evan said firmly.

"No, you don't have to-" Amanda started to protest, but Evan had already hung up. She sighed and leaned back in her seat, her heart still racing. What had she seen on the road? It had looked almost like a person but moved far too quickly. A chill ran down her spine that had nothing to do with the cold rain now seeping in through the cracked windshield. She was pinned, making it harder and harder to breathe, but she didn't hurt. Why didn't she hurt?

Amanda became aware of an eerie stillness settling over the scene. The rain continued to pour, but there were no other sounds - no distant traffic, no animals, nothing. Just an unnatural quiet broken only by the occasional rumble of thunder.

She peered out into the darkness beyond her headlights, straining to see anything. *Wait, those aren't headlights.* Her panicked eyes darted all about as the lights grew brighter. For a moment, she thought she glimpsed a shadowy figure standing at the edge of the trees lining the road. But when lightning flashed again, there was nothing there.

Her phone rang again. "Evan," she gasped into the phone, "something…"

Amanda shivered, suddenly her beleaguered car was tossed into the air.

The car flipped end over end, metal shrieking as it tore apart. Amanda's world spun violently, her body jerking against the seatbelt, yet still pinned by the steering wheel. With a final thunderous crash, the vehicle came to rest on its roof.

Dazed and disoriented, Amanda hung upside down, the seatbelt digging painfully into her chest. Blood dripped from a gash on her forehead, obscuring her vision. She could hear Evan's frantic voice still coming from the phone, now lying shattered on the roof of the car beneath her. Her battered body now twisted within the small confines of the destroyed car, her head touching the roof of the upside-down vehicle.

"Amanda! Amanda, can you hear me? What's happening?"

She tried to respond but could only manage a weak groan. The interior of the car was rapidly filling with water from the torrential rain pouring in through the shattered windows. Amanda fumbled with trembling, broken fingers of her shattered right arm, trying to release the seatbelt.

A flash of lightning illuminated a dark figure approaching the wreckage. Amanda's heart leapt with hope - had help already arrived? But as the figure drew closer, an inexplicable dread settled over her. This was no rescuer.

The shadowy form reached the car, peering in at Amanda with eyes that seemed to glow an unnatural pale blue in the darkness. A hand, unnaturally long and thin, reached through the broken window towards her.

Amanda wanted to scream, but all her fight was gone, her breathing labored. Her brain was trying to process the fear, the pain, the trauma all at the same time, each sense overlapping the other. Just as the cold fingers brushed against her face, the buckle finally released. She crashed down onto the roof of the car, crying out in pain as glass shards dug into her skin.

The dark figure was somehow entering the small crevices of the car with unnatural fluidity, as if its body wasn't constrained by normal human limitations. It was vaguely humanoid in shape but seemed to be composed of writhing shadows. Where a face should have been, there was only a swirling void, save for those eerie pale blue eyes. As she watched in horror, tendrils of darkness began stretching out from its form, reaching for her.

Her face began to relax, her eyes settling in to a fixed stare as her ragged breathing grew soft and shallow. The creature roared in fury, quickly evaporating into the night. Rain intermixed with blood as her lifeless hand clutched the phone tightly, the sound of Evan's voice vainly calling out her name.

William tiptoed as lightly as possible through the trees, trying his best to be silent. Every time he stepped on a stick it echoed as loud as a gunshot through the forest. *At least all the squirrels would be asleep, wouldn't they,* he thought for the hundredth time. Squirrels or not, he had to do this. His whole life, his future if he was ever to have one, would depend on exposing the asylum for what it was.

Getting to the asylum unseen wasn't the hard part, it was getting inside that was going to prove a challenge. Perhaps he could steal one of those swipe keys from one of the employees' cars? That might work. The one thought he had on his two-hour hike through the woods was that, whatever happened, he couldn't get caught. William knew that if he did, he would never be allowed to leave the place.

He clutched the video camera to his chest, taking a moment to rest and reconsider his plan of action. His free hand was absently fingering the scar on his temple. There was no reason he had to do any of this. If he kept silent, kept his mouth shut, then no one would ever bother him. That was something he just couldn't do. William had experienced too many horrors to keep it to himself. People had a right to know.

A low rumbling resounded through the woods, causing William to pause. He stopped moving, waiting patiently for it to happen again. It wasn't a long wait as the noise rumbled once more, this time faintly louder—thunder. William looked past the treetops, noticing for the first time the absence of the stars and moon. So focused had he been on his mission that he failed to notice the change in the weather. He needed to hurry.

William picked up his pace. He hated the lightning; it reminded him all too much of that chair he had been strapped to. Thousands of volts had been discharged into his brain, as if making it into scrambled eggs was going to cure him. He still had scars where the electrodes had seared into his flesh. The smell had been the worst; the smell of his own flesh burning that is. The pain had been awful, but even when it had gone away, he could still smell the scent of his burnt flesh. That is what William wanted to prevent happening to anyone else.

The trees came to an abrupt end at the parking lot of the asylum. There were few cars there as only those working the late shift remained. William counted ten cars in all. He crept up to an old beat-up blue Nova that looked as if it might be the easiest to break into. He tried the door and was astonished when the door came open. A giddy smile formed on his lips and William immediately got to work searching the car for a pass. The smile faded a few moments later when he couldn't find one.

Well, there are plenty more cars, he thought hopefully.

William checked the other cars to see if any were unlocked like the first one. When it was obvious none were, he picked one at random. He was no car thief, nor did he have the tools to do so. However, there was more than one way to do it.

A flash of lightning, followed a few seconds later by a louder rumbling of thunder, told him his time was running out. Even the wind had started to pick up. Luckily, it hadn't begun raining yet. He still had time. William searched the parking lot and found just what he needed, a large rock. Picking it up, he was sure it was heavy enough to do the job.

William took a deep breath; it was now or never. He raised the rock at the offending car window. This was it. The rock felt like it weighed a ton as the consequences of what he was about to do threatened to stall his courage. *Now or never, William,* he thought as he took a deep breath, *now or never.*

With a heave born of determination, Will brought the rock down towards the glass. Out of the corner of his eye, he saw something moving. He pulled the rock out of its trajectory at the last second, which nearly forced him face first into the glass. The rock and William hit the pavement with a thud just as a loud clap of thunder rumbled through the air.

William scrambled across the pavement, hiding behind the car he had nearly broken into. His eyes scanned the darkness for whatever it was that had distracted him. Was it a guard? He glanced at his watch. Couldn't be, it was too early for the lunch breaks. Maybe he had been mistaken. William was about to go back to the rock when he saw it.

At the end of the parking lot, heading down the long narrow road that led to the highway, was a sight that gave him chills. A large, heavy-set man in what he thought was an orange jump suit was striding down the tree line. Was it an escaped inmate?

Giving a glance back to the asylum, William realized that if the man was an inmate, then no one knew he was missing. He also knew this could be just the thing he needed for his proof; someone else to testify to the atrocities of Hale County Mental Institute. First thing first, William wanted to know where the man was going. *Only one way to find out,* William thought determinedly. He turned on his camera and followed him.

Jake was coming out of the Lost Night Diner, tall cup of straight black coffee gripped firmly in his hand, steam pouring into the cool rainy night. The Lost Diner was a Hale County original, long before there was a city proper, just a trading post. It was the longest running diner in the continental United States, passed down through a long family line. Its namesake served those brave souls who pioneered the wilderness, both native and pilgrim alike. As such it was the first restaurant you encountered entering town and the last as you left. It was Switzerland, all were welcome, troublemakers were quickly sent away, some not of their own volition.

He felt the hairs on the back of his neck start tingling, which the sheriff knew never to doubt. A long dark Cadillac pulled up close to his truck. Jake let out a long sigh, the last person he wanted to deal with was Mayor Grey. The scrawny old driver got out, a large black umbrella in hand, and opened the back door of the immaculate vehicle. The narrow, unnatural-looking Mayor stepped from the vehicle, even thinner looking than his driver.

Didn't these people eat, the sheriff thought grumpily.

"Sheriff, might I have a word," the mayor's smooth, deceiving voice purred.

Jake took a drink of his coffee then slowly turned to face the man he detested more than almost any human. "Go ahead."

"Has there been any word on the fate of poor Mr. Peasley?" the mayor asked, a look of unhidden knowing in his eyes. He *KNEW* what had happened to Peasley and was taunting the sheriff, Jake was sure of it. But Jake wasn't the untamed buck of his youth, he wouldn't be drawn in by the mayor's thin, taunting smirk as he leaned against his sleek Cadillac, his eyes glinting with mischief.

"Not yet," Jake said, his tone flat, giving nothing away. "But I'm working on it," he said casually then offered almost as an afterthought, "I am the best tracker in this state."

The mayor's eye's flickered briefly then his lips curled into what might have been a smile. "Wonderful," he said. "We wouldn't want any more unfortunate incidents, would we?"

"No, we would not," Jake replied cooly, never losing eye contact.

There was a long silence as both men took silent measure of the other then the mayor broke the uncomfortable silence. "You should come by the bastille, have dinner one evening. I promise, it will be one to remember," he all but hissed.

"I'm sure it would be," the sheriff replied flatly.

The sheriff kept his face unreadable, though inside he could feel his blood heating up to a simmer. He watched the mayor slip back into his Cadillac with the grace of a man who never had to run for anything in his life.

As soon as the car doors closed and the driver pulled away, Jake let out a long breath. The mayor was up to something, he just didn't know what yet. He could practically smell it on him like cheap cologne, all plans and plots and things he kept neatly locked away.

Jake stared at the darkened highway stretching out before him, rain beginning to tap gently on the brim of his hat. He'd give it another hour or two, then head back toward the asylum to see if anything turned up. Peasley missing was big because even though everyone knew Hale County was less than legit, no one ever quite disappeared like that.

He took another sip of his coffee and climbed into his truck, slamming the door against the cold night air. Whoever thought they could keep getting away with this was in for a hell of a surprise.

The thug hobbled along the lengthy driveway leading to the asylum, drenched by the relentless rain with every step. The blinding lightning and the torrential downpour made it nearly impossible for him to see anything. He was lost. If he could just find a house, he would sneak under a carport and take refuge until dawn. It would certainly be better than being caught in the current deluge.

Adding to his misery, his eye, which he was certain was fractured in multiple places, throbbed with intense pain. The Sheriff had given him quite a beating, which was another reason he needed to be gone by morning; he dreaded the thought of what the Sheriff might do if he caught up with him. Jail wasn't an option, nor was returning to Hale to retrieve his car.

Where were all the houses? He had been walking for over an hour without spotting a single one. There should have been some scattered along the highway. The rain was so heavy it felt like it was stinging him. The battered man did what he could: he pulled his soaked hoodie tighter around himself and pressed on through the storm, unaware of what might be lurking in the night.

William slipped in the mud, landing face first in the soft cold grass. He hadn't seen rain that heavy in Hale County in years. Yet there he was, sneaking after someone in a freezing downpour. Now it was all he could do to stay on his feet. Lying in the grass, he made the decision to crawl under the nearest tree. It was probably not the wisest decision, but he figured that he was in a forest so the odds of lightning actually hitting the tree he happened to be under were astronomical. So, he curled up and waited, occasionally looking at the screen of his video camera.

The night vision on his camera had proved invaluable as he skulked along in the dark monsoon. He had managed to get some footage of the large scary man in the orange jump suit before the bottom had fallen out of the sky. He had lost sight of the orange man a few minutes earlier. So, William had slowed his pace, not wanting to run across the man by accident. He wondered if anyone had noticed that the man had gone missing. If so then certainly they would send a search party after him. But that wouldn't happen until this rain slacked up.

Even as he thought that the storm began to lessen. The rain still fell at a good pace, but it wasn't the torrential downpour it had been. The rain had fallen so loudly that he couldn't hear anything but the millions of droplets pounding off everything in sight. Now though, as the rain lightened, he could hear more clearly.

There was a rustling nearby, from right behind the tree he was cowering under. William held his breath, not daring to move. It was getting closer. An eternity seemed to pass. It was all the control he could muster not to scream out when the rabbit jumped out beside him. He kicked at the animal, trying to regain his wits. Then another sound stopped him, the sound of feet on pavement.

William slowly moved the camera from under his arm, powering it on and pointing it towards the road. There, in the dark and not fifty feet from him, was a man in a hoodie staggering up the road. It was hard to tell, but something appeared to be wrong with the man. *He could have been in a car wreck and needed help,* William thought frustratingly. He couldn't leave the wounded man to wander around in the cold rain. William sighed inwardly.

"Hey," William called out to the man in a half whisper, "are you hurt?" He could see the man pause, looking around, trying to determine where the unseen voice was coming from. William walked towards him, finding his way with the help of his video camera. "Just stay there, I'll come to you," he reassured the man.

The thug looked his way, having located at least the general direction of William's voice. "Who…"

THUD

William watched in horror as a large form crashed into the hurt man. It was the escapee in the orange jump suit! William took an involuntary step back, unable to take his eyes off what he was seeing. The large man grabbed the hurt man by the head and slammed it repeatedly into the pavement, then reigned blow after blow with those massive arms upon the fallen man, twisting the man's neck at an unnatural angle.

"No!" William cried out involuntarily.

The killer saw him. He grinned a humorless grin, the smile of a predator on a hunt.

William ran.

The rain began falling in earnest once again.

Stumbling, falling, tripping, scratching his way in the dark, William ran.

The monster was after him. William felt a fear he had never known; it was seeping from every pore on his body. He could hear the man crashing through the trees behind him, not bothering in the least to mask his pursuit.

How could the man be so fast, he wondered crazily? William screwed up his courage; the one thing he could do well was run; and so he did, on and on through the forest. When he ran, he hadn't picked a path, he simply ran in the opposite direction of the killer.

Then he ran out of places to run.

William skidded to a sliding stop at the top of a large, flooded creek. Moore's creek was half as wide as a river and just as dangerous; the rain made it even more so. The water was rushing so fast and so loud that William couldn't think. He'd have to run along the bank and hope there was someplace he could cross downstream.

Lightning flickered suddenly, illuminating the quickly rising creek. What drew his immediate attention however was the figure standing on the opposite bank. Tall, lanky, and pale, silver hair whipping in the storm, stood Reverend Gillian.

"No…" William half whispered in disbelief.

The Reverend made no movement at all. He simply stared at William with his dark, hollow eyes.

William turned…

…right into the face of Psycho.

The killer had no expression on his face; William's was frozen in fear.

He dropped his camera, trying to back-peddle.

The beefy hand of the crazed escapee latched around William's throat, slowly crushing his windpipe with amazing force.

William clawed at the hand uselessly, bright spots dancing in his vision as he struggled for air.

In one motion Psycho picked up the much smaller man and tossed him into the raging water.

William gave out a shrill scream and disappeared beneath the churning rapids. He fought to stay above water, but the current kept dragging him under. His last vision was that of the Reverend's slight smile, then William was swallowed one final time by the raging rapids. Without so much as a glance back, Psycho faded back into the forest.

Chapter 7

Evan felt white hot anger pouring through him, clouding his mind and sending his blood pressure to near critical levels. His feet pounded the old floors of the dungeon, echoing off the dingy concrete walls. This was HIS work, HIS ideas, HIS theories, and no one was going to take it from him. The Benefactor was demanding more from him when his experiments were not yet ready. He had to push harder before the Benefactor decided to stop funding his work. Evan was trapped by his deal with the unseen force that had somehow wormed his way into the doctor's secret world.

Taking the large key ring from his pocket, Evan jammed one into an old metal door at the furthest end of the long hallway. His thoughts kept going back to the fight with his son earlier that night. JC was bitter, and rightfully so. Evan spent most of his time at the asylum. What JC didn't understand, and what Evan could not tell him was that he was doing this FOR his son. Mental disease had cost him his wife, it ran rampant through his family. He had lost his wife and now his son wanted nothing to do with him.

How could Evan blame him? But in the end JC would understand, this was all for him. Once Evan was successful in his experiments then his son would be safe. His son could live a happy life. Wasn't that all that mattered? How happy was he really? The image of his son's face, full of contempt and disdain, kept flooding his vision.

I did this, he thought angrily, *I did this to my family.*

Evan cleared the thoughts from his mind, disconnecting himself from any emotion. It was time to step up the treatments. Bru was fitting Wraith to a chair, securing his feet with a leather strap. Evan glanced at the doll heads that were attached to the chain. They were creepy, mangled and caked with grime and blood. Yet they were trophies of Wraith's pain. For control purposes they turned out to be quite an effective tool.

"I'll finish here, Bru. Go bring me Ronald."

Bru paused and looked at Evan incredulously. "We just got him sedated and put back in his cell. He was worked up pretty good when he came out of the tunnel. You want them in the same room together?"

"Yes," Evan responded distantly, his eyes moving around the large circular metal walled room they were in. There were three large medical chairs in the oversized room which were lit with dim bulbs kept behind steel grating. Operating lights were mounted on movable arms above each chair. Two carts full of syringes and tools were stationed by the door.

Bru nodded and was about to leave the room when Evan spoke again. "Have Rodney help you and tell Derek to pack Steven up. His time with us is done."

The large orderly stopped briefly as he passed by the cart with the syringes full of Evan's drug mixture. He cast a quick glance back to the doctor, who was obsessing over Wraith's restraints, and quickly swiped one of the dark elixirs, stuffing it into one of his pockets.

Evan reached into a cabinet and took out an old doll, staring at it as if trying to decipher the meaning the things held for Wraith. How many had there been? The heads of the previous dolls were all on a great logging chain in Wraith's cell. As dangerous as it was having that chain in there, it seemed the doll heads were the only things that kept his inner psychosis at bay. Evan was determined to find out why, and time was running out. He dropped the doll in Wraith's lap eliciting a slight movement.

Wraith's eyes focused on the doll.

"Daddy?" the little girl's voice spoke from the doll, "why do they keep hurting me, daddy?"

Wraith's breathing became labored. He suddenly lunged against the restraints, the veins in his neck threatening to explode from the pressure of the anger coursing through his body.

Evan watched with a curious detachment, studying Wraith's angered movements and the primitive snarl that was spewing from his cracked lips. He knew the risks of putting the two crazed men together, but he had little choice he told himself. Timing was running out and the Benefactor kept wanting more and more. Evan felt a familiar pain in his temple a briefly tried to massage it away.

It was at that moment that Bru and Rodney escorted the large, semi-aware, sweating Ronald into the room. The monstrous man was drenched from the rain, covered in a mixture of blood and mud that was beginning to cake in the chill dampness of the dungeon.

The drugs in the psychotic man's system barely allowed him to move under his own power. As the orderlies moved Ronald across the room his large form passed in front of the light, casting a large shadow across Wraith which seemed to draw his drug induced attention.

The two huge orderlies guided Ronald into the chair opposite Wraith.

Silence.

The two deranged men, strapped to their respective chairs, were heavily sedated. Samantha handed Evan a long needle that held a small amount of murky fluid. The nurse brushed aside some of the long stringy hair from Ronald revealing a small, sutured patch near the base of his skull. Carefully, she then proceeded to take a pair of scissors, snipping away at the three sides of the cranial patch.

Taking a pair of forceps, she pulled away the bone flap to reveal the brain of the comatose man.

Evan slipped a headlight and began gently guiding the needle deep into Ronald's traumatized brain, just past the thalamus into the Pineal Gland. The doctor slowly emptied the contents of the needle before withdrawing it, placing the used syringe on a tray as the nurse sewed the cranial flap closed once again.

Samantha, having finished her part of the procedure, noticed movement from Wraith's chair. She nodded to Evan. "Doctor, Wraith is coming around."

Bru was leaning against the wall, nervously watching the procedure. He had witnessed this many times but never with both patients in the room together. It was the sound of Wraith's name being spoken that gave him an opportunity to get his mind off the situation. "Who calls their child Wraith? Is that his real name?"

Samantha just rolled her eyes as Evan responded unemotionally, his focus more on the patients than anyone else in the room. "Of course not and therein lies the issue. Because who he knew himself to be before is foreign to him. Neither of these men remember anything of their past. THAT is what I am trying to fix."

A sudden jostle took everyone by surprise as Ronald shifted in his seat. At the same time a grunt escaped Wraith's lips.

Everything was calm, as if the air had been sucked out in a vacuum leaving the world frozen in time. No one in the room moved as Ronald lifted his oversized head, his dead eyes falling on the doll that rested haphazardly in Wraith's lap.

"Daddy..."

Wraith's head hung limply but his eyes focused on something unseen.

"...it's him daddy..."

In the large man's grime covered hands was a doll, grotesque in almost every way. The rubber baby head was ghostly pale with tacks buried into the skull. One eye was red with blood cake blood that had dried as it trickled down its face. The rest of the face was matted with grease and other varied disgusting elements. The doll was missing one arm while the rest of its body was bound by black electrical tape that was frayed and stretched by age and rough handling. It was an eerie sight.

Wraith's eyes snapped from the doll in his lap to the one Ronald was gripping in his grimy meat paw. But what Wraith saw wasn't an inanimate object, oh no, he saw two versions of the girl, *daughter?* that plagued his every moment. The one, beautiful as an angel. The other, twisted, bloodied...abused. Both cried out for him, pleading in fear. *Daddy!!!*

Ronald grinned nastily as Rodney was trying to strap his arm to the chair. He unexpectedly shoved the orderly away from him, back handed Bru across the face temporarily stunning him, and snatched the doll from Wraith's lap.

...Daddy!!!

Wraith lunged against his restraints, roaring in rage, trying to protect the girl that screamed out for him.

Evan backed into a corner, watching in mesmerized fascination, tuning out everything else but the conflict between the two deranged men.

Ronald slammed the doll into Wraith's face, gashing the restrained man's eye with a sickening thud. The insane fat man then swung the other doll catching Wraith on the cheek with one of the tacks that was buried in the doll's head which ripped a gap all the way to Wraith's lip sending blood squirting across the room. The wicked gleam on the evil fat man's face grew with each strike, drool of pleasure salivating from his mouth, drenching his unkempt beard.

Two, three, four blows rained down upon the helpless Wraith who snarled defiantly at his attacker. The fifth blow shattered his nose, sending blood in every direction.

Ronald took a step forward, dropping both dolls, grasped Wraith around the throat with both bloated hands and began to squeeze. It was a familiar feeling, his killing stroke. A twisted smile curved the corners of his mouth as he tightened his grip around Wraith's throat.

Killing excited him more-so than any sexual act. The taking of life by his own hands was the ultimate high. Ronald didn't need a weapon. Sure, they were great for softening up his prey but to end their life had to be done with his hands. He could feel their soul escaping as their bodies went cold. It strengthened him, enraged him, for he knew he had no soul. That knowledge fueled his rage.

Dr. Daniel Lane wasn't above confrontation. His quest for knowledge and his overly quizzical nature was one of the reasons he was great at his job. There was a special need that burned within him. It was a need to know what made people tick on the inside. The thrill of diagnosing a patient, of understanding them, was as much a joy as curing them. On that level, he had much in common with his protégé, Evan.

But where Evan was headed was someplace that Daniel couldn't follow, not this time, not like this. It's been said that everyone has their demons. That saying held true for Daniel as well. He had been a good friend and done as Evan had asked. *No, that's not right*, he thought remorsefully, *as Evan had begged.*

Daniel gently opened the door to the dungeon, trying to keep it from squeaking on its rusted hinges. Upon his argument with Evan in the parking lot, Dr Lane knew he couldn't turn a blind eye to what was going on below any longer. He tried to pretend he hadn't known, yet that of course was a lie.

Following that bimbo of a nurse had inevitably led him to the dungeon, an area he thought long since abandoned. Or was that merely wishful thinking once again on his part? The truth was that Daniel knew Evan couldn't quit his search for a cure to the madness, whatever the cost. And hadn't Evan paid the dearest cost of all?

As Daniel slipped through the door and made his way down the short hallway that lead to a freight elevator, the memory of that horrible tragedy ran through his mind unbidden and unwanted. It seemed he was back there again, 20 years earlier, another stormy night like this one.

The smell of the large, dank room came rushing back to his senses. It had been dimly lit, hiding all of the monitoring equipment and surgical tools in the shadows by the wall as to not upset the patient by their presence.

*The patient...**Miranda**. He tried not to think of her name, tried not to envision her strapped to that god-awful table like Frankenstein's monster. But there she was, in his mind's eye, all her beauty and intelligence swept away by the insanity that had overtaken her. Once a colleague with an unequalled mind, she had mysteriously slipped into madness. No explanation. No warning. A promising career and a marriage that held equal promise had all been lost. Miranda was dragging Evan into her insanity with her.*

Daniel remembered her last moments vividly. *The leather straps dug into her arms as she strained against them. Miranda's eyes were sunken and hollow, hair matted with sweat and plastered to her head in an inelegant manner. All semblance of beauty lost.*

Daniel tried to force the memory aside as he reached the elevator and reached out to push the button. A scream, shrill and full of terror echoed from somewhere below. He paused as the memory continued to play once more.

Evan worked frantically, trying to save her. But it wasn't just her.

Daniel leaned heavily against the wall as the memory bore its heartache. No, if it had just been her then the tragedy, as great as it was, might have been salvageable.

The desolation hung in the air that night as Daniel could only watch helplessly from the shadows as his friend fought to save his beloved wife...and their unborn son. She cussed and spit at Evan as he tried in vain to save her, tears of remorse and desperation streaming down the young doctor's face. Miranda's swollen belly was heaving on the table from the amount of force she used to struggle against the restraints that held her so tightly.

Her insanity overpowered the drugs. The harder she fought; the more stress was put on the unborn child. Evan had to make a choice. Daniel locked eyes with his friend. Never had he seen such hopelessness in someone close to him. It had never bothered him in other patients, not before or since, but seeing it in his friend was shattering.

The two men and Miranda had been working on a new compound that attacked the prefrontal cortex to heighten its activity while decreasing the activity in the basal ganglia, which would hopefully help patients with schizophrenia. While they had yet to test it, Evan was determined to find the riddle to her fractured psyche, whatever the cost.

They could have taken her to a hospital, they should have. But Evan was insistent that no one know of Miranda's illness. He wouldn't put her through that. Daniel had reluctantly agreed. Evan approached the cart with the syringe, reaching for it. Daniel stopped his hand.

"I'll do it," Daniel told him comfortingly.

Evan looked at his friend sadly, "she's, my wife."

As Daniel looked on, Evan kissed his wife on the forehead even as she continued to struggle and cuss him. Then he plunged the needle into her temple, burying it in the frontal cortex. Miranda's scream pierced the walls, forcing Daniel to look away.

The next moments were chaos that Daniel could only remember in rapid flashes: a baby crying, the heart monitor flat-lining, Evan shoving the small bundle in his arms and yelling at him to get the child to the hospital, the crazed sprint up the stairs, through the asylum, and into the driving rain.

Daniel tried to calm his breathing, to once again push the memories back into their locked cage. Twenty years later, he finally stepped back into the dungeon. This time he would stop Evan, keep him from making yet another mistake.

He reached out for the elevator button but the sound of it working its old gears and cables brought him pause.

Someone was on their way up.

The Doctor opened a door to his immediate left and darted into the old stairwell. He pressed himself against the wall as he heard the elevator doors swoosh open. A gurney was being pushed by that large orderly followed by Samantha. But who was that on it?

Whoever it was stared blankly at the ceiling. Daniel waited for them to pass and leave the dungeon, heading back up to the main patient area. As he stepped back into the empty hallway Daniel knew he had to find out just who was on the gurney and just what was wrong with him. Confronting Evan would have to wait.

Daniel gave one last look at the elevator doors before following Samantha and Bru. Luckily, they hadn't known he was there. The good doctor didn't notice the camera that sat unsuspectingly in a high corner of the dungeon corridor, watching his every movement.

Jake sat in his patrol truck, eating a thick greasy cheeseburger, washing it down with a beer. He supposed he probably shouldn't be drinking in his official vehicle, but then again there were a lot of things he shouldn't have done. Jake had a ton of regrets but drinking a beer in a patrol vehicle in a county that owed him a helluva lot more than that wasn't one of them.

The rain beat down on top of his truck as sporadic lightning occasionally lit up the area, thunder rumbling over the static of his police radio. In the darkness, out on the lonely county road, no one would notice him backed off slightly into the woods; nor did he care if they did.

His focus was on the house a hundred yards off the road. He could see the lights on in the windows. Occasionally, when the lightning was close enough, it lit up the area so he could make out the house and its surroundings. Jake didn't need lightning, daylight or anything else to tell him about the house...he knew it well. The front porch was cluttered with rustic lawn furniture. The backyard had a kids swing set, trampoline, and one of those plastic kitchen play sets. He knew enough to know the roof needed repairs, the house could use a fresh coat of paint, and the Great Dane the family had looked more like a moose than a dog.

Most nights he watched the house, unseen, unheard, and unknown. He often wondered just what went on in there, sometimes obsessively so. Sure, he could make an excuse to go knock on that door but then what? What would he say? "Hi, I'm the Sheriff and I demand you let me in so I can snoop around?"

He didn't need the city cops to get involved. Things would turn messy. There was enough messiness and mistrust without him giving those idiots any reason to turn the county against him, which Chief Malone would love. He would continue to play it silent, waiting to see what he could come up with.

Jake reached into his glove box and pulled out a small jewelry box, the old small kind that was made of felt. He opened the box and stared at the contents. He sighed, leaning his head back against the seat rest as he snapped the lid shut.

"Not tonight", he said aloud through gritted teeth, "not tonight". Rain brought out memories, the memories brought out the past, the past was nothing but pain.

It was then that his radio blared to life.

"All units, we have a wreck on county road 205. All available units please respond."

Jake picked up the mic as he stared at the house. He shoved the jewelry box back into the compartment and spoke into the mic, "This is Sheriff Hooks, en route."

"SO's 5 and 7 are also en route. Be careful out there Sheriff. By all reports it's pretty bad."

"Paramedics?"

"Almost on scene."

"Thanks Clair, Hooks out."

Jake gave one last meaningful look at the house as he silently pulled out of his hiding spot. He watched the house fade away in his rearview mirror. He waited until he was out of sight before turning on his lights. Another mile and his sirens blared to life.

It was going to be a busy night.

The bright monitors flickered from one scene to the next, keeping track of Dr. Lane as he hurried from his office and into the main hallway, swinging on his raincoat as his briefcase juggled between hands.

Another monitor flickered to life.

Wraith was sitting in a chair with thick leather straps holding him down, comatose. Blood was dripping down his face. The room surrounding him was in disarray.

A pale hand picked up a phone mounted beside one of the monitors and pushed a single button. The time for subtle moves and discretion was past. All the seeds of calamity had been sewn, watered, and nourished with precision. As the phone rang persistently on the other end of the line, grey eyes peered purposefully at the images filling the monitor.

The human psyche was a fragile thing, full of ego, regret, and desire. Powerful men were the most mentally frail. The fear of losing all that they had attained was a particularly easy pressure point to take advantage of. Even the most brilliant of minds, stoic of hearts, strength of character were at risk of such poison.

Great wars had been started over such easy manipulations. Empires had fallen, all of them, at one time or another, to that basic human greed for power and control. Only one last great empire remained to crumble- humanity.

The key was not to rush. Penultimate moments had to be groomed for years, decades…. centuries. Everything had to be moved, just like chess pieces, each one a gambit setting up other plays until…

"Checkmate…"

"NO! No, no, no!!" Evan Michaels shouted into his phone, slumping over his desk in the dimly lit office. Anyone who witnessed his outburst would have been incredulous; his usual calm, controlled demeanor had vanished. His face was livid, flushed a brilliant red from his rant. He wasn't concerned about anyone overhearing him—in the dungeon, his only worries were his experiments…and his benefactor.

His "other office" was in complete disarray, with books scattered haphazardly across the room and a rumpled bed pushed against one wall, clearly indicating that he received no visitors there. Regardless of the chaos, Evan's sole focus was on the person listening at the other end of the line.

"I will not allow it, do you hear?! I won't let you take them again! Wraith was nearly beaten to death! Psycho almost killed him. Ronald is in his room, screaming with anger because he didn't get to kill Wraith! What if something else happens?" Evan was on the brink of a breakdown, saliva spewing as he yelled into the phone. His hand gripped a crushed pack of cigarettes like a vice, trembling with rage. Yet, even as he raged, the voice on the other end remained silent.

Utterly silent.

"If I let him out now, we will lose control. Psycho is completely over the edge! We're not ready! The formula is unstable, and whatever concoction you're adding only increases that instability!" Dr. Michaels pleaded into the silent phone, wondering if he had pushed his unresponsive benefactor too far this time.

Slowly, his breathing began to normalize, and the red color slowly ebbed from his cheeks.

Then the voice finally spoke.

Evan's eyes widened in shock, nearly popping from their sockets, and the veins in his neck pulsed against his pale skin. His trembling hand nearly dropped the phone. He dared not speak; all he could do was listen to the silky-smooth voice on the other end—a sound he dreaded more than anything.

"Please," Evan begged, "not tonight. It's too much. If we push him any harder, he could suffer a permanent, complete breakdown... all my work... He's not ready. The last session took too heavy a toll." He ran a ragged hand through his hair as the voice continued. Taking a deep breath, he added, "Yes, the other patient is on his way to you."

After listening for a moment longer, Evan silently nodded and let the phone fall to the floor. He sank back heavily into his chair, running his hands through his unkempt hair.

"What have I done?"

"Daddy. Wake up, daddy."

Wraith's eyes flew open, releasing a guttural snarl from his drooling mouth, the chains clinking as they hung from his muscular arms. One eye was swollen shut, with blood slowly seeping from the roughly stitched wound on his cheek.

Wraith's eyes darted frantically around the dimly lit cell, searching for the source of the voice. His body tensed against the restraints, muscles rippling beneath his pale, scarred skin.

"Daddy, please help me," the small voice pleaded again.

Wraith's gaze fell upon a doll lying on the floor near his feet. Its porcelain face was cracked and stained with what looked like dried blood. One eye was missing, leaving a dark, empty socket that seemed to stare accusingly at him.

"No..." Wraith rasped, his voice hoarse and barely above a whisper. "Not real...not real..."

He squeezed his eyes shut, trying to block out the haunting voice and the memories it stirred. But behind his closed lids, images flashed rapid-fire:

A little girl laughing, her blonde pigtails bouncing as she ran through a sunlit field.

The same girl, older now, cowering in fear as a shadowy figure loomed over her.

Blood. So much blood.

Wraith's eyes snapped open with a roar of anguish that echoed off the cell walls. He thrashed violently against his restraints, the chains clanking loudly as he struggled.

"I'm sorry!" he screamed, spittle flying from his lips. "I'm so sorry!"

The doll's voice came again, softer now, almost a whisper: "It's okay, daddy. I forgive you."

Wraith froze, his chest heaving as he stared at the doll. Slowly, almost imperceptibly, its cracked lips seemed to curve into a smile.

And then, from somewhere deep in the asylum, a blood-curdling scream pierced the night.

"The man who hurt me is out there, daddy."

He could see Katie, just beyond the unbreakable glass, out of his reach. Wraith roared in fury, his restraints started to stretch against his rage and finally, with one last surge they snapped free. He looked around wildly.

"It's okay, daddy, get the bad man. Then come home."

Wraith's eyes darted around the room. In a distant corner, a concealed door slid open. The deranged man acted without delay. Get the bad man. Come home.

He would capture the bad man. He would harm the bad man... for Katie. Then he would return home.

Wraith glanced back at Katie, who only smiled. The crazed man let out another growl and dashed through the hidden door. He was determined to do terrible things to a terrible man.

Chapter 8

A strangled, panicked scream echoed through the dark forest. It was a sound born of primal fear but lost in the thunder of the slackening storm.

An owl, perched high on a tree, sat watching the commotion on the ground below, yellow piercing eyes narrowing as the bushes rattled angrily beneath his tree. The lightning cast eerie shadows through the large, spacious forest.

A middle-aged man, dressed in torn scrubs covered in blood and filth, stumbled through the bushes, crashing headlong into the tree in which the owl sat, his breathing came hard and fast as beads of sweat, mixed with blood, poured down his forehead. He knew he needed to keep running but his body refused until his lungs could recover from the stress they were so unaccustomed to. He dared to close his eyes for a brief moment, trying to will his body to calm itself.

Dr. Daniel Lane wiped a dirty hand across his forehead. The name Hale County Mental Institute was printed on the pocket of his shirt, though it had a jagged tear through it, as did the rest of his clothes. His shoes were caked with thick mud, which seemed to slow him down and expended even more of his precious energy.

The expression on his face portrayed one of stark terror, a wounded animal that realized that escape may be impossible. But escape from what? As he sucked in breath after breath, Daniel tried to think about what had happened.

He had discovered the identity of the man on the gurney and made up his mind to confront Evan in the morning. It hadn't been that hard actually. He simply reviewed the current patients versus the cameras and there he was. But why? Why was Evan doing this?

Daniel locked his findings in his briefcase and headed out into the rain. He'd almost made it to his car when he saw the man running wildly at him. There was no warning, no explanation. The stranger crashed into Daniel, slamming his head into the concrete parking barrier. His keys went flying from his hand and into the flooded parking lot. The next thing he knew the figure was on top of him.

Luckily for Daniel he was prepared for things to go slightly wrong with patients from time to time. He fumbled in his pocket and grabbed the taser he kept with him at ALL times. Daniel jabbed it into the man's neck. He heard a howl of rage then felt the pressure release from his chest. The older doctor had gotten quickly to his feet.

Unfortunately, the enraged man now stood between him and the relative safety of the asylum. And with his keys gone, the car was not an option. Daniels only hope was to run. And ran he did, and ran, and ran, and ran until he thought his lungs would burst. He didn't know how long he had run nor where he had run to. Thankfully the rain had finally begun to let up.

Who was that man? Was he still after him? More importantly...why??

The questioning call of the owl jolted the man yet again. He glanced quickly up into the tree, trying to spot the creature that watched him with unsympathetic eyes. Another sound reached his ears. The sound of something big, something dangerous, stalking towards him through the trees, purposefully and uncaring, sparked a new sense of urgency within him. He dared waste no more time.

The stricken man flung himself headlong into the forest, oblivious to where he might be headed but knowing full well it was better than where he had been. Branches continuously slapped him in the face as he scrambled through the murky forest, ripping little bits of flesh, the rending of which grew more frequent the faster he ran.

Daniel's foot caught a root, sending him crashing to the ground in a loud heap. The sound of crackling leaves echoed through the night as the air was blasted from his lungs. He paused, a deer in the headlights. His chest heaved greatly as he fought to keep his struggling breathing the sound of a whisper.

All was silent.

A moment, stretched by eternity, played through his mind. The horrors of what would befall him if he were caught. The man who chased him was driven by madness, that much he understood. Daniel also understood what that could do to a man. He had witnessed it firsthand, and knew, without questioning, that doom was upon him.

Still, the silence lingered.

Slowly, hopefully, he lay back on the cool ground, daring to breathe in the night air, desperate for rest. He tried to remember a happier thought, something soothing. What was his name? Could he at least remember that?

"Daniel," he whispered hollowly, "my name is Daniel, Doctor of Psychology. I'm a professional. Calm yourself Daniel."

Tears began to stream down his cheeks as the moment overwhelmed him. A short, choked sob escaped his lips.

"I have two kids. Two kids. I love my kids." His thoughts released themselves in manic whispers, the sobs wracking his entire body. "My wife," he sniffled loudly as the memory of her flooded him, "I love her." His eyes widened in realization, as if he had remembered a dream long since forgotten. "I do love her. I have to get back to her."

I'm panicking, he realized. *Anxiety, Agoraphobia, yes, yes…faintness, vertigo, it's not real. Calm yourself, Daniel, calm yourself.*

He began to breathe slowly, his mind envisioning his wife. For some reason, that thought made him laugh. It was a thought he never considered, yet it was painfully true. He had taken her for granted so many times. How often had he preached that very thing to his clients. "I'm sorry, love," he whispered with a finality that caught him by surprise. "Oh my," he said raggedly.

The snapping of a limb rang out like a shotgun blast, instantly bringing Daniel back to reality. He sat straight up, fear lighting his senses. His eyes began a slow, meticulous scan from left to right. Every hair on his neck was warning of danger.

A movement, pale and hulking, flashed through the trees on his left. Another, slow and raspy, moved through the bushes on his right. They made hardly any sounds, like phantoms. But these were no ghosts, no creatures from some late night horror film. These monsters were all too real. And they had found him. *No,* he demanded to himself, *no, get up and run!*

Daniel scrambled to his feet once more and began running blindly through the forest again. He could hear them, on either side of him, the sound of chains mixed with heavy footsteps, closing the distance. *Chains?* He didn't remember his attacker having chains. But the sound was distinctive. But he dared not look back, he couldn't.

Finally, the trees gave way.

Daniel burst into a clearing. His intense feeling of escape was quickly dashed as he skid to a halt, inches from the edge of a cliff, his feet sliding on the rain slick leaves. Panic set in anew as he peered over the edge to the dark pit hundreds of feet below. Vertigo swept over him. His stomach grew queasy as his heart sank.

"No," he said simply.

The hot, putrid breath on the back of his neck forced him to shut his eyes tightly. Daniel began to whimper, snot and tears running down his face. A dirty hand, caked with blood, latched on to his shoulder.

His eyes flared open abnormally wide.

A doe, white tail flicking in the spattering rain, drank from a large, rocky stream. The night was otherwise peaceful, save for the lightning and dull thunder that followed. A scream pierced the air. Suddenly, the doe's head whipped up and she bolted, tail flicking behind her as she leaped over trees and stumps.

A large object crashed into the stream, spraying water onto the rocky bank. The deer paused on a hill and looked back to the stream.

Daniel's small and grossly contorted body, floated, twisted and broken, in the shallow stream. His lifeless eyes stared up the walls of the cliff, never again to see the two merciless monsters disappearing back into the forest.

Red and blue lights danced off the trees as the rain fell at a steady pace. Police cars and an Ambulance were parked haphazardly on the side of the road. Bright orange road flares warned any potential passerby to be cautious. The scene was minor pandemonium as rescue workers tried to cut into the silver Honda that was folded around the base of a thick pine tree.

"I'm not getting a pulse!"

Two rescue workers ripped into the hood of the car with the hydraulic shears. They worked as fast as the shears that tore into the mangled hood would let them. The rain wasn't nearly the obstacle that time was.

For the young lady in the car, each passing second was a second closer to infinity.

Jake Hooks was oblivious to the cold rain that beat down on him, soaking his clothes and dripping off of his cowboy hat in streams. His eyes were glued to the lifeless hand that hung outside of the car, which was the only part of the woman he could see.

Memories came flooding back to him, but now wasn't the time. He forced them back into the locked closet in his mind, refusing to let them out, especially now. His focus was on the task at hand.

Metal and glass littered the tree line for a hundred feet as a result of the force. It wasn't hard to tell that the car had hydroplaned; figuring that out was the easy part. No, the difficult part was going to be getting the driver of the car out before she died, if she wasn't dead already.

As he took in the all-too-familiar scene (car wrecks were common in Hale County) his brain was busy processing the reasons why the reporter from Nashville was in his county to begin with and, more importantly, why he hadn't known about it.

"She was staying at the Skyridge Motel, sir," a squeaky voice spoke from behind him.

The Sheriff turned and stared at the skinny deputy. "The room?"

"Processing it now, sir."

"The city PD?"

The deputy fidgeted uncomfortably, remaining silent.

"Well, Sanders?" Jake asked, becoming irritated with the young deputy. The kid was always fidgeting when he was bothered by something. It pissed Jake off to no end. God, he missed Marcus.

"They, uh…they don't know anything yet, sir," he finally stammered.

"Good." *They would only screw everything up as usual,* he thought to himself.

Multiple sirens blared in the distance, catching Jake's attention. The Sheriff walked towards the road as the flashing lights of the vehicles drew near. Sanders had to move quickly to keep up with him.

The vehicles, an ambulance, a fire-rescue truck, and a city police cruiser roared past them just as he got to the road.

"Find out what's going on," Jake bit out to his deputy, never taking his eyes off the fast-moving vehicles as they disappeared in the distance.

The only call that his office received was the wreck he was working. He should have been notified if other calls had come in. And why was a city cruiser answering the call out in the county?

"Sheriff!"

Jake turned to the rescuer that had called out. The man was motioning frantically for Jake to come down.

The hood of the car had been ripped open by the powerful hydraulics of the Jaws of Life; the metal peeled back like a sardine can. EMT's were lifting the unconscious woman from the car, blood matting her long dark hair to her face. They placed her on a stretcher board and immediately began CPR. The men worked frantically yet purposefully, every second crucial.

"She's not breathing!"

"Oxygen!"

A portable respirator was slipped over her head. The men looked desperate.

"Sir, they found another body!"

Jake rounded on his deputy. "Dead?"

"Yessir," Sanders stammered out, "brutally beaten they say."

"Where?"

Sanders didn't want to answer but knew there was little choice. "The asylum."

Jake knew immediately who it was--the drug dealer. He looked once again at the paramedics working feverishly on the reporter and then back to his deputy. The dark days he feared were upon him. Hale County was drowning in blood.

Chapter 9

Little Haley Perkins pushed her baby stroller across the lawn of her tiny country home, a small beat-up doll resting comfortably in the plastic seat. Following her around the yard like an overprotective nanny was a thick German Shephard with rippling muscles. The little five-year-old girl, brunette curls bouncing on her shoulders, was doing her best mommy impersonation.

"Stop your crying!" Haley complained to the doll as she rolled her eyes dramatically, "I just fed you an hour ago."

Haley's mom chose that moment to stick her head out the window. "Haley, don't go down by the creek!"

"I won't mommy!"

Haley unbuckled the little doll and picked it up, staring stern fully into the doll's eyes.

"She always tells us not to go down by the creek," the little girl spoke knowingly to her canine companion, who just cocked her head to the side as if in understanding.

Haley was about to put the doll back into the stroller when a flash by the creek caught her eye. She looked from the creek to her house, and back again. The doll slipped from her hand as she walked warily, yet curiously, towards the slow flowing water. A low growl caused the little girl to turn, locking eyes with the dog. "Shush, Kaia," she whispered commandingly, "I think I saw something." The dog whimpered in warning but followed her lead.

Little bushes blocked most of the creek from her view, forcing Haley to make her way through the thick brush. She pushed limbs out of her face as she slowly walked through the thick mess towards the object she had seen. Her mother would kill her if she knew what she was doing. But Haley didn't care, she was a five-year-old girl with a child's overpowering curiosity.

Haley was almost clear of the bushes when her foot caught some brush. Kaia began to growl in warning. As Haley began to shush the dog once more her shoe snagged, causing her to trip. She stumbled towards the creek bank and landed half in the water, her hand smacking something moist and rubbery. Haley looked to see what it was she had grabbed and looked directly into the dead pale blue face of Dr. Daniel Lane, causing her to do the only thing she could.

She screamed.

Sheriff Jake Hooks stood over the lifeless corpse of Dr. Lane; eyes locked in concentration on the sightless vision of the pale dead man now lying on the gurney. The coroner had tried closing the man's eye lids but they refused to stay shut, as if they were still afraid of something, even in death. He studied the dead doctor's face carefully. It was frozen in a perpetual state of fear. Well, what was left of it. From the eyes down had been completely smashed it, to the point it was unrecognizable. It was something he had never seen in his career, and the Sheriff had seen a lot of horrible things over the years. Jake nodded to the coroner who immediately began zipping the body bag.

"Let me know what you find," the Sheriff said automatically before turning back to the creek embankment.

"Will do," The coroner waived for two EMT's to come get the body.

Jake examined the creek, watching it twist up the hill and disappear in the distance. He looked back up toward the house to see the EMT's loading the body into the ambulance. *Murder.* That made two in the same night. Similar types at first glance. *Connected? But who had done it? And why?* Those would be much tougher questions to sort out. He had but one clue; Hale County Mental Institute. Hell, at least it was someplace to start.

His eyes came to rest on Haley, the little girl that had discovered the body. She was wrapped in a blanket, numbly running her hands over her doll as her mother tried to comfort her. Her mom, whom Jake would have considered to be quite striking under normal circumstances, tried without fail to get through to her traumatized little girl. *Why is it always the innocent that must witness such things*, he asked himself privately. An older deputy, Lt. Mitchell, strode up to the Sheriff, studying a notepad.

"What do ya got?" Jake asked morosely.

"Not sure. It's obviously Dr Lane, but we have no idea how he got in the creek or how far the body travelled. According to the way he's dressed you think his last know whereabouts was at the asylum?"

"Looks like it. Need to check it out."

"You want me to do it?"

"Nah, I got it."

"Sir you haven't slept in over 24 hours at least; worked that car wreck and the other homicide last night."

"I'll be alright. Send deputies to his clinic and the pharmacy. Seems we lost our town physician and pharmacist all in one day. Have you contacted the institute yet?"

"I did but they weren't much help. Very short and to the point. I talked with the receptionist, explained we needed to speak to the administrator. She said he would be available in an hour or so but she wouldn't talk to me any further. I didn't elaborate. Gave her your number. The lady didn't seem interested in anything I had to say."

"Probably thought you were wanting to bring in another patient and didn't want the hassle. Well, that gives me a starting point."

Jake was about to walk away when Mitchell stopped him once more.

"Sir?"

"What is it deputy?"

"Did you see his face? He saw something bad. What could make a man look like that? What could have scared him so?" The deputy shook his head as he walked away.

The Sheriff was about to talk to the coroner one last time when another cruiser pulled up to the scene. Jake took a deep, steadying breath and set his jaw. A very tall, slender, clean-cut man, late thirties, stepped from the vehicle. His ice blue eyes and blonde slicked back hair meshed with his perfectly tanned skin. *Politician in a uniform*, Jake thought bitterly. It was the perfect way to describe Police Chief Edward Malone.

"What's that, two murders in a few short hours, Jake?" the Chief asked mockingly, voice full of bemusement.

"Well, nothing gets by you Eddie."

"Come now, how about a little inter-agency cooperation?"

"You city cops are not an agency. You're a bunch of boot lickers to that crooked Mayor."

"Watch your mouth, Hooks," Malone retorted hotly, all humor gone from his voice.

"Not my style. But then, I don't have to worry about getting replaced by a grimy swindler that owns the toilet I piss in. I answer to the people." He had a good mind to tell Eddie exactly what he had been doing with that mouth. But he didn't have the time to deal with the asshole at the moment.

Eddie closed the distance, slightly looking down on Jake. "Nobody owns me," the Chief growled dangerously.

"Why don't you go tell that to your boss."

A smirk played across Eddie's face. "Laugh it up for now. Soon though, there's gonna be changes." Eddie walked halfway back to his cruiser then turned back to Jake. "You think you're invincible. Just ask your old buddy Cutty where that got him. I hear tell that you stopped a mugging from a meth head last night. Same dealer they found beaten to death at the asylum?" Eddie didn't wait for a response. Jake's scowl was enough of an answer. Eddie just smirked and turned without another word, leaving the implied accusation hanging in the air.

Jake cast a quick gaze towards the unresponsive Haley, anger flooding through him. Fear ruled his cursed county and people like Eddie and the Mayor were reveling in his inability to stop it. He shifted his focus to the latest victim. What COULD have done that? It was the same look the meth dealer had on his face when they found him last night. How could a man, or anyone for that matter, be so scared that the fear still showed in his face even after death? Jake had no idea, but he certainly meant to find out.

The Sheriff glanced around the yard once again, eyes taking in the swing set, the trampoline, and the kitchen set. It looked so different during the day. The large German Shephard was barking wildly as it stood in the window watching all the uniformed intruders in its yard. As he looked once more to the little girl, he found her mother's piercing green eyes, full of emotion, staring pointedly back in his.

Entering the foyer of Hale County Mental Institute was much like entering a funeral home. The walls were decorated in a soothing modest shade of burgundy, not the sterile white you would expect. A low, melodic instrumental music played softly through the room.

A secretary was seated behind a glass partition that stood guard to a large set of double doors. Why Evan kept her, he couldn't really say. She was useless, spending most of her days reading those silly romance books and scribbling through a crossword. Maybe it was because she gave the place a sense of normalcy, legitimacy.

The elder lady flashed Evan with an automatic smile as he strolled by her, casually ignoring what he was sure was false platitude. It kept up appearances, and that was all that mattered.

Evan became aware of his thoughts, the anger and dread that fueled them. He wasn't sleeping. It was affecting every decision...*and yesterday, my God, yesterday. Why did I push them?! I have to regain control.* Those thoughts forced Evan to put on his own mask, to try to hide the internal conflict. He had been slipping into his own madness and not even realized it. Until last night. Perhaps it wasn't too late to regain control, to fix this. He had to talk to Daniel, confess his sins.

Daniel would know what to do. He had always known how to pull Evan back from the brink as he had when Miranda...

Miranda...

Evan felt the familiar pang of guilt but forced it away. Daniel, he had to see Daniel. Together they would fix this.

The double doors, what he had overheard some of his associates call the gates of Hell, fed into a long hallway. There were offices on either side, most of which were empty. Evan stopped at the entrance to one of the darkened offices and peered inside. The name "Dr. Daniel Lane" was etched into the placard on the desk. Evan gave the office a quick once over then began to move on down the hall.

Odd, he thought silently, *his car was in the parking lot*. Anger flared within him. He tried to fight it. That anger was mixed with fear; fear of what his mysterious benefactor was capable of. The man had eyes everywhere. He knew the conflict between Daniel and himself. Evan forced the thought out of his mind. *No, Daniel was most likely checking on some of his more meaningful patients*, he thought reassuringly.

Evan turned a corner, lost in his musings. Almost instantly he was greeted by a timid young male nurse, dressed in crisp white scrubs, barreling through the double doors at the other end of the hall.

"Morning Dr. Michaels."

"I very much doubt that," he bit out harsher than intended. The doctor was in a mood this morning. Last night's phone call left him ill, as it usually did. Evan cast a quick look back at the office. "Have you seen Dr. Lane this morning?"

"No sir, he hasn't been here nor has he called in to my knowledge."

"I see," Evan said thoughtfully, brow furrowed deeply.

The nurse handed him a clipboard full of names and charts. "Here are the charts of the morning's rounds. Everyone's had their meds."

The doctor stopped and turned a dark, questioning glare on the young nurse. The way he had said 'everyone' gave him pause.

"Everyone?"

The nurse cleared his throat nervously. "Yes sir, everyone."

"How many times have I told you to stay out of the lower levels when Bru isn't with you?" the doctor growled, low in his throat, as he got nose to nose with the nurse.

"I-I'm not afraid," the nurse managed to croak out half-heartedly.

"You are a fool," Evan looked deep into the timid nurse's eyes, "They sense your fear, smell it as if it were a perfume whipping through the air. That is dangerous, Derek. Very dangerous."

The look of fear in Derek's eyes was mixed with a false bravado. Evan slapped the chart roughly into Derek's chest and stalked off to his office. He called back over his shoulder.

"I will be in my office! See that I'm not disturbed. And do NOT venture down there again without permission! When you see Dr. Lane, send him to my office at once!"

"Yes Dr. Michaels."

Derek watched the doctor walk away and glanced down at the charts once more. He swallowed the lump in his throat then hurried off in the opposite direction.

A small truck pulled up to the police tape that cordoned off the street. City patrol cars had the streets blocked off. The sky was still overcast from that awful storm the previous night. A Fire engine was parked at an angle beside a fire hydrant. JC and Ashlyn stepped from the truck, looking in awe of the mess at 120 Norris Lane.

The windows of the remodeled two-story house had been blown out, strewing glass all across the well-kept yard. Siding had been stripped away. The front door lay flat atop the concrete steps that had led up to it. Shingles had been ripped from the roof. The flower beds decimated. It looked for all the world like a tornado had ripped the house apart, except looking around, JC could only see that house with any damage.

JC felt a tight grip on his arm. He looked down to see Ashlyn's stricken face trying to understand what she was seeing. It was a feeling he shared.

"Do you think he was in there?" she asked, voice barely more than a whisper.

"I hope not."

JC pulled her gently but urgently to a police officer that was standing by the cordon tape. "Excuse me. Was...was Professor Locke in there? Is he okay?" JC asked worriedly.

The officer, who looked put out by JC's question, answered smartly, "We don't know. We're still searching. Now, clear the area."

"He's a friend of mine. If I could just..."

"I don't care who he is, beat it."

"You can't talk to him that way! He's concerned about his friend!" Ashlyn retorted hotly.

That seemed to only agitate the officer further. "I suggest you and your boyfriend leave now before I have you removed. Got it?"

"These two are checking on their friend. Is he in there or not?"

All three turned to see a stocky, clean cut black man in a business suit. While his face was kind and rather good-looking, his voice had an air of authority to it. JC and Ashlyn seemed thrilled to see him. The officer, however, scowled and marched woodenly towards the house.

"Mayor Carson," Ashlyn said happily.

"Miss Taylor," he replied kindly. "And you can call me Marcus. Except when I beat Grey in the election, THEN you can call me Mayor," he laughed, a twinkle in his eye. "No offense to your uncle."

JC shot Ashlyn a quick glance but her fear from the night before was nowhere to be found. Had it been an illusion? She hadn't mentioned it again. No, Ashlyn was an actress. She simply put on another face.

"None taken," she said easily, her own sweet smile in full bloom.

"What happened here?"

"We don't know. We were on our way to campus."

JC scanned the street again. "His house is the only one that got hit. Isn't that weird?"

Marcus nodded slightly. "Maybe, but those storms can be freaky. Wind can do amazing things."

"But look around, there is no debris anywhere. Not one piece in anyone else's yard."

It was true. Every yard, while not perfectly manicured, was certainly free from any debris related to the previous night's storm. Everywhere they looked in any yard, bushes, garbage, leaves, all was nice and neat with the exception of the occasional puddle here and there. Yet Jason Locke's house looked as if a tornado had dropped straight down on top of it. Why would there be no fragments of it in anyone else's yard, especially the immediate neighbors?

Strange.

Officer asshole came marching back towards them, only this time he wasn't alone. He strode towards them at an awkward gait, slightly ahead of the casual Chief of Police. Whereas the beat cop wore a constant expression of irritation, Chief Malone's was measured and confident; cocky even.

The officer didn't speak a word as they stopped before the three onlookers. He simply fixed them with a contemptuous glare. Chief Malone, however, smiled his snake-charming grin at the three, especially at Marcus.

"Marcus, surprised to see you here," the Chief said smoothly.

"Just passing through, Ed, thought I'd see if you needed any help." Marcus replied easily.

"Hard to get it out of your system, isn't it? That curious NEED to know what's going on, especially when it's no longer any of your business?" The Chief's eyes cooled a bit as they locked with Marcus'. But if it got under Marcus' skin, the mayoral candidate didn't let it show.

"I like to help people," Marcus countered with a smile, "not being an officer, or Mayor for that matter, anymore doesn't change that."

"And what about you two," Chief Malone asked JC and Ashlyn, never taking his eyes from Marcus', "I suppose you're here to help as well?"

"My friend lives there," JC said shortly, anger unexpectedly boiling to the surface.

Chief Malone pulled his eyes from Marcus and levelled his gaze on JC. "And you just happened to be driving by?"

"Yes sir."

"Very neighborly of you, Mr. Michaels, to come down from your castle to mingle with us lowly common folk," said with undisguised contempt. Chief Malone didn't bother to hide his dislike for JC and his family. The air around them seemed to develop a sudden chill.

"Hey, I didn't mean…" JC began but was quickly quieted as the arrogant Chief waved away his comment.

"I don't particularly care what you meant. This is a police matter. Stay out of it. Let us do our job."

The other officer smirked, loving that his boss was putting these children in their proper place. JC clenched and unclenched his fists, wishing he could push the arrogant bastards face in. But they all knew that wasn't going to happen, which only added to his anger.

"And what IS your job, Ed," Marcus broke in smoothly, still maintaining his calm demeanor, "search or recovery?"

The Chief had seemed to forget about Marcus, but the sound of that deep baritone voice snapped him out of his arrogant ridicule. He turned his withering gaze back to Marcus who seemed nonplussed. "That's none of your concern."

Marcus gave him an easy smile. "Whether you tell me now or not, one phone call is all I need to find out. I'm curious what the press would say."

The Chief gave a quick laugh. "The press? I wouldn't consider old man Shaw's ten-page, bible thumping, pamphlet as the press."

"Nah, there's a big-time reporter in town, all the way from Nashville."

It was the Chief's turn to smile as he regained his arrogance. "Haven't you heard? She was killed in an unfortunate car wreck last night. The storm was something awful. Your best bud was on the scene, or didn't he tell you?" The Chief let that sink in as he turned back towards Jason Locke's house. The verbal sparring with Hooks may have left him with a bitter taste but the look on Marcus' face made it a distant memory. His day was indeed improving.

The jovial expression on Marcus' face was gone. He hadn't heard about the reporter. That wasn't good. He felt a sudden weight in his chest. Guilt began to overpower his thoughts, the rapid beat of his heart thundering in his ears. Mist began to fall; he could feel it tingling his skin with its cool moistness. Marcus took a steady breath. He was trying to focus when he suddenly sensed the Chief beside him, whispering into his ear.

"Outsiders don't belong in Hale County. You should know that. Her blood is on your hands," the Chief mockingly whispered into Marcus' ear.

Marcus was rooted to the spot, trying to process the information and the emotions all at the same time. When he finally regained his awareness JC and Ashlyn were on either side of him, holding him upright, and asking if he was ok. His focus was on Malone, who was walking back to the house. The Chief turned to the three once more.

"The house is empty. There was no body found." He fixed them all with an icy stare. "The next time any of you interfere in my crime scene I'll have you thrown in jail...I don't care who you are."

The fog, murky and gray, swam thick before Wraith's eyes. The soupy clouds peppered his face with sweet, cool droplets of water. But it might as well have been fire to him. The deeper the fog moved around him, the more enraged he seemed to get, the mist, acid on his flesh.

Deep, animalistic growls, roiling from somewhere deep in his soul, spewed forth in anger. He could no longer remember why he was mad, only that he was. Pain and hate flashed their venom through his already poisoned mind. Who did he hate? It didn't matter. He was angry and needed an outlet for that anger.

Sweat intermixed with his dirty brown hair, streaming its salty mix down his face and soaking the soiled gray coveralls he wore. The emblazoned HCMI logo on his front pocket was covered in blood. Hale County Mental Institute, his home. The home of the man known only as Wraith; his real name lost long ago to him. It was a place of control, a true asylum from the world, one that could sometimes contain his anger, a place where his need for violence could be satiated. And it was a need, instinctual and ancient.

Humanity?

What was humanity?

He was an animal, simplistic and efficient in nature. His mind worked on the most basic of levels, a black hole sucking the life from everything he touched. Yet there was a spark in that well of darkness he called a soul. He saw it out of the corner of his blood shot eyes.

Where had it come from?

His body went rigid as his eyes scanned the dense fog for that glimmer of light. Only his eyes moved, tracing back and forth like a feral cat, muscles tensed in anticipation, ready to uncoil. A tingle traced up his spine, giving him pause, as he spotted his quarry.

The fog parted as he pounced, cat like, towards the dancing light. His hands tried in vain to grasp it, but the small dot of light slipped lazily away from his menacing reach. He tracked its movements then pounced again. Over and over, he repeated this process. Over and over he came up short.

"Daddy"

Wraith's breathing became labored as the hate on his face grew stronger. He roared in anger then leapt as hard and fast as his tired body would let him. His grimy hands, fingernails caked with blood and dirt, closed over the light and held it fast. A twisted grin formed on his face as he stared at his closed fist.

"Daddy"

His head snapped around like a whip at the sound of the voice. Where had that voice come from? His hands dropped to his sides, although his grip on the little speck of light never slacked. The muscles in his body tensed once more, his eyes darting all around the fog.

" Why did you kill the good man, daddy?"

Good? No, not good. Couldn't be good. He killed the bad man like he was told. The bad man hurt his little girl, so he hurt the bad man. No, he couldn't have been good.

The disembodied voice floated in the air all around him. He growled low in his throat as he wheeled to and fro in search of this new tormentor. The sound of the voice was quite like that of an angel, soft and melodious. But to Wraith it was a demon sent to torture him, a staunch reminder of his past, a whisper of his diseased mind.

" *Here daddy, can't you see?*"

Wraith looked down at his fist, the one that still held the little speck of light and raised it slowly towards his face. There beside it was a darker spec, the other Katie...the darker one. They both stared at him, one pleading one sadistic.

" *Why daddy, why?*"

Blood oozed from his closed fist, slipping between his tightly pressed fingers, and began streaming down his arm. For one moment, the hate in Wraith's eyes disappeared, replaced with sorrow and self-loathing. And in that instant, the hunter tilted back his head and wailed in agony.

Chapter 10

A pale hand flicked on the computer screen in the poorly lit room. Shadows danced off high bookshelves giving a dark expanse to the room. The books themselves were ancient, sturdy bound, volume upon volume. The sole source of the shadows was caused by the low, almost evil, crackling fire in the stone fireplace. The monitor whined to life, adding a white glow that seemed to douse the dull orange light of the fire.

The stick-like fingers danced across the keyboard, typing in a web address. **The Dark Truth** website flared to life. The cursor moused over the webcast button, the soft click of the button almost echoing the crackle of the fire. Where William's face usually flooded the screen at that time, there was only offline snow with the simple text: webcast offline. William's faithful followers were none too happy, some even derisively speculating that the squirrels must have gotten him after all.

The ghostly hands typed another address in the url. This time it pulled up the local newspaper with a headline that read: **Nashville News Reporter Killed In Car Crash**. The page scrolled across the screen until it came to rest on a picture of Amanda Richardson, happy but determined. Another image showed her mangled car and rescue workers scrambling around the scene of the accident.

"Sir, your meal has been prepared," a lifeless hollow voice spoke into the silence.

The hand flicked off the screen, the pale reflection in the empty monitor window turning away to address the unseen speaker. Framed in the doorway was an extremely slender, alabaster skinned man, middle aged with slicked back snow-white hair, standing as still as a statue. His reddish-pink eyes were as lifeless as his voice. The butler outfit he wore was reminiscent of the clothing English butlers donned decades earlier.

Mayor Grey leaned thoughtfully against the high back leather chair, hands steepled below his chin. "And our guest, Geoffery or is it the good Reverend Gillian?"

The upper left corner of the Geoffery's lip twitched involuntarily, his eyes coming alive with hunger. His dual identity, part of the mayor's grand scheme, was as smooth as putting on a new suit. It was easy, comforting. But even though the thought brought a sense of pride the rest of his body remained rigidly composed. "Prepared."

The mayor let his cool eyes rest on the mesmerizing fire as if trying to look beyond it. People were growing suspicious, especially that pesky sheriff, a final string he was not quite ready to cut. It wasn't time for that yet. Soon, very soon. As careful as he had endeavored to be, the war with his desires was the toughest to overcome. Now was not the time to falter.

"Will you be venturing out tonight, sir?"

"No," he said as he continued to gaze into the fire, battling the stirring within him, "no, my attention is required elsewhere."

"Surely…" the butler began but was quickly silenced with a quick wave of the mayor's boney hand.

He wanted to go, needed to go if truth be told. The desires that compelled him were overwhelming at times, a fight between his true nature and the endgame he had worked so tirelessly to craft. Every seed was sewn just so. One mistake would destroy his plans before they could be put into play, therefore control was a necessity.

The mayor arose from his chair with a grace that seemed preternaturally fluid, crossing the room silently, as if he were weightless. Geoffery moved to the side to allow Mayor Grey to pass, but something brought the mayor to a sudden stop. He sniffed the air, whipping his head to stare menacingly at his butler, who did his best to avoid the withering admonition.

"There is a speck of blood on your neck..."

The albino swallowed quickly then answered directly, for there was no sense in lying to the mayor, he would see right through it. "Only a speck sir, nothing serious. It was an unfortunate occurrence that could not be helped."

A bony finger snapped out, tipped with an overly elongated, and very sharp fingernail. A small, quick flick of the wrist and the mayor had dislodged the blood speck from Geoffery's neck, leaving a small, burning, scratch in the butler's otherwise perfect alabaster skin. The pain, however, was immense. Geoffery, to his credit, did not flinch away because that would have shown weakness. The mayor did not suffer weakness. Sweat glistened his forehead as he stood statue still. The cold washed-out lips of the mayor were less than a hairs breadth from his ear.

"For your sake, I hope that is true," he whispered with a cold hiss.

Geoffery merely stared straight ahead into nothing. The mayor quickly turned away, moving down the hallway like a ghost. Geoffery took a quick breath as he gulped in relief. He wasn't the mayor's first caretaker, but he wanted to be the last and the mayor could be fickle. He quietly followed his master down the hallway until they came to a set of large French doors.

The butler reached out a hand to open the doors, but the mayor stopped him, a perverse smile on his face. "You may go now," Grey spoke in that eerie whisper of a voice he used when his inner nature would begin to reveal itself. Geoffery immediately turned and walked away.

Mayor Grey opened the sliding doors, allowing the pale light to sliver into the darkened room beyond. A low, unconscious moaning issued from a lump of clothing and sheets that were sprawled across a large, iron wrought bed. The pile of cloth stirred, revealing a naked male form, dark hair matted over his shoulders.

The man tried to rouse himself in an attempt to gain his bearings, a beam of light forcing him to squint at its brightness. *From one prison to another*, he thought hopelessly.

Steven looked over his shoulder at the silhouetted form of Mayor Grey. Even through squinted eyes he noticed the overly elongated teeth that shone brilliantly in that sinister smile. The poor man shrank back, trying to scream but was so caught up in his terror that the only sounds he could make were stuttering sobs. *Was this more of the doctor's torture*, he wondered in his terror?

"No need for screaming, dear one," the twisted visage of the mayor crooned, "there will be plenty of time for that."

The mayor silently closed the door, wading into the darkness where his prey helplessly awaited. A grim, sadistic smile splayed across his pale features. "Steven, is it? We're going to have such good times."

Evan leaned back in the old leather chair, eyes peering at the monitors that provided him with a view of every room and office in the mental institution. Unlike the monitors in the security office, he was the only one with access to these, the only one who knew they existed. He had eyes everywhere, but at that moment he was fixated on two rooms only.

In the dungeon Evan was God, free to create and destroy as he chose. He reasoned to himself that his experiments were justified, and never cruel. He was a scientist after all, that meant making hard choices and doing things that most people thought were inhumane. Evan had come to grips many years earlier that a few had to be sacrificed so he could cure millions. History would judge him correctly.

Mad?

Not at all, from his viewpoint. Of course, he knew what he was doing was morally wrong and that he would be condemned to Hell for it.

But I'm already in Hell, he thought bitterly, *my wife was taken from me, my son hates me, and all because of this damnable disease.*

There was no turning back for him, nor did he want to. Evan would see it through to the end, however it turned out. He had made his deal with the devil, knowing what that meant. As long as he could complete his work and free his son of this wretched legacy then it would all be worth it.

It was his sacrifice, his cross to bear.

Daniel knew him better than anyone, tried to reach out to him, to help Evan out of the pit he kept sliding further into. Daniel, his only friend and mentor, had he abandoned Evan as well? *No, he thought fiercely, Daniel would stand by my side no matter what, even if it meant having to confront and perhaps even fight me. Where was Daniel? It wasn't like him not to show up for work, the man was predictable that way.*

Evan reached for his phone and was about to call his friend when his eyes shifted back to the monitors.

"Dammit," he screamed as he looked at two empty monitors. His two most prized, and dangerous, inmates were out of their cells yet the doors to their prisons were locked up tight.

His benefactor had set them free, and right under Evan's nose. There were too many bodies piling up. That thought shifted his mind to Amanda. He called her to meet for supper while she was driving in that damn storm, losing her life in the horrible crash, a beautiful woman with so much potential. Was it his call that caused her wreck, that one instant that irrevocably changed the course of her destiny? He was accountable for her death as well as his beloved wife's. Eventually those deaths as well as the newest ones would be linked back to the Asylum, to him. Then all his work would be over, as incomplete as the rest of his life.

Evan could sense himself fading, the feelings of madness were stirring within him as surely as it was in the patients he was trying desperately to heal.

His intercom snapped him from his self-pity.

"Dr. Michaels, Sherriff Hooks is here to see you," the monotone voice of his secretary belted from the speaker.

Evan glanced once more at the empty monitors. Everything was disintegrating around him.

A tall, older, black man was running a wax buffer across the office floor, oblivious to his surroundings, semi-dancing as he pushed the machine back and forth while listening to Marvin Gaye through his earphones.

Jim worked alone, which was how he preferred it. He worked at his own pace, on the late shift, so he wouldn't have any stuck-up bosses to answer to. Jim was not a man prone to greatness, yet greatly prone to misfortune. He wasn't a lazy man, not by any stretch of the imagination could he ever be characterized as such. But for all his years of hard work, Jim now found himself a janitor in a local nut house.

A janitor.

At fifty-three years old, he knew that finding a higher paying job with his lack of education was non-existent. And to think, it was all going so well until the last couple of years. He was now as much a part of the asylum as the stone that held up the walls.

The stories he could tell.

Jim, however, never spoke to his family or friends about what went on up there. Silence meant you kept your job; he learned that the hard way when the Army forced him out after his outspoken nature ruffled one too many feathers. They used a million excuses, tried to get him to mess up. Finally, Jim decided the fight was no longer worth it so he took his retirement and came back home to Hale County...and now he was a janitor. The pay wasn't great, but it paid the bills. Combine that with his military pension and he carved out a nice little life for him and his wife. Jim wasn't going to mess that up over gossip, no matter if it was sometimes true.

When people pressured him for news the old soldier would bristle and stand to the full height of his large frame. Jim may have been in his fifties, but people knew not to get on the old soldiers bad side. His temper was short. His temper with fools even shorter.

He unplugged the buffer and wrapped the cord up neatly around the handle, then pushed it into the hallway. Jim pulled a trash-bag from his cart in the corner and changed out the used one in the small can with the fresh unused one. Not even the soothing melody of Marvin Gaye could distract him from his anger over the slight the Army gave him. The storm raging outside of the office served as a mirror for the turmoil in his mind.

"How in the hell did it come to this?" Jim mumbled bleakly as he tied the trash bag in a knot and tossed it angrily into his cart. He turned off the office light, pushing his cart into the hallway as he shut the door behind him. He jerked the key ring from his belt loop and rifled through them until he found the key he was looking for then shoved it roughly into the keyhole. "Thirty years. Thirty damn years."

Jim pulled the key from the lock and turned back to his cart. He let out a loud yell and fell back towards the door, slamming into it with a solid thud. He grasped his chest, trying to catch his breath.

"You shouldn't do that to people, Ms. Perkins!"

The small petite brunette, Kara Perkins, looked at him sympathetically. "I'm sorry Mr. Holt. I just came by the office to pick up a few things. Are you okay?"

"Yes ma'am. Just take me a moment to collect myself," he said indignantly.

"I couldn't help but overhear. Do you not like working here, Mr. Holt?" Kara asked Jim with all sincerity.

"Oh, yes ma'am. I like working here very much. Everyone's really nice it's just…" Jim shook his head in frustration, struggling to voice his angst.

"It's just that you're a janitor here whereas in your previous job you were a supervisor in charge of maintenance for the Army mobile division at Fort Benning. Am I right?"

Jim looked at her as if she were a twelve-eyed toad with eight legs. "H-how did you know that?"

Kara winked and smiled disarmingly holding up some files and tapping her name badge. "I'm the Human Resource manager, remember? I know your file backwards and forwards."

Comforting laughter escaped Jim's throat, draining him of the tenseness that had threatened to consume him. "I'm sorry, I had forgotten. Thought you was a witch there for a minute," he said conspiratorially and then busted out a deep bellowing laugh that seemed to drain the growing tension in the room.

His laughter was contagious. Kara couldn't help but join him. Tears of laughter began rolling down his face. "Some people think so!" she snorted with a laugh.

Finally, Jim began to get control of himself. "Whew, I haven't laughed like that in a long time."

Kara wiped a humorous tear from her own eyes. "Seriously, if there's anything I can do for you then just let me know. Any conversation we have will be strictly confidential."

Jim looked at her warily, but Kara flashed that warming smile again. "Jim," he said abruptly, holding out a hand, "my friends call me Jim."

She shook his hand without pause, "My friends call me Kara."

Jim smiled and glanced at her badge once again. "Perkins? You related to that little girl who found the body?"

A sad, forced smile replaced Kara's sincere one. "My daughter, Haley. Word travels fast." she said heavily.

Realization dawned on him. "Small town. I'm sorry, I didn't mean to say anything. Things come out before I think about them sometimes."

Kara's reassuring smile put him at ease. "It's okay, truly."

"How is she holding up?"

"Children," she said with a bemused shake of her head, "they are resilient. I think it's the parents who suffer the most. She was back to playing with her dolls like nothing ever happened."

"Then I think the question is 'how are YOU holding up'" he said sympathetically, his concern as much of a shock to him as it was to Kara.

"Um, well," Kara stammered as she searched her emotions, so caught up in what her daughter had gone through that it didn't occur to her that she could be suffering as well. Kara let out a quick amused sigh and a slight smile. "I was going to say I'm fine but, honestly, it saddens me that my little girl has to go through that. She's so young. Seeing a dead body like that is the last thing any child should have to witness."

"Did they ever find out who it was?"

Kara shook her head, trying to get the image of Dr. Lane's dead body out of her mind. She knew, but the Sheriff had warned everyone at the crime scene not to say a word until he had paid a visit to the asylum. Dr. Lane had always been nice to her, she could only imagine what his family could be going through. She wanted to tell someone. Perhaps she could tell Jim, he did confide in her after-all, to an extent. But no, the Sheriff had forbidden them, and she didn't want to be the one to mess up the investigation, especially considering her daughter was involved, even somewhat peripherally.

The Sheriff. That was a whole other bag of worms she didn't want to open. Kara could feel her blood pressure rising and had to force him from her thoughts.

"No," she said finally, hoping that her delay in answering didn't arouse suspicion that she did in fact know who it was. She looked back at Jim, expecting to see him peering doubtfully at her, but Jim's focus was on something beyond her, out in the storm.

Jim moved past her, almost robotically, towards the office window, eyes straining to see something in the darkness.

"Mr. Holt, Jim, what is it?"

"I'm not sure," he finally answered, nose almost pressed to the cool glass. He had seen something pass by the window while Kara had been talking. It was big. *But who would be out in that monsoon?* "I thought I saw someone."

Kara joined him at the window, peering out into the storm trying to see what he saw. A huge clap of thunder shook the windows as a simultaneous flash lit up the night, startling Jim and Kara.

The lights suddenly went dark. Neither one spoke as an eerie silence crept over the asylum. Inmates began stirring, yelling deliriously into the pitch of the mental institute, one voice becoming two, two becoming a multitude. Kara and Jim shifted their attention from the window to the darkened hallway.

There was a loud patter of feet that kept drawing closer, flashes of light bouncing in the lightless hallway. There was no organization to the footsteps making it impossible to tell how many were running free.

Had the inmates somehow gotten out of their rooms?

Kara and Jim involuntarily moved closer together as the pounding of feet on tile grew closer. Jim's military training instantly kicked in. He may have gotten older, but he wasn't going down without doing some serious damage. His senses began tingling with the anticipation of the encounter.

They were almost upon them. There was a disparate grumbling coming from the approaching group.

Jim tensed.

Kara grabbed a lamp from the desk.

Jim nodded in approval as the lightning lit up the room. *Kara was a tough lady, no fear. She will need that,* Jim thought proudly.

The unseen group came running up to the office...and immediately past, flashlights bouncing in their hands.

Orderlies.

Jim and Kara breathed a sigh of relief. They turned from the hallway to stare back out the window, as lightning continued illuminating the stormy night.

The distorted face of Wraith was staring at them, eyes ablaze with hatred, long wet hair hanging woefully against his grime-stained jumpsuit.

Kara screamed.

"Oh shit!!" Jim yelped in surprise, leaping back from the window.

Lightning flashed.

The visage of Wraith was gone.

"Damn, one got loose! We gotta tell somebody!" Jim yelled, as he tried to pull Kara along with him.

Those eyes.

The image of Dr. Lane's death face came instantly to her mind. *"What could cause a man to be so afraid?"* the deputy had asked the Sheriff. Now she knew. For the first time in her life, Kara was afraid.

Evan peered across the desk; fingers folded under his chin in thought. The news was unexpected yet at the same time it was something he feared might happen. Too many eyes seeing every tiny thing that was going on. Daniel had been digging into things, things he should have left alone.

"When?" he asked, fighting his composure. It was a simple question that carried so much weight. The timing was everything.

Jake glared back at the doctor, studying his emotions. The reaction was genuine. Dr. Michaels didn't know anything about Daniel Lane's death. But someone at the asylum might. The forest around the old mental institute was vast and thick. Dr. Lane's car was still in the parking lot. Therefore, to Jake's way of thinking, somebody at the institution knew what had happened to Daniel. It was simply a matter of finding that one clue, that scent that put him on the trail. Once that happened, the culprit was his. Dr. Michaels was a cool customer who had always seemed to hide his emotions very well, at least in their previous dealings. This news seemed to crack that façade. Dr. Michaels may not be involved but he could very well lead Jake to who was.

"Last night," Jake finally said, no emotion in his voice.

"Where?"

"Does it matter?"

"Hell yes, it matters."

There it is, Jake thought, knowingly, *the crack in the armor.* "His body was found in a creek by a little girl. His neck was snapped."

"Neck snapped?"

"And he was beaten…extensively." Jake let that last part hang in the air.

Evan shut his eyes trying to block out the news the sheriff had given him. "Daniel…"

The doctor slumped back in his chair, all pretense of professionalism and composure sapped from him. Daniel, his friend and mentor, gone. Evan seemed to float out of his body, his hearing a constant ringing as he tried to focus. But all his mind could see was the twisted corpse of his friend...and he knew he was responsible. Why? Why Daniel? Evan had been so careful.

Or had he?

Doubt racked him as he tried to remember where he possibly could have slipped. He knew suddenly, in that moment, that it wouldn't matter, not for any of them. They were all being watched and when HE decided it was time for someone to go, they went.

Time. Everyone in Hale County was on a timer, they just didn't know it. Another garbled sound tried to break through the ringing. Evan tried to refocus as the sound struggled to break through.

"Doctor."

Evan physically shook his head as the sound of the Sheriff's voice finally got through to him. The doctor didn't bother to hide his emotions as he exhaustedly rubbed the bridge of his nose, trying to relieve some of the pressure.

"I look into the eyes of normal and all I see insanity" Evan said, voice full of exhaustion.

"What do you mean?"

It was Evan's turn to study the Sherriff. He knew of the man's reputation, what he was capable of. Jake Hooks may come across as a backwoods country Sheriff in a hick town, but Evan knew, just from the short time they had been talking, that it was the furthest thing from the truth. The Sheriff feared very little (the naturally inquisitive part of the doctor wondered just what that might be), by all accounts was as tough as they came, and had an instinct for reading people. What an ally he would make...or a troublesome enemy. The doctor could have just lied to the man but what good would it have done? Jake was no fool. The best way to deal with a man like that was the truth, or at least a satisfactory version of it.

"You've noticed it, haven't you?" the doctor said, rising from his chair to peer out into the storm. "The people are afraid, on edge. Some have gone missing others have been murdered."

Jake nodded slightly, "I wouldn't expect any less from these people when bodies are turning up like they are. Why wouldn't they be nervous? It happens everywhere from time to time."

"Not like this."

"What do you know?"

Evan didn't turn at the accusation, and he was certain that it was just what it was. "I know it's not something in the water. I know it's not mass hysteria. Something is preying on the people in this county. They are terrified. People are afraid to close their eyes at night for fear they may never have the chance to open them again. These aren't random deaths. You know that."

"I do. But I'm wondering how you know that."

"It's what I'm trained for, the human condition, to see and study what others won't. My singular goal, my life's work, is to find a cure for the insanity inside of us. It's a fool's quest but if I can find the common thread that binds the madness then we can begin to unravel it. We all have it you know, floating just beneath the surface. Certainly, you've felt it."

Jake couldn't deny it. He fought the rage to lash out at least once a day. His eyes fell on a picture sitting on the corner of the doctor's desk: the doctor himself, a beautiful dark-haired woman, and a boy he recognized. "Nice family."

Evan glanced at the picture then back to the sheriff. "The great lie," the doctor continued, "is that we have convinced ourselves that we are sane rational beings. The Universe was born of chaos and darkness. That darkness is in every one of us, even the supposed innocents. Innocence, is there really such a thing?" Evan turned to the Sheriff, once more locking eyes. "There is a madness running through this county and it WILL consume everyone no matter where they run or how they choose to hide. It will find us all."

"Okay," Jake scoffed dismissively, rising from his chair.

He didn't have time for ridiculous nonsense when someone out there was killing people on his watch at will. Was the doctor succumbing from too much time spent with his trouble patients? It didn't remotely jive with what he had heard of the even-keeled psychiatrist. Perhaps people in that profession were all a little off. Either way, he didn't have time to listen to horror stories. He had real issues, like finding Daniels killer. The good doctor just jumped to the top of his very short list. Hell, he was the ONLY one on the list...so far.

"You can doubt it now Sheriff but there will come a time, very soon perhaps, that you won't be able to deny it."

"Just what do you mean by that?"

Evan took a step towards him, a look of pleading that was palpable. His voice took on a low, desperate whisper, "Don't trust anyone, watch everything...evil is here."

"Alright, look..."

Jake was about to say more when the lights went out almost immediately followed by the emergency generator roaring to life, bathing the office in an amber glow.

The door to the office burst open. Samantha looked panicked as she shouted at Evan, "The doors to Ward D were all unlocked and opened somehow. Those patients are destroying everything on that block!"

Evan flew past Jake, following Samantha into the hall. He looked over his shoulder as he began to run towards the end of the corridor. "You coming?!"

Jake stared after him for a brief second, cursing under his breath, "Dammit," before sprinting after them.

The security camera in the corridor followed his path until he disappeared beyond the far doors. Thunder rumbled loud enough to shake the walls, causing the emergency lights to flicker. The chaos was just beginning.

The cold glass perspired as he took a sip of the bitter amber liquid. JC couldn't prevent his face from puckering at the taste. Still, the alcohol was needed. His dad wasn't likely to be home anytime soon and he needed to release some tension after what Ashlyn had told him about the mayor. It had been on his mind all day and then there was that episode with the cops at the professors.

Ashlyn...

He hurt me, she had said. It wasn't until after the mayor left that JC pried further. At first, she was reluctant to talk about it so he dropped it but as he was getting into his car to go home she pulled him to her, wrapping her arms around him in an unwillingness to let him go.

Then there was the look the mayor had given him, piercing, cold...and taunting? Yes, there was no other word for it. The pale Mayor was taunting JC with a smirk, either figuring Ashlyn had told JC about the Mayor or that the young man simply had a wary feel about "Uncle Grey". Either way, the mayor made it perfectly clear with a single glance that he wasn't to be trifled with.

JC downed the liquid at the thought. Ashlyn was hurting, the mayor hated him, he somehow got cast as the lead in the play, his professor and friend was missing...and then there was his dad. He set the empty glass on the table and filled it half full once again. *I shouldn't be drinking*; he thought in a moment of clarity that was quickly pushed back behind the walls of his burgeoning depression.

He wanted to forget. He wanted to just get lost in the bottle of whiskey. JC brought the glass to his lips when his eyes settled on the picture of him and his father. High School graduation, one of the last times they had smiled together. His thoughts drifted to other families, normal families. JC wanted normalcy. He craved it as much as most people craved excitement.

There were moments like shards of a broken mirror where he could remember brief times of having that ordinary life. The early days, catches with his dad, birthday parties, Christmas. He had no memories of his mother. She had died soon after he was born. His dad kept pictures of her for a while until they just became too painful. Evan packed them all away and refused to talk about it. His dad refused to marry again, shutting himself off from the possibility and denying JC that important part of his life that was missing, having that mother figure that could provide what his father seemed incapable of, love.

JC rested his head back on the leather chair, twirling the glass of alcohol in small aimless circles as the lightning flashed outside. Every once in a while, the room would illuminate with the lavender white glow of the storm, echoed by the low rumbling thunder. At first, he was unaware of anything else lost as he was in his alcohol-induced moroseness.

Then he saw it.

It was that shadow, the one in the corner of your eye that always disappeared when you turned to look at it. Except this one didn't disappear. It was there. It was moving.

Lightning lit up the room, but the shadow remained. It was formless, without detail.

JC stared at it blankly, his mind trying to cut through the alcohol-induced fuzziness. He tried to sit up in the chair, but his body wouldn't respond. He felt sluggish…entranced. There was a sound, raspy and sporadic. He listened intently only to realize it was him. His chest was heaving quickly from panicked breaths. The young man closed his eyes, controlling the panic was important. His dad had taught him that when he was young after the night terrors had begun. It worked then. His night terrors had stopped shortly thereafter.

Was this them returning?

It had been over ten years since the last one, so long so that he couldn't remember what they were about. He steeled himself, mentally imagined his chest rising and falling normally. JC shut out everything else and just concentrated on his breathing. The room seemed to fade away as his body seemed to right itself. He slowly opened his eyes.

The shadow was gone.

JC let out a long sigh of relief and brought the glass to his lips letting out a small, relieved laugh. The cool of the glass touched his lips followed quickly by the bitter alcohol.

Across the room.

There.

Standing there.

The shadow.

The glass slipped from his paralyzed grasp. His heart thumped wildly, electric shivers shot up his spine. He tried to take a breath. The glass shattered on the floor spilling its amber liquid everywhere. JC didn't hear it. He didn't hear anything.

The shadow moved…

…and the world went black.

The door shut on the last patient's room. Jake wiped the moisture from his brow, he had worked up quite a sweat rounding up the escapees, the ancient AC unit going out didn't help. The doctor leaned heavily against the wall opposite him and took a deep breath. There wasn't much time for talk once the round up of the patients began.

The sheriff eyed the tired doctor, "is this a regular occurrence?" Jake's voice was laced with weariness and suspicion.

Evan matched his look, "No. Not since we put in all these safety measures."

"Intentional."

The doctor nodded his head in the affirmative, "makes sense. Daniel goes missing and now this. I don't believe in coincidences, Sheriff, not in my line of work."

Jake glanced at the patients' rooms, "me either, doc, me either."

Jake eyed the exhausted doctor warily. Something wasn't adding up, but he couldn't quite put his finger on it. The patients' escape seemed too convenient, coming right on the heels of Daniel's murder. And Evan's earlier ramblings about evil and madness in the county… the man was either losing it or hiding something. Possibly both.

"So doc, care to explain exactly how all these safety measures failed at once?" Jake pressed.

Evan ran a hand through his disheveled hair. "I wish I knew, Sheriff. The locks, the alarms, the cameras - it's all state of the art. For everything to malfunction simultaneously... it shouldn't be possible."

"And yet here we are," Jake said flatly.

"If that, in fact, is then true..."

"...then it was most certainly deliberate," the sheriff finished for him.

Thunder rumbled ominously outside as the two men stared each other down in the dim emergency lighting. The air felt thick with tension and unspoken accusations.

Jake rubbed his chin thoughtfully, studying the doctor. "So who would have the ability to override your security systems and unlock all these doors at once?"

Evan sighed heavily. "Very few people have that level of access. Myself, of course. My head of security. And..." he trailed off, looking troubled.

"And who?" Jake pressed.

"The board chairman. But surely, he wouldn't..." Evan shook his head. "No, it must have been some kind of malfunction or hack."

"Why wouldn't he?"

"Because that would mean getting off his boney ass and paying us a visit."

Jake raised an eyebrow at Evan's uncharacteristic display of frustration. "Not a fan of the chairman, I take it?"

Evan let out a bitter laugh. "Let's just say we have our disagreements on how this place should be run. He's more concerned with the bottom line than patient care."

"And what exactly does the chairman do?" Jake probed.

"Technically he oversees operations, finances, that sort of thing. But in practice..." Evan trailed off, his expression darkening. "Let's just say he has his fingers in a lot of pies around the county. The kind of man who likes to pull strings from the shadows."

Jake's eyes narrowed. "You're talking about Mayor Grey, aren't you?"

Evan nodded grimly. "One and the same. Though how he finds the time to run both the town, and this place is beyond me."

Jake's mind raced as he processed this new information. Mayor Grey as the board chairman of the asylum? That connection hadn't come up in any of his investigations so far. It added a whole new layer of complexity - and suspicion - to the recent events plaguing Hale County.

"And just how long has the good mayor been involved with this place?" Jake asked, his tone deceptively casual.

Evan shrugged. "Longer than I've been here. Decades, from what I understand. The asylum's been in his family for generations."

"Interesting," Jake mused. "Very interesting indeed."

A loud crash from down the hall interrupted their conversation. Both men tensed, exchanging a wary glance before hurrying towards the source of the noise.

They rounded the corner to find an orderly sprawled on the floor in front of a large iron door, a shattered meal tray beside him. The man was trembling while trying feebly to pick up the mess he made. "Sorry sir," he half-whispered to the Doctor, not daring to meet his gaze, "I slipped."

"No worries, Gary. Get it picked up and finish your rounds." Evan then turned to the Sheriff, gesturing down the hallway, "I appreciate your help tonight, we'll take care of the clean-up and if there is anything else I can find that might help your investigation I'll get it to you ASAP."

Jake spared a look back, his eyes fixing on a single word above the door: oubliette. This place just kept getting odder and odder.

"Hey mom, how's my baby," Kara asked into the phone she held precariously to her ear with her shoulder as she walked across the Hale County Mental Institute parking lot, hands full with her purse, coat, and a box of paperwork.

"I know," she said as she fumbled with her keys while expertly balancing the familiar items she carried on a seemingly nightly basis. Thank God the rain had subsided long enough for her to get to her car. Thunder still rumbled and lightning flashed in sporadic bursts but nothing like earlier. "I'll be careful. It's been a hectic night. We lost power and had a minor riot."

Kara clicked the keyless remote as she approached her car listening patiently to her mother's insistent and, as usual, overprotective concerns for her safety. She grasped the handle with the only two free fingers she had, popping the door open and tossing in one item after the next. She was about to answer her mother's concerns when she noticed movement along the tree line.

"Mom, I'm going to have to call you back." She hung up and stared after the large man. Another escapee perhaps? She thought they had all been accounted for. It was still chaos inside. Kara pulled the taser from her purse. She'd had to use it on more than one occasion and certainly had no qualms with doing so again. Kara was a country girl at heart, her daddy made sure of that, so she wasn't afraid to stand up to anyone. Her daddy made sure of that as well.

She didn't take her eyes off the man in orange. That would have been a mistake. Self-defense 101, always keep your eyes on your opponent.

"What are you doing?" a deep voice spoke authoritatively from behind her.

Kara jumped and swung her arm with the taser at the unknown voice, her eyes mixed with fear and desperation.

A strong hand caught her arm, avoiding contact with the potent little weapon.

"Whoa! Calm down!"

Kara realized in an instant who the voice belonged to which only seemed to anger her. "Goddammit Jake!! Shit! Are you trying to give me a heart attack?!?"

"I called your name twice!" the sheriff said defensively. Why did all their conversations begin in anger? It was always that way between them. That bitterness just never seemed to go away.

"You should have said it louder!" she half screamed, trying to collect herself in the process.

"Relax" he retorted, trying to maintain so semblance of calmness. She was wound tightly tonight, understandably so after the events of the past two hours. Everyone was on edge. "Why did you have your taser out?"

The change that came over her was off putting as she transitioned from hostility to concern. "A patient. I think we have another escapee. But I've never seen him before."

"Where?"

Kara pointed to the tree line. "Over there."

"What did he look like?"

She looked at him matter-of-factly. "Scary. Big...big and scary."

"Great."

Jake pursed his lips, ran to his truck and grabbed his Mag flashlight. Snapping on the button, the intense LED beam cut through the darkness. He started to step past Kara when he felt her grip on his arm.

"Be careful", she said seriously, "he was huge."

Jake paused for a moment as they locked eyes. Kara. He felt his stomach tighten at the mere thought of her name. He shook it off. Now wasn't the time.

"I will. Let Dr. Michaels know I'm in pursuit of another one of his patients and get me some backup. You remember how to use the radio in my truck?"

"Yes, of course.", she said, immediately heading back towards the building. Kara paused at the entrance, looking back towards Jake as he approached the area where the inmate had disappeared. A whirling of emotions rose within her as she watched him enter the woods. Small towns. You could never escape your past.

As Kara slipped back into the asylum, she was unaware of a second set of eyes that had been watching her. Eyes of vengeance, eyes of hate...eyes of death.

Wraith stepped from the shadows. With grim purpose a feral snarl escaped his lips. Like a seasoned predator he quietly entered the woods in the same area Jake had only moments before, retribution was his singular focus. He paused only briefly casting a quick glance behind him.

She was there as always, his dark angel, watching over him. "The bad man, daddy…the bad man" She smiled wickedly at him.

Wraith's face twisted in morbid determination. In one cat like move he stealthily disappeared into the dark forest.

Jake shined his giant mag flashlight on the ground, following the footsteps of guy that was hiding in the trees. Kara was right, the man was big. As for the scary part, well, that was debatable. Still, he needed to be on guard. The last thing he wanted was to be taken by surprise.

As he tracked the big man something kept weighing on him, something about Evan Michaels. He figured the doctor wasn't being totally honest with him. Hell, he expected that. No, there was something else, something in the doctor's mannerisms that reminded him of someone else, but he couldn't quite put his finger on it. The doctor *wanted* to say something, even managed to go on a rant about evil taking over the county or some such bullshit. Perhaps he was simply as crazy as his patients.

You hang around the nut cases long enough you become one, the sheriff thought to himself.

Then there was Kara. He paused in his tracking as his mind flooded with nothing but her. All these years later she could still piss him off and turn him on all at the same time. What was it with her?

Really? You want to blame her? That voice he hated, the honest one wasn't having any of it. *She did the best she could. And what you did to her was beyond sorry. And you wonder why she never came back for those earrings…*

"I know goddammit!" Jake hissed out loud. The sound of his voice startled him. He hadn't meant to react that way. He was wrong, maybe it was him who was nuts.

A limb snapped a few feet to his right.

Jake stopped thinking and listened intently.

Nothing.

Rain began to fall again. He would have to pick up his pace or lose the ability to track the escapee. The rain was falling hard as the thunder picked up. The lightning became consistent and almost strobe-like.

Concentrate.

Do the job.

He could hear Cutty's slow growling drawl in his head reminding him in no uncertain terms to stay focused. *Not staying focused gets you sloppy. Sloppy gets you killed. Ain't no time for female problems.* Cutty had lived his life with that old school mentality. He died the same way, old school and stubborn.

Still, the old man wasn't wrong. Jake needed to be sharp and on alert. The storm was picking up again. It had already been the wettest year he could remember, and it just kept coming. He wasn't sure about El Nino or whatever the hell it was called, he simply knew it wasn't normal.

A darkness is coming.

The doctor's words kept coming back to him. Normally it wasn't the kind of crazy talk he focused on but there was a sincerity to the doctor that gave Jake pause. Probably because Jake had felt the change as well. It was like when you just knew your spouse was cheating on you or that you were about to get pulled over.

There was no proof, it was a feeling, a thickness that hung in the air like a smothering blanket.

Hale County, his county, was being strangled.

SNAP

Jake stopped moving.

He didn't move, didn't think. He just listened.

With all the rain there shouldn't have been a dry limb to on the ground to break. Someone had to have intentionally broken a limb.

Intentionally…

Jake's eyes went wide as he threw himself onto the wet leafy ground of the forest. He felt a breeze by his ear as he completed a full roll coming up on his knees.

He whipped the flashlight up in time to see the large man in the orange jumpsuit barreling towards him impossibly fast for a man his size. Jake barely had time to brace himself as the crazed man dropped his shoulder and rammed it into his chest sending the sheriff flying into a tree and knocking the breath from him. There wasn't time for Jake to attempt a breath as another solid blow caught him in the ribs, forcing him into the air before crashing onto his back. He lifted his head…

WHAM!!

The world seemed to explode before his eyes as a large meaty fist caught him squarely in the nose causing a spray of blood to erupt, painting his face and clothes a crimson sea.

The attack had only lasted a few seconds, and Jake knew it was over. He had never been hit so hard in his life.

Blow after blow rained down on him. Thankfully, he was almost unconscious. *Good*, he thought offhandedly, *at least there won't be any more pain...*

Jake felt his soul leaving his body and gave into it. It was over, he was done. A coolness spread over him, comforting and strange. The ringing in his ears was replaced by rumbling. *Odd, that's not what I thought angels would sound like.*

He could tell he was moving; the strange floating sensation wasn't as smooth as he had assumed a floating soul would be. The rumbling grew louder, the coolness felt like being dipped in a frigid bath.

Pain shot through his ribs. *You're not supposed to feel pain when you die...*

Jake's eyes snapped open. Lightning flashed wildly in the sky above him as the rain poured like a monsoon.

He was being carried by the crazed man. Carried where? Then Ronald had him pressed over his head. Jake turned his head as the lightning flashed, illuminating the area.

Oh shit...

...a cliff.

It was then Jake realized he was still somehow holding the flashlight. He brought it down with all of his strength on the insane man's temple. Jake heard a grunt and gravity took hold, his body crashing to the soft earth.

Jake fought the pain, rising to his feet. The inmate wouldn't be stunned long. The sheriff swung the flashlight again, catching Ronald on the jaw and sending the man staggering backwards. Jake knew he couldn't hesitate. Once, twice, a third time he hit the man with the heavy flashlight causing the inmate to stumble.

What the hell is keeping him up...

Change of plans. Jake swung as hard as he could and crushed the flashlight into Ronald's knee.

It worked.

The big man hit the ground on his knees, a weird howl of pain coming from his crazed mouth.

Jake didn't let up. He kept hitting the big man, blow after blow, until finally the escapee hit the earth and remained still.

The sheriff fell to his knees as well drinking in the air. When the pain finally hit it was going to be bad. He needed a vacation.

"Sheriff?"

He unhooked the walkie-talkie from his belt. "I'm fine. I got him."

"Where are you sir?"

I don't know," he said looking around, "by a cliff. Can't be that far away."

"On our way, sir."

Jake put the walkie-talkie back on his belt breathing a sigh of relief in the process. That's when he saw it. It was so strange that it took him a moment to realize what it was...a doll. The head of it was pasty white and mutilated with dried blood. There were nails and tacks jammed into the head in random areas.

"What the hell..."

The sheriff felt the blow before he saw it. The inmates oversized foot shot out, catching him in the stomach and sending him reeling. He tried to scramble to his feet. He almost made it. As he looked towards the crazy bastard that refused to stay down, he saw the pale face of the doll coming at him.

Pain exploded in his head once again as the head of the doll caught him just above the eye. One of the nails dug into his flesh and as it was pulled away cut a swatch across his nose and over his opposite cheek. The agony was unbearable. Jake lost his footing and stumbled back over the cliff facing.

He dug his hands into the earth as his feet dangled over the abyss. Desperately he tried to pull himself up but his strength was gone. *Where are my goddamn deputies...*

The lightning flashed to reveal the psychotic inmate standing above him, a sick smile playing on his bloodied face.

There was no getting out of this one.

Ronald lifted a huge limb over his head, his intention obvious.

Jake Hooks was not a begging man and he certainly wasn't a coward. No one was going to take his life, no one but himself, in his own way...just like he lived. A blur of movement suddenly appeared out of nowhere, barreling into the large, crazed human sending him tumbling out of site as the Sheriff desperately tried clinging on to the cliff.

Ronald hit the ground hard but quickly rolled to his feet, snarling in anger at whatever had attacked him while trying to finish his prey. There, dressed in bloodied scrubs of his own, blonde hair matted in dirt and mud, crouched in a feral attack posture, stood Wraith. Drool dripped from the smaller inmate's mouth while the hellish hatred in his eyes burned unequalled. This was round 2, and there were no chains to hold him down this time.

The two crazed inmates charged one another through the downpour. Ronald's massive arms reached out to grab his enemy in their deadly embrace, but Wraith had slid beneath him, shoving both fists into the bigger man's groin. Letting out a howl of anger and pain, Ronald tried to pivot in the slog, but the smaller inmate was just too quick, rolling once more to the side Wraith brought his legs up, jamming them both into the left knee of his opponent. He could feel ligaments tearing beneath his feet as he forced Ronald's joint into a direction it was never meant to go, sending another howl of horrific agony echoing through the woods.

Hurt as he was, Ronald refused to stay down, staggering up to his feet, facing his mortal enemy once more, hatred fueling his every movement. He lunged towards Wraith with a quickness that surprised the smaller man. The meaty paw of Ronald closed around Wraith's neck, driving him down to the rain-soaked earth. Wraith twisted to and fro, writhing under the insane strength of the crazed man. But the smaller man countered the larger man's strength with a wild fierceness. He grabbed a handful of mud, grass, and leaves and shoved them into Ronald's mouth and down his throat. The psychopath gagged in anger, picked up Wraith and launched him into a tree with bone-crushing force.

Blood, mud, leaves and bile poured out of Ronald's mouth as he gagged in unbridled rage. He was no longer having fun. His eyes snapped to the crumpled form of his opponent, lying in a heap beneath a small tree. Another primal yell and the big man charged like a berserker towards his prey.

Wraith winced in agony, trying to shake away the pain. "He's coming, daddy!" The tiny voice warned him urgently. The large body of Ronald barreled into the tree with a groan as Wraith narrowly rolled out of the way. He was still weary from being tossed into the tree but reaching out his hand fell across something solid.

Ronald let out another fierce insane battle cry and rushed as fast as he could on his broken knee, ignoring the pain. Wraith waited until the last possible moment, spun, and brought the limb Ronald was going to use on the sheriff swiftly across the back of the man's neck. His eyes rolling back into his head, the deranged man refused to stay down. He pushed himself back to his feet, but

Wraith swung the branch full force into Ronald's pudgy jaw. The resulting strike fractured the killer's jaw and sent pieces of bone, mixed with saliva and blood, across the rain-soaked forest, leaving the inmate unconscious.

The smaller man wasn't finished. He lifted the branch high above once again, years of fury, rage, captivity, loss pouring through his veins. It was finally time to let it all out. One perfect strike on the piece of evil incarnate lying at his feet.

"Don't do it daddy," the voice spoke softly. Wraith shook his head, as if pushing aside the disembodied voice. "Please, daddy, let's go. Others are coming." He dropped the limb, breathing raggedly when another sound caught his hearing. He walked to the edge of the cliff and looked down. The sheriff was struggling to hang on.

They locked eyes.

"Who the hell are you?" Jake asked the bloodied and muddied form standing over him. The sheriff knew instantly that it was another escapee. *Because of course it is*, he thought bitterly, *can this day get any better? And yet...*the sheriff squinted, trying to see beneath the mud, blood and sweat. The escapee was almost...familiar.

To his surprise, the inmate reached out a hand. *Thank God*, Jake thought, exhaustion tearing at his muscles. Reluctantly, he reached out a weary hand to his rescuer when suddenly Ronald crashed into Wraith with a full body check. Wraith had nowhere to go, nothing to stop his sudden momentum. His body was launched off the cliff, up and over the sheriff, and into the darkness below.

Ronald looked down at the sheriff. There was no pity in his expression, no anger, just relish in the kill. He bent down and picked up the limb once again. There was no one else to save the sheriff as Ronald lifted the limb high above once more, drool and blood mixing in with his horrible, twisted grin.

With his last bit of strength Jake brought his feet up as high as he could and planted them on the cliff wall. He stared into the eyes of the crazed inmate in sheer defiance which caused Ronald to pause. He had never known anyone not to fear him.

Ronald smiled sickly and raised the limb higher.

Jake smiled too, "fuck you."

The sheriff let go of the cliff and kicked backwards as hard as he could. As he did, he unsnapped his holstered gun, whipping the barrel around to the surprised man. A flash of lightning ripped through the storm, the roar of the .357 magnum drowning out the thunder. Jake's last vision as he fell was of Ronald's head exploding like a watermelon, mist of blood mingling with the down pour…then the darkness took him.

Jake, finally, was at peace.

Book 2: Awakenings

'It is a man's own mind, not his enemy or foe, that lures him to evil ways'- **Buddah**

Chapter 11

Ragged boots dug into the damp, soggy, earth, kicking up dirt and leaves as each frantic stride moved at an ever-quickening pace. Twigs snapped, echoing off of the leafless skeletal trees in the dull grey morning.

Everything was enveloped in a foggy haze.

The figure, with sagging jeans and an oversized sweater as badly damaged as the boots he wore, plunged headlong into the ghostly maze of the forest. His breathing was labored, stinging his lungs as he tried to force more of the lifesaving air into his exhausted body.

The boots slipped on the dewy grass, sending him crashing to the wet earth.

Pale hands with long uncut fingernails, caked with dirt and blood, reached blindly until they found the base of a tree. The man drug himself up to a sitting position at the base of a tall, dead oak.

He squeezed his eyes tight, trying to will the air, molecule by molecule, to feed his starving body. His facial hair was so overgrown from what seemed like an eternity of neglect, that barely any flesh could be seen. The skin that did show was covered in blood and grime.

Time didn't exist for him.

He was free, that's what mattered.

Memories of his captivity threatened to consume him. He couldn't let it.

This was his first taste of freedom in weeks but instead of the crisp, clean, fall air the only smell that permeated his senses was the molded, rotting planks of the cellar he had been kept in. It was an ancient smell, the odor of a room that hadn't tasted clean air in centuries.

He couldn't think about that now.

But those thoughts, in his exhausted state, forced their way in, just like his captives.

No, he thought wearily, *don't think of them.*

Yet there they were, drifting across his mind's eye with horrific clarity, dark and malicious. He was never able to see their faces, nor did he want to. The fear of what lie behind those dark hoods was worse than not seeing them at all.

The shadows never spoke to him, not once. They merely slinked into the room to make sure he was alive, leaving only bitter water and bread for sustenance. At first, he had refused to eat, but it wasn't long before his body's instincts of survival kicked in. He was unable to refuse the food, regardless of its putridness.

Soon he was like a dog, scrambling for the meal he detested but needed; his mind giving in to thousands of years of primitive instinct. That was his torture—at first.

The dark ones had only begun his slow descent into madness.

A dirty finger traced over fresh scars on his forearm, one of many that now etched his body in a chaotic tattoo of pain. He could see the rusted metal, feel its scouring pain, hear the sound of his own anguish as it echoed throughout his prison.

SNAP!!

He jerked his head up, searching for the location of the noise. The fog made it difficult. His eyes scanned the dead trees with a feral intensity. There was no doubt he was the prey. Overworked leg muscles flexed, ears perked and aware. If they caught him, there would be no second escape.

A dark flash bolted through the fog to his right.

Another to his left...

They were here.

The skin on the back of his neck tingled, hair standing on end.

The air around him grew cold.

More shadows flitted in the thick fog.

He saw an opening, his one chance. They would see him, but there was no other option. With a snarl born of defiance, William darted once more into the fog.

The sounds of mismatched singsong echoed in disjointed waves throughout the old historic theatre. It was a small thing, the Playhouse, but rich in history. At one time it had almost become a relic of the ages, but a resurgence by a couple of determined citizens had not only brought the Playhouse back to a full-time functioning theatre, they had given it a makeover that surpassed anything in its glory years.

Upon entering its preserved lobby, you could not help but be struck by the flavor the little theatre contained. As with everything in Hale County, it had a reputation for being haunted. But as JC sat in the green room, going over his lines, he sensed the only thing that haunted the Playhouse were the performances of the past.

JC was anything but nostalgic, but even he couldn't deny the sense of awe that fifty years of performances permeated through the building. But now wasn't the time to dwell on those. No, JC had his own performance to worry about, such as it was. He snarled silently at the thought of what would take place in a few short hours—opening night.

For a moment he let his mind stray away from his lines as he sat in the dimly lit green room all alone. He could hear Ashlyn's voice amongst the others, beautiful and melodic. It was a voice that he could pick out of a crowd, calm and sweet. But even her voice couldn't stem the rogue thoughts that swirled within him.

Things had changed in the last few weeks, and not for the better. His thoughts turned to Jason Locke, his professor and friend. He hadn't been heard from in almost three weeks. No one spoke of it aloud for some reason. Of course, that didn't keep people from whispering behind closed doors, or on social media.

Many rumors circulated around the community as to what had happened to him. Some rumors had him running away with a mistress while others said he had been murdered. Certainly, from what the city police had said they found at his house it didn't sound good, blood, but no body.

A couple of students who had almost run over him the night he disappeared said he was acting strange. They were questioned but it was fairly clear early on they had nothing to do with it. Halloween had come and gone, leaving those who knew him to spend the next few weeks mourning the beloved teacher's disappearance.

JC let the sounds of the vocal warm-ups from the stage settle in the periphery of his mind. He missed Jason more than any of the others. While they weren't the best of friends, they were certainly more than acquaintances. Jason had become a mentor to him, always pushing JC to chase his own dreams and goals and cautioning him never to settle for less than what he wanted out of life. He had been the one to convince JC to try out for the play, even though Ashlyn had been after him for months to do it.

Then there was that stalker. No one believed him except Ashlyn of course. But even he didn't tell her the truth about what he had seen that night. There were limits to her faith in him, as there were for any sane person trying to understand what he said he had seen. He had been drinking, *just your imagination*, they would say. He saw the shadow everywhere, its smokiness wafting in every corner. Telling his dad would only get him his own personal suite in the asylum. *No thanks*, he thought sourly, *this play is enough to contend with.*

The play, he didn't want to think of it. But there it was, always in the forefront of his mind. He had finally gotten over the embarrassment of what they had done to him. Although the director swore someone had hacked his computer and made changes to the cast list before it was put online for the world to see, JC couldn't help but feel there was something more underhanded. He could tell by how they looked at him, especially Myers, the supposed top stud of that theater.

Ashlyn told him not to be concerned about their petty jealousies but that was easier said than done. Their animosity was palpable, bubbling just below the surface. At first, it was amusing, then annoying; now it was straight up just pissing him off. He had the lead for all of two days until the director called and informed him of the error.

JC would have (and should have) quit right then but he had already promised Ashlyn that he would do the play. *If you quit then they win*, Ashlyn's words echoed in his mind. *Why is it when something like that happens everyone says that? It's a dumbass saying*, he thought bitterly.

Ashlyn, that's who kept him sane. She was the only one in his life who hadn't let him down. She certainly had no problems putting him in his place when he needed it or letting him vent his frustrations. It was scary how well she could read him.

JC closed his eyes, shutting out the lines of dialog in the script he had folded at his side. He visualized them in his mind. He knew them backwards and forwards. He knew everyone's lines, but there was still that doubt that lingered. JC didn't want to give them anymore fuel to hate him with. His dad gave them plenty enough reason for that. His dad, yet another thought he had to forcibly bury, which led him back to his nemesis.

JC had to fight every impulse not to beat the hell out of Myers the first time the idiot had to kiss Ashlyn on stage. But Ash, as she always seemed to be able to do, quickly diffused the situation by immediately going over to JC and showed the theater how a real kiss was done.

A smile came to his face at the thought, and he had to force the chuckle that threatened to spill out of him as the look of shock on Myers' face appeared comically in his mind.

Myers, what a douche...

The hair stood on the back of his neck. There was a noticeable chill in the air, as if the universe had suddenly switched and was not his own. JC tried to adjust his eyes as he sat up a little straighter, his body tense, anticipation burning his senses.

The green room was large and full of costumes, props, tools and hundreds of other things needed to make the theatre operate. It was also full of shadows, some deeper than others. The feeling of danger was thick about him. JC pushed himself off of the small couch he had been sitting on.

It was in the corner of the room, in the blackest of shadows. Perhaps the Playhouse was haunted after all. Haunted or not, he had to know what it was, curiosity overrode his fear. He carefully pushed props out of his way, the nerve endings on his neck were on fire.

There...

...the darkness seemed to fold in on itself. Every sense screamed danger but JC, almost trance-like, kept moving towards the foreboding veil that shimmered in the corner.

He wanted to stop. HAD to stop! Yet, he couldn't. His body was pulled forward by an unseen hand that seemed to press against his will.

One foot forward...

...sliding across the rough concrete floor...

Something hard clamped firmly upon his shoulder.

JC, with an unexpected burst of energy, spun to confront his attacker. His hands, balled into fists, were already flying towards the unseen enemy before he even realized it.

CRUNCH

The feel of flesh exploding beneath his knuckles was followed quickly by a large grunt of pain that was not his own.

"What the hell man?!?"

JC's chest heaved from the adrenalin rush. All that left him when he saw Myers spread eagle on the floor, a hand instinctively covering his nose which was a bloody mess.

"Are you insane?!? You broke my nose!"

Reality suddenly restored; JC turned back to the shimmer that drew him over to the corner. The power of the storm matched the oppressiveness of the dire mental institution. It would stand strong against this tempest as it had so many others. For what fortified the walls of the asylum was buried deep in the sinful dungeons far below.

Gone.

What the hell was going on?

"Oh my God! JC!"

He knew that voice all too well, and it was NOT happy. Ashlyn, as well as the rest of the cast, were now crowded around Myers who was looking as if he were about to pass out from the sight of his own blood.

"I'm sorry. I thought…Myers, man, I'm sorry."

But Myers, who was beyond consoling, was having none of it. "Get away from me you freak! You did this on purpose!"

As JC looked into the eyes of his cast-mates, he could tell they thought the same. Even Ashlyn gave him a disapproving look. *Not her too.*

"What's all this commotion?"

Eric Haynes, the director who had been busy prepping the box office, bolted into the room. He knew full well the history between his star and JC.

"Mr. Haynes," JC began, but that's as far as he got.

"Don't bother explaining," the agitated director ground out, "you're out of the show."

"But…"

The director ignored him as he focused on his star. "Ashlyn, please show your boyfriend the door! Let's hope we can salvage this! Two hours before show time for God's sakes!"

JC felt himself being pulled roughly through the building; the only sound was the pounding of his heart roaring in his ears. The chaos was surreal as everyone rushed around Myers, trying to patch his nose up and get the bleeding stopped. The power of the storm matched the oppressiveness of the dire mental institution. It would stand strong against this tempest as it had so many others. For what fortified the walls of the asylum was buried deep in the sinful dungeons far below.

He stopped moving.

Ashlyn was in front of him, yelling and despondent. But even she couldn't shift his focus, her words were silence to his ears. For in the corner the dark thing watched him, and, for a moment, JC could see it perfectly clear. It was back.

The world turned upside down and all went black.

Jake stared out of his office window, watching the foreboding dark grey clouds rolling in from the North-west, heavy with rain. It was a system that hadn't been in the forecast. It appeared as if by its own will, to torment Hale County with a depressing monsoon—insult to injury. The weather was a point-blank reflection of the chaos his county was in.

He could see the dark grey sheets of rain in the distance, stretching across the wide borders of his county, and only thus. Jake wasn't a superstitious man, but even he knew the unnaturalness of the storm. His fingers traced absently along the path of the scar that marred his otherwise perfectly chiseled face. The Sheriff tried to shake the ridiculous thoughts from his mind, rubbing his aching lower back. The sciatica was flaring up, although, truth-be-told, it probably wasn't healed all the way in the first place. It had only been a few weeks after all.

Jake had been in many fights, none of which had even sparked the slightest fear that he might lose or had ever been in danger. Not until that one.

That was a hell of a fall he had taken. Jake was lucky to be alive and he knew it. Oddly enough it was because of the rain that he survived that plummet from the cliff. The creek he had fallen into had risen enough to take some of the force. The resulting impact had pinched his sciatic nerve, causing his legs to temporarily lose their feeling. On top of that he ended up with one hell of a concussion, along with spotty memory loss. He had thought for a moment he had broken his back and would spend his life in a wheelchair, maybe even die on that cold wet earth far off in those woods. Jake didn't normally give in to fear, but being helpless was an enemy that he didn't want to ever face again.

His nemesis was gone by the time he regained feeling in his extremities and climbed up the muddy hill to get help, disappearing like he had never existed. Jake searched everywhere. He had even brought his deputies out in force. He tore the asylum apart, all but accusing Dr. Evan Michaels of ordering the man to assault him. Those few hours between his fall and the search had made all the difference. Someone had covered their tracks very expertly. But in the end, there was nothing to be found, leaving Jake to look the part of the hysterical fool. No one would say it to his face, but he knew they were thinking it all the same.

Now this storm, coming on the heels of more bodies and disappearances, was driving the people in his county to paranoia. The sun hadn't shone in weeks as the disappearances moved from the county to the city. The thunder reflected the fear in the citizens.

Outsiders would call it coincidence, or a sudden freak weather occurrence; but Jake knew better than anyone that Hale County was different. It was different in ways that normal folks everywhere else in the world would call it fantasy, tall tales, imagination. The people here had another word for it...horror.

In all his years though, it had never been like this. The disappearances, the bodies, the change in people's demeanors; something was happening. Someone was playing on people's fears and he was going to find out whom.

The door to his office opened, the old hinges on the doors creaking in protest. Jake silently echoed their feelings; he didn't want to be disturbed either.

"Sir," his deputy's voice cracked with nervousness, "she's waiting."

"Send her in," was Jake's hollow response as he continued his observation of the coming storm.

He heard the distinctive clip of high heel shoes on the old tile floor as his visitor stepped into his office. Jake didn't face his uninvited guest at first, his vision enthralled by the lightning flashing in the roiling thunderhead.

"Sheriff Hooks..."

"I see you've recovered from your accident," Jake said, cutting her off. He finally turned to face the woman that had been bombarding his office with phone calls the last three weeks; phone calls he purposefully ignored.

"How do you know about that," the female voice ground out.

The woman stood there defiantly, arms crossed angrily, wearing a scowl of indignation. Her dark hair was cut short thanks to the hundred or so stitches that had to be stapled to her scalp to keep it together, making her features more angular than was most likely usual. She was thinner than her sister, Amanda. A testament to a lifestyle lived in a warzone instead of luxury. There was a pain in her eyes she tried to cover. It was a pain Jake could relate to. The IED had done its job; it took her off the playing field. Full recovery was still a long way off, but Laurel Richardson had never been one to sit idly by when there was a story to uncover.

"We're in the backwoods, not cavemen. We DO have television. I know who you are. I know what you've done. I know what happened to you. You survived. You don't seem that happy about it, Miss Richardson. Shouldn't you be resting?"

"Fuck that."

Jake looked at her with a bemused expression. *Reporters*, he thought sourly, *nosey vindictive reporters.*

She stepped towards the desk, a slight limp to her once fluid gate. The screws still gave her fits, but she was getting used to it. Laurel leaned across the desk, as much to take the pressure off of her leg as to convey her anger. "You intentionally ignored my calls."

Jake slid easily into his chair, never taking his eyes from hers. "And?"

That seemed to catch her off guard. "You're not going to deny it?"

"I don't see the point, Miss Richardson. I have quite enough to keep me busy without having to worry about playing tag with a reporter's feelings and lying about it."

Laurel's mouth opened and closed a few times, no sound coming forth. Jake thought, in that moment, that she looked like a big mouth bass he had caught a few months back. The difference was that fish couldn't talk. He knew from his research that the human fish standing before him was like a piranha, and she wouldn't hesitate to bite if it meant getting her story.

She closed her eyes as a stab of pain shot up her leg. Her hand began massaging it absently.

"Need to sit?"

She shook her head, waving the gesture away. Laurel was angry. How could she have let this happen? Her carelessness had cost her *the* story that would have handed her a second Pulitzer. Well if the Sheriff thought this was over then he was sadly mistaken. *A Pulitzer? Could that replace my sister?* Laurel chastised herself for such a thought. *That was the whole reason her sister had been in this God-forsaken town to begin with*, Laurel thought angrily, *my incessant need to be the best.*

"I want my sisters belongings," she finally managed to grind out, glaring her best withering gaze at him. But if it was having an effect, the Sheriff wasn't showing it.

"I don't have anything of hers here, Miss Richardson," He said coolly, eyes never leaving hers.

Silence hovered between them as each held the other ones stare, refusing to be the first to blink. A brilliant flash of light poured into the dimly lit office, followed by a roaring clap of thunder that broke her accusing glare.

"I demand you return them immediately!"

"You demand?" he asked, voice low and purposeful.

There was something in his voice that stopped her, a silent warning that there was more to the Sheriff than she initially thought, which wasn't the first time that had happened to her in Hale County. *What was with the people here*, she fumed silently. Laurel believed at first that he was just some back woods hick Sheriff. But his eyes, those dark eyes, they belied something altogether different. The problem was it wasn't in her nature to turn tail and run.

"I know you took Amanda's things from her room," she stated matter-of-factly, arms crossing as she spoke. "Her notes, recordings...everything."

Jake said nothing. His eyes were expressionless.

"That was all her research, contacts, interviews, personal belongings...you have no right." She uncrossed her arms and leaned across the desk towards him, the knuckles of her balled fists lying heavily on the Formica top, supporting her weight. "Or are you afraid of what she was going to uncover? Of what she HAD uncovered?"

Laurel let that last bit hang in the air, the subtle threat of exposing the nasty underbelly of Hale County.

"Miss Richardson, I really don't give a damn what you find. I don't care what she found. You can dig until Hell freezes over and it wouldn't mean a goddamn thing to me."

Rain began to slowly pelt the window.

The usually unflappable reporter felt her throat go dry. She was out of her element. *Was it a result of the IED? The ensuing surgery? Her sister's sudden and tragic death in this God forsaken place? Was that it? Was it Hale County itself?* Laurel felt off, like she was standing outside of herself. She knew, just by the look in the Sheriff's eyes, that he meant what he said.

"You don't..."

But Jake cut her off, leaning over the desk and matching her intensity with his own. "Do you think anyone gives a damn what happens here? We're a backwoods town cutoff from the rest of the civilized world, stuck in the middle of nowhere. No one gives a shit."

"Someone took her things, raided her hotel room," she said somewhat off kilter.

"I know."

That got her attention again.

"You know??"

Jake nodded his head.

"How?"

"Because someone beat me to it."

The asylum moaned in protest as the fierce, howling winds of the approaching storm battered its weary concrete walls, each gust echoing like the anguished cry of a forsaken soul. Massive raindrops, as if hurled by a vengeful giant, began to thud relentlessly against the timeworn facade, each plop punctuating the silence until, in one sudden, overwhelming moment—a deluge akin to a faucet gushing unchecked—the dark, restless clouds unleased torrents of water upon the bleak, grey surface of the mental institution. Though the venerable stone edifice had stoically endured numerous merciless tempests since its inception, this storm, charged with an otherworldly menace, felt markedly different. If the ancient building possessed even a spark of life, it would have quivered in trepidation, its reinforced stone walls shuddering with foreboding dread, mirroring the anxious tremors of the patients huddled within its confines.

The corridors soon resounded with the anguished symphony of wailing and crying, interspersed with the sporadic, uncertain flickering of the power. Nurses and orderlies, their faces etched with desperate determination, surged from room to room. They administered medications with hurried precision to calm the frantic patients, restraining those whose terror and agitation surged uncontrollably as the building's electrical lifeline faltered under the storm's relentless onslaught.

In the midst of it all, Samantha's voice cut sharply through the cacophony as she barked orders, her tone a blend of authority and urgency. She fought to keep her crew anchored in the chaos, acutely aware that the raw fear permeating them was no less potent than that infecting the patients. The old wives' tale of a full moon awakening madness was quickly forgotten in the face of this tempest—its savage power had stirred the inmates into a frenzy far beyond anything she had previously witnessed. It was as though the storm itself had become an alchemist, transforming latent psychosis into palpable chaos.

Her gaze drifted downward, seemingly peering through the aged, cracked tiles of the floor, lost in thought. If these "nut jobs" were already spiraling into madness, what turmoil might be unfolding in the depths below? Her mind wandered to the institution's secretive cohort, the specially chosen patients, those unspoken treasures of the asylum. Wraith was conspicuously absent, and Ronald, poor, ill-fated Ronald, was gone forever. Now, there were newer subjects, some freshly acquired, and others recently elevated in status: Pappy, Jai, Chop—each one distinct and disturbingly unique.

Evan, ever the fervent devotee of the program, was plunging himself ever deeper into its clutches. The loss of Daniel had struck him with an intensity that left an indelible mark. "Good riddance," Samantha thought bitterly, her mind laced with venom. The decrepit old man's lingering influence had been a hindrance, and now, as Evan sought solace, it was she who filled that void—her smile turning devilish at the thought. The mastermind had assured her of such a destiny. The curious case of Ronald's absence from the Hale County Institutes system had been orchestrated entirely by her cunning hand—a plan as simple as it was brilliant. A new transfer, a wild, unannounced storm; the elements were aligning with her intentions. With a self-assured smirk, Sam pressed her hand against the cold, unyielding stone wall, drawing strength from its ancient, enduring presence.

The raw, elemental power of the tempest mirrored the oppressive atmosphere of the beleaguered institution. The asylum would, as it had countless times before, stand resolute against the onslaught of nature's fury. For within its depths, hidden away in the murky abyss of its sinful dungeons, lay the secret core that fortified its walls—an enduring, malevolent strength born of its darkest, most forbidden realms.

.

Richard Porter doused the portable lantern, taking shelter behind the makeshift bar in the old hunting cabin. His palms began to sweat, gripping the .30-06 rifle in his hands as firmly as possible. He tried to control his breathing, remain focused on the situation.

Although the fifty-year-old man hadn't been in the military in twenty-five years, he still remembered a few things from Uncle Sam's Army. The number one thing: don't panic. But if there were ever a time to panic, then this was it.

He wanted to peak out the window but resisted the urge. They were out there, stalking him in the hellish thunderstorm that raged. He knew that without having to see them. It was time to collect. Richard thought he could hide from them, disappear into the dense forest until he could figure something else out.

Time had gotten away from him. The years, they had passed by so quickly. No his time was up. Whatever wealth he had amassed wasn't going to buy him out of this predicament. At least his wife and kids would be well looked after. In the end that's all that ever mattered to him.

A loud crash sounded from the back of the cabin where the guest hunting quarters were located. They were in.

Richard backed slowly along the far wall, quietly, his gun leading the way, safety off. He had to get to the stairs. The lone, tiny, upstairs room had the rest of his ammunition. If they were coming for him, he wasn't going to make it easy on the bastards. Richard was a fighter, always had been.

A dark figure moved in the kitchen.

Richard fired. The thunderous report of the rifle rattled the windows. Dishes exploded where the lead bullet made impact, sending glass shrapnel flying all around. He didn't dare breathe.

All was quiet.

Had he somehow hit it?

The silence lingered, seconds seemingly lasting for hours.

Then...

...movement!

A quick flash of a jet-black shadow zipped into the living room.

Richard fired again. He didn't wait to see if he had hit anything. The grey-headed lawyer bolted up the stairs as fast as his short dumpy body would take him. He could feel the pursuit behind him; the rank breath that was bearing down upon his back.

He reached the top step, grabbing the open door before he had even cleared the threshold. As he lumbered into the room, he slammed the door shut, locking both the door handle and the deadbolt.

Something slammed hard against the door, almost taking it off the hinges.

Richard yelled defiantly, firing into the door until his ammo was spent.

There was a moment of silence.

Richard dropped his gun.

His eyes were transfixed upon the door. Black mist oozed through the holes his bullets had made.

His body began to shake uncontrollably as he backed away. Richard suddenly had a thought: the window. But as soon as he went to open it he knew it was too late. Down below, standing amongst the trees, staring up at him, was his fate.

In his nightmares it was the same vision, the same evil that always came to collect him. The crystal blue eyes, pale skin, the smile of a snake; hell itself had come. Richard screamed as the mist enveloped him, his last vision on earth was the hell that danced in the pale man's eyes.

Chapter 12

A single cool drop of perspiration trickled down the neck of the brown glass that contained the dark Mexican beer. It was bitter, not even remotely pleasant to the taste which mirrored the way Jake was feeling as he sat at the bar trying to convince himself things couldn't get worse. Normally his drink of choice was a glass of Tennessee Whiskey with a shot of coke, just enough to dull the tart smoothness of the well-aged alcohol. Tonight though, Jake was on a slow buzz, his thoughts a whirling mess of uncertainty.

The sheriff stared at the bottle, slowly rotating it absentmindedly in his large hands. He was at a loss on how to proceed with his investigation having been stonewalled by the mayor and the city police. He took a long swig of the awful beer. Bodies. Disappearances. With the exception of the missing college professor all had occurred outside of the city limits. That new reporter was another issue as well.

"That bad, huh?"

Jake nodded his head dejectedly, not bothering to look up.

Marcus set down on the stool beside him. Jake made a small waving gesture with his thumb at the barkeep who immediately grabbed a beer, popped the top, and set it in front of his friend. Marcus picked up the beer and frowned. "You must really be in a helluva mood to drink this shit."

"Yeah" Jake responded with a non-committal sigh.

"Still no leads?"

Jake took another swig as he shook his head.

"Damn man. Somebody HAS to know something."

"The mayor does. Malone does. Hell, that son-of-a-bitch all but admits to it when I see him. They're untouchable. This county is dying because of it."

Marcus clapped him supportively on the shoulder. "That'll change when I beat Grey in the election tomorrow."

Jake let out an unintended snort of doubt. Normally he was supportive of his friend but tonight he just wasn't feeling it. Marcus was kidding himself if he thought for a moment he was going to win and Jake told his friend as much. "There is no way in hell they will let you win that election, Marcus."

"You're wrong, I've got a lot of support. The mayor is so arrogant he doesn't even campaign. The people are tired of him. They want a change. They want me back."

"Perhaps they do. But they will never vote against him. I know what they tell you to your face but once you turn your back they show their fear. Make no mistake, they ARE afraid. The mayor plays to it. He has Malone and his paid city thugs reinforcing that fear. You can't win."

Marcus looked as if he had been punched in the gut. Under different circumstances Jake would have felt bad for him, but the sheriff had his own problems. He had no more shits to give.

"What about you? You scared too?" Marcus asked with a simmering anger.

Jake took another swig, sloshing the nasty beer in his mouth before swallowing it. "Nope, you've got my vote. Just don't be surprised if it's the only one you get. I've got your badge waiting on you at the station."

Marcus slammed the beer on the counter followed quickly by a crisp ten-dollar bill. He stared at his friend in undisguised anger.

"Keep it" he told the bartender before rounding on the sheriff, "Not all of us are quitters, Jake." With that the hopeful Mayoral candidate stomped out of the bar. For a moment Jake thought about going after him.

"You treat all your friends that way?"

Jake didn't bother to hide his aggravated sigh. "Lady, I am not in the mood."

Laurel took Marcus' vacated seat snatching up his unfinished beer in the process and took a long swig, killing the rest of the foul liquid. She set the empty bottle down and faced the sheriff. "Neither am I. But I figure we can help each other."

"Really?" Jake scoffed.

"I'm an investigative reporter. I've probably investigated more crime scenes, been in more close calls, seen more action than any of you hick cops combined."

Jake wasn't sure whether to be insulted or impressed. He massaged his temples, trying to fight the migraine that was getting progressively worse. "Congratulations," he sighed sarcastically as he motioned the bartender for another bottle.

"I've been in war zones and seen shit that would put most people in therapy for the rest of their lives," she pressed on, "I'm no amateur, sheriff."

"Is that supposed to impress me, lady, because it doesn't." Jake took the beer from the bartender and drank half of it without pausing. "Great, you've seen dark shit, witnessed human beings torn apart. Your bedside manner could use a little work though."

"I don't care if you like me or not sheriff. I've seen every kind of horror imaginable and had my ass blown up in my last assignment in rock shithole in Afghanistan only to have my sister murdered in this back ass country you local yokels call civilization. I don't scare easily and I'm damn sure not scared of you. So, you can help me or I can be a pain in your ass. Your call."

Jake's eyebrows were the only thing that showed his surprise at her brass balls. Laurel Richardson was tough as hell; he sensed that about her. His eyes traveled up to her scar which caused his to tingle and burn. She might be of use. Still, if she stayed, she could become the next casualty. He didn't need that. *Better to run her off. Provoke her, piss her off, send her packing.* "What makes you think she was murdered? It was raining that night. She was on her phone. Confirmed that with her boss. Car wreck. Pretty simple. Took her eyes off the road. Happens all the time."

Laurel was about to hurl another insult at the sheriff when it hit her. He *knew*. He knew and was just as stumped as she was. Or was he? "You've known all along," she said pointedly.

Damn, he thought begrudgingly, she just wasn't going to bite which meant there was no getting rid of her. "I suspected."

"Why?"

"Besides the fact that someone completely wiped her room of all her belongings there was another set of tires on the shoulder of the road, grooved into the mud. Probably stopped, checking to make sure she was dead. I was first on the scene so there should have been no other tracks except for hers and mine."

Laurel thought about that, trying to process the information. "What else?"

"There is no 'what else'. That's it."

The reporter's mind was doing what it did best, it processed the information and began working on the problem, trying to find a pattern where none existed. "Maybe not." She fixed her eyes on Jake's questioning gaze, all animosity gone. Laurel was in full investigative mode. "Her boss told me she was going to see a local named William Tyler. He runs some kind of conspiracy site."

"William Tyler? Never heard of him."

"You know everybody in this county?

"Pretty much."

Laurel hopped off the stool, ignoring the pain that shot down her leg. She had the sheriff's attention. She needed him if she was going to get to the bottom of her sister's death. "Sounds like that's our only lead."

"Ours?"

"Ours. You're not getting rid of me. You know that. I know that. So the games can stop right here. You're not as dumb as you pretend to be." She headed towards the front door without waiting.

"Thanks," he replied sarcastically as he threw a wad of money on the counter.

"Well, you coming?" she asked impatiently before disappearing through the door and into the rain.

Jake cursed under his breath. He was wrong. Things just got worse.

The cave was dark and cold. Nighttime had fallen along with the relentless rain. None of that mattered to Wraith. His body was curled up in a fetal position on the dirt floor shivering not from the cold but from the withdrawal of the medication the doctor at the asylum had kept constantly pumping into his body. Most withdrawal symptoms could be overcome within days but whatever god-awfulness they had plied him with over the months wasn't willing to release its grip quite so easily.

There were moments when Wraith had some lucidity. In those moments he hunted for food wherever he could find it; hunting cabins, trash cans...animals. The corner of the cave was a morbid shrine of animal skins and bones, mostly deer and squirrel, except for the one pile that was off to itself wrapped in ripped shreds of cloth. He had pulled the body of the fat evil man into the cave to rot, but also as a warning to other predators that might come lurking. The stench would have been overwhelming to ordinary people, but to Wraith it was just another part of his misery, one he welcomed. He untied the bottom of his grimy scrubs and pissed on the corpse in what had become a ritualistic marking of superiority over the man that had attacked him while he was tied down in that room.

His mind was a maelstrom of chaos with fragmented moments of serenity. Those instances were like dreams, flashes of a life he couldn't fully remember, of a time before the asylum. He reached for the back of his head, feeling about under the hair, feeling the regrowth of hair that had once been a doorway for the experiments. The stitches had fallen out days ago. Shakes from the withdrawal were starting to ease up, his lucidity lingering longer and longer even though his memory refused to resurface except for brief shadows.

His body stopped quivering as a flash of memory burst through the fog of his corrupted mind. The spasmodic breathing slowed into a seemingly long-drawn-out inhale of lucidity. His muscles went limp with exhaustion as Wraith gave himself over to the dream.

A house.

It was old. Rustic. The white painted boards that framed the house were aged and cracked. There was a long overhang porch that ran the width of the front of the house, its narrow-planked wood slats painted a weird bluish grey. An old metal swing sat on the porch just off to the right of the torn screen door. The yard was overgrown with weeds which were dying and drooping limply over an old broken stone walkway.

Wraith stood at a rusted chain link gate that was flung open, one corner dug into the earth as it hung by one partially attached hinge. The crazed man seemed to recognize the house, staring at it in wonder. He knew that place. If only he could remember how.

He glanced down at himself, no longer was he dressed in the grimy scrubs of the asylum. Dark denim jeans that were fastened around his waist with a black belt with silver ringlets and a dual buckle seemed to be a natural fit. The dark grey gothic t-shirt he wore that stretched over his well-toned chest was emblazoned with a medieval cross with widespread angel wings.

Who was he? What was this place?

Daddy.

Wraith looked up to see a little girl standing at the bottom of the steps leading up to the front porch. The child, no more than eight years old, had a gaunt haunted look to her. Her hair was dirty blonde, hanging almost to her waist. It was unkempt and unruly as if it had never experienced a good brushing. She could have been pretty, but Wraith's memories couldn't comprehend such things.

Daddy.

She spoke without speaking.

He tried to speak, tried to form words with a mouth that was out of practice. "K...K..." He blinked and she was gone. Desperate eyes searched wildly all about.

Here daddy.

Yes. There, just behind the screen door. Was she smiling? He took a step towards her then another until each step made her face clearer. She *was* smiling. He remembered that smile. "K...Ka..." he tried again.

Good daddy...almost home.

He was on the porch reaching for the screen door handle. Home. This was home. Wraith pulled the door open.

She smiled.

Suddenly he was standing in the middle of a bare living room filled with dust and cobwebs. Chains lined the walls. The room had no windows. He turned quickly to the door. She was standing on the outside of a door that resembled the one from the asylum. Black, red-tinged mist swirled just beyond her. She stared at him through the glass partition. Her voice was clear in his mind, her smile gone.

Welcome home, daddy.

Wraith let out a howl as he found himself chained to the wall. *NO!! No, no, no, nooo....*

On the floor of the cave his body began shaking uncontrollably as the nightmare once again took its toll. Little pale arms wrapped themselves around him. "It's okay, daddy, it's okay".

He pressed on through the downpour, making one final sprint for the door. His dirt-caked nails grasped at the handle, trembling with both relief and apprehension. Weeks without his medication had left William doubtful about nearly everything—everything except the undeniable truth that he had escaped and finally found his way back home. Sanctuary.

The doorknob clicked, and the door, left untouched since his disappearance, creaked in a quiet welcome. Hidden beneath the hoodie he'd snatched from a clothesline during his escape, William paused and listened intently, trying to detect sounds beyond the pounding rain. Only his bloodshot eyes peeked out behind his scruffy beard.

Nothing.

Not even a squirrel.

He quickly slipped into the old house, securing every latch, then collapsed onto the floor as he battled a panic attack. Tears streamed down his face, each sob wracking him with waves of fear and anguish. He needed to regain control—even as disturbing visions spiraled unchecked in his unstable mind.

The things they had done to him...

His eyes darted to every corner of the room.

...the shadows...

...the darkness...

Everywhere...

yet nowhere.

In a sudden burst, William leaped to his feet and switched on the light. No shadows now. "Get rid of the shadows," he pleaded desperately between convulsive sobs. He staggered through the small house, turning on every light, before eventually collapsing by his computer.

Then his gaze fell upon the medicine bottles on the desktop. He grabbed them quickly. Under normal circumstances, opening these childproof containers was challenging enough; with his hands trembling violently, it was nearly impossible. Miraculously, he freed the pills and poured a few of each into his hand, unconcerned about the possibility of overdosing. Without water, he swallowed them dry as he sank back to the floor, waiting for the medication's effects.

Slowly, as the pills began to work their pharmaceutical magic, the memories crept in—memories of what they had done to him, of what they truly were. They were beings that dwelled in darkness, lurking in shadows within shadows. He could feel them writhing all around him: the prick of hair on his neck, shivers down his spine, movement just out of sight, always lurking at the edge of his vision. They used fear to strip him bare, and only then would the true nightmare commence.

As the sedative effects softened his terror, William felt his mind cloud over with a sense of relief. Yet, the scars beneath his rain-soaked clothes still burned. "Hellfire," he mumbled incoherently as he slipped further into unconsciousness. Soon, all memories dissolved as he surrendered to a blissful sleep.

Safe.

At least, he was safe...for the moment.

JC sat straight up in bed. "Where..." he said aloud in confusion. He was shocked when he heard the response.

"Home" a voice answered tiredly in the dark.

He flicked on the lamp on his nightstand, the forty-watt bulb softly illuminating the room in a warm glow. The storm outside barely registered to him. His sole focus was on his dad who sat in a chair across the room at JC's computer desk nursing a glass of bourbon. The doctor was just beyond the reach of the light, so he was difficult for JC to see clearly but there was no disguising the fact something was wrong with his father.

"How?"

"Your girlfriend called. Said you passed out at the theater. They called an ambulance, but I got there first and sent them away. It was obvious you didn't need one." Evan took a slow sip of the whiskey. "Overreacted. Everyone always overreacts."

"Ashlyn?"

Evan gave a derisive snort. "The show must go on."

JC felt that all-too-familiar anger rising. "What is your issue?"

Evan stood up and moved into the light which gave JC a good look at just how disheveled the man was. He apparently hadn't shaved in days. The man's hair looked like it hadn't seen the sharp end of a barber's scissors in weeks either. But it was the eyes that seemed to reveal the biggest change. Lines wrinkled the corners of the doctor's once ever youthful appearance. There was an anger there that JC hadn't seen before. Evan took another sip, allowing the beverage to be indulged by every taste bud. When he finally spoke JC wasn't sure if that was really his father or not. "You. You're my issue."

"What..." JC began before Evan abruptly cut him off.

"Shut up. I'm not finished" the doctor growled dangerously which caught JC off guard. "Everything I've done has been for you, yet you have the audacity to look at me with loathing. And for what?! Huh? Did I beat you? Did I ever tell you that you couldn't do something? Have I not given you everything you could ever want?!"

Evan was worked up almost to a frenzy. JC had never seen his dad that way. The words stung far more than he could have imagined. It made him feel like a little kid again that had just gotten in serious trouble; except he wasn't a kid and damn sure wasn't about to take that from his absent father. "Everything except a dad!!" he shouted back angrily.

If that was meant to hurt Evan it wasn't working. "Who in the hell do you think provides all of this? Do you think I just sit in a comfy chair at that hell hole simply because I don't want to be here?! You think it doesn't bother me to have to miss ball games, school plays, awards programs? Someone has to put food on the table, and I don't see anyone else stepping up to do that!" Evan killed the rest of the bourbon in one long gulp. He was seething.

JC let the words slip before he could stop himself. He knew it was wrong the instant he said it but all he could think of doing was hurt his dad the way he felt he had been hurt. "Mom would have if you hadn't killed her!!"

There was no going back from that statement. He had put it out there. It couldn't be undone. Evan felt the world fall away. His anger became a fire smoldering from lack of oxygen. And JC, JC was burning with his own anguish.

"You were gone all the time!! If you had been here, she wouldn't have gotten sick! You could have saved her!!" JC stood up, was almost chest to chest with his father as he breathed his last condemnation upon him, "You let her die..."

There it was, the statement that allowed the oxygen back in the room, that turned a smoldering pile into a violent backdraft. Evan's head snapped to attention. A crazed look raged in his eyes forcing JC to take a step back at the intensity of it. The back of Evan's hand caught JC square on the jaw, sending him reeling back atop the bed.

"Don't you ever!!" Evan screamed in a near inhuman shrill. "I tried to help her! I stayed with her every moment! I saw her deteriorating!" Froth spewed from his mouth with every screeching protest like a rabid dog ready to bite anything that moved. JC was scared. For the first time in his life, he knew real fear. His dad took a step toward him, the madness fully taking ahold. "I was there the night she killed herself goddammit!!" Evan hurled the glass he had been holding. It whizzed by JC's head and shattered on the wall. JC ducked as shards of glass exploded everywhere.

Silence.

The air was still.

Nothing moved.

Time ticked by infinitely slow.

When JC finally turned back to his father he was floored by the sight. Evan stood there; tears were rolling unchecked down his cheeks. The doctor's face was a mask of defeat and sorrow. Years of pent-up anguish had been released leaving him a tattered mess. In that moment JC finally saw the man her remembered, the man who raised him. His father sank to his knees…broken. "I couldn't saver her…."

His mother had killed herself. He didn't know that. He thought she had simply gotten sick, and his dad had sent her off to die. But no, his dad had tried to save her. Tried and failed but tried nevertheless. Evan had carried the burden so JC wouldn't have to. Finally, he understood.

"Dad…"

Evan, head bowed, tried wiping the tears from his eyes. "I'm sorry" he managed to say quietly. JC helped him to his feet. Evan wrapped him in a hug, "I'm so sorry."

JC hugged him back, tears stinging his own eyes. "It's okay, dad. It's okay."

The thing in the shadows knew it wasn't okay. It was never going to be okay. Before the night was over their lives were going to be changed—forever.

Chapter 13

A long bony finger swirled the thick crimson liquid that languished in the old skull. The skull was ancient, tracing back beyond biblical times. It wasn't one of those shiny fake looking things that were found in Hollywood B-movies. This particular skull was stained with layers of blood, grit, and other bodily fluids that had been so generously given from thousands of donors throughout the centuries, that is what gave the old artifact its power.

Mayor Grey pulled his finger from the bowl bringing it towards his lips as he repeated a low murmured chant spoken in the long dead language of the fallen. To human ears the words had a strange cadence with a dialect that was Gaelic in origin, a tongue seldom used anymore. They were trance inducing. The mayor finished his chanting as a wisp of black smoke wafted from his blood-soaked finger. The old man flicked a serpent like tongue that encircled the blood covered digit sighing in satisfaction at the taste copper mixed with soul. When he withdrew his tongue the finger was clean. A quick flash of red danced across his dark eyes, a malevolent smile turning up the corners of his extremely thin lips.

The gaunt old man, dressed in his finest pin stripped suit, turned to the figure on the stone table. He held the blood-filled skull in one hand as he removed the gag from the naked pencil thin man lying bound before him. The eyes of the man were sunken, his skin once white had taken on their own greyish tones. He was unhealthy, almost anorexic and unrecognizable, a skeleton with a covering of skin. The man tried to whimper as Grey stooped over him, but all will to resist was gone.

"It's time, Steven" Grey spoke soothingly, "all of your agony, your sacrifice, your hurt will soon be ended."

Steven wanted to protest, to rage against what he knew was coming but there was simply no will left within him. Truthfully, he only wished for it to all end, and sooner rather than later. His whole body seemed desensitized from pain. The straps that bit into his bruised and chafed skin felt as if no more than a light touch. He couldn't have resisted even if he wanted to which he honestly didn't. The end, that was his only desire.

A muffled sound echoed from across the perfectly round room which had been dug deep below the backyard of the mayors mansion. There were no structures in the small room other than the stone table, a large stone fireplace and a stone pedestal that had just enough room for the skull artifact and a very menacing knife. The rest of the room was rather unspectacular as far as décor went. Grey had no use for any such frivolities down there.

The old man turned his attention to one odd bit of scenery, the source of the muffled cry. Richard Porter was chained like an animal to the damp dirt floor of the room. The pitiful man was stripped bare, covered in dirt and dried blood. He seemed to Grey much like a hog ready to be skewered and roasted over a fire pit, a thought which wasn't too far from the truth. There would be time for him later. For now, though he needed to finish the ritual. He turned once again to the poor bastard strapped to the table.

The table itself seemed as if it could have been a part of Stonehenge but infinitely older. The table had a slight downward tilt. The head of the table was within a hand's breadth of a large stone fireplace. A small obsidian chute ran from beneath the table directly into the fireplace. Etched deep into the old stone were strange sorts of hieroglyphs that looked like fairies, goblins, even some that resembled Angels and Demons.

The stones of the fireplace were crafted from the same stone as the table taking up half the expanse of the earthen wall. The firebox was easily the strangest part of the fireplace for in its massive expanse raged a fire of darkness. Black flames with occasional flecks of red crackled within the stone encasement. The dark flames resonated with no heat instead crackling with wickedness and hatred.

The mayor lifted the knife from the pedestal in reverence. The exquisitely crafted bone handle, etched with ancient Enochian runes, was formed precisely to fit his grip. The blade was the darkest of obsidian, polished naturally in the depths of the volcano. It was foraged from giving it a mirror like finish. The curved tapered edge cut finer than the sharpest razor. If death were an artist that knife would have been its brush.

With a sensuous delight Grey stroked the blade, biting his lip as if embraced by a lover. After a moment he leaned over Steven, his foul breath causing the near catatonic man to flinch in revulsion. The mayor looked deep into Steven's eyes, holding the broken man's gaze.

It was hypnotic...trancelike.

While holding Steven's gaze the mayor flipped the knife over so that the duller spine side was resting against the trapped man's crotch. Slowly, tauntingly, he pulled the knife over Steven's exposed genitals expertly so as not to pierce the flesh. Grey drew the knife around the pubic bone, across the soft flesh of Steven's slightly distended stomach, up the rib cage and paused at the sternum with the tip of the knife biting slightly into the flesh. Through it all Steven didn't so much as whimper held as he was by the mayor's intoxicating stare.

Grey was lost in the moment as well. It was one of his guilty pleasures of which he had many. But those were the moments that were truly special, the moment life transitioned and the soul transferred from one vessel to the next.

"Sir"

The mayor broke his gaze and glanced at the source of the interruption. Geoffrey was standing at the bottom of the earthen stairs that lead back up to the mansion. Grey was not happy about being disturbed, especially in those vital desirous moments. "Geoffrey…" he began, voice a dangerous hiss.

"Sir," the butler continued unfazed, "it is time. Any longer and you risk ineffectuality. The way MUST be prepared."

Grey's eyes snapped back to Steven's who seemed to be coming out of the trance, fear growing in the tormented man's face. With an almost imperceptible movement the mayor whipped the deadly knife through the air.

The room was silent.

Still.

For a moment Steven was unsure of what had happened. Had he been spared? He felt strangely at peace. It was in that instant he realized it was all over, his eyes flared in sudden recognition as the cold shadow of death enveloped his body. A thin red line appeared from one side of his neck to the other. Gravity took hold. The impossibly sharp obsidian blade had severed both carotid arteries as well as the muscle and sinew that kept the head firmly attached. Grey had almost decapitated him.

The blood didn't spray forth as one would normally expect but rather flowed out as if someone had turned on a nozzle from a pitcher of sweet tea. The crimson river flowed down the obsidian chute directly into the black flames. As more and more of the blood emptied into the dark fire the flames became a deep red. Charcoal-colored smoke thickened within the firebox then shot up through the stone chute and into the stormy night skies.

A wickedly satisfied smile played on the mayor's face. *All according to plan.*

"We had a deal..." the portly man whimpered from the dirt floor.

Grey stood over him, observing the pathetic man begging in the dust. *Humans*, he thought with disgust, *pathetic and greedy*. "Yes. We did." He stepped past Richard, making his way to Geoffrey.

"Why??" Richard cried desperately.

The mayor stopped by his butler and cast a humorous look back over his shoulder. "Because," he said unsympathetically, "your wife made me a better one." Grey gave a short snort of laughter as he walked up the steps to his mansion leaving the desolate businessman to mourn his fate. The end was drawing near. After centuries of planning, it was finally time. His power was reaching its zenith. Soon, all would know his retribution. "Dispose of this," he mewed, turning a sinister grin towards the whimpering businessman, "all of it."

Geoffrey watched his master disappear through the upper doorway then turned his attention to Steven as the final drops of life were leaving the helpless man. "I do loathe waste."

"Thank you, Coach Wilson. Give your wife my regards and thanks again for your vote. We will make a change together!" Marcus said happily as he shook the elder man's hand. Mr. Wilson had long been a proponent for Marcus. As the long-tenured football coach he had seen that spark within Marcus since day one. He knew the young man's potential and encouraged it.

The coach had the ability to see beyond the superficial and into the very makeup of a person. All were welcome at his table. Every athlete knew that whatever your background you could always turn to coach. That was something Marcus had never forgotten.

When he became a deputy Coach Wilson had pulled him to the side. "Son," the wizened southern gentleman spoke to full effect, "people aren't going to hate you because of your color, they are going to hate you because of that badge. But as long as you are fair and stick to your principles then you will earn their respect and more importantly, you'll earn your own. That's all a man can do." The coach had always reminded him of that doctor in Field of Dreams, spry and caring with that constant twinkle in his eye.

Marcus let go of his hand and faced the rain that was steadily falling just outside the safety of the porch. He popped open his umbrella but turned back towards his mentor. "Thanks coach, I would never have had the courage to run again without you."

Mr. Wilson cracked one of his trademark self-deprecating smiles. "No son, you always had the courage. Now kick the mayor's ass in the election tomorrow. Take back that office he stole from you."

"Yes sir," Marcus laughed then darted into the rain. There were a few more stops he needed to make, and it was getting late. He hated to admit that Jake had a point earlier about the people in Hale being afraid. That only added to his resolve to push harder. The people deserved better. The county had been crooked for as long as anyone could remember. There were a lot of good people not just in the city but in the whole of Hale County and they needed a leader that could help give their children a brighter future.

With the rash of deaths and disappearances and the mayor's inability, *or unwillingness,* to help Sheriff Hooks, Hale's once untouchable leader finally appeared vulnerable. When the chaos was mostly outside of the city of Hale all blame could be pushed on to Jake's shoulders but with the disappearance of Jason Locke, the professor at the community college who was beloved by his students, and a few other citizens as well as the death of the reporter doubt had begun to creep into the city proper. People didn't come right out and challenge the mayor or his police force but there were whispers, lots and lots of whispers. The polls were their opportunity to make that change and get themselves out from under the controlling Mayor's constrictive grip.

Marcus wasn't afraid of the challenge and the people knew it. He would fight and he would win. There was no other option. As those thoughts danced in his head, the rhythmic beating of the rain put him in a very upbeat mood. Walking down the sidewalk he began to whistle an old Fat's Domino tune, *Ain't That A Shame*. He let his mind drift as he let the tune mix easily into the stormy night.

The sounds of a police siren interrupted his relaxation. The bright reflection of the red and blue lights bounded off the buildings and streets like bad seventies disco. The patrol car pulled up just ahead of him and stopped. Chief Malone stepped from the vehicle with his wide flat-brimmed hat and a rain poncho stamped with the word "police". *Well now*, Marcus thought sourly, *this really is a shame.*

"Getting late isn't it...Marcus." Chief Malone remarked with false kindness.

"Finishing up my rounds. Big day tomorrow" Marcus said happily without stopping.

Eddie moved to block him. "I've gotten some complaints you've been bothering our fine citizens."

Marcus stopped and squared up to Eddie. "The only complaint you've had is from your boss. Old man Grey is scared."

Eddie snorted his derision. "Scared? You ain't seen scared yet. Just wait til after the election. Everything is gonna change."

Against his will, in spite of it, Marcus was fuming. It was as if the outcome of the election was already determined and everyone knew it, everyone but him. He couldn't stop himself. "Enjoy your last night as police chief," he said as he dropped his umbrella and stepped-up nose to nose with the arrogant bastard.

"You really think you gotta chance, don't ya…" Eddie grinned darkly, pausing for effect before twisting the final screw, "…boy."

That was it. Eddie had pushed him too far. Marcus' hands clinched into fists. He knew he shouldn't, that that was the excuse Eddie was looking for. He had been goaded one too many times.

"I'm not your damn boy. And I sure as hell ain't one of those bottom feedin' pansies that kiss your wrinkled white ass."

Eddie's cocky grin was gone, replaced by white hot anger. His hand went for his gun, thumb unlatching the leather strap that held the 9mm in its holster. The move was second nature, something he had done many times.

Marcus had no weapon. He had one option and one only. He tensed his muscles, ready to launch himself at the bigger man. Yet Marcus had no fear. There was a tingling in the back of his mind, a quick whimsical thought that was there one second then gone the next. *Fear was that of the fallen.* He winced internally at the thought, tried to trace its origins.

Woop woop!!

Both men involuntarily flinched as the sharp shrill of the police siren cut through the storm. Headlights blinded the men as a patrol car pulled up next to them.

The oversized head of Archibald Brubaker peered out of the driver's side window. "Hey Marcus, Sheriff Hooks has been looking for you!"

Eddie's thumb casually clipped the leather strap back around his gun as Marcus relaxed his posture as if nothing was the matter. The chief's eyes narrowed as he whispered in a low growl so that only Marcus could hear him, "soon," was all he said before turning on his heel and climbing into his own vehicle.

Marcus watched him drive away as the hulking form of Bru stood next to him. "You need to be careful, man" the deep voice said cryptically.

"Careful?" Marcus asked quizzically. But as he turned the deputy was already back in his vehicle and pulling away from the curb. He watched the vehicles disappear into the rain as he picked up his umbrella and continued down the sidewalk. Each step was quicker than the one before. As his adrenalin calmed down, he realized just how close to a very bad ending he had come. Still, Eddie and the mayor weren't about to scare him off.

Marcus arrived at his car but stopped to look back down the road, the lights going off in his old coach's house as he did. There were people who would stand beside him no matter what. He could win the election, he knew it. What he didn't know, what he couldn't see through the downpour, was the dark, red-tinged smoke that was snaking down his coaches chimney. The screams of an honorable man were drowned out by the pounding of endless thunder.

Kara locked up the medicine cabinet with an exhausted sigh. Her shift was over, *finally*, a full three hours after it had been scheduled to end. The asylum was short staffed, and as a trained nurse the HR Manager was pulling double duty. They kicked her pay up to match their staffing deficiency, she understood that well enough and the overtime was great but after six straight nights of it with only one day off in between she was in desperate need of some down time.

Time, she shook her head in frustration, *that's something I don't have.*

By the time she got off work Haley was already in bed. Moving to the day shift was supposed to have given her more time with her daughter who had been struggling ever since she discovered Dr. Lane's body.

Dr. Michaels assured her that kids were resilient and that she would bounce back quickly but that hadn't been the case at all. Kara's mom was doing the best she could with Haley when she wasn't there but there was so little improvement. The sight of the dead man had shaken the bubbly child. She stopped playing with her dolls, stopped watching cartoons. All Haley would do is sit in front of the window looking out into the rain snuggled up to her faithful dog Reese. The Great Dane wouldn't leave the child's side as if it instinctively knew that Haley needed her.

Kara felt lost with it all. She had to work. Bills had to be paid. *But at what point is it just not worth it?* She had asked herself that question so many times over the last few weeks. Her mother was the only family she had so she couldn't pick up and leave. There was nowhere else left to go. Hale County was it.

She stopped by the locker room to get her belongings, mindlessly tossing her stethoscope, thermometer, pen light, and pulse oximeter onto the top shelf. It was so routine that she didn't have to think about it. *If I hurry, I can probably get home before Haley goes to bed*, the worn-out nurse thought with a surge of hope.

Slamming the locker with more urgency than she realized, Kara attached the lock, put her purse on her shoulder and turned to the door. She hadn't gone two steps when Samantha walked in.

"There you are. I'm glad I caught you before you left," Sam said as she quickly assessed Kara's posture.

"Is there a problem?" Kara asked unsurely. She was fairly certain everything was in its rightful place, all paperwork complete. She was always thorough with not even the smallest complaint on her record. Actually, if Sam wasn't already then it was well believed amongst the rest of the employees that Kara would be running the staff. It was no secret to anyone what Sam's relationship to Evan was. It was also well known that you didn't cross the young nurse. She wasn't blatant about her dislike for people who didn't respect her, she was far cleverer and conniving. You would either get few hours, the late shift, or the worst jobs on duty rosters, sometimes all three. Still, the two women had never had cross words or hard feelings, not that Kara knew of anyway.

"Oh no, nothing like that" Sam assured her. "I hate to ask this because I know the amount of hours you've been keeping but could you possibly stay on for another couple? I just had a call in. I managed to get ahold of Derek, but it'll be about two hours before he's able to get here."

Kara felt her composure slip but quickly recovered. She felt sick, another night without seeing her little girl to sleep. *Say no,* her inner voice screamed at her. *What about you? What about Haley??* "Yeah, no problem"

"Oh, thank you!" Sam spun on her heel to leave but then a thought occurred to her. She turned back to Kara, who was opening her locker and retrieving the instruments she had just placed in there moments earlier, and smiled warmly, "We have some new employees starting soon. I'll talk to Dr. Michaels about getting you some paid vacation leave so you can have some quality time with your daughter. You've earned it."

"Thanks," Kara said returning the smile. Vacation would be extremely welcome, so would the help. She looped the stethoscope around her neck and stepped past Sam and onto the ward. Maybe tomorrow she would get to tuck Haley in. It seemed as if tomorrow was always just out of reach.

Sam watched Kara leave. As soon as the nurse was out of sight her smile quickly morphed into one of disdain. She hated all those do-gooder nurses on her staff. They went about their unimportant little lives as if that was all there was to the universe. But not Sam. Samantha knew what life was, what it could be, and what lie beyond. She thought of Evan briefly then pushed the thought away.

The nurse cocked an ear, listening for the sounds of people nearby. When all she heard was the rumbling of the thunder outside the stone walls she went to Kara's locker. Sam studied the lock for the briefest of seconds then quickly turned the dials until the combination clicked and the lock sprung free. *He was right. Of course*, she chided herself, *he's always right.*

She opened Kara's purse and went through her wallet until she found the prize she was instructed to retrieve. The little girl in the picture was beautiful, her hair in pigtails and smiling as though she didn't have a care in the world. If Sam were capable, she would almost consider the picture sweet.

What was his fascination with the girl, she wondered. It wasn't her business, she decided. There were far more important things happening for her. Sam put everything back just like it was and reattached the lock. A smile, genuine and vile, pulled at the corners of her pink full lips. He would be pleased. She let Evan take over her thoughts. Perhaps it was time to go see her lover. There was a fire in her belly. Whether it was from her successful mission or the storm or even some weird combination of the two she needed that desire quenched. Sam grinned once more and slipped onto the ward.

The paved road ended at an old cattle gate that was chained shut between two huge oak posts that were embedded deeply into the hard earth. Most of the greenish paint had been peeled away by time leaving only patches of steel and rust. No Trespassing signs were posted all over the gate and the surrounding trees.

Jake dimmed the lights to his truck as he pulled up next to the gate, his heavy mud-grip tires biting into the soggy dirt road that lead from the gate into the woods. Red led lights marked the cameras that were nestled in the trees. Whoever was watching knew they were there.

"A little paranoid, don't you think" Laurel asked sarcastically.

"Conspiracy nuts" Jake retorted, "they think the whole world is out to get them."

"Isn't it," she asked with a sardonic smile.

Jake snorted at her, furrowing his brow. "Awesome, now she's a comedian."

Laurel almost chuckled at his look. "What do we do now?"

"We walk."

Jake was half expecting her to drop the smile and complain but was not at all surprised when she opened the door and stepped into the rain. He reached behind the seat and grabbed a poncho. He slipped his on as he got out of the truck then tossed the other to Laurel. She looked questioningly at him. "I get it, your tough. You don't need a man's help. But you don't have to go and die of pneumonia just to prove it."

Laurel put on the poncho and shot him a look of thanks. "Don't we need a warrant?"

"For what?"

"We can't just barge in and search his place."

"We're not. He's obviously in danger and in need of assistance. I'm doing my civic duty. Unless you think we should just go back to town and wait til tomorrow and hope the mayor's judge will issue said warrant."

"Nope, this works for me."

Jake scaled the fence then helped Laurel over the slick metal. He heard her give an involuntary whimper as her bad leg landed awkwardly but he kept the thought to himself. She was a very proud woman, very determined. He wasn't going to insult her by questioning her toughness. He flashed his mag light up the curvy dirt road. It was going to be a long walk, especially in the mud.

"You can ask" she said as if reading his mind.

"That's okay, you'll just snap at me again. I got enough people doin' that."

Laurel actually laughed. "I was doing county hall pieces, corruption stories, I even did a few activist things but one day I was at an airport sipping a latte getting ready to fly out west to cover yet another Hollywood scandal when I looked out the window and saw something that completely put my life in perspective."

"And what was this life changing event" Jake asked, surprised to find himself curious.

"A plane had just taxied up to the gate, I'm not sure now if it was our plane or not. They had just landed. A hearse had pulled up along with some service men. The crew opened the cargo hold. Everyone came to attention. They wheeled out the flag draped casket of that young soldier and performed a ceremony, honoring his service and his sacrifice. You see it all the time online but in person...people around me were crying. Family members met and escorted to the body. That's when it hit me. I became a journalist to make a difference. Instead, I got caught up in other people's bullshit, into their narratives, and pathetic petty squabbles for likes and shares. The money had become important. It was an easy life. I could get to a story as naturally as breathing. It came easy to me. But when I saw that crew and the soldier's military family honor him, when I saw how it touched everyone in that terminal, it woke me up. I called my boss and quit. All the red carpets and social hobnobbing parties became irrelevant in that single instant. Two weeks later I was headed overseas to cover the wars, the skirmishes. Wherever our troops went I went. I felt they needed a voice. The politics didn't matter. The religious implications didn't matter. Their sacrifice to people they would never meet, dying freely for those people, that's what mattered."

"I didn't know that" Jake said solemnly.

"So, does that answer your question? Why does someone like me do these things?"

"No, I was just going to ask if you really liked that nasty ass beer you drank at the bar."

Laurel gave him a sideways look with a half-smile, "I've had worse".

Jake felt a begrudging like for the reporter. She was feisty, determined, and simply didn't give a shit about anything but getting what mattered to her. The soldiers mattered. She told their story. Her sister mattered. She was damn sure going to get to the bottom of her death. That was something Jake could sympathize with. He was about to say just that when the muddy road ended into a gravel driveway. He stopped her with a slight motion of his hand and pointed towards the small little house.

A light was on in the front window.

He switched the flashlight off and carefully stepped as softly as he could towards the house, Laurel following silently behind him. Luckily the storm would hide most of the sound, so Jake wasn't worried about being overheard. His biggest concern was the cameras mounted on each corner. There was no doubt more cameras on the backside of the house. *This guy was beyond paranoid*, he thought sourly, *which made him dangerous.*

The sheriff drew his gun as they neared the side of the house. A door was slightly ajar. A dim soft light poured from the crack the opened door made. Jake peeked through the crack. The room was a mess. He gripped the door and gently pushed the door open. It made the slightest of creaks and was then silenced.

Conspiracy posters littered the walls. Bigfoot, the grassy knoll, the moon landing, even that one from that old FBI spook show was on there, 'I Want To Believe' it read. *I believe you're nuts*, Jake thought as he scanned the room. In the far corner was a desk that had empty drink bottles on it.

Laurel saw an object on an end table and picked it up. It was a big round stone with drawings on it. "What is this?" she asked, pitching it to Jake.

The sheriff caught it and examined it with surprise. "It's called a Cherokee Marble. It has a white owl on one side and a brown cougar on the other. This one is old. Where'd he get it?" Jake wondered aloud as Laurel checked out the desk.

"Over here!" Laurel shouted as she pointed to a figure slumped on the floor.

Jake rushed to the man's side, holstering his gun. He was covered in a hoodie and dark clothing. Saliva drenched William's long unkempt beard. So, this was him. The sheriff thought he knew everybody in Hale County, but he didn't recollect ever seeing this character. The man was obviously in a bad way, so Jake didn't have time to put any more thought into it.

Laurel snatched up an empty pill bottle as Jake checked for a pulse. "Oh my God" she said, voice full of shock "he took Olanzapine...and a bunch of it."

"What is that?" he questioned, half-listening as he checked for a pulse.

"It's an antipsychotic. I've seen them give patients this crap overseas. This is powerful stuff. If he OD'd on this there isn't a cure. We have to get him to a hospital now!"

Jake reached down and grabbed the man by the front of the hoodie to pull him up so he could lift him over his shoulder. That was when the sheriff finally got a good look at William's face. He hadn't paid attention before while he was checking for a pulse. But now, seeing past the beard, there was no doubt. Jake's face was twisted with confusion, a look Laurel didn't miss.

"What is it? I thought you didn't know him."

"This isn't possible..."

"What?! What's not possible??"

"This is the missing professor" Jake said with absolute certainty.

"Jason Locke?" Laurel looked from Jake to William and back again. "That's the name on the prescription. What the hell is going on?"

Jake couldn't answer that and the only person who could, might already be too far gone to give them any answers. He hoisted the comatose man over his shoulder and ran out the door. Hale County continued to get stranger and stranger.

Chapter 14

"How are you feeling?"

JC looked up to see his dad standing in the doorway with a tray of food. He could smell it from across the room. He was hungrier than he'd realized. "Hungry."

Evan sat the tray by the bed and handed his son the bowl. "Careful, it's hot. Chicken noodle soup. Sometimes the best cures are the old-fashioned ones."

The soup was tasty. It had been years since JC had eaten it, but it definitely hit the spot. He pointed to the glass on the table. "Sweet tea?"

"Of course. Can't have one without the other."

"Uncle Daniel wouldn't have agreed."

Evan laughed, "No, no he wouldn't. Daniel thought the only drink we should ever consume was water. 'All natural, Evan' he used to say, 'that's how we should treat our patients.'"

JC smiled, "I miss him."

"Me too, son. Me too".

Father and son sat there in silence for a moment while JC ate his soup. It was a rare moment of happiness, and both men were afraid of shattering it. The world had been spiraling out of control for so long that neither was sure how to react, so they simply enjoyed it. Not even the storm outside could dampen their spirits. Oddly enough it was the doorbell echoing through the massive home that broke the quiet atmosphere.

They both looked at one another questioningly.

"Are you expecting anybody?" Evan asked JC.

"Nope. You?"

"Nope. Hmmm, be right back." Evan left to answer the door, leaving JC alone to finish his meal.

JC couldn't help but wonder at the sudden switch in character, for the both of them. The bitterness and anger on both their parts seemed to just vanish. *Okay, it might have taken some yelling and harsh words but hey, it worked*, he thought with his first bit of real humor in a while.

"Hey…"

Ashlyn stood in the doorway, a hopeful smile on her face.

JC hadn't expected to see her especially after what had happened earlier. "Um, hey, uhhh" he stumbled over his words as he set the soup on the nightstand. "Come in".

Evan popped his head around the doorframe. "I'll be downstairs if you two need anything." He smiled at Ashlyn, "it was great to finally meet you. Officially."

"You too, Dr. Michaels" she said with a smile.

Evan left the young couple alone and wandered serenely down the staircase. *This is my Christmas Carol moment, my awakening to a new day.* There was a lightness to his step. The heavy cloud that had been weighing him down seemed to lift. A song sprung to mind from the 'King of Cool' Dean Martin as he hit the final step. He began humming to the rhythm of one of Dino's greatest songs, 'Sway'. *God, I'm actually happy*, he thought as he began lazily dancing along to the tune he was humming.

He had no destination in mind as he danced around the bottom floor of the mansion and was almost surprised to find himself in his bedroom at the south end of the large home. Evan stopped humming as he entered his large walk-in closet. Set back in the far corner was a small safe. His hands instinctively worked the combination causing the door to pop open with a metallic sigh of gratitude.

There was a small wooden box inside the safe which Evan removed with much care and reverence. He sat down on the soft beige carpet and opened the lid. A picture, slightly curled up at the edges, sat facing up at him. The doctor removed the old photograph and stared at it, willing himself back to the day it was taken. Miranda, wearing a slimming light blue dress, was smiling blissfully as she held their infant son. The picture was taken just before JC's second birthday. Bad days would come soon after but right then, at that moment, life had been perfect. Evan kissed the picture, trying to reach back through time as he did. The memory, like so many others, had faded with time but he could still smell how Miranda's perfume swirled in the air that day. He could still feel the warmth of her lips and the softness of her cheeks.

Evan smiled as he put the picture back in the wooden box. Normally sadness would have overcome him but not then. "I have him back, honey," he whispered as looked at her smiling face once more, "I haven't lost him after-all." He shut the box securely in the safe once again and began getting undressed for bed when the doorbell rang. The clock by the bed showed it was almost midnight. *Who in the hell could that be? Two guests in one night...well, I'm not getting dressed again,* he thought stubbornly without bothering to button his shirt as he made his way down the hall.

Samantha smiled at him as he opened the door, partly because of the look of surprise on his face and mostly because he was halfway undressed...it would save her time. She brushed past him, stepping into the foyer. The long greyish pea coat she was wearing held tiny droplets of water from the rain which had dampened her usually tight kept blonde locks.

The doctor looked fidgety as he cast a nervous glance upstairs. Outside of Daniel none of his employees had ever stepped foot in his home. There was a reason for that. Home was his escape from the asylum, from the screams of the inmates...from himself. He couldn't help but cast an appreciative glance over Sam. *And away from other temptations*, he thought uncomfortably.

"Is there a problem at the institute? I never got a call..." Evan said letting his questions hang in the air as he checked his phone. He was finally reconnecting with his son and didn't need or want the anxiety of an unannounced rendezvous to reignite any lingering tension. No one knew about his affair with Sam, and he intended on that remaining the case. The last time they had been together was months earlier and he hadn't honestly given it another thought.

Sam stopped midway through the living room and turned to face him with a concerned look, her smile as well as her calm demeanor was gone. "Yes," she said softly, "but I couldn't tell you over the phone."

"Why not" the doctor asked taking a curious step towards her?

She looked nervously around the room for a moment then gulped forcibly as if she were afraid to answer. "Because...because someone is always listening."

Evan understood. *The Benefactor.* The secretive man always had eyes watching them. He knew every move made inside the walls of the mental institute. The doctor took Sam by the arm and led her into his study. He closed and locked the doors behind them then guided the frazzled nurse to a chair at his desk. Evan clicked on the desk lamp. He poured them both a drink from an old bottle of scotch he kept on a bookshelf with other antique bottles he had collected over the years then took a seat opposite of his frazzled nurse. He took a long sip of the smooth liquid and leaned towards her. "Okay, tell me what's going on."

Sam tasted the alcohol as she wrestled with what she should say. Finally, she put the half-empty glass on the desk and reached into her coat pocket. "This," she said as she handed the photograph to Evan.

"I don't understand" he said confused, looking at the photograph of a beautiful young child with dark hair. "What does this have to do with...him," he bit out after a pause.

He had never seen her look uncomfortable. Sam had always been overconfident if anything. Evan even wondered at times if the young woman had a conscious at all. Yet here she was, barriers down, struggling with herself over something that twisted son-of-a-bitch was having her do. How long had the bastard had his claws in her? He reached out and put a comforting hand on hers. "Sam, what is it?"

The warmth of his touch seemed to rouse her from the quandary she found herself in. She met his dark eyes with her own. "She's the little girl that found Dr. Lane's body," she said in a whisper.

Evan was taken aback by that news. "What..." was all he could manage to say. He hadn't expected that response. Sweat prickled his forehead. Heat rose at the back of his neck, tingling his ears. He grasped Sam's hand tighter than he had intended. She flinched under the pressure but didn't attempt to pull away. "He's not going to hurt her...," he said probingly.

Samantha shook her head slightly as she said, "He, he didn't say. He only said he needed her."

No, no that was too far. Not a child, Evan thought fiercely. He felt as though his head was swimming. He would do anything to cure the world of the horror that took his wife, but a child was just too far, even for him. "I can't."

"But you know what he will do," she pleaded.

"We know what he *says* he'll do! We don't know for sure! Hell, we don't even know who he is for that matter!" He felt he was drowning in quicksand. Evan's brief moment of happiness, the reconnection with his son that sparked it, was slowly being pulled from him. *Why?! He thought wildly, why, why, why?!* He felt a strange warmth spreading within as a light pressure seemed to drape over him. He raised his head and took a sharp breath.

Sam was in his lap, her hands caressing his chest. The room seemed different, foreign. Evan's mind grew fuzzy, not quite his own. He felt her hands on his neck. He wanted to protest, to deny what was happening. There was a sweet smell in the air, intense and overpowering. Her moist lips pressed against his. Evan felt an uncontrollable need for her far beyond any sexual desire. Any awareness of reality faded from him. His tongue danced with Sam's as she swayed slightly above him.

Evan didn't remember getting undressed, he had no concept of the world around him. He felt the silky heat of Samantha's lithe body as she twisted in her own nakedness above him. Their eyes met. For a moment Evan's mind seemed to clear, his heart skipping wildly as he saw the devilish fire in her eyes. He wanted to protest, to push her away, but as she lowered herself upon him, taking him fully into her, he knew he couldn't resist...nor did he want to.

Samantha weaved her fingers in his hair, pulling herself tighter against him with each of his uncontrollable thrusts. She smiled wickedly. Bringing her lips to his ear she whispered the words she had bargained her soul for, "you're mine..."

Jake peered out of his truck windshield through the seemingly never-ending storm. He was exhausted. All he wanted to do was drift into a peaceful dreamless sleep and rest, just a few blissful hours were all he asked. Insomnia, his inescapable nemesis, forbade it. He cast a quick glance to the glovebox, tempted to take the pills that would force sleep upon him, but Jake couldn't chance it. Laurel was at the hospital with William. She promised to notify him the moment William, Jason, whoever the hell he was, woke up. Jake had questions...lots of questions.

He took a tired breath, squirming around in the seat until he found the sweet spot. The lights from the house reached out to him through the rain. He hadn't spoken to Kara since that night at the asylum. She had tried to call him but Jake, in all of his male macho bullshit stubbornness, wouldn't answer. It was stupid. He knew that. But talking to her was...

Bump bump bump!

Jake jumped in his seat, hand flying towards his pistol, before the last bump of the glass faded. It had caught him off guard. He was never caught off guard. The beating of the glass rattled in his ear as the gun cleared the holster. The sheriff froze, easing his gun back in its holster as the awareness of who was standing there dawned on him. He tapped the button on the door, letting the window roll down.

"Hungry?" Kara asked, holding up a brown bag and a fountain drink.

"Dammit, Kara..." the flummoxed sheriff sputtered.

"What? Big tough emotionless sheriff frightened by a little ole helpless nurse?"

"Very funny," he frowned at her condescending sarcasm, "get in."

Kara walked quickly around to the passenger door and casually slid into the seat, tossing the brown bag filled with a burger and fries into his lap. "It's cold. I was going to eat it but looks like you could use it more than me, especially if you insist on staying out here all night."

"I wasn't. Been a long night. I was on my way to the hospital to question a suspect and was falling asleep, so I pulled over," he lied, turning his head so most of the ugly scar was hidden in the low light of the truck cab.

"Do you just happen to fall asleep here EVERY night?" Kara retorted matter-of-factly.

Jake opened his mouth to respond, to deny the implication, but his exhaustion wouldn't let him continue the fruitless denial. His shoulders dropped with a sudden sigh of surrender. Besides, he couldn't lie to Kara. She always seemed to see through it. "I haven't slept in days…and I have to make sure y'all are safe."

She studied him for a moment. "That's not your job."

He tapped his badge and looked away from her, forcing himself not to stare into those deep hazel eyes. "Sheriff."

"You know what I mean," Kara said with a hint of touchiness in her voice. It was also accusatory.

The tone didn't pass Jake's ears unheeded. She was getting mad. Kara always seemed to get frustrated with him rather easily. He couldn't blame her. There was also nothing he could do about it no matter how much he wished things could be different. Jake was as much of a badass as they came. He was also human, with human emotions that made logic into distorted fantasy. "I do."

"'I do'. That's all you can say?" Yep, her blood pressure was rising. The fiery red head was living up to the stereotype. "What the fuck, Jake?!" she practically shouted at him. "I called and called after you got hurt that night and you couldn't be bothered to answer your damn phone?! Did you ever stop for one second to think people actually give a shit about you?! Especially me?!"

She was seething. Pissed. But his own anger was taking hold. "You know why! You're the one who ended it!" he shouted back defensively.

"That's such bullshit!"

No one talked to him that way. Ever. Except her. Jake couldn't maintain his false anger and looked away, absently rubbing a finger across his facial scar. The pain was deep and searing, a reflection of his feelings for Kara. What happened had to be done. He hated it, with every fucking breath he hated it. Every moment was regret dipped in acid and it burned away at the only piece of his heart that refused to die. But he was given no choice then and he wasn't given a choice now. If he hadn't walked away...*No! No, you had to. It was the only way.* He reached into the bag, unwrapping the cold wet burger, and took a tasteless bite as he forced the guilt back into its own private hell.

"You're right," he mumbled as he choked down the burger, "it *is* cold."

Kara slapped the burger from Jake's hands sending the contents exploding through the cab of the truck in a shower of greasy waste. "You son-of-a-bitch," she shouted as she angrily opened the door then slammed it with as much hatred as she could muster before marching stiffly through the rain towards her home.

Just as he had years earlier, Jake didn't chase after her. He didn't yell. He didn't scream. He didn't do anything. He just watched the only woman he ever loved walk away hating him for the second time. It was the right decision then. It was the right one now. It was for her safety. Hers as well as the daughter he would never get to know.

Darkness, its blanket of secrecy basting the fever of every human's deepest fear...the unknown. Real fear doesn't hide in the brief jump-scare of a Hollywood horror flick. Sure, cinematic monsters can be good for a quick fright but nothing lasting or substantial, nothing that keeps you up at night. But the darkness, it's always there hiding unseen secrets, prickling the back of your neck with an unknown danger that only your subconscious can seem to detect. That movement out of the corner of your eye, that trepidation of crossing into a darkened room, the oppressiveness of a silent home at night when the electricity is out and only the storm rages, when you can hear those peculiar noises that are usually drowned out by the normalcy of everyday life, *that* is the power of the darkness. And in that darkness, there are worlds beyond worlds hiding terrors that nip at the psyche of human existence.

That was the terror that Wraith knew well as he looked out from his cave, eyes peering into that darkness through the pouring rain, sensing the opening of that preternatural rift. The mad man had been tormented with it in his darkest hour before becoming the instrument of fear himself. His mind, no longer clouded by the buffer of the usual fog of the everyday mundaneness of the world, could feel the subtle drop in temperature, the tingling of the molecules that sent chills through normal people. They were nowhere, and they were everywhere. The keenness of his sight picked out the black, red-tinged mist that almost blended with the night sky as it whipped over the trees, hidden by the onslaught of endless rain. It was both familiar and unfamiliar.

They're here.

The tiny voice whispered through the lifting fog of his mind...and it was terrified. Wraith felt his heartbeat quicken as he crouched in a feral stance, ready to pounce on whatever was foolish enough to come out of the shadows. The hair on his scarred, muscled arms was standing on end, as if realizing the danger his broken mind refused to process.

A low growl issued from his grinding teeth...

...daddy...

...his calloused hands clenched and unclenched...

...please, daddy...

...bare, muddied feet dug into the earth...

...stay with me...

Wraith's head snapped around. He saw her, in the corner, little arms stretched towards him, begging as she clutched a doll in her hands. He had seen her before, in the same living room, hadn't he? Except this time, it was different. A large duffel bag was slung over his shoulder as he stood in the middle of the living room staring into her sad blue eyes. Sun streamed through the windows of the small room. Tears stained her cheeks as she cried out over and over for him not to leave, her breath choked from incessant crying.

"Daddy, please..." the sad little girl cried as she ran up to him and latched on to his leg. "Please don't leave me daddy."

He knelt down on his knees, taking her little cherubic face in his hands. The smile that touched his face was the first in years. It affected him more than any horror he had endured. He brushed her golden hair out of her face as she fought to stop crying. How could he have forgotten? That thought sickened him. He should never have forgotten. The realization embarrassed him. It angered him. But before the rage could reassert itself the little girl sniffled, failing in her struggle not to cry.

"You said you wouldn't leave anymore," she stammered between sobs.

Wraith looked deep into her eyes and smiled as he tossed the duffel to the side. "Katie, I'm never leaving you again. I promise." *Katie! That was her name!* He knew that, he had always known that.

Katie leapt into his arms, dropping her doll onto the hardwood floor. He held her tight as tears of his own stung his eyes. Katie. His little girl, his sweet precious little doll. He remembered. He remembered and vowed silently to never forget again. Wraith's senses came alive with sudden memories: the smell of her hair, the sound of her voice, the warmth of her heart. She was his angel. She was what he lived for.

A disturbing thought suddenly replaced the happiness. He *knew* her name was Katie. He *knew* she was his daughter. He *knew* he loved her as he had never loved anything in his god forsaken life. But there was something he didn't know.

"Who am I?" he whispered into her hair as he held her.

Katie looked at him with a sweet smile that was both familiar and new, "your daddy, silly."

"My name," he said, panic racing through him, "I don't know my name."

The front door rattled with a sudden boom, almost knocking it from its hinges, startling Wraith and Katie. The little girl's eyes grew wide with terror.

"Daddy…"

"Run! Hide in daddy's closet!"

Katie stood rooted to the spot as a louder jolt slammed into the door causing a large crack. The lights dimmed all around them.

Wraith took her by the shoulders. "Baby, go get in daddy's closet. I'll come get you when it's safe." The sunlight was gone. All light in the house vanished except for the flashing of lightning, casting the room in eerie blues and grays, while the rain beat hard on the old glass, which seemed to creak under the pressure.

The scared little girl took a couple of involuntary steps backward, her hand slowly pointing to something behind him.
"Daddy...daddy, stay with me..."

Wraith looked over his shoulder and saw only menacing yellow eyes glaring hatefully back at him. The blood pumped so loudly through is head he could barely hear anything else over the anxious drumming of his heartbeat. They wouldn't take her, not now. He would protect her this time. His muscles tensed in unbridled rage. *No. They won't take her from me again.*

"Daddy..."

Cool rain began pelting his skin as he growled menacingly outside the mouth of the cave. To Wraith, he was still standing in that living room protecting the only person he ever loved. The shadowy thing with the yellow eyes had barely emerged from the trees when Wraith launched himself at it, growling, punching, and biting with all he had.

Don't go, daddy...

Wraith and the shadow tumbled out of sight, down the side of the steep hill, through the mud and rain, as the ghostly form of Katie smiled in hatred.

The old fluorescent lights in the long hallways of the Hale County Community Hospital flickered as the storm played havoc on the outdated power grid. Laurel cut her eyes down the vacant hallways of the minimally staffed facility. She hadn't seen a nurse or a doctor in over an hour. Her ass was getting numb sitting on the hard orange plastic seat outside of William's room, which was just around the corner from the nurse's station and on the upper end of a long hallway that ended with a set of double doors that were for "medical personnel only". The reporter stretched her neck from side to side, trying to keep it from cramping up as she nodded in and out of sleep.

As an "embedded" reporter she had slept under far worse conditions. Her thoughts drifted to Fallujah, Pakistan, Kabul, Syria…so many battlefields, so much death. *Death*, she thought derisively, shifting her aching body to find a temporary respite from the discomfort, *death was for the lucky ones*. Laurel had come to know and admire so many men and women who put on the uniform to serve their country. While politicians argued the pros and cons of being overseas fighting a war so far from home, the soldiers were entrenched in skirmishes with people who wanted to kill them based on a simple difference in ideology. There was never any warning as to when an attack might come or what the face of that attacker might look like. Over there, it could be anyone. Sometimes the worst thing you could do was survive. It changed you…forever.

Horrors that the majority of people couldn't possibly imagine she experienced firsthand. She was a witness to death in all its gruesome insanity. Acquaintances, friends, strangers, they all looked the same in the end, potential wasted, a life that could have been, gone in an instant of misunderstood hatred. At least in that backwater hospital she didn't have to concern herself with sudden mortar bombardments in the middle of the night. The worst thing Laurel convinced herself she might have to face would be an invasion of cockroaches. She hurled an empty Dr. Pepper can at one of the disgusting little creatures that poked its head out from behind the tarnished metal of an opposing chair. The can missed its mark, echoing off the dingy floor tiles, the roach scampering back into the shadows. Laurel doubted anyone in the hospital even heard it, much less cared.

The hospital itself was massive...and mostly empty. Basically, a two-story coffin. Budget cuts, and the lack of funds and staff meant that only a handful of rooms and the most vital services remained functional. As such, the hospital seemed like a self-contained ghost town. The doctor had come and gone leaving only one nurse to check the patients. The only other person was an overweight security guard asleep in a chair outside the break room. The tired reporter stood up sluggishly, stretching out each body part in exaggerated fashion. *Where the hell is that sheriff,* she thought, exasperated. He was a different kind of customer than she was used to, someone who just straight up told you how he felt and didn't care whether you liked it or not. Laurel admired that. At that instant, however, she just wanted to punch him in that handsomely scarred face.

Time to check on the patient.

Laurel pushed open the door to the stairwell as the elevator had long since been condemned and out of order. She hurried as fast as she could up the old concrete steps, the echo of her shoes only managing to make the stairwell even more creepy. As she pushed through the door onto the second floor, she found herself incredibly grateful that it was so close to the patients' rooms, just passed the empty nurses station.

The reporter poked her head in the room where William...*Jason*...was lying in a comatose state. Even asleep the man looked paranoid, whoever he really was. She noticed his clothes piled somewhat folded in a somewhat open closet on the opposite side of an even smaller bathroom. Glancing down the hallways, Laurel crept across the old dull floor tiles to the closet, quietly taking out the pants they had found him in. The sheriff and her had been in such a rush to save his life there hadn't been time to search him. She found a rather nice, slender, leather wallet in the back pocket. Taking it out, she let the pants fall to the floor.

Laurel opened the wallet and noticed rather quickly that the nasty mess they found him in was the direct opposite of the well-conditioned leather billfold and its contents. There was nothing out of place, the few dollars that the man kept were placed in order of denomination, unfolded. There were no crammed receipts, business cards, or random gift cards. The man had one bank card. She slipped it out and looked at the license in the see through flap. The names matched: Jason Locke. *So, who in the hell is this William Tyler person?* She was about to close the wallet when she noticed something folded in another pocket. It was a paper slip for an appointment at the Hale County Mental Institute.

Hale County Mental Institute, all leads consistently back to that place, she thought bitterly, knowing where her next stop would be. Putting everything back in its proper place, she put the clothes back in the closet and crept out of the room.

The lights in the hospital flickered again, longer than the previous times, causing the machines to bleep as they reset. Laurel heard the double doors clicking shut at the end of the long hallway. No one had walked past the room, at least not that she noticed, and no one was walking up the hall towards her.

Laurel felt a chill run down her spine as she peered down the empty hallway. The flickering lights and eerie silence heightened her unease. She took a few cautious steps, straining to hear any sound of movement.

Suddenly, a loud crash echoed from William's room behind her. Laurel spun around, her heart racing. She rushed back to the doorway and froze.

William was no longer in his bed. The IV stand lay toppled on the floor, fluids pooling on the linoleum. The window was wide open, curtains billowing in the wind and rain.

"Shit," Laurel muttered, rushing to the window. She leaned out, squinting through the downpour, but saw no sign of the escaped patient. How had he woken up and fled so quickly and quietly? More importantly, how was he able to land two stories down and not get injured?

A flicker of movement caught her eye in the door frame. The anxious reporter whipped her head around but saw nothing. She slowly made her way to the door, her breathing quickening. Reaching into her pants pocket she pulled out a mini taser and held it close to her breast. Finally, one agonizing second later, she peered into the hallway. Nothing.

Laurel felt a sudden chill run down her spine. Something wasn't right. The flickering lights, the eerie silence, the sense of being watched - it all added up to trouble. She instinctively reached for her phone, only to find the battery had died. Cursing under her breath, she glanced back at William/Jason's room, debating whether to go back inside or investigate the hallway.

Her journalistic instincts won out. Cautiously, she crept down the dimly lit corridor towards the double doors, her footsteps echoing in the empty hall. As she neared the doors, she noticed a faint red glow emanating from beneath them.

Laurel's heart raced as she pushed one of the doors open slowly, peering through the crack. What she saw made her blood run cold.

Standing in the middle of the room beyond was a figure, tall, thin, and dressed in a grimy white, tattered jumpsuit. He wore a long, scraggly beard that looked matted with saliva and mucus, his bald head dulled with dirt and sweat. In his left hand was a weird, very old-looking clown doll with an evil smile.

Laurel's instincts screamed at her to run, but her feet remained rooted to the spot. The figure slowly turned, revealing a face that was more monster than man. His skin was a sickly grey, eyes sunken and lifeless. A wicked grin spread across his face, revealing rows of rotting, jagged teeth.

"Hello" the creature rasped in long drawn-out syllables, his voice like nails on a chalkboard. "Want to play?"

Laurel's paralysis broke. She slammed the door shut and sprinted down the hallway, heart pounding in her ears. The sound of inhuman cackling echoed behind her as she ran.

She rounded a corner and collided hard with a solid figure. Laurel stumbled back, raising her taser defensively.

"Whoa, easy there!" Jake exclaimed, grabbing her shoulders to steady her.

Laurel's eyes were wide with panic as she gasped for breath. "Jake! There's something... someone back there!" She pointed frantically down the hall.

The sheriff's hand went instinctively to his holstered weapon. "Slow down. What did you see?"

"William... Jason... whatever his name is - he's gone! The window was open, he must have jumped out of it because he couldn't get past me without me seeing him. And there was this... this person-thing in the other room down the hall. It wasn't normal!" Laurel's words tumbled out in a frenzied rush.

Jake's brow furrowed as he tried to make sense of her rambling. "Okay, let's take this one step at a time. Show me Jason's room."

Laurel nodded, still trembling slightly as she led Jake back to William's room. *Get ahold of yourself*, she thought angrily, *you've been through worse*. The window remained open, rain splattering onto the empty bed. The IV stand lay toppled on the floor, bed sheets thrown on the floor. Sure enough, there was no sign of Jason.

The sheriff took in the scene quickly, etching it into his mind, then shifted gears to the current problem at hand. "Damn, he leapt out of a two-story window. Those meds must be working overtime. Now tell me about this man you saw." Jake watched the slight flicker in her eyes when he said man. "It was a man, right?"

Laurel matched his stern gaze with one of her own, knowing what he was getting at. "Sheriff, Jake, I don't know what the hell it was but I know he wasn't normal and he sure as hell wasn't here to play nice. Maybe methed out of his mind, I don't know."

The lights flickered again, this time more rapidly as they stepped back out into the corridor. Their eyes quickly shifted to the double doors Laurel had come from when Jake found her. They locked eyes again. "There's something in there," Laurel said breathlessly, pointing back down the hallway. "Some kind of... something."

Jake's hand instinctively went to his holster. "What do you mean 'something'?"

Before Laurel could respond, an inhuman shriek echoed through the corridor. The fluorescent lights flickered violently, plunging them into darkness for several seconds before sputtering back to life.

"We need to move," Jake said firmly, drawing his weapon. He grabbed Laurel's arm and began leading her towards the stairwell. His scar was burning like crazy, as if it were some early warning system. At first, Jake was practically dragging the reporter to the stairwell but in impressively short fashion she took the lead and barreled into the stairwell, skipping steps as they quickly hit the first landing. Drug head psycho or not, they couldn't stay there.

Jake and Laurel burst out of the stairwell onto the first floor, hearts pounding. The fluorescent lights flickered ominously overhead as they rushed down the hallway.

"We need to evacuate the building," Jake said firmly, his gun drawn. "How many staff did you see earlier?"

"Just one nurse and a security guard," Laurel replied breathlessly. "But they could be anywhere now."

They rounded a corner and nearly collided with a startled nurse pushing a cart of supplies.

"Sheriff? What's going on?" the young woman asked, eyes wide.

"We need to get everyone out of here now," Jake ordered. "Where's the security guard?"

"I-I'm not sure. He was by the break room earlier..."

A blood-curdling scream echoed from down the hall, followed by the sound of shattering glass. Jake's grip on the pistol tightened as he flicked off the safety. He shared a look with Laurel, "there's no way he made it down here before us."

"Two?"

The sheriff nodded and slowly made his way towards the break area.

Jake turned to Laurel, his expression grim. "Go to my truck. Here are the keys. Lock yourself in and don't open the door for anyone but me."

Laurel hesitated, torn between fleeing to safety and staying to help. "What about you? I can help."

"I've got a gun," he said with a smirk, half-trying to belay her fears and half his own. "I'll be right behind you with the staff. Now go!"

Reluctantly, Laurel nodded and sprinted for the exit. Jake watched her disappear through the doors before turning back to face the darkened hallway.

He moved swiftly but cautiously, checking each room as he went. The flickering lights and eerie silence set his nerves on edge. His scar burned fiercely, a constant reminder of the danger lurking in the shadows.

As he rounded a corner, Jake came face to face with the night nurse. She let out a startled yelp.

"I thought there was only one nurse on duty," the sheriff exclaimed, quickly moving the gun out of the terrified nurses face.

"I'm the night nurse. The doctor called the other nurse in when you brought that patient in," she said, voice trembling.

"How many patients?"

"Just yours."

"Have you seen the security guard?"

"No, I heard him scream and came running this way."

"Where is the break room?"

The scared nurse pointed a shaking finger across the way to a darkened room with a flickering light. A chair was turned over just outside the doorway to the break room.

"And no one came past you?"

"I was in my office charting," she said on the verge of hysteria.

Jake rubbed his jaw uneasily, feeling the stubble of his beard. "Okay, listen to me. Get out of the building, now. Don't stop for anything or anyone else. Got it?"

The nurse nodded quickly and took off sprinting down the hallway to the front entrance. The sheriff took a calming breath, raised his pistol before him, and slowly moved across the room to the break area.

Jake approached the break room cautiously, gun raised. The flickering fluorescent light cast eerie shadows across the overturned furniture. He could hear labored breathing coming from inside.

"This is Sheriff Hooks," he called out. "Anyone in there?"

No response, just more ragged breaths. Jake stepped into the doorway, sweeping his gun across the room. What he saw made his blood run cold.

The security guard lay crumpled on the floor, a pool of blood spreading beneath him. Standing over him was a figure that could only be described as monstrous - grey skin, sunken eyes, almost balding at the top of his scalp with long matted hair trailing down his shoulders and a mouth full of jagged teeth. The dark blue jumpsuit it wore was in tatters, caked in blood and grime. In its hand was a blood-soaked teddy bear, missing parts, covered in black tape and tacks.

The creature's head snapped up at Jake's entrance, its lifeless eyes locking onto him. A wicked grin spread across its face.

"Want to play, Sheriff?" it rasped.

Jake knew by the look in the crazed man's eyes where this was headed, it was an instant understanding that made his scar sting in anticipation and memory. The psycho on the hilltop had the same look. "That fucking asylum," the Sheriff grunted angrily. He raised his gun, stone-faced with determination, mind made up before he even had time to process the question, and squeezed the trigger. But, before he could pull the trigger something solid slammed into him, driving Jake back into the hallway, gasping to catch his breath.

As he began to push himself off the floor, everything went dark.

JC gazed at Ashlyn's sleeping figure as he lay beside her. The storm had picked up, pounding the house with wild winds and rain. But inside Laurel Rose Manor, tucked away in his bed with only the soft glow of the lamp barely illuminating the room, JC marveled at the young woman snuggled up next to him and shut out the raging world around him. The night had been a roller coaster of emotions; the Playhouse fight, the fight with his father...the reconciliation as his father opened up for the first time in JC's life. Yet, as he tried to savor the moment, that prickling on the back of his neck wouldn't go away. It sat there, tingling his senses with a dread unspoken premonition.

As he absently stroked Ashlyn's hair he caught movement from the corner of his eye. JC jerked his head up to track the motion. There was nothing there. The door, closed tightly only seconds earlier, stood ajar. A shadow seemed to move on the other side of it.

"Dad?" he asked in hushed tones so as not to wake his girlfriend.

No response.

A nondescript figure moved on the other side of the door. JC could make out something dark, not quite like a shadow but like nothing else he knew of. It was almost a dark cloth-like material that seemed to billow like smoke.

JC slowly got out of bed, careful not to disturb Ashlyn. He crept towards the partially open door, his heart pounding. As he reached for the doorknob, a chill ran down his spine.

The shadow seemed to retreat further down the hallway. JC stepped out of his room, peering into the darkness. The house was eerily quiet except for the storm raging outside.

"Hello?" JC called out softly. No response.

He took a few more steps down the hall. The shadow appeared to be moving towards his father's study. JC followed, his unease growing with each step.

As he approached the study, he heard muffled voices coming from inside. One was clearly his father's, but the other was unfamiliar - a woman's voice.

JC hesitated outside the closed door, unsure if he should interrupt. But something felt very wrong

JC stood frozen outside his father's study, torn between respecting his father's privacy and investigating the strange voices and shadows he had seen. His instincts were screaming that something was very wrong.

Taking a deep breath, JC gently turned the doorknob and cracked open the door. What he saw inside made his blood run cold.

His father was locked in a passionate embrace with a woman JC didn't recognize. But it was more than that - there was an otherworldly quality to the scene. A faint reddish mist seemed to swirl around them, and the woman's eyes flashed with an inhuman light.

JC stumbled backwards, his mind reeling. This couldn't be real. He blinked hard, hoping the bizarre vision would disappear. But when he looked again, the disturbing scene remained.

Just then, the woman's head snapped towards the doorway.

JC's blood ran cold as the woman's inhuman eyes locked onto him. Her lips curled into a wicked smile, revealing unnaturally sharp teeth. In that instant, JC knew with absolute certainty that this was no ordinary woman - this was something else entirely.

His father remained oblivious, seemingly in a trance-like state as the creature caressed him. JC wanted to cry out, to warn his father, but fear paralyzed his vocal cords.

The woman's form began to shift and writhe, her human visage melting away to reveal something monstrous underneath. Her skin took on a sickly grey hue, her limbs elongating into grotesque appendages.

JC stumbled backwards, electricity shot up his spine, tingling the back of his neck, his heart pounding wildly in his chest. He had to do something, had to save his father. But how could he fight against something so unnatural?

Just then something moved to his right, a dark shadow like he had seen earlier darted outside the corner of his vision. The young man barely had time to react when the dark mass was upon him. It had no tangible weight or form. JC couldn't grasp it, his hands passing through the cloudlike being as if it were air yet at the same time it felt as if he were being crushed.

JC struggled against the oppressive darkness, his lungs burning as he fought for air. The shadowy mass seemed to be pulling him away from the study door, away from his entranced father and the monstrous creature.

Panic gripped him as he realized he was being dragged down the hallway. JC thrashed wildly, his fingers scrabbling against the walls, desperate for purchase. But the shadow's grip was unyielding. He was pulled back up the staircase and down the dark upper hallway. As they passed his room JC managed to grasp onto the doorframe, using all his strength to fight against the force tugging against him.

"Ashlyn," he managed to croak out. Through the dark cloud he could see her stir, eyes fluttering open in confusion.

"JC? What's wrong?" she mumbled sleepily.

He was about to answer when he noticed an arm wrap around her waist from the opposite side of the bed. When the head slowly came into view gazing down at Ashlyn it was his own eyes that took in her countenance, his own voice that reassured her.

"It's okay, go back to sleep," his doppelganger spoke comfortingly to her. Then those strange but familiar eyes met his, and the imposter's smile twisted inhumanly.

JC tried to scream but lost his grip on the doorframe, the cloud pulling him into an unending darkness.

Chapter 15

Jake blinked rapidly, trying to clear his vision as he struggled to his feet. The hallway was pitch black, the only sound his own ragged breathing. He fumbled for his flashlight, cursing under his breath as he realized it must have fallen when he was knocked down. It was at that moment the emergency generators kicked in just enough to cause the emergency lighting to barely illuminate the surroundings.

Suddenly, a high-pitched giggle echoed through the darkness, sending chills down Jake's spine. He raised his gun, spinning in place, trying to pinpoint the source of the sound.

"Come out where I can see you," Jake growled, his voice steadier than he felt.

Another giggle, closer this time. Jake's finger tightened on the trigger.

A flash of movement to his left - Jake fired instinctively. The muzzle flash briefly illuminated the hallway, revealing nothing but empty space.

"Missed me," the creature's raspy voice taunted from behind him.

More movement to his right, causing the sheriff to fire wildly in that direction.

"Missed me too," a higher pitched screechy voice responded.

The second one, he thought. *That must have been the one who blindsided me.* Jake was at a severe disadvantage. Jake's mind raced as he tried to process the situation. Two hostile entities, possibly more, in a darkened hospital with limited visibility. He was outmaneuvered and outgunned. The sheriff took a deep breath, forcing himself to think rationally despite the adrenaline coursing through his veins.

"Alright, let's talk this out," Jake called out, keeping his gun raised. "What do you want?"

A chilling laugh echoed through the hallway. "Want? We want to play, Sheriff. Isn't that what everyone wants? Excepts we want your blood, your soul. We wants to watch the light burn out of your eyessss..." the thing hissed in the dark.

Jake's grip tightened on his weapon. "I'm not here to play games. You've hurt people. That ends now."

"Oh, but we likes games," the raspy voice replied, seeming to come from everywhere at once. "we likes to hurt the normies."

Suddenly, Jake felt a presence directly behind him and instinctively rolled back to his left to avoid the on-coming blow. He heard the whistle of air rush over his head, felt the wind the wake made. As he stood up he saw exactly what it was, a hatchet. It was in the hand of the of the white jumpsuit guy. That was close, way too close for his liking. He was outnumbered and outmaneuvered in unfamiliar territory against opponents that seemed to defy logic. His police training hadn't prepared him for anything like this. But he'd be damned if he was going down without a fight.

"Chop, chop," the hatchet man, hissed, drool dripping from his beard.

"You want to play?" Jake growled, his voice low and dangerous. "Okay, let's play."

In one fluid motion, Jake dropped and rolled, coming up in a crouch with his back against the wall. He fired three rapid shots in the direction of the hatchet-wielding maniac, the muzzle flashes briefly illuminating the grotesque figure.

The creature howled in pain and rage as at least one bullet found its mark. But instead of dropping, it charged at Jake with inhuman speed, hatchet raised high.

Jake dove to the side, narrowly avoiding the whistling blade as it embedded itself in the wall next to where his head had just been.

Jake rolled to his feet, heart pounding. The hatchet was stuck in the wall, the creature struggling to yank it free. Jake seized the opportunity, tackling the monster with all his strength. They crashed to the floor in a tangle of limbs.

Up close, the stench of decay and madness overwhelmed Jake's senses. He grappled with the creature, its inhuman strength nearly overpowering him. Rotting teeth snapped inches from his face as Jake struggled to keep the monster at bay.

Suddenly, Jake felt sharp claws dig into his back. The second creature had joined the fray, cackling maniacally as it raked its talons across Jake's flesh. Pain exploded through his body, but Jake refused to let go of the first monster.

With a roar of effort, Jake managed to slam the hatchet-wielder's head against the floor. The impact stunned it momentarily, giving Jake a chance to reach for his fallen gun.

His fingers closed around the grip just as the second creature leapt onto his back, its weight driving him to the ground. Jake twisted, bringing the gun up and firing blindly over his shoulder.

A shriek of pain told him he'd hit his mark. The weight on his back lessened as the creature stumbled away, howling.

Jake scrambled to his feet; gun trained on the two monstrosities. Both were wounded but still very much a threat. Blood dripped from the bullet holes in their bodies, but it was a strange, dark ichor that seemed to move with a life of its own.

"What the hell are you?" Jake growled, his voice raw with pain and exertion.

The creatures exchanged a look, their inhuman faces twisting into grotesque grins.

"We are the forgotten ones," the hatchet-wielder rasped. "The ones they locked away and tried to break."

"But we broke free," the other giggled. "And now we play!"

"Play the game of the Sluagh na marbh," the hatchet man spat.

"From the aisle of the Sidhe to do thee harm," the greasy one gleefully added.

They lunged at Jake simultaneously, their monstrous forms blurring with unnatural speed. The Sheriff knew what being hyped up on some of these manufactured drugs could do to people, make them almost unstoppable, immune to the pain and reality around them. What the hell kind of drug was "Sidhe" and what was in it that kept these two monstrous men coming after him despite the damage he was inflicting. One thing was certain, he felt everything they were doing to him. He knew he couldn't outlast them.

This had to end. Now.

Jake steeled himself, knowing this could be his last stand. As the creatures charged, he fired his remaining bullets in rapid succession, aiming for center mass. The impacts slowed them but didn't stop their advance.

With no time to reload, Jake hurled the empty gun at the hatchet-wielder's face. It connected with a sickening crunch, buying Jake precious seconds. He dove for the fallen hatchet, wrenching it free from the wall.

The sheriff spun, swinging the weapon in a wide arc. The blade bit deep into the greasy creature's side as it lunged for him. Dark ichor sprayed from the wound as the monster howled in agony.

Jake didn't hesitate. He brought the hatchet down again and again, hacking at the writhing form until it stopped moving. The hallway echoed with wet, meaty thuds and inhuman shrieks.

Panting heavily, Jake turned to face the remaining creature. The hatchet-wielder's eyes blazed with hatred and something akin to fear.

"What are you?" it hissed.

Jake's face was a mask of grim determination. "I'm the goddamn sheriff," he growled, "and this is my county."

With a roar, Jake charged. The creature raised its claws, but Jake was faster. The hatchet cleaved through rotting flesh and bone, nearly severing the monster's arm.

They grappled, crashing into walls and medical equipment. Jake felt claws raking his skin, tearing flesh. But adrenaline and rage drove him on. He brought the hatchet down again and again until finally, mercifully, the creature stopped moving.

Jake stumbled back, his breath coming in ragged gasps. Blood - his own and the creatures' - soaked his clothes. Every inch of him screamed in pain. But he was alive.

As the adrenaline faded, exhaustion threatened to overwhelm him. But Jake knew he couldn't rest yet. He had to make sure the hospital was clear, had to find Laurel and the others.

Gritting his teeth against the pain, Jake retrieved his gun and reloaded. He cast one last look at the motionless forms on the floor before moving deeper into the hospital's shadows.

The night was far from over.

Dan Roundtree drove slowly along the boundary of the Rez, as was his practice when the spirits whispered in his dreams, leaving him unable to rest. They had been especially vocal tonight. He took a swig of the white man's coffee. "White man's coffee," he scoffed amusedly. "Not even the white man knows where this awful stuff comes from," he laughed aloud from the warm confines of his brand-new Dodge Ram. Dan loved the ways of his people, and his house was a living monument to the love of his ancestors and their history, but that didn't mean the Cherokee Elder couldn't enjoy the modern comforts and it sure beat freezing his native ass off on the back of a cold saddle.

He laughed again at the thought of being an "Elder". Dan was only in his mid-forties, but it was his love of his people, the strive to make sure on this stretch of land they called the Rez, all the families who lived there would flourish. It wasn't an official reservation, but they and the locals treated it as one, they even had their own little police force, much like the Sheriff's Department, that was written into County Law over a century and a half earlier. Dan was the official Mayor of the Rez as elected by the people who resided there. They trusted him and thrived under his leadership. It was a world unto its own, it protected its own, and it protected their neighbors who looked out for them. In that, Dan Roundtree found tremendous pride.

But darkness was now upon them, the evil his ancestors who had inhabited that land spoke of since they laid claim to it.

Dan slowed the truck as he approached the edge of the Rez boundary. Something didn't feel right. The air seemed heavy, charged with an energy he couldn't quite place. He pulled over and cut the engine, listening intently.

At first, all he could hear was the patter of rain and the low rumble of thunder. But then another sound reached his ears - a low, keening wail that made the hairs on the back of his neck stand up. It wasn't human, nor any animal he recognized.

Dan reached for the rifle he kept under the seat, his hand closing around the familiar wood stock. As he did, movement caught his eye at the tree line. A silverish line of energy seemed to move through the woods and across the land before him. The light vanished as quickly as it had appeared but, in the afterglow, a dark shape emerged from the shadows, shambling and unnatural.

His breath caught in his throat as he made out more details. The thing was vaguely human-shaped, but twisted and wrong. Its skin was a sickly grey, hanging in tatters from an emaciated frame. Empty eye sockets glowed with an eerie light.

"Tsalagi Tsunsdi," Dan whispered, invoking the protection of the Little People. This was no ordinary threat - this was something born of ancient evil, the darkness his ancestors had warned about.

The creature's head snapped towards him, a lipless mouth opening in a silent scream. Dan raised his rifle, knowing instinctively that normal weapons would have little effect. But he had to try.

The thing had barely taken a step towards him when another figure leaped out of the forest upon the creature's head, wailing wildly. Through his scope Dan could tell it was a man, a wild, psychotic looking man with dirty blonde hair, and wearing torn inmate scrubs, caked in blood. The fight between the two was visceral, as though they were mortal enemies.

Dan watched in shock as the wild-looking man and the grotesque creature grappled violently. The inmate was fighting with unnatural strength and ferocity, landing blow after blow on the monster. But the creature seemed unfazed, its elongated limbs wrapping around the man as it tried to crush him.

Dan knew he had to act. He took careful aim with his rifle and fired, the shot echoing through the night. The bullet struck the creature's shoulder, causing it to release its grip on the inmate momentarily.

The wild man seized the opportunity, driving his thumbs into the creature's glowing eye sockets. An inhuman shriek pierced the air as the monster thrashed in pain.

Dan fired again, this time hitting the creature's chest. Dark ichor sprayed from the wound as it stumbled backwards.

Suddenly, the inmate got the upper hand, wrapping his arms around the creature's neck in a chokehold. With a sickening crack, he wrenched the monster's head to the side. The creature went limp, collapsing to the ground.

The inmate stood over his fallen foe, chest heaving. Then his gaze snapped to Dan, eyes wild and feral.

Dan tensed, finger hovering over the trigger. But something in the man's expression gave him pause. Behind the madness, there was a flicker of... recognition? Pain?

"Who are you?" Dan called out cautiously.

The man tilted his head, brow furrowing as if struggling to understand. His mouth worked silently for a moment before he managed to rasp out a single word:

"Daddy..."

"Daddy," Dan echoed, trying to decipher what the crazed man meant. He was about to ask another question when the inmate suddenly grasped his head as in terrible pain.

Finally, as if forcing every fiber of his being to speak, the man said to Dan in a pained voice, a pain that was echoed in his eyes, "daughter."

Then he turned and bolted into the woods, disappearing into the shadows.

Dan lowered his rifle slowly, mind reeling. What in the name of the spirits had he just witnessed? And who was that man? One thing was certain - the evil his ancestors had warned of was no longer lying dormant. He needed to warn the others. Dark days were coming to Hale County. No, they were most definitely here.

The dawn of a new day was finally rising, but for Marcus the election he had so patiently but nervously awaited for was upon him. His sleep had been fitful, so he finally just got up, showered, brewed a fresh pot of coffee and sat at his kitchen table, sipping coffee and listening to the rain outside as election day dawned. Despite his efforts to stay positive, a sense of unease gnawed at him. The conversation with Jake echoed in his mind - something was very wrong in Hale County.

As he stared out the window, Marcus couldn't shake the feeling that dark forces were at work. The strange incidents, the unexplained deaths and disappearances, the corruption that seemed to infect every level of local government - it all pointed to something sinister lurking beneath the surface.

He thought back to his encounter with Chief Malone the night before. The man's arrogance and thinly veiled threats made it clear the current administration would not give up power easily. Marcus knew his campaign for change had made him a target.

With a sigh, Marcus stood and walked to the window. The rain showed no signs of letting up. It was as if the weather itself reflected the gloomy mood hanging over the county. But Marcus refused to give in to despair. He had come too far, fought too hard to back down now.

Whatever forces were aligned against him, whatever darkness threatened to engulf Hale County, Marcus vowed to stand against it. The people deserved better, and he would do everything in his power to bring about real change. For a moment, he could have sworn he saw something shift in the darkness - something that didn't belong.

Shaking his head, Marcus chalked it up to lack of sleep and pre-election jitters. But as he poured himself another cup of coffee with slightly trembling hands, he couldn't fully dismiss the feeling that unseen eyes were watching him.

"Get it together," he muttered to himself. "Today's the big day. Focus."

But even as he tried to psych himself up, Marcus knew this election day would be unlike any other. Something was coming - he just didn't know what. He just needed to get a little breakfast and get to the polls. Making an actual appearance and being present to greet and reassure the voters would be critical.

A knock on the door interrupted his musings. He wasn't expecting anyone this early in the morning so he sat the coffee down and quickly moved to see who it could possibly be. As he pulled the door open to say hello, his voice caught midway through the first word, "Good…," his voice trailed off in stunned silence. Marcus took a shocked step backwards, his incredulous eyes taking in the sight before him.

The tall, leggy dark-skinned beauty that stood before him almost matched him in height. Her deep brown almond shaped eyes bore into his own as her smile held him rooted in place. Her black and blonde curls of hair trickled around her shoulders giving the mysterious lady an otherworldly look, shaping her angular face with grace and confidence.

"Hello, Marcus," her silky voice purred.

"Char..." he managed to sputter in shock, "how, why, are you here?"

Charlotte smiled warmly as she stepped inside, raindrops glistening on her dark curls. "I couldn't miss your big day, Marcus. Not after everything we've been through."

Marcus stood frozen, his mind reeling. Charlotte had been his rock during his first campaign, his confidante and strategist. But she had left Hale County years ago, driven away by the corruption and darkness that seemed to permeate every corner of local politics. Her sudden reappearance on election day felt almost too good to be true.

"I... I can't believe you're here," Marcus stammered, finally finding his voice. "How did you know?"

Charlotte's smile faltered slightly. "I've been keeping tabs on things here. When I heard you were running again, I knew I had to come back. Hale County needs you, Marcus. Now more than ever."

There was an urgency in her voice that sent a chill down Marcus's spine. He studied her face, noting the subtle lines of worry etched around her eyes.

"What aren't you telling me, Char?" he asked softly.

Charlotte sighed, her shoulders sagging slightly. "There's so much, Marcus. So much darkness here. I've uncovered things... terrible things. But I couldn't warn you from afar. I had to come in person."

Marcus felt a pit forming in his stomach. "Tell me everything," he said, leading her to the kitchen table.

As Charlotte began to speak, Marcus knew that whatever happened at the polls today, nothing would ever be the same in Hale County again.

Jason's head was pounding.

He was sitting on something hard, his muscles felt cramped and on fire. Forcing his eyes open despite the headache he could see a small amount of light coming through a cross shaped hole. Where was he? Why couldn't he remember what happened? Slowly, he began feeling around him. The room was small. "Room," he though quizzically, "more like a closet maybe…" his thought trailed off as he tried coming out of that groggy state. It finally struck him; he was in a confessional. And he had been there before, except he hadn't. Had he?

He was so confused. Maybe he had gone mad. "Why would you think that?" he thought to himself. "At least it's not squirrels," another part of his mind whispered. "Squirrels? What the fuck?" finally said out loud, giving breath to the chaos he felt.

"It is good to see you again, my son," a strange but familiar voice spoke from the other side of the partition nearly causing Jason to jump out of his skin.

Jason's heart raced as he tried to place the familiar voice. "Father...?" he ventured hesitantly.

"Yes, my child," the Reverend replied gently. "You've returned to us once again."

Jason's mind reeled. He had no memory of ever being here before, yet something about this felt achingly familiar. "I...I don't understand. What's happening to me?"

The Reverend Gillian was silent for a long moment. When he spoke again, his voice was heavy with sorrow. "The darkness that plagues Hale County has touched you, William. It fragments the mind, and twists reality. But you are safe here, for now."

"William?" Jason echoed, a chill running down his spine, "My name is Jason. Jason Locke"

"Evil forces are stirring, William" the Reverend continued. "The veil between worlds grows thin. You have a role to play, though you may not remember it."

Jason's head throbbed as he struggled to make sense of the Reverend's cryptic words. Flashes of memory teased at the edges of his consciousness - a little girl's laughter, the acrid smell of smoke, a teddy bear with button eyes. But they slipped away before he could grasp them.

"I'm not William!" Jason shouted; his voice not able to mask the fear.

"Not now, perhaps, but rest," the reverend replied. "When the time comes, you'll know. But beware the shadows, William. Not all is as it seems in Hale County."

Jason took a shaky breath. "I've seen things...terrible things. Monsters. Shadows. I don't know if they're real or if I'm hallucinating. And there are gaps in my memory - whole chunks of time just...missing."

"The mind is a fragile thing," the Reverend said. "Sometimes it fractures to protect us from truths we are not yet ready to face."

"What truths?" Jason asked desperately. "Please, I need answers."

There was a long pause before the Reverend spoke again. Geoffrey knew the line was thin and he had to be careful, one push in the wrong direction would undo everything. "The darkness in Hale County runs deep, William. Deeper than you can imagine. You've glimpsed it, haven't you? The true face of evil that lurks beneath the surface?"

Jason nodded, then realized the Reverend couldn't see him. "Yes," he whispered.

"And the marble, you still possess it?" the Reverend's voice asked with unhidden need.

Marble? Jason thought for a moment before realization struck. *The Marble!* He quickly checked his pockets. Empty. "I...I must have dropped it."

"You must find it, everything depends on this," Geoffrey told him, pleadingly, almost letting his carefully crafted reverend persona slip. "You've felt its pull, yes?"

"I have," Jason whispered knowingly, eyes glistening with tortured tears.

"Then you know your role in all this is only beginning," the Reverend said ominously. "The choices you make from here will determine not just your fate, but the fate of many others."

Before Jason could respond, the partition slid open. He found himself staring not at a priest, but at his own reflection in a small mirror.

The confessional was empty. He was alone.

CHAPTER 16

Ashlyn awoke to an empty bed. Her mind raced back to last night, how everything was finally coming together. She had officially met JC's dad and was treated as well as she had ever been in her life, and fallen asleep in the arms of the man she loved. It couldn't have been better if it had been planned. So why was she feeling a prickling on the back of her neck warning her to flee this house and never come back?

Ashlyn sat up slowly, trying to shake off her unease. The room was quiet except for the patter of rain against the windows. She called out softly, "JC?"

No response.

She climbed out of bed and padded to the bedroom door, peeking out into the hallway. Empty. The house felt strangely still.

"JC?" she called again, louder this time. "Dr. Michaels?"

Only silence greeted her. Ashlynn's heart began to race as she made her way down the stairs, checking each room. No sign of JC or his father.

In the kitchen, she found a note on the counter in JC's handwriting:

"Ash - Had to run an errand with Dad. Back soon. Love you."

She should have felt relieved, but something about the note felt off. The handwriting was JC's, but the words didn't sound like him. And hadn't Dr. Michaels mentioned having to go to the hospital early?

Ashlyn's skin prickled with goosebumps. She couldn't shake the feeling that something was very wrong. Grabbing her phone, she dialed JC's number with shaking fingers. It went straight to voicemail.

As she lowered the phone, movement outside the window caught her eye. A shadowy figure darted across the lawn, there and gone in an instant.

Ashlyn's breath caught in her throat. She needed to get out of this house. Now.

She quickly went back upstairs to JC's room to gather her things. She would text him later about leaving, make something up, anything. But right then her only thought was to leave. Making sure she hadn't left anything she bolted out of the door and into the hallway.

When she reached the top of the grand staircase, Ashlyn paused. The foyer below was bathed in the grey light of the rainy morning. Nothing seemed out of place, and yet...

A floorboard creaked behind her. Ashlyn whirled around, her heart pounding.

There at the end of the hallway stood JC, watching her with an unreadable expression.

"JC!" Ashlyn exclaimed, relief flooding through her. "You scared me. Where were you?"

As JC slowly walked towards her, Ashlyn felt her relief give way to unease. There was something off about the way he moved, the look in his eyes.

"JC?" she asked hesitantly. "Is everything okay?"

He smiled, but it didn't reach his eyes. "Everything's fine, Ash. Why don't we go back to bed?"

Ashlyn took an involuntary step backwards. "I...I should probably get going. My mom will be wondering where I am."

JC's smile widened, revealing too many teeth. "Oh, I don't think you'll be going anywhere."

As he lunged towards her, Ashlyn's scream was cut short by a hand clamping over her mouth. The last thing she saw before darkness claimed her was JC's face shifting, melting into something inhuman and monstrous.

The front door to the cabin swung open heavily without a sound. Although constructed out of a sheet of solid white oak the hinges were industrial strength. Nothing was knocking that door down outside of a stick of dynamite, and even then the odds were iffy. The rest of the house was much the same, hand-built from the foundation up, none of that cheap thrown-together, toilet paper mixed particle wood or aged out two by fours. The cabin could have been a fortress, and Jake had built it as such not long after becoming Sheriff. He wanted to be sure that when he was at home there was nothing to worry about outside of a complete world collapse.

After the events of last night, he was doubly glad of his decision. All he wanted now, as he tossed his jacket and hat on the counter, was a hot shower and at least a thirty-minute nap. He pointed down the hallway as he spoke to his guest that followed closely behind. "Down on the far left is the guest room. There's a bathroom with a shower through the doorway before that. If you're hungry the kitchen is full of," he paused shaking his head, "well, whatever you can find. You were imbedded with the military, so eating what I eat should be okay. Make yourself at home." Jake half-grinned at his guest, half-grunted. There wasn't a centimeter of his body that didn't ache.

Lauren took in her surroundings as Jake was painfully crawling out of his boots. The windows were triple paned. There was probably a panic room though, now that she thought about it, this cabin was one GIANT panic room. "Paranoid much," she asked amusedly with a hint of sarcasm.

Jake sighed as he gave his last boot a final pull, letting it thud to the floor. He gave a shrug of his shoulders with slight grin, "people don't like me."

Lauren gave a small laugh, fully understanding and sympathizing with the pain he was feeling, "I can't imagine why." Jake looked like shit. "Go take care of yourself, I'm good in here. Anything I need to be aware of?"

He returned her laugh with a half-laugh of his own as he walked down the hallway to his room. "Yeah," he called back over his shoulder, "I don't have cable."

Laurel chuckled softly as Jake disappeared down the hallway. She took a moment to survey her surroundings, impressed by the sturdy construction of the cabin. After the harrowing events at the hospital, she was grateful for a safe place to regroup.

She made her way to the guest room, eager to clean up and change out of her bloodstained clothes. As she passed by a window, movement outside caught her eye. Laurel froze, peering intently into the misty forest beyond the cabin. For a moment, she thought she saw a shadowy figure dart between the trees. But when she blinked, it was gone.

Shaking her head, Laurel chalked it up to exhaustion and nerves. She continued to the guest room, locking the door behind her out of habit. As she showered, her mind raced with questions about the nightmarish creatures they'd encountered. What were they?

Where had they come from? And most importantly, were there more out there? What had they witnessed at the hospital? Those creatures defied explanation. And William - or was it Jason? - had vanished without a trace. None of it made sense.

One thing was clear: there were dark forces at work in Hale County. Forces that didn't want their secrets exposed. Laurel's investigative instincts tingled. She was onto something big here; she could feel it. But at what cost?

Shutting off the water, Laurel dried off and slipped into the clean clothes Jake had lent her. They were comically large on her slender frame, but she was too tired to care. She padded down the hall to the guest room and collapsed onto the bed.

As sleep claimed her, Laurel's last thoughts were of her sister. Whatever was happening in Hale County, she would get to the bottom of it. For Amanda's sake, and for all the others who had suffered at the hands of this insidious evil.

But for now, she slept. The real battle was just beginning.

The door to the kitchen of Kara Bennett's house opened up and a giant mass of fur bolted into the yard followed closely by little Haley Bennett, dressed in her Princess Leia Halloween costume, arms wrapped tightly around one of her many dolls. Kara was close behind, an umbrella in hand, as the three of them walked quickly to her car.

"Hurry, mommy," Haley shouted out, a light bark from Kaia, the German Shephard, seemingly echoing the sentiment as a light rain descended upon them.

Kara hurried after her daughter and their overeager dog, fumbling with the car keys as she tried to keep the umbrella steady. The morning air was thick with humidity, the rain a constant drizzle that seemed to match her gloomy mood.

"I'm coming, sweetie," she called out, unlocking the car door with a beep. "Kaia, in the back!"

The German Shepherd obediently hopped into the backseat, tail wagging as Hailey climbed in after her. Kara helped her daughter buckle up before sliding into the driver's seat, shaking droplets from the umbrella.

As she started the engine, Kara caught sight of her reflection in the rearview mirror. Dark circles shadowed her eyes, a testament to another sleepless night. Her thoughts kept drifting back to Jake, to their heated exchange outside her house. The hurt and anger in his eyes haunted her.

"Mommy, are you okay?" Haley's small voice piped up from the backseat.

Kara forced a smile, meeting her daughter's concerned gaze in the mirror. "I'm fine, honey. Just a little tired."

She pulled out of the driveway, trying to focus on the road ahead. But as they drove through the misty streets of Hale County, Kara couldn't shake the feeling that something was terribly wrong. The town seemed too quiet, the few people out and about moving with an air of unease. It was an election day, there should be far more bustling about.

As they neared the school, Kara's grip tightened on the steering wheel. A police cruiser was parked outside, lights flashing. A knot formed in her stomach as she pulled up to the curb.

"Wait here with Kaia," she told Hailey, unbuckling her seatbelt. "I'll be right back."

Kara approached the school entrance, where a small crowd of parents had gathered. Officer Malone was speaking in hushed tones to the principal, his face grim.

"What's going on?" Kara asked another mother.

The woman shook her head, fear evident in her eyes. "They're saying there's been some kind of incident. The school's closed for the day."

Kara's heart raced as she pushed through the crowd, desperate for answers. As she neared Officer Malone, she overheard snippets of his conversation with the principal.

"...can't rule out a connection to the hospital attack..."

"...keep the children safe..."

"...Sheriff Hooks is investigating..."

At the mention of Jake's name, Kara felt a mix of relief and apprehension. Whatever was happening, Jake was on the case. But the thought of him in danger made her blood run cold.

Officer Malone noticed her approach and broke off his conversation. "Nurse Bennett," he greeted her, his tone professional but strained. "I'm afraid we're going to have to ask you to take your daughter home. School's cancelled today due to some... security concerns."

Kara's eyes narrowed. "Security concerns? What's really going on here, Officer?"

Malone glanced around nervously before leaning in closer. "Look, I can't say much, but there was an incident last night. Some kind of attack at the hospital. The Sheriff's ordered extra patrols around town, especially near schools and public buildings."

A chill ran down Kara's spine. "An attack? Was anyone hurt?"

"I don't have all the details," Malone replied evasively. "But it's best if everyone stays home today if they can. We'll put out an official statement once we know more."

Kara nodded slowly, her mind racing. She needed to talk to Jake, to find out what was really happening. But first, she had to get Hailey somewhere safe.

"Thank you, Eddie," she said, turning back towards her car. As she walked away, she couldn't shake the feeling that Malone wasn't telling her everything.

Haley's face was pressed against the window as Kara approached, eyes wide with curiosity and concern. "What's wrong, Mommy? Why are the police here? Are we not going to the Halloween party?"

Kara forced a smile as she climbed back into the driver's seat. "I'm sorry, sweetie. School's cancelled today, so we're going to have a fun Halloween day at home instead. How does that sound?"

Haley's face showed her disappointment then quickly lit up. "Can we bake cookies and bob for apples?"

"Of course we can," Kara replied, her voice steadier than she felt. As she pulled away from the curb, she caught sight of Officer Malone watching them leave, his expression unreadable.

The drive home was tense, with Kara constantly checking her rearview mirror for any signs of trouble. Haley chattered away in the backseat, oblivious to her mother's anxiety.

As they pulled into their driveway, Kara made a decision. She needed answers, and there was only one person she trusted to give them to her.

"Honey, why don't you and Kaia go inside and pick out which cookies you want to make?" Kara suggested as she helped Haley out of the car. "I need to make a quick phone call."

Once Haley and the dog were safely inside, Kara pulled out her cell phone and dialed Jake's number. Her heart pounded as the phone rang once, twice...

"Come on, Jake," she muttered. "Pick up."

A groggy voice answered on the other end.

"Hello."

"Jake," Kara said with more agitation than she meant, "what the hell is going on at the school?"

"At the school?" Jake asked in surprise.

"Come on, Jake, don't play dumb with me," she shot back accusingly, "I'm not some stupid barfly bimbo. What is happening? Is that why you've been guarding the house?" Her voice was rising with each word. Kara was getting riled up and she knew that meant Jake was going to get angry, he hated anyone mouthing off at him like he was beneath them. It had always been a sore spot with him. At the moment she didn't care.

There was a long silence on the other end. *Here it comes,* she thought expectantly, steeling herself for the verbal lashing sure to erupt. But it never did. There was another deep sigh. She could hear sheets rustling and it dawned on her that he must have been asleep when she called.

"Kara," Jake said tiredly, *"I honestly don't know about the school. My first time hearing about it. I've been dealing with an..."* he paused, not sure how in the hell to describe what had transpired without freaking her out or getting yelled at again for being a liar. The truth was just too crazy. *"...incident at the hospital all night. I came home, tried to get a nap in and now here you are telling me something new."*

The school.

Haley!

Jakes voice changed from weary to worry in the span of a moment, *"Haley, is she..."*

"She's fine, Jake," Kara reassured him, all anger subsided. Jake honestly didn't know what she was talking about. "I'm sorry to come at you like that. Just, after last night, then being woken up by mom about the hospital and going to the school and that happened I..." she paused as realization dawned on her.

"Kara, what is it?" Jake asked concerned at her sudden silence.

"Jake," she breathed heavily, "Malone said you were looking into the school incident and wondered if it had anything to do with the hospital."

"But I told you..." she could almost hear Jake's eyes narrow on the other end of the phone. *"That son-of-a-bitch."*

Jake's mind raced as he processed what Kara had told him. Malone was lying, using Jake's name to lend credibility to whatever was happening at the school. But why? What was he trying to cover up?

"Kara, listen to me carefully," Jake said, his voice low and urgent. *"I need you to stay home with Haley. Lock the doors, don't answer for anyone you don't know. I'm going to look into this school situation."*

"Jake, what's really going on?" Kara asked, fear creeping into her voice. "First the hospital, now the school... Is Haley in danger?"

Jake hesitated, torn between his desire to protect Kara and Haley, and his need for their trust. *"I don't know,"* he admitted finally. *"But I'm going to find out. Just... be careful, okay? And call me if anything strange happens, no matter how small. Understand?"*

"Okay," Kara replied softly. "You be careful too, Jake. Please."

As Jake ended the call, he felt a mix of emotions - concern for Kara and Haley, anger at Malone's deception, and a growing sense of dread. Whatever dark forces were at work in Hale County, they were escalating their activities. And Jake had a sinking feeling that this was just the beginning.

He quickly got dressed, wincing as his battered body protested every movement. The events at the hospital had left him bruised and exhausted, but there was no time to rest. Not with Malone up to something at the school.

As Jake strapped on his gun and badge, he glanced at the guest room where Laurel was sleeping. He debated waking her, but decided against it. She needed the rest, and he wasn't sure he could trust her completely yet. She would be pissed at him when she woke up. This was police business, after all. Jake scribble out a message and laid it next to her phone, explaining what he could and apologizing, telling her he would be back soon.

Grabbing his keys, Jake headed out into the misty morning. As he climbed into his truck, he couldn't shake the feeling that he was walking into something far more dangerous than he could imagine. But he had no choice. The people of Hale County were counting on him, whether they knew it or not.

With a deep breath, Jake started the engine and pulled out of his driveway, ready to face whatever darkness awaited him at the school.

Marcus slid his Crown Vic into an empty parking space near the courthouse. Char, driving a brand-new cobalt blue Charger, took the space right next to his. As a matter-of-fact it was dealer's choice on parking as the town looked eerily vacant. *What the hell is happening*, he wondered in disbelief. Marcus popped open his umbrella, moved to Char's car, waited for her to exit, and hurriedly led them to the front doors of the old courthouse.

"Where is everyone?" Charlotte whispered as they reached the doors. "It's election day. There should be lines of voters, campaign volunteers..."

Marcus shook his head, a knot forming in his stomach. "I don't know. Something's very wrong here."

They entered the courthouse, footsteps echoing in the empty marble foyer. A lone security guard sat at the desk, looking bored and slightly nervous.

"Morning," Marcus called out, forcing a smile. "We're here to vote. Where's the polling station set up?"

The guard blinked at them; confusion evident on his face. "Voting? There's no voting today, sir. Election's been postponed, so has Halloween. My son is gonna be pissed."

Marcus felt as if he'd been punched in the gut. "Postponed? On whose authority?"

"Mayor's office put out the order last night," the guard replied. "Said there was some kind of security threat. Polls are closed until further notice. Strange incidents been happening all over town. Ain't you heard?"

"This isn't right," Marcus muttered, pulling open the heavy wooden door to the interior of the courthouse. "There should be voters, poll workers, protestors even. Where is everyone?"

Charlotte frowned. "Shouldn't the judge be here by now?"

Marcus nodded, a knot forming in his stomach. He rapped loudly on the door to the judge's chambers, the sound echoing in the empty square behind them. After a moment, they heard shuffling from inside. The door creaked open just enough for them to see Judge Hawthorne's worried face.

"Marcus, Charlotte," the judge whispered urgently, "get inside, quickly."

They slipped through the narrow opening, and Judge Hawthorne immediately bolted the door behind them. Inside, the courthouse was dimly lit and eerily quiet. A small group of poll workers huddled near the center of the room; their faces etched with fear.

"What's going on?" Marcus demanded. "Why aren't the polls open?"

Judge Hawthorne ran a trembling hand through his silver hair. "There's been... incidents. All over town. The mayor's declared a state of emergency. He's postponed the election indefinitely."

Marcus felt a surge of anger. "He can't do that! It's election day!"

"He can and he has," the judge replied grimly. "Said it's for public safety. But something's not right, Marcus. This feels... wrong."

Charlotte stepped forward, her eyes narrowing. "What kind of incidents?"

Before the judge could answer, the courthouse phone rang, startling everyone. Judge Hawthorne hurried to answer it, his face growing paler with each passing second.

"Dear God," he whispered as he hung up. He turned to face the group, his eyes wide with shock. "There's been an attack at the school. And reports of... of citizens just missing from their homes."

Marcus and Charlotte exchanged alarmed glances. This was worse than they had imagined. Whatever dark forces were at work in Hale County, they were making their move now.

"We need to do something," Marcus said firmly. "We can't let them steal this election and terrorize the town."

Charlotte nodded in agreement. "But we need to be smart about this. If what the judge says is true, we're dealing with something far beyond normal politics."

As they stood there, trying to formulate a plan, a commotion outside caught their attention. Through the courthouse windows, they saw a group of figures emerging from the mist, moving with an unnatural gait towards the building and then just as suddenly disappearing.

Judge Hawthorne's face went ashen. "What was, who, there was" he stammered. "You gotta save me, Marcus," the judge whispered hoarsely.

Marcus felt a chill run down his spine as he watched the judge lose his sanity before their eyes. He stepped towards the trembling judge, trying to project a calm he didn't feel. "Judge Hawthorne, we need to focus. What exactly did you see out there?"

The older man's eyes were wild with fear. "Shadows... moving on their own. And faces... terrible faces in the mist. They're coming for us, Marcus. They know we're here!"

Charlotte moved to the window, peering out cautiously. The street outside was eerily empty, shrouded in a thick fog that seemed to writhe and shift unnaturally. "I don't see anything now, but... there's something off about that mist."

Marcus felt torn. Part of him wanted to dismiss the judge's ravings as the product of stress and fear, but after everything he'd learned from Jake and Charlotte, he couldn't ignore the possibility that there was real danger lurking outside.

"Okay, here's what we're going to do," Marcus said, taking charge of the situation. "We need to get in touch with Sheriff Hooks. If there's been an attack at the school, he'll be investigating. And we need to find a way to get word out to the citizens about what's really going on with this election."

One of the poll workers, a middle-aged woman named Susan, spoke up hesitantly. "I might be able to help with that. My son works at the local radio station. If we can get there, we could broadcast a message to the whole county."

Marcus nodded approvingly. "Good thinking, Susan. Charlotte, can you try to reach Jake while I work on getting us safely to that radio station?"

As Charlotte pulled out her phone, Judge Hawthorne grabbed Marcus's arm. "You don't understand," he hissed. "The mayor... he's not who you think he is. He's in league with them!"

"With who, Judge?" Marcus asked, growing increasingly concerned about the man's mental state.

"The shadows," Hawthorne whispered, his eyes darting around the room. "The ones who've always been here, waiting. They're waking up, Marcus. And they're hungry."

Marcus stared at the elder judge for a moment, hardly believing what he was hearing. It was nonsensical, superstitious, children's stories. "Sir, surely you, of all people, don't believe that. Whoever is behind this wants us in a state of panic for sure, but make no mistake, they are just human."

The judge looked at him with pity, which took Marcus by surprise and made him feel small, like an adult trying to explain basic concepts to a newborn. "Son, this county has a history, a very complicated, dark history, hidden by our founders. Most people here have no idea of the terrible past that formed this town, this county. We were arrogant. We tried to hide it, tried to bury our failings and our shortcomings. It was believed if we removed all traces from the public, we could effectively close that door, bar our past from returning. We were wrong."

A chill ran down Marcus's spine at the judge's words. He was about to press for more information when Charlotte interrupted.

"Jake's not answering," she reported grimly.

Marcus took a deep breath, trying to process all the information and formulate a plan. "Alright, here's what we're going to do. We'll split into two groups. Charlotte, you take Susan and try to get to that radio station. The people need to know what's happening. I'll take Judge Hawthorne and head to the school to meet up with Jake. Maybe together we can figure out what the hell is really going on in this town."

Charlotte stepped forward, her voice low and urgent. "We need to barricade the doors and windows. Whatever's out there, we can't let it in."

Marcus nodded, springing into action. "Everyone, help us move these desks and filing cabinets. Block every entrance!"

As they worked to secure the courthouse, Marcus's mind raced. This had to be connected to the mayor's sudden postponement of the election. But how? And why?

Just as they finished barricading the main entrance, a loud bang echoed through the building. Everyone froze.

"What was that?" one of the poll workers whispered.

Another bang, louder this time. It was coming from the back of the courthouse.

"They're trying to get in," Charlotte hissed.

Marcus looked around frantically, searching for a weapon, anything they could use to defend themselves. His eyes landed on the American flag standing in the corner. He grabbed it, wielding the pole like a staff.

"Everyone, stay together," he ordered. "We're going to make our way to the basement. There's an old tunnel down there that leads out of town. It's our best chance."

As they moved towards the stairs, the banging intensified. The sound of splintering wood filled the air.

"They're breaking through!" Judge Hawthorne cried.

Marcus gripped the flagpole tighter, positioning himself between the group and the source of the noise. "Char, lead them down. I'll hold them off as long as I can."

Charlotte hesitated, her eyes meeting his. In that moment, all the years of friendship and unspoken feelings passed between them. "Be careful," she whispered before ushering the others towards the basement.

Marcus stood alone in the darkened courthouse, his heart pounding as he faced the unknown threat. Whatever came through that door, he was determined to protect the people of Hale County - even if it cost him everything.

The wood of the back door splintered and cracked. Marcus raised the flagpole, ready to strike as the door finally gave way.

Laurel took a swig of beer, standing on Jake's front porch, as she desperately tried to get a signal on her phone. She wasn't happy about waking up to find Jake gone without her, although she was appreciative of the rest. He wrote something about an incident at the school. Coincidental? Highly doubtful. She would Uber back into town, *if only I could get a damn signal long enough to make a fucking call*, she thought irritably.

A nice Dodge truck drove by the house, put on its brakes, and slowly backed up, coming to a stop not a hundred feet from where she stood on the porch. Laurel was immediately on alert at the suddenness of the stop. The driver's side door quickly opened to reveal a native man in a cowboy hat, dressed somewhat nicely in a deputy outfit that wasn't too different from Hale County's deputies, exit and hurry towards her.

"Hello," he called out as he approached her, "Do you know where Jake is at the moment?"

Laurel eyed the man warily, her guard up. "I'm afraid I don't know exactly where Jake is at the moment. He left earlier to investigate some incident at the school. Who did you say you were again?"

The man stopped at the bottom of the porch steps, sensing her caution. He held up his hands in a placating gesture. "Dan Roundtree. I'm the elected leader of the Cherokee reservation nearby. Jake and I go way back. There's something urgent I need to discuss with him."

Laurel's investigative instincts kicked in. "Laurel Richardson, I'm a journalist. What kind of urgent matter? Does it have anything to do with what happened at the hospital last night?"

Dan's eyes widened slightly. "You know about that? Were you there?"

Laurel nodded slowly. "I was. Saw things I still can't explain. Strange people, like they were on those synthetic drugs that make you damn near impervious to pain, and sanity."

Dan's expression grew grim. "Then you've seen it too. The darkness that's awakening in Hale County."

"What do you mean, 'awakening'?" Laurel asked, her curiosity piqued.

Dan glanced around nervously before lowering his voice, forcing himself to say the crazy part out loud. "There are forces at work here, ancient and malevolent. My people have known about them for generations, but now... now they're stirring. And I fear it's only the beginning."

Laurel felt a chill run down her spine. "Forces?"

"I know how it sounds," Dan said understandingly, "but if I were to say what I really believe you would no doubt have me locked up. I know I would."

Laurel studied him for a moment, "What can we do?"

"First, we need to find Jake," Dan said firmly. "He needs to know what's coming. And we need to warn the town."

Laurel made a quick decision. "I was about to head into town myself but I can't get a damn signal. Why don't you give me a ride? We can look for Jake together."

Dan nodded, relief evident on his face. "Gladly. But we need to be careful. Phones are down all over. The shadows have eyes everywhere." It was Dan's turn to study her. "Richardson? You're that other lady reporter's family?"

Laurel acknowledged with a slight nod, "Sisters."

"I am truly sorry for your loss," he said sincerely.

"You think these events are related..." she said, more statement than question.

"Don't you?"

As they hurried to Dan's truck, Laurel couldn't shake the feeling that she was stepping into something far bigger and more dangerous than she had ever imagined. But she was determined to see it through, for her sister's sake and for the truth.

The truck's engine roared to life, and they set off towards town, the mist swirling ominously around them as they drove into an uncertain future.

Book 3: Oncoming Storm

Isaiah 54, 'No weapon formed against thee shall prosper.'"

CHAPTER 17

I'm a scientist.

That thought kept rumbling through Evan Michaels head, trying to cut through the fog that weighed down his independent thought. That fog, swirling through his senses, subjugating his clarity, his control. It was as if he was experiencing everything in third person through a hazy filter. He had been at home, happy for the first time in ages, he and JC finally on good terms and then...

...then what, he thought manically, *what happened to me...*

His hands were working rapidly, combining additive after additive to a strange fogger contraption that looked like one of those old pesticide containers, they used to drive through town to kill all the mosquitos and bugs when he was younger. But, while he knew he was doing it, he wasn't purposefully guiding his body. He was a puppet to a master that could tap into his psyche. How had he given over that type of influence?

Dr. Evan Michaels struggled against the fog clouding his mind, desperately trying to regain control of his own body. He watched helplessly as his hands continued to mix chemicals and adjust the strange fogger device. Part of him recognized the components - a potent combination of hallucinogens, stimulants, and other mind-altering substances. But the formula was unlike anything he'd ever created before.

"What am I doing?" he mumbled, his voice sounding distant and unfamiliar to his own ears.

A dark chuckle echoed through his mind in response. "You're fulfilling your purpose, Doctor. Just as you were always meant to."

Evan's blood ran cold at the inhuman voice invading his thoughts. He tried to stop his hands, to step away from the device, but his body refused to obey.

"Who are you?" Evan demanded, panic rising in his chest. "What have you done to me?"

"We are not of this plane, we are from that next place, the one that runs parallel to this one, banished so long ago that our existence has been relegated to myth and lore, mere children's stories." the voice replied, dripping with malice. "But you, Doctor, are our instrument, the author of a new history for our people. Your brilliance will usher in a new era of life."

Flashes of memory assaulted Evan's mind - secret meetings in shadowy rooms, arcane rituals performed in the bowels of the asylum, a contract signed in blood. He had willingly given himself over to these forces, blinded by ambition and the promise of unlimited power. He saw brilliant dots of light in the shadows of the room, blurry movement he couldn't quite fixate on.

"No," Evan whispered, horrified by the realization. "This isn't what I wanted. I'm a scientist, not a... not a monster. I just wanted to heal."

"But you ARE healing, doctor. You are healing a wrong that is thousands of years old," the voice hissed then became all too familiar as Samantha stepped out of the shadows to guide his hands, the hissing voice becoming that of the lover he had known for years. "The process has already begun. Soon, lover, all of Hale County will be under our control. And you, Doctor, will be remembered as the architect of our rebirth."

Evan wanted to reel away in anguish and betrayal, but his hands finished the final adjustments on the fogger. He watched in stunned horror as his body moved of its own accord, hefting the device and heading towards the door.

"Please," he begged, tears streaming down his face. "Don't make me do this. Think of my son, of all the innocent people..."

The blonde, leggy nurse laughed cruelly. "With change comes suffering. And your precious son? He has a special role to play in all of this."

"No!" Evan cried out, summoning every ounce of willpower he possessed. For a brief moment, he felt his fingers loosen on the fogger. But the reprieve was short-lived.

"Foolish human," she snarled. "You cannot resist us."

An agonizing pain ripped through Evan's skull, driving him to his knees. When he stood again, his eyes were blank and lifeless.

"I'm a scientist," he muttered again, clinging to that identity like a lifeline. "This isn't me. I don't do this."

But even as he said the words, a part of him knew they weren't entirely true. He had done things, terrible things, in the name of science and progress. The experiments, the unethical trials, pushing the boundaries of what was possible - and legal. Had he gone too far? Opened a door that should have remained closed?

A chill ran down his spine as he remembered snippets of conversations with his dead friend, warnings he had ignored:

"The human mind isn't meant to be tampered with like this, Evan."

"You're meddling with forces you don't understand."

"There are some lines that shouldn't be crossed."

But he had crossed them, hadn't he? In his arrogance, his quest for knowledge and recognition, he had ignored the risks. And now something dark and ancient was using him, puppet-mastering his body to carry out its sinister plans.

The fogger device hummed to life, a sickly dark mist beginning to seep from its nozzle. Evan wanted to scream, to smash the machine, to run far away from this nightmare. But his body wouldn't obey.

Instead, he found himself walking towards the window, the fogger in hand. Outside, he could see figures moving in the mist - patients and staff, their movements jerky and unnatural. They too were under the influence of whatever malevolent force had taken hold of the institute.

As Evan watched in horror, unable to stop himself, he opened the window and began to spray the dark mist into the air. It mingled with the natural fog, creating swirling patterns that seemed almost alive

"What have I done?" Evan whispered, a single tear rolling down his cheek as he realized the full extent of his role in unleashing this darkness upon the people of Hale County. "Samantha, you have to stop this. This isn't you."

The woman turned and with unnatural strength snatched him by the back of his collar, easily pulling him from his feet. The doctor had no time to react before he was being drug deeper into the underground maze below the asylum, a section he hadn't seen in years. He heard the sound of an old door creek open, felt his body lift into the air, then crash against the far wall, dazing him and knocking the wind from his lungs.

As he struggled for breath, he felt Samantha's warm touch on his cheek, saw her eyes bore kindly into his. When she spoke her voice was full of empathy, the woman he remembered. "Evan," she whimpered in fear, "you're right…"

The doctor watched the abject sorrow on her face twist into an unrivaled coldness, her grip tightening on his jaw as she slowly twisted his head away from her. "…I'm not Samantha…that is…"

Evan's eyes locked on the frail husk of a woman, slumped in a corner. Their eyes met. He knew those eyes, that hair. Their gazes locked. Samantha's were a mixture of regret and resignation; Evan's were of horror and confusion. But if that was Samantha...

The imposter released her grip on him and casually strolled to where the real Samantha lay whimpering. Evan could only watch in disbelief as the imposter knelt down to the real Samantha and pulled her face close. Evan had seen terror before, but nothing that had ever matched the look in Samantha's gaunt face.

"Her life force is almost empty," imposter Samantha spoke hungrily. She pressed her lips to the real Samantha's. The nurse's eyes rolled into the back of her head as her body seemed to cave in on itself. Her empty husk fell to the floor with a dry, dull finality. The imposter then turned to Evan, its oversized smile of needle-like teeth sending a shiver of dread throughout his body. The fake nurse walked past Evan and to the cell door. It paused to speak to the doctor as it grabbed the handle. The imposter's head twisted unnaturally to meet his disbelieving stare. "Feasting on your essence is far more fun..." it hissed as she locked the door behind her, leaving the doctor to revel in his own fear.

The mayor descended deeper into the tunnels beneath his home, feeling the barrier between worlds grow thinner with each step. Specks of otherworldly power shimmered in the air around him, bleeding through from the realm of Tír na nÓg.

He smiled grimly, knowing the time was nearly upon them. The human form he inhabited was almost spent, its essence drained to maintain his disguise among the mortals. But it mattered little now. Soon, he and his people would be free.

Tír na nÓg was calling to him. His people, the true Tuatha Dé Danann, would finally be free of their millenias's old prison, not those that claimed its legendary beauty for themselves, leaving the true Sidhe, the Slúagh na Marbh, to dwell in the darkest parts of Tír na nÓg. His people had mastered the ley lines all over the Earth but were still cursed with having to exit through fairy mounds. That was about to change as well.

The tunnels opened into a vast underground chamber; its walls carved with ancient symbols. At the center stood a ring of standing stones, pulsing with eldritch energy. The mayor approached reverently, feeling the pull of his true home.

"Soon, my brothers," he whispered. "Soon we will reclaim what was stolen from us."

He began the final preparations, knowing that with each passing moment, the veil between worlds grew weaker. The dark power of the Slúagh na Marbh would soon engulf Hale County, paving the way for their triumphant return.

As he worked, the mayor's thoughts turned to the humans above, blissfully unaware of the fate that awaited them. A cruel smile twisted his lips. Their ignorance would be their undoing. Ironically, it was the human's thirst for understanding that made it all possible. The doctor he had groomed, devastated by the loss of his precious wife, was driven beyond reason to find a cure, to delve into the untapped truth of the human mind and unlock secrets that humanity was far to ill-equipped to understand.

Humans were easily manipulated, the seat of their undoing lay within their own hubris, the self-centered need to satisfy their greedy appetites. A poke here, a prod there and just like that the most meager among them became the most dangerous.

Geoffrey suddenly appeared by his side. "Lord Bres," the wily butler began, "we are nearing completion. The spells and wards are all but completed, we need only the last trinket to begin. Samhain is upon us."

The mayor, now revealed as Lord Bres of the Slúagh na Marbh, nodded grimly at Geoffrey's words. "Excellent. And what of our human pawns? Are they playing their parts as planned?"

Geoffrey's lips curled into a cruel smile. "Indeed, my lord. The doctor continues to spread our influence through his infernal device. The sheriff and his allies scramble in confusion, unaware of the true threat that looms. And the would-be savior of this pitiful town? He walks right into our trap."

Lord Bres chuckled darkly. "Marcus Thompson. Such potential, wasted on these mortals. He may yet serve a greater purpose in our new world."

As they spoke, the air in the chamber grew heavy with otherworldly energy. The standing stones hummed with power, casting eerie shadows that seemed to move of their own accord.

"What of the final piece?" Lord Bres asked, his voice tinged with anticipation.

Geoffrey's expression turned serious. "It is nearly within our grasp, my lord. However, the girl, Haley Bennett, possesses the innate power we need to complete the ritual. Her mother's protective instincts have made acquiring her... challenging. But not for much longer."

Lord Bres nodded; his eyes gleaming with malevolent purpose. "See that it is done, Geoffrey. The veil grows thin, and Samhain approaches. We must not fail when we are so close to our goal."

As Geoffrey bowed and retreated into the shadows, Lord Bres turned his attention back to the ancient stones. He could feel the pull of Tír na nÓg growing stronger, the whispers of his kin echoing in his mind.

"Soon," he murmured, running his hand along the cold surface of the nearest stone. "Soon we will reclaim what was taken from us. The banished will have a new kingdom to rule, and this world will know the true meaning of fear."

The chamber trembled slightly, as if in response to his words. In the tunnels above, dark shapes began to coalesce, drawn by the promise of freedom and the scent of mortal fear. The Slúagh na Marbh were stirring, ready to unleash their vengeance upon an unsuspecting world.

As Lord Bres began the final preparations for the ritual, he allowed himself a moment of dark triumph. Centuries of planning, of manipulating events from the shadows, had led to this moment. The humans of Hale County had no idea that their quaint little town sat upon a nexus of otherworldly power - or that their lives and souls would soon fuel the rebirth of a long-forgotten race.

Jake moved cautiously down the darkened hallway, his flashlight beam cutting through the shadows. The silence was eerie - no sounds of children or staff, just the faint echo of his own footsteps.

When he had arrived the first thing his noticed were the glass security doors ripped from their hinges. Chief Malone and his officers were mulling around outside, doing nothing other than talking to the principal and teachers who had found the situation in the building.

“What's the situation,” Jake asked Malone without preamble.

“Cleaning up your mess, as usual,” Malone quipped sarcastically, as he was writing something down on a pad.

But this was NOT the day. Without so much as a warning Jake backhanded the notebook away from the surprised Chief of Police and stepped-up nose-to-nose with a growl, "I don't have time for your shit, Eddie, not today. What's the fucking situation?"

Malone took a surprised step back in shock, realizing he had pushed the sheriff one step too far. He tried regaining his composure, but he knew he was about to cross a bridge he had no desire to be on. "Easy, Jake, just trying to lighten the mood with all the hell breaking loose. We aren't sure. We haven't gone in. We DO know there were a handful of children and some teachers inside."

Jake glared at him, "but you haven't gone in to check."

Malone, usually one for snarky banter, only shook his head, face turning red. "We couldn't be sure of the structure's durability. I mean, look at it, it looks like a tornado hit it. There were no reports of high winds this morning. You're the lead. This is a county school."

That had never stopped him before. Something else was going on here. Chief Malone's discomfort was palpable. Jake simply nodded and took out his gun and his flashlight, all the power to the building was out. "My deputies are on the way. Fill them in for me. I can't wait, not if there are children in there."

Jake moved cautiously down the darkened hallway, his flashlight beam cutting through the shadows. The silence was eerie - no sounds of children or staff, just the faint echo of his own footsteps.

As he rounded a corner, Jake froze. The beam of his flashlight illuminated a scene of utter chaos. Desks and chairs were overturned, papers strewn across the floor. But it was the strange, dark substance splattered on the walls that made his blood run cold. It looked like blood, but something about its consistency was... off.

Jake approached slowly, his senses on high alert. As he approached one of the stains, he noticed it seemed to be... moving. Tiny tendrils writhed and pulsed, as if the substance was alive.

"What the hell..." Jake muttered, reaching out to touch it.

Suddenly, a child's scream pierced the silence. Jake whirled around; gun raised. The sound had come from further down the hall.

Without hesitation, Jake sprinted towards the source of the cry. He burst through a classroom door, flashlight sweeping the room.

In the far corner, a young girl cowered behind an overturned desk. Her eyes were wide with terror as she stared at something Jake couldn't see.

"It's okay," Jake said softly, approaching slowly. "I'm here to help. What's your name?"

The girl's gaze snapped to him. "Emily," she whispered. "Please, you have to run. They'll get you too!"

"Who, Emily? Who will get me?"

Emily opened her mouth to reply, but her words were drowned out by an inhuman shriek from the hallway. Jake spun around, positioning himself between Emily and the door.

What he saw emerging from the darkness made his blood run cold. It was vaguely humanoid, but its proportions were all wrong - limbs too long, joints bending at impossible angles and yet it was shadowlike, wispy yet solid. But the teeth, those jagged arrowhead-like teeth were plenty real.

Jake aimed his gun at the monstrous figure, his mind reeling at the impossibility of what he was seeing. The creature's form seemed to shift and waver, as if it wasn't fully anchored in reality.

"Emily, stay behind me," Jake ordered, his voice steady despite the fear gripping his heart.

The creature let out another bone-chilling shriek and lunged forward with inhuman speed. Jake fired twice, the muzzle flashes briefly illuminating the classroom. But the bullets seemed to pass right through the shadowy form.

"It doesn't work!" Emily cried out. "Nothing hurts them! When the lights come on, they go away!"

She was right, every time his flashlight beam hit it or his muzzle flashed it would simply evaporate and appear elsewhere. Jake grabbed Emily's hand and pulled her towards the door. "Run!" he shouted, firing again to buy them time.

They sprinted down the hallway, the sound of the creature's pursuit echoing behind them. Jake's mind raced, trying to process what he was dealing with. This was beyond anything he had ever encountered; beyond anything he thought possible.

"In here," he said, pulling Emily into a nearby classroom. He quickly barricaded the door with desks and chairs. He grabbed his mic from his collar, "Bru, get me a damn generator to the school, now!"

"What are those things?" Jake asked Emily, trying to catch his breath.

The girl's eyes were wide with terror. "They came with the fog," she whispered. "They... they took the others. I hid, but I could hear them screaming."

Jake's blood ran cold. "The others? How many people were in the school?"

"A few teachers and some kids, maybe, maybe twelve," Emily replied, her voice shaking. "We were here early for a special Halloween program. Then the fog came, and... and those things..."

A loud bang on the door cut her off. The barricade shuddered under the impact. Apparently, they could disappear but not go through solid objects. That, at least, was good news. The sheriff quickly surveyed his surroundings, he was in a history classroom and the teacher obviously loved antiques. He spotted an old iron axe on the wall and snatched it down.

Jake gripped the old fire axe tightly, positioning himself between Emily and the door. "Stay behind me," he ordered. "When I say run, you run. Don't look back, just get out of the building. Understand?"

Emily nodded, tears streaming down her face.

The door splintered as the creature burst through. Jake swung the axe with all his might, feeling a moment of resistance as it connected with the shadowy form. The creature let out an unearthly wail, recoiling as if it had been doused in acid.

"Run!" Jake shouted.

As Emily darted past him, Jake swung the axe again, only slightly connecting but still causing a wild reaction from the thing. But he knew he couldn't hold it off forever. Whatever these things were, they were unlike anything he had ever faced before.

The creature was injured, keeping its distance. From deep in the school, he could hear more coming, banging up against lockers. With one last swing, Jake turned and sprinted after Emily, praying they could make it out of this nightmare alive.

Jake raced down the hallway after Emily, the iron axe clutched tightly in his hand. He could hear more of the shadowy creatures converging on their position, inhuman shrieks echoing through the school.

"Almost there," Jake called out encouragingly to Emily as they neared the main entrance.

Suddenly, a dark shape materialized in front of them, blocking their path. Emily screamed as Jake skidded to a halt, raising the axe defensively. He could hear the sounds of pursuit echoing behind them, inhuman shrieks mixed with the clatter of overturned furniture.

Jake pulled Emily close to him. They were so close. Another shadow creature popped up beside the one in front of them, then another. There was no way through.

"Sheriff! We've got the generator hooked up!"

Relief flooded through him. "Emily, cover your eyes!" he warned as he threw open the doors.

Bright floodlights illuminated the school grounds, cutting through the unnatural fog. The shadowy creatures pursuing them let out piercing wails of agony as the light touched them, their forms dissipating like smoke.

Jake scooped up Emily and sprinted towards the safety of the police barricade. As they reached it, he set the girl down gently and turned back to face the school.

In the harsh light, he could see dark shapes retreating into the building's shadows. Whatever these things were, they couldn't stand the light.

"Keep those lights on!" Jake barked to his deputies. "And get some more generators here ASAP. We need to light up every inch of this place."

As paramedics rushed to check on Emily, Jake took a moment to catch his breath. His mind raced, trying to make sense of what he had just experienced. This was beyond anything he had ever encountered as a sheriff. But one thing was clear - the threat was real, and it was spreading. Jake knew he needed answers, and he needed them fast.

The sheriff shot a look at Bru. "Where is Rodney," he asked with an exasperated sigh, already knowing the response.

Bru shut his eyes, pissed that Rodney had once again put him in this situation, then looked directly at this boss, "he's at the asylum."

The sheriff dug a heel into the ground, forcing his anger elsewhere. Now wasn't the time. With grim determination, Jake turned to his deputies. "Alright, listen up. We've got a situation here unlike anything we've ever faced. We have missing children and teachers inside. Approximately twelve. Fan out, sweep pattern, two by two. Call out as you clear each space. Do NOT leave your partner's side. Got it?"

Each deputy nodded in the affirmative. "Alright, let's go!"

The deputies wasted no time plunging into the school. Jake turned to the principal and asked him about Chief Malone.

"He, he…he bugged out as soon as you went inside the school. Took his men and said he was needed on another matter," the shocked man managed to spit out.

Jake just shook his head, clutched the axe, and prepared to go back into the school when the screeching of tires caught his attention. "Awww, god, now what?"

The familiar truck skidded to a halt only a few feet away. Dan and Laurel practically leapt from the truck and quickly joined him, both faces wondering the exact same thing, *what in the hell was going on?*

Jake quickly filled Dan and Laurel in on the situation - the shadowy creatures in the school, the missing children and teachers, and how light seemed to repel the entities.

"This is worse than I feared," Dan said grimly. "The old stories speak of shadow beings that prey on the living, but I never thought..."

"You're saying you've heard of these things before?" Jake asked incredulously.

Dan nodded. "My people have legends of dark spirits that emerge when the veil between worlds grows thin. But they were just stories - or so I thought."

Laurel's eyes widened. "The veil between worlds? Dan, what exactly are we dealing with here?"

Before Dan could respond, one of Jake's deputies called out from inside the school:

"Sheriff! We found something - you need to see this!"

Jake exchanged a look with Dan and Laurel. "Stay close," he warned as they headed back into the building.

The deputy led them to a classroom on the second floor. Inside, Jake's breath caught in his throat. Symbols were carved into the walls and floor, forming an intricate pattern. In the center lay a small object - slightly bigger than a child's marble, glowing with an eerie light.

"What is this? That looks familiar." Jake muttered, crouching down to examine the scene.

Laurel nodded in agreement, "almost like the one we found on that Jason guy."

Dan's face had gone pale. "That's a Cherokee Marble within a summoning circle," he said quietly. "Someone deliberately opened a doorway for those creatures."

"Those marbles are magic?" Laurel asked in surprise.

"No," Dan replied, "they are simply marbles created by our people as a game." It suddenly hit Dan, "those marbles are made from stone, from the earth. They could be used as a spiritual conductor if one knew the way."

Jake stood; his expression grim. "Then we need to find out who - and why. Because this is just the beginning, isn't it?"

Dan nodded solemnly. "I'm afraid so, Sheriff. Whatever's happening in Hale County, it's far bigger than any of us realized."

As they contemplated the implications, Bru's voice crackled over the radio, *"Boss, we found the missing people, but you're gonna want to see this. Something ain't right."*

Jake, Dan, and Laurel exchanged worried glances before hurrying to follow Bru's voice. As they made their way through the eerily quiet hallways, Jake's grip tightened on the iron axe. The bright lights from the generators kept the shadows at bay, but he couldn't shake the feeling that they were being watched.

They found Bru and another deputy standing outside the school's gymnasium. The look on Bru's face told Jake that whatever was inside wasn't going to be pleasant.

"What have we got?" Jake asked, bracing himself.

Bru shook his head grimly. "It's... you need to see for yourself, boss."

Jake nodded and pushed open the gym doors. The sight that greeted them made Laurel gasp and Dan mutter a prayer under his breath.

The missing children and teachers were there, but they were... changed. They stood in a perfect circle, their eyes vacant and unseeing. By all accounts they were perfectly fine and unharmed, yet they just stood there, like statues, unmoving.

"Dear God," Laurel whispered, her hand flying to her mouth.

Dan stepped closer; his expression grim. "The shadows have taken hold of them," he said softly. "We need to act fast if we hope to save them."

Jake turned to his deputy. "Bru, get the paramedics in here now. And tell them to bring every light source they can find."

As Bru hurried off, Jake crouched down in front of one of the children, a young boy no older than ten. "Can you hear me?" he asked gently.

The boy's head snapped up, his eyes suddenly focusing on Jake with an intensity that made the sheriff's blood run cold. When he spoke, his voice was not his own.

"The veil grows thin," the boy intoned, his words echoing with an otherworldly resonance. "The Slúagh na Marbh will rise again."

"The Slúagh na Marbh?" Jake asked in confusion. "What is that," he asked the boy, putting a comforting hand on the kid's shoulder. But as he did the axe accidentally bumped against the child's skin, causing him to roar in pain and pull away from the sheriff. The spot where he had been touched by the axe was hissing and smoking. "Just like the shadows..." he mumbled, staring at the weapon in his hand. "Iron...," he said, looking at Dan.

The elder Chief's eyes widened in disbelief. He reached out for the axe, which Jake handed over and studied it a moment. He looked to the Sheriff, then to Laurel, "I know this..." Suddenly, and without warning, Dan arched the axe through the air as people began screaming in realization and buried it in the skull of the boy.

"Dan, no!" Jake shouted, lunging forward. But it was too late.

The axe connected with a sickening thud, burying itself in the boy's skull. Jake braced himself for the horrific aftermath, but what happened next defied all logic.

Instead of blood and gore, a dark, oily substance erupted from the wound. It writhed and twisted in the air, letting out an otherworldly shriek that made everyone's ears ring. The boy's body turned a sickly greenish grey then shrunk in on itself like liquified clay and melted to the ground, lifeless.

"What the hell?!" Jake exclaimed, stumbling backward.

Dan stood firm, his face a mask of grim determination. "It wasn't a boy anymore, Jake. These creatures, they're using human bodies as vessels. Changelings. They take the place of their victims, copying them in every way. Taking over their lives while the victims are spirited away elsewhere. We have to stop them before they can fully manifest in our world."

Laurel's face had gone pale. "So, all of these people... they're already gone?"

"They could be anyone," Jake said in a whisper. "If that boy was a changeling then..."

They all turned at once to see the rest of the children and teachers staring at them, their mouths forming abnormally large, grotesque smiles full of jagged teeth.

Laurel grabbed a discarded baseball bat, gripping it tightly as she stood beside Dan.

"If we survive this," she said through gritted teeth, "you and I are going to have a long talk about everything you know."

Dan managed to smile grimly. "Assuming we live, I'll tell you everything."

Marcus wasn't sure how long he had been fighting off the shadow people, but it felt like an eternity. His arms felt heavy, like he could barely lift them. The others had made it to the door that lead outside but Marcus didn't dare turn his back to his pursuers. Something innately told him it was a bad idea, as though the glimpses he caught of unnaturally shaped and elongated teeth hadn't already convinced him. *But why hadn't they just overpowered me*, he thought.

Marcus's arms burned as he swung the flagpole again, keeping the shadowy figures at bay. Their inhuman shrieks echoed through the courthouse, sending chills down his spine. He could hear Charlotte and the others fumbling with the door behind him, trying to escape.

"Hurry!" he shouted, not daring to take his eyes off the writhing mass of darkness before him.

The shadows seemed to pulse and shift, tendrils of inky blackness reaching out towards him. But each time they got close, Marcus would swing the flagpole, and they would recoil with an unearthly wail.

It was then that Marcus noticed something odd. Despite their overwhelming numbers and apparent strength, the shadow creatures weren't pressing their advantage. They kept their distance, testing his defenses but never fully committing to an attack.

"They're afraid," he realized with a start. But of what?

Marcus glanced down at the flagpole in his hands. It was at least a century old, made of solid oak with old iron fittings. Could it be...?

"It's the wood!" he called out to the others. "Or the metal, or both - they don't like it!"

Marcus's mind raced. They were trapped, but he had inadvertently discovered a weapon against these things. If they could just hold out long enough...

"Come on!" he shouted, his voice hoarse. "Is that all you've got?"

He could feel the pull of something sinister teasing the back of his mind, as if trying to tempt him into their waiting embrace.

Marcus stood his ground, flagpole raised defensively. "Who are you? What do you want?

As if in response, one of the creatures lunged forward, its claws raking across Marcus's chest. He cried out in pain, stumbling backward. The flagpole slipped from his grasp, clattering to the floor.

Marcus braced himself for the end, but it didn't come. The shadows hesitated, their forms writhing and shifting as if uncertain. That's when Marcus realized - they were afraid of him. Or rather, something about him.

He quickly picked up the pole, held it up, and quickly thrust it forward like he was jousting. He felt the tip hit something solid. The shadows recoiled, hissing in what sounded like pain and anger.

Marcus didn't waste any time. He pulled back the flagpole and ran for the exit, praying the others had made it to safety. As he burst through the doors into the misty morning air, he saw Charlotte and the rest of the group huddled near Dan Roundtree's truck.

"Marcus!" Charlotte cried out, relief evident in her voice. "Thank God you're alright!"

Before he could respond, the sound of screeching tires filled the air. A police cruiser skidded to a halt nearby, and Chief Malone leapt out, his face a mask of barely contained panic.

"Thompson!" he shouted. "We've got a situation at the school. Shadow creatures, missing kids - it's a goddamn nightmare. Sheriff Hooks is there now, but he needs backup."

Marcus exchanged a look with Charlotte, both of them realizing the gravity of the situation.

He looked at the small crowd of people they had gotten to safety, or what they assumed was safe. "Get to your homes, lock yourselves in." Something else occurred to him, "keep your lights on, they don't seem to want to be seen." He then turned to the judge, "you're with us, I need some answers of some kind."

Wraith ran through the forest, chasing the strange creature it had been fighting. Katie wanted the bad man gone and he would be. Her voice was like an echo chamber in his mind, begging, pleading, demanding. *Wraith*, the thought drifted through his mind while in pursuit, *why was I called that? It's not my name. My name*, the question persisted, *what is my name? Who am I?* He stumbled as the questions shifted his focus.

Daddy, he's getting way, Katie's voice pierced his turmoil.

He refocused on the shadow thing that he somehow knew he couldn't let escape. It had almost killed the man in the field, he could feel its hunger, its wanting.

Wraith shook off his momentary confusion and redoubled his pursuit of the shadowy creature. His bare feet barely made a sound as he raced through the underbrush, leaping over fallen logs and ducking under low-hanging branches with inhuman agility.

The creature ahead of him moved with an unnatural, jerky gait, its form seeming to flicker and shift as it darted between the trees. But Wraith could sense its fear, its desperation to escape.

"No escape," he growled, his voice a guttural rumble that barely sounded human.

As they burst into a small clearing, Wraith saw his chance. With a feral roar, he launched himself at the creature, tackling it to the ground. They rolled across the forest floor in a tangle of limbs, the shadow being's cold, oily substance seeping into Wraith's skin where they made contact. As they grappled, flashes of memory assaulted Wraith's mind. A little girl's laughter. A woman's smile. The smell of gunpowder. Blood on his hands.

"Who am I?" Wraith growled through gritted teeth as he struggled with the creature.

The creature's only response was to sink its teeth into Wraith's shoulder. Pain exploded through him, but it was different from anything he'd felt before. It was as if the creature was trying to devour not just his flesh, but his very essence.

Wraith felt a jolt of... something... course through him at the touch. More images flashed through his mind - a dark realm of writhing shadows, ancient rituals performed in secret, a veil between worlds growing thinner.

The creature beneath him let out an unearthly shriek and tried to dissolve into mist, but Wraith's grip remained firm. He could feel Katie's presence in his mind, urging him on, lending him strength.

"End it," Katie's voice whispered. "Before it can hurt anyone else."

Wraith didn't hesitate. His hands found the creature's throat - or what passed for a throat on its amorphous form - and began to squeeze. The shadow being thrashed wildly, its claws raking across Wraith's arms and chest, leaving trails of icy fire in their wake.

But Wraith didn't relent. He poured all of his rage, all of his confusion and pain, into his grip. The creature's form began to waver, then crack like glass under the pressure.

With a final, ear-splitting shriek, the shadow being shattered into a thousand inky fragments that dissipated into the air. Wraith collapsed to his knees, panting heavily.

As the adrenaline faded, the questions came flooding back. Who was he? Why could he do these things? And who was Katie, this presence in his mind that felt so familiar yet so alien?

"You did it," Katie's voice said softly. "You saved them."

Wraith looked down at his hands, which were trembling slightly. "Who am I?" he asked aloud, his voice hoarse and uncertain, the sound of own voice was odd to his ears.

There was a long pause before Katie's voice responded, tinged with sadness. *"You're my daddy. And... and you're a hero."*

Wraith nodded grimly, even as part of him wondered why he was obeying the voice of a child he couldn't remember. But before he could dwell on it, a new scent caught his attention. Human. Familiar.

Without fully understanding why, Wraith began moving through the forest again, drawn towards the source of the scent. Towards answers he both craved and feared.

 As he moved silently through the trees, Wraith's fractured mind tried to piece together the fragments of his identity. He knew he was dangerous - his skills and instincts spoke of years of training and experience. But for what purpose?

A new smell wafted through the air, once again familiar, sending pangs of hunger through him. He finally focused on his surroundings. It was a small clearing with an old cabin. There, on the front porch, a large grill was seeping smoke out of a stack and sitting beside that grill was a short, rotund man in overalls with a grin on his face, sitting in a rocking chair, a lit tobacco pipe clinched between his teeth.

"We have to leave, Daddy..." Katie silently urged him but something in Wraith, something about THIS particular person, stirred something within him, something lost.

The cherub faced man shined a wide-eyed grin at Wraith, "It's about time you found your way home, my friend. Pappy's got some smokin' ones on da grill. But we gotta get you cleaned up," he laughed wildly, "you look like shit."

"Daddy, we have to leave NOW," the girl in his mind proclaimed desperately.

Without consciously meaning to, Wraith found himself moving towards the man, *his friend?* Yes, that was it! A friend. After all this time, someone knew him, someone could help him remember.

With each step he took, Katie's pleas to leave became nothing more than whispers, then silence. For the first time in years, the only voice in his head was his own.

Jason Locke burst into his home, everything was cold and dark. His mind was on fire. Nothing made sense. The blackouts, waking up in odd places, weird memories. The church, what was up with that and the weird pastor. *Reverend*, a strange but familiar voice, spoke in his head. The professor went straight for his liquor cabinet and with trembling hands poured himself a quick shot of cool nasty bourbon.

That...reverend kept calling him William, who the hell was William? He downed another shot, wiping the excess away that had dripped down his chin. His head felt as though it was literally splitting in two. He staggered into the bathroom. What had that reverend said...the marble, *do you have the marble?* Jason tried remembering what happened but couldn't quite grasp the answer. *Let me back in, you're messing it up, always messing it up.*

"William," he said aloud, staring into the bathroom mirror.

Jason stared in shock as his reflection rippled and changed before his eyes. The face looking back at him was both familiar and strange - older, with haunted eyes and a scar running down one cheek.

"I am William," the reflection said, its voice echoing strangely.

Jason stumbled back, his head spinning. "What's happening to me?" he gasped.

The reflection seemed to flicker between his face and the other. "We are fractured," it said. "Torn between worlds. The marble...we must find the marble."

"What marble?" Jason demanded. "Who are you?"

"I am you," the reflection replied. "Or rather, we were once one. But the rituals, the experiments...they shattered us across realities."

Memories flashed through Jason's mind - dark chambers, arcane symbols, searing pain as something was torn from him. He clutched his head, overwhelmed by the conflicting images and sensations.

"No," he moaned. "This isn't real. It can't be."

"But it is," the reflection insisted. "And now the veil grows thin. We must become whole again, or all will be lost."

Jason looked up, meeting the gaze of his other self. "How?" he whispered.

"Find the marble," William urged. "It's the key to everything. When you find it, let me in, I'll take care of it."

With that, the reflection faded, leaving Jason staring at his own pale, shaken face. He gripped the edges of the sink, his mind reeling as he tried to process what he had seen and heard.

One thing was clear - he needed answers. And he knew just where to start looking.

With trembling hands, Jason grabbed his keys and headed for the door. The asylum held secrets; he was sure of it now. And he was going to uncover them, no matter what the cost. But first, he had to get that marble. He remembered the sheriff. He had to find the sheriff. Only then could he make himself whole. He didn't understand why, only that he had no choice if he wanted to live.

CHAPTER 18

Ashlyn's head throbbed as she struggled to open her eyes. Her mind was fuzzy, she tried to remember what had happened to her. As her vision came into focus a wild, coppery flower smell permeated her senses. It was unlike any smell she had ever inhaled, at the same time calming yet suffocating. Then, she heard a voice that make her heart almost stop...the mayor.

Her eyes flew open as the mayor's voice registered. She found herself in a dimly lit room, surrounded by strange symbols etched into the walls. The coppery floral scent was overwhelming. Through barely open eyes, she could make out dark stone walls - some kind of underground chamber.

"Ah, you're awake," the mayor said, his tone oddly cheerful. "I do apologize for the rather... abrupt way we brought you here. But you see, you have a very important role to play."

Ashlyn tried to move, only to find her wrists and ankles bound to a chair. Panic rose in her throat. "What do you want from me?" she demanded, her voice shaking.

The mayor smiled, but it didn't reach his eyes. "It's not about what I want, my dear. It's about what you are. You see, you possess a certain... spark. An energy that is vital to our plans."

As he spoke, Ashlyn noticed movement in the shadows behind him. Figures lurked just out of sight, their forms shifting and writhing unnaturally.

"Our plans?" Ashlyn repeated, her mind racing. "Who are you really?"

The mayor's smile widened, revealing teeth that seemed too sharp, too numerous. "We are the Slúagh na Marbh. The Host of the Dead. And you, my dear, are going to help us reclaim this world."

Ashlyn felt a chill run down her spine as the shadowy figures began to close in around her. She knew then that her life would never be the same again.

The mayor was speaking to someone else, his tone cold and authoritative.

"Is everything prepared for the ritual?" he asked.

"Yes, Lord Bres," came the reply. "We await only the final piece."

Ashlyn fought down a wave of panic. Ritual? Final piece? What were they planning? Lord Bres?

She shifted slightly, trying to get a better view without alerting them to her consciousness. As she did, she felt something digging into her hip - her phone! They hadn't taken it from her. If she could just find a way to contact JC or the sheriff...

And that's when she remembered...JC! The way he looked at her, that, that oversized, evil smile...

The man she knew as mayor seemed to sense her thoughts and motioned across the way.

Ashlyn felt her heart sink as JC appeared, standing next to the man she had known as the mayor. His eyes were cold and empty as he gazed at her, nothing like the warm, loving look she was used to seeing.

"JC," she whispered, "what's going on? What have they done to you?"

Lord Bres chuckled darkly. "I'm afraid your dear JC is no longer with us, at least not in the way you knew him. He serves a greater purpose now."

Ashlyn struggled against her bonds, anger and fear warring within her. "Let him go! Whatever you've done to him, undo it!"

"JC, please," she pleaded softly. "If you're in there somewhere, fight this. I know you can."

"Oh, my dear," Lord Bres said, his voice dripping with false sympathy, "what's done cannot be undone. Perhaps I misspoke, you humans and your overly complicated language. What I mean to say is that this is not the young man you knew. This is a changeling, a part of the Sidhe, a dark fae of my world. He is a better version of your JC, unbound by humanity."

"Are you a demon?" she managed to blurt out.

Lord Bres looked disgusted at the very notion. "Demon? Angels? THIS is why you pathetic mortals don't deserve to live. Your ego! They are from another plane adjacent to this, as MY people are also from a neighboring universe connected to your own. And there are infinitely more, yet you humans and your ignorance only acknowledge Angels and Demons, though you don't believe in them half the time, and relegate MY people to myth and fantasy. There was a time we all shared this plane, but it was bequeathed to YOUR kind," he spat at her, eyes brimming with a rage that shook her to her core, as he stood a hairs breadth away.

Ashlyn couldn't comprehend anything he was saying in her terror; it was all so surreal. This HAD to be madness, some crazed nightmare.

The wiry looking man leaned in, lips only an inch from her ear, and whispered conspiratorially, "oh what pleasures I have to show you…"

JC stepped closer, that unnatural smile still plastered on his face. "Don't fight it, Ashlyn," he said, his voice so familiar yet oddly flat. "It's better this way. You'll see."

Ashlyn recoiled from his touch, tears stinging her eyes. This wasn't her JC. Whatever they had done to him, whatever ritual they were planning, she knew she had to find a way to stop it - not just for her sake, but for JC's as well.

"I'll never be what you want!" she screamed at him angrily.

The changeling simply looked at her with a neutral expression and cocked his head sideways, "but you already are."

From behind Ashlyn another figure appeared and brushed up next to the thing that looked like JC. Her mouth dropped, tears stinging her eyes in disbelief, as the copy of herself put her arm around the image of her boyfriend. This changeling, however, didn't just stand there, oh no, she smiled a truly wicked smile and flicked a forked tongue slowly alongside JC's neck. The last thing Ashlyn heard before she passed out once more was a hissing laugh that sounded just like her.

The gnawing and gnashing of teeth seemed to be all around the small group of people, fighting desperately to fend off the weird creatures that looked so much like regular people. It was that one little detail that made it so difficult for Jake and the rest to truly fight back. The fear was palpable, even from someone like Bru, the hulking deputy who swung his muscular arms for all they were worth yet coming up empty. Dan was having more luck, however, with the axe. Something about the iron in it caused the creatures to retreat from its dull blade.

The gymnasium echoed with inhuman shrieks as Jake and his companions fought desperately against the horde of changelings. The iron axe in Dan's hands seemed to be their only effective weapon, the creatures recoiling from its touch with hisses of pain.

"We can't keep this up forever!" Laurel shouted, swinging her baseball bat wildly to keep the creatures at bay.

Jake nodded grimly, his mind racing for a solution. They were outnumbered and outmatched, their human strength no match for these otherworldly beings. But there had to be a way...

Suddenly, an idea struck him. "The lights!" he called out. "They hate the light - we need to make it brighter in here!"

Bru caught on quickly. "The emergency flood lights in the storage room!"

"Go!" Jake ordered. "Dan and I will cover you!"

As Bru sprinted for the storage room, Jake and Dan formed a protective circle around Laurel and the few unaffected children they had managed to gather. The changelings pressed in, their twisted forms writhing as they sought an opening.

"Hold on," Jake muttered through gritted teeth. "Just a little longer..."

A piercing shriek filled the air as Dan's axe found its mark, cleaving through one of the creatures. It dissolved into a puddle of dark ichor, but two more quickly took its place.

Just when it seemed they would be overwhelmed, the gym was suddenly flooded with blinding light. The changelings wailed in agony, their forms beginning to smoke and disintegrate under the harsh illumination.

"It's working!" Laurel cried out. "They're retreating!"

As the last of the creatures fled, melting into the shadows, an eerie silence fell over the gymnasium. Jake surveyed the scene, his heart heavy. They had won this battle, but at what cost? And how many more fights lay ahead?

"We need to warn the town," he said finally. "Whatever's happening, it's bigger than just this school. We need to get everyone prepared."

Dan nodded solemnly. "The veil between worlds is thinning. I fear this is only the beginning."

As they gathered the survivors and prepared to leave, Jake couldn't shake the feeling that they were stepping into a war unlike anything Hale County had ever seen before. And he wasn't sure they were ready for what was coming.

A thought occurred to the sheriff, "Why does light affect them?" His gaze turned to Dan, the only one he felt who had any inkling of just what in the hell was going on.

Laurel chimed in, "because it doesn't affect them all. Why just these?"

Dan pondered a moment, thinking back on something from his childhood, one of the many memories he had of his grandmother telling him stories of the little folk in the forest. He could still hear her voice as they sat on the porch of her cabin, shucking corn for her home brew. The fireflies were dancing wildly in the summer air, a fire crackling in the front yard as rabbit roasted on the pit.

"Danuwoa," she spoke, her soft voice full of warmth and wisdom, "the time of the Yunwi Tsunsdi is upon us. The Nunnehi travel soon, through our lands, to celebrate the Solstice, as do our people. You must stay out of the woods. Understood?"

"But why, Nisi," Dan could hear his younger self ask.

The old Cherokee woman's eyes drifted to the pit, past the roasting rabbit, and into the fire, seeing something only her eyes could comprehend. "The veil of worlds thins. The Yunwi Tsunsdi are an ancient people. They do not like outsiders interfering in their customs. To anger them is to bring a curse upon our people."

The young boy was enthralled with her story, "what kind of curse?"

She looked at him with a stern, almost haunted, expression. "They take our children and leave something else in return, a creature."

"A creature," the wide-eyed boy asked, no longer shucking the corn, completely caught up in the tale.

"The Kith, a changeling, it takes the shape of a person. It looks like that person in every way but something in the mind is missing."

Dan shook himself out of the memory, realizing Jake and Laurel were looking at him expectantly. He took a deep breath before speaking.

"My grandmother used to tell stories about the Little People - the Yunwi Tsunsdi. She said they were ancient beings who walked between worlds, especially during certain times of the year when the veil was thin."

Jake's brow furrowed in resigned disbelief. "Fairies, you're talking about fairies. You think that's what we're dealing with here? Awesome."

Dan nodded grimly. "Not exactly the Yunwi Tsunsdi themselves, but something similar. Creatures from another realm breaking through into ours. The light affects them because they're not fully of this world yet. They're still... transitioning."

Laurel's eyes widened. "So, the more they manifest in our world..."

"The less vulnerable they'll be," Dan finished. "We need to stop this incursion before they can fully cross over."

Jake ran a hand through his hair, looking exhausted. "How do we even begin to do that? This isn't Dungeons and Dragons or Harry Potter! This is real life and we can barely hold them off as it is."

Dan's expression was grim. "We need to find the source - wherever they're coming through. And we need to seal it, fast."

"But how?" Laurel asked, looking as perplexed by this whole situation as the sheriff. "I HEAR what you're saying but my mind is having a real hard time processing..." she couldn't force herself to say it.

"Fucking fairies," Jake finished for her.

Dan hesitated before answering. He understood how hard this was for them to believe. He had grown up with these stories, these beliefs, so he could only imagine how hard it was for them. Still, here they were, confronted with the hard truth that these things wanted them gone. "There are... rituals. Ways to strengthen the barriers between worlds. But it's dangerous knowledge, passed down through generations of my people. Using it comes with a price."

Jake met Dan's eyes, understanding the weight of what he was saying. "Whatever it takes, Dan. We can't let these things take over our town."

As they spoke, Bru approached, his face pale. "Sheriff, you need to see this."

He led them to a corner of the gym where a strange symbol had been carved into the floor - a complex pattern of interlocking circles and lines.

Dan's sharp intake of breath told Jake all he needed to know. "What is it?" he asked.

"A gateway," Dan replied, his voice barely above a whisper. "They're not just coming through randomly. Someone is deliberately opening doors for them."

The implications hit Jake like a punch to the gut. This wasn't just some supernatural event - it was an organized invasion. And someone in Hale County was helping it happen.

As they stood there, contemplating their next move, Jake's radio crackled to life.

"Sheriff? Jake? You there?" Marcus's voice came through, sounding strained. "We've got a situation at the courthouse. You're not going to believe what we just saw."

Jake exchanged a look with Dan and Laurel. Whatever was happening, it was spreading fast. And they were running out of time to stop it.

"We're on our way," Jake replied, already moving towards the exit.

"Actually," Marcus spoke quickly, "we are almost to you."

"Alright, see you soon. Getting everyone out of this damn school. Actually, Head to my office, lock it down. You know what to do."

"10-4, amigo," Marcus said, voice hyped on adrenalin. "And Jake," he paused, "what the actual fuck?"

The sheriff let out a long sigh, watching his people carefully back out of the room where the changelings just tried ripping out their throats. "Brother, beats the shit outta me."

As they hurried out of the school, Jake couldn't shake the feeling that this was just the beginning of a very long, very dark day for Hale County.

Evan felt his senses starting to clear. Whatever they had done to him was beginning to subside. He needed to escape that cell. The doctor knew that further down the tunnel was a way out, his only way out, the passage that his special inmates took to do the benefactor's bidding.

The doctor slowly got to his feet, his limbs still feeling heavy and uncoordinated. He stumbled to the cell door, examining it closely. It was old, rusted in places - perhaps not as secure as it appeared. He began searching for any weakness he could exploit.

As he worked, Evan's mind raced. He had to warn someone about what was happening, about the dark forces that had taken hold in the asylum. But who would believe him? He had been complicit in so much of it, blinded by his own ambition and grief.

A scraping sound from further down the tunnel made Evan freeze. Something was coming. He redoubled his efforts on the lock, desperation lending strength to his trembling hands.

Just as the approaching footsteps grew louder, Evan felt something give way. The door swung open with a groan of protest. Without hesitation, he slipped out of the cell and hurried deeper into the tunnels, praying he could find his way to freedom - and redemption.

He made his way down the long corridor, knowing he had to hurry. Voices ahead of him gave the doctor pause. He was trapped. His eyes landed on a rusty grate in the corner - perhaps part of an old drainage system. With trembling hands, he began to pry at the edges, hoping against hope that it wasn't stuck shut with grime and years of neglect.

To his surprise, the grate came loose more easily than expected. Evan peered into the dark opening, heart pounding. It was a tight fit, but it might just be his only chance.

Taking a deep breath, Evan squeezed his body into the narrow passage. The smell of damp earth and mold assaulted his nostrils as he crawled forward on his hands and knees. He had no idea where this tunnel might lead but anywhere was better than that cell.

As he inched along in the darkness, Evan's mind drifted to all the terrible things he had done in the name of science and ambition. The unethical experiments, the lives ruined - how had he let himself go so far? And now, something ancient and evil was using his work for an even more sinister purpose.

"I have to make this right," Evan muttered to himself as he crawled. "I have to stop them, whatever it takes." His thoughts went to Sam and her dead body crumpled like so much trash on that cell floor. He was having trouble, despite what he had seen, in reconciling her death and the thing that caused it. The doctor wanted to tell himself that monsters weren't real, not that kind of monster. Yet he had seen it, witnessed it. *Could it have been a figment of my drugged mind?* Sure, it could have been, but the doctor knew better.

After what felt like hours of slow progress, Evan saw a faint glimmer of light ahead. Hope surged through him as he quickened his pace. But as he neared the opening, he heard voices echoing from beyond - familiar voices that made his blood run cold.

Evan froze, hardly daring to breathe as he strained to listen. Whatever was happening out there, he knew it was crucial to the dark plans unfolding in Hale County. And he might be the only one who could stop it - if he could find the courage to face the monsters he had helped create.

Wraith stared at the plump, smiling man sitting at the end of the table. *Pappy*, he said to himself, *his name is Pappy.*

The craze man sat across from Pappy at the small kitchen table, his mind a whirlwind of confusion and fragmented memories. The smell of barbecue filled the air, reminding him of...something. A life he once knew, perhaps.

"You look like you've been through hell and back, my friend," Pappy said, his jovial tone at odds with the concern in his eyes. "But you're safe now. You're home."

Home. The word stirred something deep within Wraith. But was this truly home? And if so, why couldn't he remember it?

"Who...who am I?" Wraith managed to ask; his voice rough from disuse.

Pappy's smile faltered for a moment. "You're you, of course. My old friend. The man who's saved more lives than he can count." He paused, studying Wraith's face. "But something's happened to you, hasn't it? Something that's made you forget."

Wraith nodded slowly, grateful for any scrap of information about his past. "There was...a voice. A girl. Katie. She was in my head, guiding me. But now she's gone."

Pappy's expression darkened. "Ah. I was afraid of that. Sounds like you've had a run-in with some nasty folk. But don't you worry. We'll get you sorted out."

As Pappy spoke, Wraith felt a sense of comfort wash over him. This man knew him, cared for him. Maybe here, in this cozy cabin, he could finally find the answers he sought.

But a nagging doubt lingered in the back of his mind. Why had Katie's voice been so insistent that he leave? And what were the "nasty folk" Pappy had mentioned?

Wraith knew he couldn't rest until he uncovered the truth about his identity and the forces that had shaped him into the man he was now.

He fixed his eyes on the rotund man across from him. Pappy. The name felt familiar, yet distant, like a half-remembered dream.

"Eat up, son," Pappy said cheerfully, gesturing to the plate of food before Wraith. "You look like you haven't had a decent meal in ages."

Wraith stared down at the heaping plate of barbecue and sides. His stomach growled, reminding him how long it had been since he'd eaten. But something held him back.

Wraith asked, the weirdness of hearing his own voice giving him pause. "How do you know me?"

Pappy's smile faltered slightly. "Well now, that's a complicated question. But I reckon the important thing is you're here now."

Wraith's eyes narrowed. "That's not an answer."

Pappy sighed, setting down his fork. "No, I suppose it's not. Truth is, I've known you a long time. Longer than you might believe. But your memory... well, let's just say it's been through the wringer."

As Pappy spoke, flashes of memory assaulted Wraith's mind - a dark forest, the taste of blood, a little girl's scream. He gripped the edge of the table, fighting off a wave of dizziness.

"Easy there, Dean" Pappy said, concern evident in his voice. "Don't try to force it. The memories will come back in time."

Wraith looked up at the mention of the name, meeting Pappy's gaze. *Dean*. That seemed right. "Why should I trust you?"

Pappy's expression turned serious. "Because right now, I'm the only friend you've got. And believe me, son, you're gonna need friends for what's coming."

As if on cue, a distant howl echoed through the trees, sending a chill down Wraith's spine. Whatever was out there, he knew instinctively it wasn't natural. And somehow, he knew it was coming for him.

———

Jim Holt laid the flowers gently on the headstone. The day was nasty, but which days weren't anymore? He wasn't going to miss the anniversary no matter what. His wife had long since given up the annual trip, not that Jim blamed her, but he couldn't bring himself to stop. His wife, God bless her, she understood. Vivian always knew what he needed.

The tall black man knelt beside the grave, wiping off the stone. *James Earl Holt III*, the name read. His son died following in his father's footsteps, putting his service of God and Country above his own life, and though Jim missed his son terribly, he was incredibly proud of his sacrifice. People were alive because of that. Jim knew that his son didn't hesitate when the mission went south, his squad buddies telling him as much at the funeral. There was no braver soldier. That thought gave Jim comfort. But Jim knew he hadn't been the best father, although his wife disagreed. The military kept him on the move, once tour after the other, which left him little time at home.

Jim Holt stood slowly, his aging knees protesting the movement. As he gazed at his son's headstone, a familiar mix of pride and sorrow washed over him. The misty rain seemed fitting for his mood, matching the gray heaviness in his heart.

He was about to turn and leave when something caught his eye - a flicker of movement at the edge of the cemetery. Jim squinted through the drizzle, his old military instincts kicking in. There was definitely someone - or something - lurking among the gravestones.

"Hello?" he called out, his deep voice carrying across the silent graveyard. "Is someone there?"

No response came, but Jim could have sworn he saw a shadow dart between two nearby mausoleums. His hand instinctively went to his hip, reaching for a sidearm that was no longer there. Old habits die hard, he thought grimly.

As Jim took a cautious step forward, the air around him seemed to grow colder. The mist thickened, swirling unnaturally. A chill ran down his spine as he realized this was no ordinary fog.

"Show yourself," Jim demanded, his voice steady despite the growing sense of unease. He had faced down enemies in the jungles of Vietnam and the deserts of Iraq. Whatever this was, he would not be cowed by shadows and mist.

A low, inhuman growl answered him. Jim's blood ran cold as a figure emerged from behind a nearby tombstone. It was vaguely humanoid, but its proportions were all wrong - limbs too long, joints bending at impossible angles. Its face was a twisted mockery of human features, with too many teeth gleaming in a grotesque parody of a smile.

Jim stumbled backward, his mind reeling. This couldn't be real. It had to be some kind of hallucination, a trick of the light and his grief-addled mind. But as the creature took a shambling step towards him, Jim knew with sickening certainty that this was no illusion.

"What in God's name are you?" he whispered, crossing himself instinctively.

The creature's mouth opened wider than should have been possible, revealing row upon row of needle-like teeth but no sound came out.

As more shadowy forms began to materialize from the mist, Jim realized with growing horror that he was surrounded. He cast one last glance at his son's grave, silently apologizing for what he feared might be his final visit. It was only then that he noticed the other graves in the old cemetery. There were an abnormal amount of freshly dug graves. There hadn't been a new one dug there in years, not since the new cemetery had been built on the other side of town. Only those with plots purchased long ago, waiting rest next to loved ones, would be buried in this one.

Then, drawing upon years of military training and the strength that had seen him through countless battles, Jim Holt prepared to face this new, impossible enemy. Whatever these things were, whatever they wanted, he would not go down without a fight. But fight what? Shadows? Had Jim worked at that asylum so long that he had finally lost his own mind?

Another shadow moved through the mist. Then another.

No, this was no figment of his imagination. It was real.

Jim knew he had to run, to regroup. His military training kicked in as he quickly assessed his surroundings. The cemetery gate was too far - he'd never make it before these things caught up to him. But there, about 20 yards away, stood the old groundskeeper's shed. It wasn't much, but it might buy him some time.

As he ran his foot caught on something solid, sending him crashing to the soggy ground. He knew he couldn't hesitate but as he quickly tried pushing himself off the ground his eyes made contact with another set of eyes, only these were faded blue recessed back in the skull. Jim tried to keep calm and not cry out but his natural instinct betrayed him. It was the corpse of a sheriff's deputy, except that it looked like it had been completely drained of fluid, almost like human beef jerky. That thought disgusted him. While his stomach was threatening to betray him, the growling of the mist creatures snapped him back to reality. A thought snapped into place as Jim reached out and quickly grabbed a radio off the dead deputy's belt.

Without hesitation, Jim sprinted towards the shed. He could hear the inhuman shrieks of the creatures behind him, their unnatural movements creating a cacophony of snapping twigs and rustling leaves. Jim's heart pounded in his chest as he reached the shed door, yanking it open and throwing himself inside.

He slammed the door shut just as one of the creatures slammed into it from the other side. The thin wood creaked and groaned under the assault. Jim quickly scanned the dimly lit interior, looking for anything he could use as a weapon or to barricade the door.

His eyes landed on an old shovel leaning against the wall. Jim snatched it up, wedging it under the door handle to reinforce it. The pounding outside intensified, accompanied by inhuman howls of frustration.

As Jim backed away from the door, his foot knocked against something metallic. He looked down to see an old toolbox. Kneeling quickly, he rifled through its contents, his hands closing around a hefty wrench. It wasn't much, but it was better than nothing.

The shed's single, grimy window rattled as one of the creatures peered in, its distorted face pressed against the glass. Jim's grip tightened on the wrench as he stared back at the monstrosity.

"What do you want?" he shouted, more out of desperation than any expectation of an answer.

To his shock, the creature spoke - its voice - a grating, unnatural sound that seemed to bypass his ears and resonate directly in his mind.

"We want what was taken from us," it hissed. "This world. Your lives. Your souls."

Jim felt a chill run down his spine at the creature's words. This was beyond anything he had ever faced in his long military career. But he'd be damned if he was going to let these things take over without a fight.

"You'll have to go through me first," Jim growled, raising the wrench defensively.

The creature's twisted mouth curled into what might have been a smile. "With pleasure," it rasped.

As the assault on the shed intensified, Jim Holt steeled himself for the fight of his life. He may not understand what these things were or where they came from, but he knew one thing for certain - he would not let them desecrate this place, this final resting place of his son and so many other brave souls.

Whatever was coming, Jim was ready to face it head-on. For his son. For Hale County. For humanity itself. But he was going to need lots of help. He felt the weight of the radio in his hand and glanced at it. "Who in the hell is ever going to believe this?" he asked himself, clicking on the radio as the storm outside grew in angst.

CHAPTER 19

The smell of fresh coffee permeated the air, wafting around the conference room of the sheriff's department. The rain had picked up, but that eerie mist kept hanging around and with Dan reiterating the story he had told earlier to the fresh ears of Marcus, Char, and the Judge, it only added to the heaviness that loomed about all their shoulders.

Jake refilled the coffee as the others listened to the tales in disbelief, Laurel helping by finding whatever snacks she could and placing by the freshly brewed pot. She leaned into Jake, whispering, "I feel like I'm in the Twilight Zone. Does this happen all the time around here?"

The sheriff actually smiled and whispered back, "it DOES explain a lot of things."

Jake and Laurel watched as the others absorbed Dan's incredible tale. Marcus sat with his head in his hands, while Charlotte paced back and forth, her brow furrowed in concentration. Judge Hawthorne simply stared out the window, his expression unreadable.

"So let me get this straight," Marcus said finally, looking up. "We're dealing with some kind of... fairy invasion? Like Tinker Bell and shit? Ancient beings from another realm trying to take over our world?"

"But not so cute," Jake tossed in deadpan.

Dan nodded grimly. "I know how it sounds, but after what we've all seen today, can you really deny the possibility?"

Charlotte stopped pacing and turned to face the group. "Assuming this is all true, what's our next move? How do we stop these things?"

Jake stepped forward; his expression determined. "We need to find the source - wherever they're coming through. Dan mentioned rituals and gateways. We close those, we might have a chance of stopping this before it gets worse."

"And how exactly do we do that?" Judge Hawthorne asked, his voice tinged with skepticism.

Dan hesitated before answering. "There are... ways. Ancient Cherokee rituals passed down through generations. But they're dangerous, and they come with a price."

"What kind of price?" Laurel asked, her reporter's instincts kicking in.

"The kind that could cost a person their soul," Dan replied solemnly.

A heavy silence fell over the room as they all contemplated the gravity of the situation.

Marcus was the first to break it. "We can't just sit here and do nothing. Whatever the risk, we have to try."

Jake nodded in agreement. "Marcus is right. We need a plan of action. Dan, what do you need for these rituals?"

Dan suddenly remembered his earlier conversation with them at the school. "You mentioned you found one of those marbles, like at the school."

Laurel nodded, "Yeah, but the one we found is bigger and made different, it's more of a stone."

The native's eyes widened excitedly, "do you have it with you?"

"Of course," Jake said, fishing around in his pocket. He tossed the marble to Dan who snatched it out of the air, immediately feeling his demeanor change. "What is it? What's wrong?"

"Jake," Dan said, voice full of fear and awe, "this is a summoning stone. It looks like a traditional Cherokee Marble, but it's made of infused granite."

"What do you mean, infused," Jake asked, confoundedly, feeling way out of his league.

Dan pointed to the images of the owl and the cougar. "These are part of the stone, they were not carved or painted. They were imprinted into the stone through ancient blood magic, there is even a trace of it here, embedded in the stone as well," his finger traced to the rusty discolored spot.

"Magic?" Marcus scoffed. "I'm trying here, I am, but fucking magic?"

"I share your skepticism," Dan spoke softly, voice full of understanding, "but you can't think of magic like hocus pocus or wizards with pointy hats. Magic is energy. Energy makes up the universe, both light and dark. Lightning is energy yet we don't call it magic. If you were to show a lightbulb to someone from 400 years ago you would be burned at the stake for witchcraft."

"What are you saying?" Laurel asked.

"I'm saying that to these creatures, the use of magic is nothing more to them than what science is to us. And whoever made this, was very powerful and very knowledgeable."

"So we can use that to shut off this portal, bridge, whatever you want to call it, right?" Jake chimed in.

Dan nodded, "I believe so."

"Great, what do you need?"

As Dan began listing off ingredients and preparations, Charlotte's phone buzzed. She glanced at it, her eyes widening.

"It's a message from one of my sources at the asylum," she said urgently. "Something's happening there - patients going missing, staff acting strangely. And there's mention of Dr. Michaels being involved somehow but no one has seen him."

Jake's expression hardened. "Alright, we need to split up. Dan, you and Judge Hawthorne start gathering what you need for the ritual. Marcus and Charlotte, head to the asylum and see what you can find out. Laurel and I will try to track down Dr. Michaels - he might have answers we need."

Before anyone could answer, the radio on Jake's belt crackled to life. "Sheriff? Hello. Anyone out there?! My name is Jim Holt. I've got a situation at the old cemetery. You're not going to believe this, but I'm under attack by... well, I'm not sure what they are. But they ain't human. I promise you I ain't been drinking."

Jake grabbed the radio. "Jim, hold tight. We're on our way."

"You believe me," Jim asked, his mildly shocked voice coming through the radio perfectly.

"Sir, after the day I've had you could tell me a blind elephant was running down Main Street shitting out nuns and I would believe you. Are you somewhere safe?"

"I locked myself in the caretaker's shed. But sheriff, there's something else." There was a long pause. "I found this radio on the body of a deputy. He...he looked...like a husk. I'm sorry, sir, but he's dead."

Jake let that information sink in before replying. "Thanks, Jim. Hold up in there, I am on my way to you."

He turned to the group. "Alright, people. Plans have changed. Laurel and I are heading to the cemetery to get Jim. Let's go."

As they all prepared to move out, Jake couldn't shake the feeling that they were racing against time. Whatever was coming, it was clear that Hale County - and perhaps the entire world - hung in the balance.

"One more thing," he added as they headed for the door. "Keep your eyes open and trust your instincts. If something feels off, it probably is. And whatever you do, stick together. We don't know how many of these... changelings... are out there."

With grim determination, the group dispersed, each heading off to face the unknown threats that awaited them.

William watched from his perch atop the building across from the Sheriff's Department. The rain was soaking him yet he stood there, statuesque and unmoving, transfixed by the call of the stone the native man held in his hand. While everything else seemed a blur, William could see it clearly, like a lighthouse in a storm, guiding him home.

Home, he thought suddenly, *Rachel*. The name took him aback. *Rachel? Who's Rachel?*

You KNOW her, another strange but familiar voice echoed in his broken mind. *She's our wife.*

Jason! But he didn't exist. He was the other, the sick version of himself. The pretend one.

No! YOU are the pretender, the fraud. I want my life back! The voice in his head demanded in silent fury.

He shook away the intruding demands, forcing them deep. He had a mission. It was important. Nothing could be allowed to stop him.

William stood motionless atop the building, rain cascading down his pale face. His eyes remained fixed on the sheriff's department across the street, tracking the movements of the people inside. But it wasn't the humans that held his attention - it was the stone in the native man's possession.

He could feel its power calling to him, a siren song that resonated deep within his being. The stone was a beacon, a link to the world he had left behind so long ago. William's fingers twitched involuntarily, yearning to grasp the ancient artifact.

As he watched, the group inside began to disperse. William's eyes narrowed as he saw the sheriff and the reporter woman heading for a patrol car. The native man and the judge moved towards another vehicle.

A low growl escaped William's throat. They were splitting up, making it harder for him to track them all. But the stone - he couldn't let it out of his sight.

With inhuman grace, William leapt from his perch, landing silently in the alley below. He moved swiftly through the shadows, trailing the native man's car as it pulled away from the curb.

As he ran, William's form seemed to flicker and shift, sometimes appearing almost translucent in the misty rain. He was caught between worlds - not fully of this realm, but not yet able to fully manifest his true form. The stone was the key to changing that.

William's mind raced as he pursued his quarry. He knew the reverend would be pleased if he could secure the artifact. But a part of him, a part that still clung to his fading humanity, whispered doubts. Was this truly the right path? Or was he merely a pawn in a game beyond his comprehension?

Pushing aside his uncertainties, William focused on the chase. Whatever came next, he knew one thing for certain - he could not let that stone slip away. The fate of two worlds might well depend on it.

Evan's lungs burned as he pushed himself to keep running through the dense forest surrounding the asylum. His mind raced almost as fast as his feet, trying to process everything he had seen and heard in that underground chamber.

The experiments, the rituals, the otherworldly beings - it was all connected somehow. And he, Dr. Evan Michaels, had played a crucial role in unleashing this nightmare upon Hale County.

"I have to warn them," he gasped between ragged breaths. "Have to stop this before it's too late."

But who would believe him? He was complicit in so much of what had happened. His reputation, his credibility - all of it was in tatters. And yet, he was possibly the only one who truly understood the scope of the threat they faced.

As he ran, Evan's thoughts turned to his son, JC. Was he safe? Or had he already fallen victim to the dark forces that were spreading through the town like a cancer?

A branch whipped across Evan's face, drawing blood. He stumbled but forced himself to keep moving. He had no idea if he was being pursued, but he couldn't risk slowing down.

Suddenly, the trees thinned out and Evan found himself on the outskirts of town. Lights glimmered in the distance, a beacon of normalcy in a world that had gone mad.

Evan paused, trying to catch his breath and get his bearings. Where should he go? The police station? The hospital? His own home?

Before he could decide, a police truck came flying up the road, lights flashing through the rain. Evan began waving his arms wildly.

The truck slid to a stop and the sheriff emerged from the driver's side, a mixture of amazement and anger on his face. "Dr. Michaels? Is that you?"

Evan, his heart leaping into his throat, ran towards the sheriff. Relief flooded through Evan. If anyone would listen, if anyone could help, it would be Jake.

"Sheriff," Evan croaked, his voice hoarse from exertion. "Thank God. We have to talk. Something terrible is happening - something I helped cause. And if we don't stop it soon, it might be too late for all of us."

Jake's expression hardened as he took in Evan's disheveled appearance and wild eyes. "Alright, Doc. Get in, Hell has literally broken loose. Talk as we drive, we are headed to the cemetery."

Evan scrambled into the back of the police truck, his heart pounding. As he settled in behind the reporter, Laurel, a flicker of recognition passed through him. There was something familiar about her, but he couldn't quite place it.

"Dr. Michaels," Jake said as he pulled back onto the road, lights flashing, "start talking. What the hell is going on at that asylum?"

Evan took a deep breath, trying to organize his scattered thoughts. "It's... it's worse than you can imagine, Sheriff. The experiments, the patients - it was all a cover for something much darker."

"What kind of experiments?" Laurel asked, her reporter's instincts kicking in despite the bizarre situation.

Evan's voice shook as he replied. "We were trying to unlock the hidden potential of the human mind. Push the boundaries of consciousness. But we went too far. We opened a door that should have stayed closed."

Jake's knuckles whitened on the steering wheel. "A door to where, exactly?"

"Another world," Evan whispered. "A realm of shadows and ancient beings. They've been waiting, biding their time. And now they're coming through."

Laurel turned in her seat to face Evan, her eyes wide. "The changelings. The shadow creatures. That's what we're dealing with?"

Evan nodded grimly. "Yes. But it's more than that. There's a plan, a ritual. They need certain... components to fully manifest in our world."

"Components?" Jake pressed. "What kind of components?"

Evan hesitated, shame and guilt washing over him. "Human sacrifices. Specific individuals with... certain qualities. I don't know all the details, but I know they've been planning this for years."

The truck swerved slightly as Jake processed this information. "Jesus Christ," he muttered. "And you were involved in all this?"

"I didn't know," Evan pleaded. "Not at first. By the time I realized what was really happening, I was in too deep. They... they had leverage over me."

"What kind of leverage?" Laurel asked softly.

Evan's voice broke as he replied. "My son. JC. They threatened him. I thought I was protecting him, but now... I'm not sure he's even still himself anymore."

A heavy silence fell over the truck as they sped towards the cemetery. Jake's mind raced, trying to fit all the pieces together. The asylum, the changelings, the rituals - it was all connected. And now they were racing against time to stop whatever dark plan was unfolding.

"Alright, Doc," Jake said finally. "We're headed to the old cemetery. There's a man there, Jim Holt, who's under attack by these... things. You're going to help us deal with that, and then you're going to tell us everything you know. Every last detail. Understood?"

Evan nodded, "Jim works for us. He's a good man, if they hadn't already gotten to him."

Jake cut his eyes once more into the mirror, locking them on Evan. "How long have you known they were..." the sheriff struggled to say it, casting a quick glance at Laurel who was biting her lip to keep from laughing.

"...they were what?" the doctor dead panned.

Jake shook his head and took an angry breath. "Fairies, doc. Fucking...fairies."

An uncontrolled burst of laughter escaped Laurel, who quickly turned away as Jake shot her a look. She didn't trust herself to meet his gaze. It was all too much.

Evan lowered his head as he answered, his voice barely above a whisper:

"They're not fairies, Sheriff. At least, not the kind from children's stories. These beings are ancient, powerful, and utterly alien to our world. They've been waiting for millennia to return, and now they've found a way."

Jake's grip tightened on the steering wheel. "Return? You're saying they've been here before?"

Evan nodded grimly. "According to the texts we uncovered, they once ruled this world. But something drove them out - sealed them away in another realm. Now they want to reclaim what they see as rightfully theirs."

Laurel turned in her seat to face Evan, her reporter's instincts overriding her fear. "And the asylum? How does it fit into all this?"

"It was built on a nexus point - a place where the barriers between worlds are naturally thin," Evan explained. "The original founders knew this. They've been working towards this moment for generations, refining techniques to manipulate human consciousness and open gateways."

Jake's mind reeled as he tried to process this information. "So, all those patients..."

"Test subjects," Evan finished, his voice heavy with shame. "We thought we were expanding the boundaries of human potential. Instead, we were just softening them up for possession."

"How long have you known about this?" Jake demanded.

Evan shook his head wearily. "I didn't fully understand until recently. It started small - strange occurrences, patients with impossible abilities. These seemingly miracle plant compounds I had never heard of. But over time, the truth became clear. They were using us, manipulating our experiments to create openings between worlds."

"These experiments, what kind were they," Laurel asked curiously.

The doctor let his gaze fall on the passing trees zipping by the window. When he finally spoke, it was with a voice laced with regret and pain. "We delved deep into the human psyche. Further than morally accepted science and practice would allow." He could hear Daniel's words echoing in his head even as he spoke. His best friend, dead, because of him.

"What do you mean," Jake asked.

"The Pineal Gland is called the 'Seat of the Soul'. It's a small, pea-sized gland that looks like a tiny pine cone, sitting deep in the brain. It controls your circadian rhythm which can affect sleep cycles, melatonin, that sort of thing. It was called the Third Eye because of its location in the brain. We still have no idea what all it does, what other purposes it serves, but many beliefs think that it also touches on our spiritual communication between the physical and spiritual worlds. And if that's true and the fractured part of the mind exists at a quantum level or different plane then perhaps, we could rejoin the broken halves and heal it. That was the basis of my work. When they brought their ideas that so resembled mine, I was hooked. The results were unbelievable...at first. Then they turned monstrous, dangerous."

"And you just went along with it?" Laurel asked incredulously.

"You've never gone after a story you were warned not to, never pushed forward in your field, expanded the limits of journalism because you knew, you KNEW, with every fiber of your being that you were right?" Evan retorted bluntly against her condemnation.

Laurel understood his point as well as his perspective, that pursuit of something bigger than oneself, that need to go places and face experiences where normal people balked. "I do get that, Dr. Michaels, I do but once you saw how they were twisting your work..." she spoke again, this time softer.

"I told you, they had leverage," Evan replied, his voice breaking. "My son... and my wife. They promised to bring her back."

Jake's grip tightened on the steering wheel. "Bring her back? From where?"

"From death," Evan whispered. "They said they could restore her, make her whole again. I was a fool to believe them, but grief... grief makes you do terrible things. And I had glimpsed of the wonders they were capable of, wonders that gave me hope, faulty, foolish, hope."

The truck fell silent as they all absorbed this information. The rain intensified, pounding against the windshield as they neared the cemetery.

"I've got to find my son, sheriff. He's all I have left."

Laurel and Jake shared a knowing look.

"We're almost there," Jake said grimly. "Whatever's waiting for us, we face it together. Got it? First, we deal with whatever's happening at the cemetery. Then we figure out how to stop this invasion before it's too late. I have people searching for options, but I need to know, right now, if you're in or out."

Evan nodded, steeling himself for what was to come. As they pulled up to the cemetery gates, he couldn't shake the feeling that this was only the beginning of an eternal night for Hale County.

CHAPTER 20

"The doctor is with us," Jake's voice blared from the radio, "there's a nurse there, the head nurse, Samantha, blonde, you won't be able to miss her. She isn't who she appears to be. They've already replaced her and who knows how many others. It's compromised."

Marcus listened intently, sharing a look with Charlotte, "Shit show?"

"Shit show," she agreed.

"So, what now?" Marcus asked, "Two of us going in there is suicide."

There was silence on the other end for a minute then the radio crackled back to life. "Find Malone, he's probably at the hospital, cleaning up the evidence. I think it's time to put a foot on his weaselly throat. You up for it?"

"It's way overdue," Marcus retorted.

"We are here at the cemetery. Watch your back. I'll join you when I'm done."

"10-4". Marcus dropped the mic and was about to fishtail the car when he noticed something in the parking lot of the asylum.

"Why the Chief of Police, Marcus?" Charlotte asked, reading his tense body language.

Marcus gripped the steering wheel tightly as he slowly crept up the drive. "Malone's been dirty for years," he explained grimly. "Always covering things up, making evidence disappear. But this... this is a whole new level."

Charlotte nodded, her mind racing. "You think he's involved with whatever's happening at the asylum?"

"I'd bet my life on it," Marcus replied. "The question is, how deep does it go? And what are we walking into?"

As they neared the parking lot, Charlotte's eyes widened. "Marcus, look!"

Through the misty rain, they could see Chief Malone's cruiser parked haphazardly near the front entrance. The driver's door was open, and there was no sign of Malone. As a matter of fact there were empty cruisers everywhere, red and blue lights flashing off the building.

Marcus pulled up beside the cruiser, his hand instinctively going to his weapon. "Stay alert," he warned Charlotte as they exited the car. "No telling what we might find in there."

They approached the asylum entrance cautiously. The emergency room seemed eerily quiet, with no staff visible at the reception desk. They ducked out of sight when a figure passed by a window. Malone. But why was he just staring into nothing like that. After a few moments he disappeared into the dark of the room.

"I don't like this," Charlotte muttered.

Marcus nodded in agreement. "Let's check Malone's car first. Maybe we can figure out what he was after."

As they neared the cruiser, a muffled thump from inside the trunk made them both freeze. Marcus and Charlotte exchanged a wary glance before Marcus slowly approached, gun drawn.

"Hello?" he called out. "Who's in there?"

Another thump, louder this time, followed by a muffled voice. "Thompson? That you? Get me the hell out of here!"

Marcus hesitated, looking to Charlotte. She shrugged; her expression uncertain.

"Chief?" Marcus asked finally. If this was the Chief, then…the changelings were already inside. "We're opening it up. But no funny business, you hear?"

As Marcus reached for the trunk release, Charlotte tensed, ready for anything. Neither of them could shake the feeling that they were walking into something far more dangerous than they had anticipated.

The trunk popped open with a loud click. Marcus and Charlotte stepped back, weapons drawn, as Chief Malone slowly sat up, blinking in the dim light. He looked disheveled and confused.

"Thompson? What the hell is going on?" Malone demanded, his voice hoarse.

Marcus kept his gun trained on the Chief. "That's what we'd like to know. Why were you locked in your own trunk?"

Malone rubbed his head, wincing. "I... I'm not sure. Last thing I remember, I was heading into the hospital to check on some reports of strange activity. Then everything went black."

Charlotte's eyes narrowed. "And how do we know you're really you?"

Malone looked at her incredulously. "What the hell kind of question is that? Of course I'm me! How do I know you're you?!" the grumpy chief retorted hotly.

Marcus and Charlotte exchanged a wary glance. After everything they'd seen today, they couldn't be too careful.

"Alright, Chief," Marcus said finally. "We're going to need you to come with us. There's a lot you need to be filled in on."

As Malone climbed out of the trunk, Marcus noticed something odd - a small, dark stain on the Chief's collar. It looked almost like...

"Chief," Marcus said slowly, "don't move."

Malone froze, his eyes widening. "What is it?"

Marcus leaned in closer, studying the stain. To his horror, it seemed to be... moving. Tiny, oily tendrils writhed just beneath the fabric.

"Charlotte," Marcus said, his voice tight. "Get back. Now."

Before either of them could react further, Malone's form suddenly blurred and shifted. His face contorted impossibly, jaw unhinging to reveal rows of needle-like teeth.

"Run!" Marcus shouted, firing his weapon as the thing that had been Chief Malone lunged towards them.

"Why are we running into the asylum?!" Charlotte shouted at him.

"Because of that," he shouted back, pointing behind her. More police officers with the same crazed faces emerged from the vehicles. The ONLY place left to go...was inside.

As they sprinted towards the mental health institute's entrance, Marcus realized with grim certainty that the situation was far worse than they had imagined. The changelings weren't just infiltrating - they had already taken over key positions of power in Hale County.

And now, Marcus and Charlotte were trapped between the monsters outside and whatever horrors awaited them within the asylum's darkened halls.

——

Judge Hawthorne stared at the porch as he climbed the steps. Dan noticed his inquisitive look. "Something wrong, Judge?"

"This is a nice house you have here, Mr. Roundtree," he stated, obviously impressed with the nice little cottage style home.

"You know we aren't actual savages, right?" Dan asked him, stone faced.

The judge turned a few shades of red, realizing he had insulted the man who was inviting him into his home. "I am so sorry, I..."

Dan suddenly laughed, "I'm just messing with you." He clapped the judge on the shoulder, "come on in."

Judge Hawthorne followed Dan inside, still looking a bit sheepish. The interior of Dan's home was warm and inviting, with a mix of traditional Cherokee decor and modern furnishings.

"Make yourself comfortable," Dan said, gesturing to the living room. "I need to gather a few things for the ritual."

As Dan disappeared into another room, the judge took a seat on the couch, his eyes roaming over the various artifacts and photos adorning the walls. One photo in particular caught his attention - a younger Dan standing next to Jake, both in police uniforms.

"I didn't know you used to be on the force," the judge called out.

Dan's voice drifted back from the other room. "A lifetime ago. Jake and I go way back."

The judge nodded, processing this new information. As he waited, his mind wandered to the incredible events of the day. Changelings, ancient rituals, doors between worlds - it all seemed impossible. And yet, he had seen enough to know that the threat was very real.

Dan returned, his arms full of various items - herbs, candles, and what looked like an ancient leather-bound book. He stuffed them all into a leather-bound knapsack.

"Alright," Dan said, setting the swollen bag down on the coffee table. "That should be everything."

"So how exactly does this ritual work?"

"Well, we have to focus our energies, pour everything into the marble, it's the focal point. It's going to take all of us."

"You've done this before?"

"Nope. First time."

"First time," Judge Hawthorne sputtered, "how do you know it's going to work?"

Dan looked at the judge, a twinkle in his eyes, "I don't, but I have faith in my people, their knowledge. For my people, the passing of knowledge is a sacred thing, it keeps our ancestors alive within us. For most peoples a story is simply a tale to be forgotten. To us, it is history, our way of life."

The judge nodded slowly.

Dan paused, meeting the judge's eyes. "It's not going to be pleasant. And once we start, there's no turning back. Are you sure you're ready for this?"

Judge Hawthorne took a deep breath, stealing himself. "If it means saving Hale County - saving our world - then I'm in. Whatever it takes."

Dan nodded grimly. "Then let's gather with the others," the native elder spoke firmly, hearing the thunder rumble forebodingly outside, "we've run out of time."

———

Jake peered through the window of his truck as they came to a stop at the front gate. Nothing really looked out of place but with the heavy rain and wind it was hard to tell.

Laurel asked, eyes surveying the old grounds, "what's the plan?"

"We get to the shed, grab Jim, and don't get killed," replied without much emotion, his mind fully focused on the task at hand. He reached behind his seat, pulling out a pipe wrench, and handed it to Laurel.

"And just what do you want me to do with this?" she scoffed. "You've got a damn gun, and I get this?"

He looked at her knowingly, "iron."

The reporter nodded in understanding as he reached under the seat and pulled out a rusty old pipe with a taped handle. Roughly etched into it was the word "Adjuster".

"Adjuster?" Evan asked from the back.

"Attitudes, Doc," he said simply, "You have your methods, I have mine."

"Do you have something for me?"

Jake thought for a moment then hopped out of the truck and reached into the bed. He slipped back into the seat and handed Evan the tire iron. "Alright, let's go. Don't hesitate. If you're not sure, hit it anyway, you can apologize later."

The three of them stepped out into the rain, weapons in hand. Jake led the way, moving cautiously through the cemetery gates. The old graveyard was shrouded in mist, tombstones looming like silent sentinels in the gloom. The trees were old and ancient, some drooping like bent old men.

"The shed should be over there," Jake whispered, pointing toward a small structure about fifty yards away. "Stay close and keep your eyes open."

Laurel gripped the pipe wrench tightly, her knuckles white. "I don't see anything moving out there."

"That doesn't mean they're not here," Evan murmured. "These things... they can hide in plain sight."

They moved forward slowly, weaving between gravestones. Jake noticed something disturbing - fresh dirt piled beside several graves, as if they had been recently dug up.

"Jim?" Jake called out softly as they approached the shed. "Jim Holt? It's Sheriff Hooks."

A muffled voice came from inside. "Sheriff? Thank God! They're still out there - I can hear them moving around."

Jake tried the door, but it was barricaded from within. "Jim, it's safe. Open up."

After a moment of hesitation, they heard the sound of something heavy being moved. The door creaked open just enough for a weathered face to peer out.

"How do I know it's really you?" Jim asked suspiciously.

Jake held up his iron pipe. "Because if I wasn't me, I wouldn't be carrying this. It's made of iron."

Jim looked puzzled for a moment before relief washed over his face as he pulled the door open wider. "That explains why they backed away when I tried to hit them with a shovel. Sheriff, you won't believe what I've seen. Those things... they're not human."

"I know," Jake replied grimly. "We've encountered them too. We need to get you out of here."

As Jim stepped out of the shed, a low growl echoed through the cemetery. They all froze, scanning the misty grounds. He snatched an old scythe out of the shed.

"Too late," Evan whispered. "They know we're here."

Shadowy figures began emerging from behind tombstones, their movements jerky and unnatural. They formed a loose circle around the group, cutting off their escape route to the truck.

"Stay together," Jake ordered, raising his pipe. "Back-to-back. Don't let them separate us."

The first creature lunged forward, its face a twisted parody of humanity. Jake swung his pipe, connecting solidly. The thing shrieked in pain, its flesh sizzling where the iron made contact.

More of them moved in, emboldened by their numbers. Laurel swung her wrench wildly, managing to keep them at bay. Evan and Jim stood shoulder to shoulder, facing outward.

"We can't fight them all," Laurel gasped as she beat back another attacker.

Jake knew she was right. They were outnumbered, and eventually, the creatures would overwhelm them. That was when Jim noticed the iron wrought fencing surrounding the cemetery. It was mostly intact.

"The fencing," Jim suddenly said. "Drive them towards the fencing!"

Jake nodded grimly, understanding Jim's plan. "Everyone, move towards the fence! Use your weapons to herd them!"

The group began to slowly back up, swinging their iron implements to drive the creatures towards the wrought iron fencing. The changelings hissed and snarled but seemed reluctant to directly touch the iron weapons.

As they neared the fence, Jake called out, "Now! Push them into it!"

With a coordinated effort, they lunged forward, forcing several of the creatures to stumble backwards into the iron fencing. The effect was immediate and horrifying. Where the changelings touched the iron, their flesh sizzled and smoked. They let out inhuman shrieks of agony, their forms seeming to melt and dissolve. Wails of pain echoed through the old cemetery followed by a sudden stillness.

They had left.

The group looked at one another, shock followed by relief. They had beat them back, but for how long? It was then that Laurel noticed all the freshly dug graves. "Y'all certainly have a lot of deaths in this town."

Jake looked at her in confusion, "what?". It was then he saw what she saw, one fresh grave after the other.

Jim spoke up warily, "the last person to be buried here was my son, five years ago. Anyone else would be on the other side of town at the new cemetery."

"You said there was a deputy's body. Where was it?"

The war vet pointed to a dark mound only twenty feet away.

Jake approached the spot Jim indicated, his steps cautious. The rain had tapered to a drizzle, but the eerie mist still hung heavy among the tombstones. As he reached the dark mound, the sheriff crouched down, his iron pipe at the ready.

"Jesus Christ," he muttered, taking in the deputy's desiccated form. The body looked as if all moisture had been completely drained from it, leaving behind a leathery husk that barely resembled a human being. "That's Deputy Wilkins. He went missing three days ago."

"He was just like that when I found him," Jim explained, keeping his distance. "Like something... fed on him."

Laurel stepped closer, her reporter's instinct overriding her fear. "Jake, look at his neck."

The sheriff leaned in, noticing several puncture-like marks on the deputy's throat. "What the hell?"

"It's how they feed," Evan said quietly, his face ashen. "The changelings. They don't just replace people - they need sustenance to maintain their form in our world."

Jake stood; his expression grim. "And all these fresh graves? There must be hundreds of them. What's that about?"

Laurel swallowed hard. "They're gathering bodies. Vessels. The more they have, the stronger their foothold becomes in our world."

"It's more than that," Evan stated assuredly, "I think they are combining the energy from their world with this one, to change them, make them more powerful."

"We need to check the graves," Jake decided, though the thought made his stomach turn.

Jim nodded, gesturing to a nearby maintenance shed. "There should be shovels in there."

As they gathered tools, Jake's radio crackled to life. "Sheriff? It's Marcus. We've got a situation at the asylum. The changelings - they've taken over. Malone is one of them. We're trapped inside."

Jake cursed under his breath. "Hold tight. We'll get there as soon as we can."

"There's more," Marcus continued, his voice tense. "We found something in the lower levels. Some kind of... altar. I think they're planning something big, and soon."

Jake exchanged a worried glance with Evan who appeared just as shocked at that information. "How soon?"

"Man, I have no idea but as many of those things as we just saw I would say tonight. The whole damn police department are those things."

"Doc," Jake asked, "what the hell are they walking into?"

Evan shook his head emphatically, "Sheriff, I have no idea. I've never seen an altar down there."

The sheriff looked up at the darkening sky, thunder rumbling in the distance. "Alright. Find somewhere secure and stay put. We're on our way."

Jake's radio crackled to life once again, making them all jump. "Sheriff?" Dan's voice came through, strained and urgent. "We've got the ritual items. Where should we meet?"

Jake grabbed the radio. "Dan, the situation's worse than we thought. I'm looking at a hundred plus freshly filled graves. We need to move fast. Marcus and Char are trapped at the asylum."

There was a pause before Dan responded. "We need to know what's in them. That cemetery. It sits on a nexus point, like the asylum. If we're going to close these gateways, we need to know what those graves mean. We will head to the asylum. Be sure to bring the marble."

"We'll meet you there," Jake confirmed. "Be careful. These things are everywhere."

As they hurried back to the truck, Evan grabbed Jake's arm. "Sheriff, I need to find my son. If these creatures are taking over the town, JC could be in danger."

Jake hesitated, torn between sympathy for the doctor and the urgent need to stop the invasion. "Doc, the best way to help JC is to shut down whatever portal these things are using. Once we do that—"

"You don't understand," Evan interrupted, his voice breaking. "JC is... special. They've been interested in him from the beginning. If they've taken him..."

"Doc, I can't reallocate sources for one person. I'm sorry."

"If you had a child, wouldn't you do whatever it took, sheriff?!" Evan all but screamed at him.

Jake turned to back to Evan, eyes ablaze "well I certainly wouldn't knowingly put them in harm's way. I wouldn't help some crazed psychopath who thinks he's some kind of god destroy my town with lunatics!"

As Evan is about to fire back, Laurel spoke up. "What about the graves?"

Jake hesitated, torn between investigating the cemetery and rescuing Marcus and Charlotte. Before he could decide, Jim's shout drew everyone's attention.

"Sheriff! Over here!"

They rushed to where Jim stood beside an open grave, his face a mask of horror. Inside the grave, instead of a coffin, was a strange, pulsating mass of darkness. It writhed and shifted like living shadow, emitting a low, humming sound. It was solid and then ethereal, as if it were phasing in and out of two different worlds.

"What in God's name is that?" Laurel whispered.

Evan stepped forward, his scientific curiosity momentarily overriding his anger. "It's the mutation of a changeling."

"You mean it's copying somebody? Right now? As we watch?"

The doctor nodded slowly.

"The fuck it is," Jake growled, snatching Jim's scythe and burying it inside the mass. The changeling screamed and dissolved away to nothingness.

The sheriff unclipped his radio with a determined look. "Bru, get me some deputies out here at the Old Gatewood Cemetery. Take the rest of them to the asylum. Keep your distance and make sure you arm yourself with anything made of iron, it's the only thing that seems to work. Raid the hardware stores, raid the barns, I don't give a damn, just get yourselves armed. Understood?"

"Gotcha, boss," sending units your way.

Jake turned to the others. "I need you all to go rendezvous with the others at the asylum, I'll be there shortly. Mr. Holt, you've been recruited. Doc, don't make me fucking regret this."

Evan nodded brusquely, following Jim out of the cemetery.

"One more mission. We can take my car," the old vet said without argument, it's exactly what his son would have done.

The sheriff fished the marble from his pocket and gave it to Laurel, "look after this."

"What the hell, Jake?"

"I have to find out what these graves are and what their purpose is. You're one of the few I trust."

Their eyes locked and Laurel knew he meant it. Whatever else was happening, that's all she needed to know. "Watch your ass."

Jake nodded as the group bolted to Jim's car. "Cutty, what the hell have you gotten me into now," he said aloud, knowing his mentor couldn't hear him but sensing his response just the same. *"It's good for ya, kid. It'll build character."*

The sheriff set his jaw and walked back to his truck to wait for the deputies as late afternoon in Hale County began to push away the daylight. Whatever happened next, he knew it would change their cut-off community forever.

———

Jason ducked behind a gravestone as the others drove away, leaving the sheriff alone. His heart pounded in his chest, a mix of adrenaline and the constant battle for control raging within him.

"The marble," William's voice echoed in his mind. "She has the marble. We need to follow her."

"No," Jason muttered aloud. "Something's not right. There is something more going on here. Something..."

He peered around the stone, watching as Jake paced near his truck, radio in hand. The cemetery was quiet now, but Jason could sense the lingering presence of the shadow creatures—the changelings, as they'd called them.

"They're afraid of iron," Jason whispered to himself, filing away that crucial piece of information.

William's voice grew more insistent. "The marble is our priority. It's the key to everything."

"To what?" Jason demanded silently. "What happens when we get it? What are you planning to do?"

William's response was a surge of anger that made Jason's head throb. Images flashed through his mind—ancient rituals, doorways between worlds, beings of shadow and light locked in eternal conflict. "Let me take control," William's voice echoed inside his head. "I know what to do with the stone."

"No," Jason whispered fiercely. "I don't trust you. I don't even know who you are."

"We are the same," William insisted. "Two halves of one whole, torn apart by their experiments. I am the stronger half - the one who understands what's at stake." Dean heaved, mind fighting against itself as William's voice grew more urgent. "You don't understand," William hissed. "You're just a fragment, a piece broken off. I am the whole. I need to be complete again."

Jason clutched his head, fighting to maintain control. The conflicting memories and identities threatened to tear him apart. He was a professor, a respected academic. But he was also... something else. Something older, something that didn't belong in this world.

The professor clutched his head, trying to silence the voice. The pain was intensifying, threatening to split his skull. "Leave me alone!"

"You fool," William hissed. "You have no idea what's coming. The veil is thinning. Soon they'll be here in full force, and that marble is the key to stopping them - or helping them."

Jason's attention was drawn back to the sheriff, who was now examining another grave. The man seemed utterly alone and vulnerable. It would be so easy to overpower him, to follow the others and take the marble...

No. Jason shook his head, trying to clear it. Those weren't his thoughts. They were William's, seeping into his consciousness like poison.

"I won't hurt innocent people," Jason insisted. "Whatever you want, we'll find another way."

William's laughter echoed in his mind. "Innocent? No one in Hale County is innocent. They've all been complicit, whether they knew it or not. And now they'll pay the price."

Jason watched as the sheriff returned to his truck, presumably waiting for backup. A decision crystallized in his mind. He needed answers, and the sheriff might have them. But he'd do this his way - not William's.

Steeling himself against William's rage, Jason emerged from his hiding place and began making his way toward the sheriff's truck. As he approached, he raised his hands to show he was unarmed.

"Sheriff Hooks?" he called out. "I need to talk to you. It's about the marble."

The sheriff whirled around, his hand instinctively going to his weapon. His eyes narrowed as he took in Jason's disheveled appearance.

"Professor Locke? What the hell are you doing here?"

Jason took a deep breath. "I'm not sure I can explain it. But I think I'm part of whatever's happening. And I think I can help."

As the words left his mouth, William's presence surged within him, fighting for control. Jason staggered, nearly falling to his knees as pain lanced through his head.

"Professor?" The sheriff approached cautiously, his hand still on his weapon. "Are you alright?"

"No," Jason gasped, fighting to maintain control. "There's someone else... inside me. He calls himself William. He wants the marble. I don't know why, but I know it's important."

Jake's expression hardened. "You had it on you when we found you overdosed."

Jason clutched his head, wincing. "He knows. William knows. He says you took it from us. He's been... guiding me. Or trying to control me. I'm not sure anymore."

Jake kept his distance, iron pipe at the ready. "Are you one of them? A changeling?"

"No!" Jason's voice was desperate. "I'm me, but I'm... fractured. Split. The experiments at the asylum—" He broke off with a cry of pain as William fought harder for control. *Changelings, yes, that's what they were called. Not squirrels!*

Jake's eyes widened. "You were a patient at the asylum?"

"Not exactly," Jason managed. "A... subject. Voluntary at first. Dr. Michaels recruited me for cognitive studies. But it became something else. Something darker."

The sheriff studied him intently, weighing his options. "Alright, Professor. I'm going to need you to be very honest with me. What does William want with the marble?"

Jason shook his head, sweat beading on his brow from the effort of keeping William at bay. "He says it's a key. A focal point for some kind of ritual. But I don't think he's telling me everything."

Thunder rumbled overhead as the storm intensified. Jake glanced at the darkening sky, then back at Jason.

"Come with me," he decided finally. "But I'm warning you - one wrong move, and I won't hesitate to put you down."

Jason nodded gratefully. "Thank you. I just want answers. I want to be whole again."

As they moved away through the gravestones, he couldn't shake the feeling that he was being watched—not just by the changelings that lurked in the shadows, but by something else. Something ancient and patient, pulling strings from behind the veil between worlds.

And somewhere deep in his fractured psyche, a third presence stirred—neither Jason nor William, but something else entirely. Something that remembered the truth about who they really were, and why they had been broken apart.

———

"Dean…"

Dean? Who is Dean? That's right, I'm Dean, Wraith thought quietly, trying to come to terms with who he is versus who he was. The silence in his mind and the ghostly howling in the forest, made it difficult for him to focus. And what of Katie? Where had she gone?

Daddy? Please, don't make me go!

He shook is head frantically, her pleas tearing through his fractured mind. Wraith didn't want to let her go, she was part of him. He needed her, didn't he? She. No, not she. Katie. Katie meant something to him. It was important. At the same time the man he was knew it wasn't real.

NO, daddy. Don't let me go!

"You have to concentrate, Dean," Pappy spoke with conviction, yet he could not hide the underlying tone of concern for his once lost friend. His friend was struggling, and he wished to all that was Holy that he could give him the time to heal, but time was something they were out of. The forest path below them would soon be alight with dazzling lights, like fireflies in the spring. Only, these weren't fireflies. No, these were the folk of old, the ones from the other place. Tonight, they would cross between the worlds, following the ley lines, aglow with glimmer, deep into the forest.

Pappy's weathered hands gripped Dean's shoulders. "Look at me, son. Dean. That's who you are. Not Wraith. That's what they made you, not who you are. Dean Cutler."

"I'm trying," Dean replied, his voice rough from disuse. "Things are... jumbled. I remember bits and pieces, but nothing whole.

Cutler…" his mind flashed to an older man, slightly pudgy but full of life and spunk. "My father," he whispered, looking expectantly at Pappy.

Dean's mind struggled to make sense of the fragmented memories. Flashes came to him - a military uniform, a mission gone wrong, a laboratory, and pain. So much pain. Funerals. Two caskets, one regular size, one small being lowered into the soft earth.

"I remember... pieces," Dean said, his voice hoarse. "They did something to me. Changed me."

Pappy nodded grimly. "The project. A blend of this world and the next. They took good soldiers and tried to make them better. Faster. Stronger. But they didn't count on what would happen when they opened doors that should've stayed closed. You were a weapon, my friend. The best hunter they had." Pappy stirred the stew again. "But before that, you were Dean Cutler, your dad was the sheriff. You worked with him after the military, the best damn tracker in three counties. You even taught Jake Hooks how to track. And we all thought that was impossible," he finished with a laugh. "You certainly fill out your clothes better," the round man admired happily, "you were nothing but stick and bone before."

The clothes were a refreshing change from the old, dirty scrubs. A sudden thought occurred to him, "I lived here…"

A sad look flitted across Pappy's eyes but the man quickly brushed it aside. "For a little bit, right after the accident."

The forest around them seemed to pulse with an unnatural energy. The wind carried whispers that weren't quite human.

"They're coming," Pappy said, his usual jovial demeanor replaced by grim determination. "The folk from the other side. They've been waiting for a night like this, when the veil is thin."

"Katie," Dean suddenly said. "The girl in my head. She was real, wasn't she?"

Pain flickered across Pappy's face. "Yes. Your daughter. She died three years ago in the accident. That's when they took you - when you were broken with grief. They used that connection, that love, to control you."

Dean felt something crack inside him - a dam breaking, memories flooding back. Katie's laughter. Teaching her to ride a bike. Her small hand in his. And then the crash. The screams. The silence.

"I couldn't save her," he whispered.

"No one could," Pappy said gently. "But they used her memory, created a psychic echo to keep you in line. To make you hunt for them."

Dean looked down at his hands - hands that had killed, that had torn shadow beings apart. "What am I?"

"You're still human," Pappy insisted. "But enhanced. Connected to both worlds. That's why they want you. You're a bridge."

In the distance, strange lights began to flicker among the trees. Beautiful, entrancing, and utterly wrong.

"They're coming," Pappy said, reaching for the shotgun leaning against the cabin wall. "And they'll be looking for you."

Dean stood, something resolute hardening in his eyes. "Let them come."

"That's the spirit," Pappy grinned, though his eyes remained serious. "But we can't fight them all. Not here. We need to get to town, find the sheriff."

"Sheriff?" Dean asked, stirring another memory. A stern face, but kind eyes. Someone he trusted. "Father needs to know."

Pappy's face took a sudden sad turn. "Jake is the sheriff now, kid. I'm sorry, but your daddy passed not long after you went missing. It's been hard on all of us." The portly man stopped stirring, seemingly making up his mind about something.

Dean felt the hurt deep inside, he also felt guilt for not being there, for not remembering more.

"Jake Hooks," Pappy ladled stew into a bowl and handed it to Dean. "Eat. Then we prepare."

Jake Hooks, that name was familiar. As Dean ate, Pappy retrieved an old wooden chest from beneath his bed. He opened it reverently, revealing an assortment of unusual items - knives with strange symbols etched into the blades, vials of powder and liquid, and what appeared to be a very old revolver.

"The Sidhe fear iron," Pappy explained, lifting the revolver. "This here's been in my family for generations. Bullets are iron core, blessed by my grandmother."

Dean felt drawn to the weapon, memories of using something similar flickering at the edges of his consciousness. As he reached for it, Pappy pulled back.

"Not yet," the older man cautioned. "You need to be sure of who you are before you take up arms again. These weapons require intent, focus."

Dean nodded slowly, understanding more than he could articulate. "The town. Are they safe?"

Pappy's expression darkened. "I doubt it. These folk have been planning this for a long time. Infiltrating, replacing people with their changelings. By now, they could be anywhere, wearing familiar faces. From what I heard on the radio earlier the Sidhe are no longer hiding."

"How will we know who to trust?" Dean asked.

"Iron reveals them," Pappy explained. "They can't stand its touch. Burns them something fierce. And there are other signs - they can't cross running water in their natural form, and they can't abide certain herbs and symbols."

"The folk," Dean said suddenly. "I've hunted them before. Not just recently, but... before. When I was younger."

Pappy's eyes widened slightly. "You're remembering. Good. Yes, your daddy was a Warden - one of those who kept the boundary between worlds. And he trained you to be the same."

"A Warden," Dean repeated, the word feeling right on his tongue. Something clicked into place. "That's why they took me. Why they changed me. I already knew about them."

Pappy nodded grimly. "You were a threat. So they turned you into an asset instead. Used you to hunt down any of their kind who went rogue or threatened their plans."

The lights in the forest were growing brighter, moving with purpose. Dean could feel them now - a pressure in his mind, a calling.

"They want me back," he said.

"They need you for what's coming," Pappy confirmed, stuffing supplies into a backpack. "The grand crossing. Tonight's the night they've been planning for - when enough of their kind will cross over to take back this world."

Dean absorbed this information, his tactical mind already formulating strategies. "We need to warn the sheriff. Jake."

Pappy nodded, finishing his own bowl of stew. "That's the plan. But first, we need to make sure you're ready." He reached into the chest again, pulling out a small leather pouch. "This might help you remember more clearly."

Inside the pouch was a simple silver locket. Pappy handed it to Dean, who took it with trembling hands.

"Open it," Pappy urged gently.

Dean fumbled with the clasp, finally managing to open the locket. Inside was a tiny photograph of a young girl with his eyes and smile. Katie. His daughter. His heart.

The moment he saw her face, something broke free inside Dean's mind. Memories cascaded through him - not just fragments, but whole scenes from his life. His childhood in Hale County. Meeting his wife, Sarah. The birth of their daughter. His work with the sheriff's department. The accident that took Katie and Sarah from him. And then the darkness that followed.

"I remember," Dean whispered, clutching the locket tightly. "I remember everything."

Pappy's face split into a relieved smile. "Welcome back, son."

But along with his identity came the knowledge of what he had done as Wraith - the hunts, the kills. He had been used as a weapon against his own kind, manipulated through his grief and rage.

"They're going to pay for what they did to me," Dean growled, his voice taking on a dangerous edge. "For using Katie like that."

"And they will," Pappy assured him. "But we need to be smart about this. The whole town could be at stake."

He reached into the chest once more and pulled out a small velvet pouch. From it, he withdrew a simple silver chain with a pendant - a small iron arrowhead wrapped in silver wire.

"Your father's. And his father before him. The mark of a Warden."

As Pappy placed the chain around Dean's neck, something seemed to settle within him. The pendant felt warm against his skin, familiar and right, resting alongside the locket of his daughter.

"Thank you," Dean said simply.

Pappy nodded, tears in his eyes. "Let's go save our home, shall we?"

Dean nodded, slipping the locket around his neck. "Then let's go find the sheriff."

As they prepared to leave, Dean paused at the door, looking back at the cabin that had provided brief sanctuary. "Thank you, Pappy. For bringing me back."

The round man clapped him on the shoulder. "What are friends for?" he smiled, disappearing into the back of the house once more.

Dean looked out at the approaching lights, a fierce determination replacing his earlier confusion. He was Dean Cutler. Son of Sheriff Cutler. A Warden of the boundary. And he had a job to finish.

When Pappy reappeared, he looked wholly different. Sure, he was still the same large, rotund man but his long, greasy hair was tied back, and he wore dark fatigues and a tighter fitting shirt that belied a strength that Dean didn't realize existed before. He had this man pegged all wrong. "We served together…"

Pappy guffawed and clapped his friend again before picking up his weapon and a rucksack, "Now you're getting it!"

As they slipped out the back of the cabin, the forest around them came alive with whispers and movement. The hunt was on - but this time, Dean was no longer the hunter. He was the hunted.

And he wouldn't go down without a fight.

CHAPTER 21

The group huddled in Jim's car, rain pattering against the windows as they watched the imposing structure of the asylum looming in the distance. Emergency lights pulsed dimly through the mist, casting eerie red and blue shadows across the grounds.

"I don't like this," Laurel muttered, clutching the marble tightly in her palm. "Where's Dan and the Judge?"

Jim checked his watch, brow furrowed with concern. "They should have been here by now."

"Maybe they ran into trouble," Evan suggested, his voice tight with anxiety. His eyes remained fixed on the asylum buildings, somewhere in there was his son—or whatever had taken his place.

Jim drummed his fingers on the steering wheel, military instincts on high alert. "We can't wait forever. Your friends are in there, and from what I gather, time isn't on our side."

Laurel's phone buzzed with a text message. "It's from Charlotte," she said, relief evident in her voice. "They're holed up in the east wing, bottom floor, sub-basement. Some kind of old records room. She says they found something important."

"The old annex," Evan mused, "that's where the oldest files were kept when the asylum was first built. No one ever goes down there. Records of radical experiments, patient histories, strange diagnosis, everything."

"Is there another way in?" Dan asked. "One of these things might not be watching?"

Evan nodded slowly. "The service tunnels. They run throughout the facility, connecting to the old boiler room. The entrance is hidden in that grove of trees," he pointed to a dense copse about fifty yards off the main road.

"Alright," Jim said decisively. "We go in through the tunnels, find your friends, and figure out our next move."

As they prepared to exit the car, headlights appeared behind them. Everyone tensed until they recognized Dan's truck pulling up alongside them.

"Sorry we're late," the Judge said as he rolled down his window. "Roads are getting worse. And we had to dodge some... unfriendly faces in town."

"They're spreading," Dan muttered grimly.

"What's the plan?" the Judge asked.

Jim quickly briefed him on their intended route through the service tunnels. The Judge nodded, retrieving a leather satchel from his passenger seat.

"Dan, you got everything we need for the ritual?"

Dan patted his own bag. "Everything but time and luck."

"Then let's move," Jim ordered, his military bearing evident as he took charge of the situation. "Stay close, stay quiet, and remember—iron hurts these things."

As they made their way toward the grove of trees, Laurel fell into step beside Evan. "Dr. Michaels," she whispered, "what should we expect in here?"

Evan's face was a mask of anguish. "I don't know. Chaos. Disorder." His own mind was in disarray, he had failed his son, and that failure was being used for evil, there was no other way to put it.

The group crouched in the underbrush beside the access road, rain dripping from the leaves above them. The asylum loomed in the distance, its windows glowing with an eerie light that seemed to pulse in rhythm with the distant thunder.

Laurel clutched the marble tightly in her palm, feeling its unnatural warmth against her skin. "How much time do we have?"

Evan shook his head grimly. "Not much. The storm is intensifying. They'll use its energy to complete their transition."

As they made their way through the woods, Evan led them to a rusted metal door set into a small hillside, nearly invisible beneath years of overgrown vegetation. "This was used for supply deliveries back when this was a prison. Later on it was abandoned when the mental institute was built," he explained, pulling a key from his pocket. "Later, it became... something else."

The door creaked open, revealing a dark, narrow passageway sloping upwards.

"How do we know this isn't a trap?" Laurel asked, eyeing Evan suspiciously.

"You don't," he replied honestly. "But right now, I'm just a father trying to find his son before it's too late. Let's be clear. They know we're coming; it's going to be a fight from here all the way through."

Jim Holt produced a flashlight from his pocket. "I'll take point," he offered, his military training evident in his posture.

"I'll bring up the rear," Dan added, pulling a small iron knife from his belt.

With a deep breath, the group entered the tunnel, the heavy door closing behind them with an ominous thud. The beam from Jim's flashlight illuminated a narrow corridor with pipes running along the ceiling, the walls slick with moisture.

"Where does this lead?" the Judge whispered.

"Directly beneath the main building," Evan replied. "There's a main tunnel that stretches from here all the way up to the main floor. This used to be a prison. This narrow passage goes on for a hundred feet or so then opens up into a proper hallway. There will be rooms on either side…"

"You mean cells," Laurel said matter-of-factly.

"…ROOMS, almost all the way up then it opens to a small foyer with a boiler room to one side and a couple of medical offices to the other. Past that there is a small flight of stairs to a large steel door that opens onto the main floor, just past the visitor check in."

Jim cast a look to Evan, "I never knew that. Why would you need…" He let the question die on his lips, they all realized the answer together. "The rumors 'bout them experiments are true," he said bitterly, disbelief changing to scorn.

Evan stopped the group, eyeing each one of them, "Think whatever the hell you want to, judge away. But what you are about to see in here, don't let it distract you from our goal. If you let this get to you, it WILL consume you and we will lose."

That point, no one was arguing. Exchanging one last look they took off up the musty passage.

They moved cautiously, the only sounds their footsteps and the occasional drip of water from the ceiling. The tunnel stretched before them, a damp, claustrophobic passage that seemed to breathe with malevolent life. Their flashlight beams cut through the darkness, revealing peeling paint and decades of neglect.

"Stay close," Jim whispered, his military training evident in every precise movement. "And keep those iron weapons ready."

Laurel felt the marble pulse warmly in her palm, almost like a heartbeat. She couldn't shake the feeling that it was responding to their surroundings, becoming more active as they ventured deeper beneath the asylum.

"Dr. Michaels," she whispered, "what exactly were you doing here? What kind of experiments?"

Evan's face was a mask of shame in the dim light. "We thought we were expanding human consciousness, breaking down the barriers of perception. But we were really..." he trailed off.

"Opening doors," Dan finished for him. "Doors that should have stayed closed."

"How is any of this legal," Jim asked in a low whisper.

"It's not," Laurel replied, casting a suspicious glare at Evan. Every bit of this situation could be place on his doorstep, and she wasn't about to pretend otherwise.

As they moved up the dark passage, Jim suddenly raised his hand, signaling for them to stop. Ahead, the tunnel opened into a larger hallway, just like Evan described it. Strange symbols had been painted on the walls - elaborate spirals and interlocking patterns that seemed to shift and move in the wavering flashlight beams.

"What is this place?" the Judge asked, his voice barely audible.

"This is the hallway," Evan replied. "But I've never seen these markings before. They're new."

Dan moved forward, studying the symbols with a look of grim recognition. "These are binding sigils. Ancient ones. Someone was trying to keep something contained."

A low moan echoed through the hallway, causing everyone to freeze. It seemed to come from everywhere and nowhere at once - a sound of pain and rage that set their teeth on edge.

"We need to keep moving," Jim urged. "Your friends are waiting."

The old stone walls seemed to suck in the fluorescent lighting that was fixed to the stone ceiling like matchsticks, casting odd shadows through the dim light. The rooms closest to them still had their iron cell doors attached from a century earlier.

"What were these for?" Laurel asked, shining her light into one.

"Storage," Evan answered too quickly, not meeting her eyes, "mostly."

But as her light swept across the back wall of the alcove of the misshapen cells, Laurel saw scratch marks - dozens of them, carved deep into the concrete. Human fingernails had left those marks. Someone had been imprisoned here, desperate to get out. Was those shackles on the wall?

"My God," she whispered. "What did you people do down here?"

Before Evan could answer, a shuffling sound came from up ahead. Everyone tensed, weapons raised.

"Who's there?" Jim called out, his voice steady despite the tension.

A figure emerged from the shadows - a woman in a nurse's uniform, her movements jerky and unnatural. As the light hit her face, they could see her eyes were yellow, the iris completely black, her skin too pale, almost translucent.

"Evan, lover..." she said, her voice a rasping parody of human speech, igniting a strange set of emotions from Evan. On the one hand she was the exact image of Sam, his head nurse, and sudden lover, which the doctor couldn't quite wrap his head around. Yes, they flirted often, even had taken it a little further a few times, but nothing like the other night. On the other hand, he knew this wasn't her, it was some creature that had taken her image and it reviled him.

Sam seemed to read his thoughts, his feelings, and laughed out loud in derision. "You think I'm a changeling," she laughed sardonically, voice laced with derision, "no, Evan. I was me all along. I'm no changeling, nothing so small." A weird glimmer seemed to shimmer around her, barely visible but there as her voice took on a sultry tone, "Oh lover, what I am your mind couldn't comprehend. You humans and your ego. If it makes any difference, you were quite the challenge, one I loved every second of."

Evan's face twisted with horror and disbelief. "No," he breathed, his voice a choked whisper.

The others looked at him, then back at the thing that wore Sam's face. Its laughter rang through the tunnel, a sound like breaking glass.

"Did you think you could hide from me down here?" Sam taunted, taking a jerky step forward. "Did you think your little escape plan would work? The others are waiting for you to come back, Evan. And we will make sure you do."

Evan felt a wave of nausea. He raised his iron pipe, conflicting emotions tearing at him.

"Don't listen to her!" Jim barked. "These things lie." Jim raised his iron pipe threateningly. "We have to get past her," he said, determination cutting through the doubt that clouded the group.

Sam's laughter echoed off the walls, a sound like brittle glass shattering. "Lies?" She glided closer, the air around her vibrating with menace. "Why don't you ask him about Project Gatekeeper?"

Laurel turned to Evan, eyes wide with shock and accusation. The marble in her hand pulsed faster, a desperate warning.

"There's no time for this," Dan insisted. "We need to find the others!"

But Sam blocked their path, her presence warping the air like a heat mirage. "You'll never make it," she taunted, arms outstretched as though to embrace them all. "You can't even save yourselves."

Sam's eyes flicked to Jim, Laurel, Dan, and the Judge before settling back on Evan with a chilling intimacy. "Your friends will betray you," she said, her face suddenly twisting in concern. "You've been promised to me. All will be forgiven."

Evan shook his head as if trying to clear it of cobwebs. "I want my son!" he shouted suddenly, lunging toward Sam with reckless abandon, his own iron knife arcing through the air.

The Sam creature screamed in pain as the weapon slashed through its arm, then vanished into the shadows, her agonized scream echoing off the stone walls.

"We have to hurry!" Jim yelled, "more have to be coming!"

Laurel clutched the marble tightly, feeling its heat intensify as they ran quickly through the hallway.

Behind them, they heard another moan—closer this time—and a skittering noise that filled the tunnel like an infestation of locusts.

"They're coming for us," Dan realized grimly.

The Judge glanced over his shoulder but kept running, his breath coming in ragged gasps. "Keep going! Don't look back!"

They passed by another odd room where rusted machinery loomed like ancient sentinels against the walls. More symbols covered every surface, vibrating with an energy that made Laurel's skin crawl.

The noise behind them grew louder as they plunged headlong up the narrow hallway before finally coming to the small foyer Evan told them about. Strange noises were reverberating from the boiler room. Here, the walls were riddled with cracks and fissures that seemed to bleed darkness itself.

"Faster!" Jim urged.

A shriek pierced the air—a sound of fury and loss that reverberated through their skulls—and Laurel risked a glance back. She saw shapes moving in the gloom: indistinct figures with eyes like burning coals and mouths stretched wide in silent screams.

She stumbled but caught herself before she fell. "They're everywhere!" she cried out.

Dan's face was pale beneath his mop of hair as he pushed himself to run harder than he ever imagined possible.

"We're close," Laurel insisted desperately, trusting the marble's strange guidance even as everything else crumbled into chaos around them.

Jim pulled ahead, his determination a tangible force. He saw the last staircase looming before him. "We have to keep moving!" he shouted, but his voice was nearly drowned out by the cacophony behind them.

The lights were dimming, the monsters were getting closer. The exhausted group could feel the putrid breath of the strange beasts pursuing them.

Just when it seemed the hallway would never end, Laurel felt a surge from the marble—a hot pulse of urgency—and veered toward the spiral staircase that twisted upward like a rusted corkscrew. They took the stairs two at a time, stumbling and breathless.

The Judge lagged behind, gasping with every step. "Help me!" he wheezed as Dan turned back and hauled him up by the arm.

"Almost there!" Dan urged.

The shrieks and skittering noises reverberated beneath them, an unholy choir growing louder and more insistent. But above, there was light—or something like it—glowing dim but steady through the grimy glass ceiling of an abandoned lobby.

They burst into the room just as the sound reached a fever pitch below. Dan chanced at glance at their pursuers, little goblin-like creatures with dark red skull caps. Jim slammed the heavy door behind them, jamming his iron pipe across it as a makeshift barricade.

Laurel doubled over, clutching her knees and trying to catch her breath. The marble in her hand cooled, its frantic pulsing finally slowing.

"Will it hold?" she asked between gulps of air.

"It has to," Jim replied grimly.

The Judge leaned against a wall, his face ashen. "What were those things?" he whispered.

"More of the Sidhe, the little folk, those ones are called red caps," Dan said shakily. "We got away."

But even as he spoke, they all knew how fragile their reprieve was. The vibrations in the floor beneath them told of Sam's promise, echoing through every crack and corner: they will come for you too.

They huddled together in the lobby's eerie half-light, fear drawing them closer despite everything that divided them.

"What now? Where is everyone?" Laurel asked quietly.

"We have to find that altar," Dan said with more confidence than he felt. "None of this will mean anything if we don't shut it down."

The Judge shook his head, eyes full of doubt. "What about Marcus and Charlotte? How do we know they're even alive? How do we know anything isn't just another lie?"

"Because we don't have a choice," Jim snapped back. "I'm not giving up on them."

"And we have a radio," Laurel chimed in, cutting a look to Dan.

Dan straightened up slowly, wiped sweat from his brow, ashamed that he had forgotten. "Damn, I forgot," he said, embarrassed. "This place does something to the mind."

Evan looked at them all sternly. "The thing we are looking for has to be up stairs, on the parapet. But don't get confused, this place is a maze, hallway upon hallway of patient rooms. There are stairwells at the end of hallway's two and five, both will lead to the roof. That's where we will find most of the resistance. Keep trying the radio."

Laurel looked at each of their faces in turn and nodded slowly. She opened her palm where the marble lay cool and still against her skin—the only thing they had left for guidance—and felt for its pull once more.

It was subtle now but there: a quiet insistence-like whispers in the dark.

"This way," she said softly, leading them toward another series of hallways that might spiral back into nightmare—or maybe freedom—until they vanished from sight like ghosts themselves.

———

Marcus and Charlotte could hear the ominous footsteps and guttural growls of the police—or whatever those monstrous entities were—closing in on their trail. They had delved deeper into the eerie asylum's hallways, but neither had a clear plan of action. Earlier, they had explored the shadowy lower levels, stumbling upon bizarre, makeshift altars, but their stay was cut short by the presence of goblin-like creatures lurking in the darkness. Suddenly, Marcus's radio crackled to life, slicing through the tension-filled silence.

"Marcus, it's Dan. Where are you guys?" came the familiar voice, crackling with static.

"We're trying to keep our distance from the police. They're not human, they're all creatures. This is some fucked up Lord of the Rings shit in here. Where are y'all?" Marcus replied, his voice edged with urgency.

"We made it to the main floor, it looks relatively empty," Dan responded, the words echoing slightly as if bouncing off damp, claustrophobic walls.

"That's because they are all chasing us," Marcus retorted.

Charlotte's eyes widened with alarm. "Marcus, that's where those goblin things were…"

Marcus's voice turned sharp as he spoke into the radio, "Dan, y'all gotta get outta there, there is…" His sentence was brutally cut off as the radio emitted a harsh squelch and then died, leaving an unsettling silence.

Charlotte turned to him, her expression a mix of fear and determination. "What are we going to do? There's no way out of here that doesn't get us killed."

Marcus paused, his mind racing through possibilities, then looked at her with resolve. "We release the patients," he declared, the weight of his decision hanging heavy in the oppressive air.

She blinked at him, disbelief etched across her features. "Are you serious? This is an ASYLUM! These people are whacked out of their minds!"

"It's the only way," he insisted, urgency rising in his voice. "If this place is crawling with those things, we let everyone loose. They're not ready for that."

Charlotte hesitated, torn between fear and the flicker of a plan. The chaos of it all. The unpredictability. "It might just work," she agreed finally.

They sprinted down the hallway, shadows looming larger than life against the cracked and peeling walls. Their footfalls echoed like war drums as they passed rows of locked doors, each one hiding the tormented souls they hoped to set loose. The sounds of moaning and wailing reverberating from the rooms was soul-crushing.

They finally found a security guard looking for all the world like a lost child in a zoo full of monsters. Marcus ran up to him, "where is the security room?"

The security officer looked at him blankly, lip quivering as if trying to find his words but fear made it impossible.

"Security room!" Marcus shouted again, "Where?"

The guard managed to raise a trembling arm and pointed down an opposite hallway. Marcus snatched the keys off the man's belt and bolted in that direction, Charlotte right behind him, the poor security guard too overwhelmed to give chase.

"This'll shift their focus," Marcus panted as they reached a heavy steel door labeled SECURITY.

He fumbled with the key ring, hands slick with sweat, heart pounding in his throat. Charlotte twisted around nervously, eyes on the corridor behind them.

"Hurry," she urged.

The lock clicked open; they tumbled inside and slammed it shut against any immediate pursuit. Banks of monitors flickered in the dim room, wires snaking like vines through a jungle of machinery. Marcus's eyes landed on the large control panel in the corner.

"There," he said, rushing over to it.

Tapping frantically at switches and buttons, he worked to override whatever system kept this place contained. Red lights flashed warnings—LOCKDOWN DISENGAGED—and an alarm began blaring overhead. Inmates' howls joined its mechanical wail as doors thudded open one by one throughout the asylum.

Panic spread fast and wild: human stampede mixing with inhuman fury as creatures turned from hunting to desperate containment efforts.

"Time to go!" Charlotte shouted over the noise.

They bolted back into chaos incarnate: patients surging like a tidal wave through every passageway, a thousand voices raised in madness or triumph or both. As they were swept along with the tide, Marcus held tight to Charlotte's hand.

"Stairs," he yelled over bedlam, pointing to an exit sign barely visible through the clamor.

But nothing was simple here—nothing was straightforward—and even as they pushed toward what might be freedom, those same forces pulled them deeper into confusion. The old asylum had been a prison, and before that a fort, and was part of the underground railroad. There were too many underground passages to name and the upper floors were just as bad, wing after twisting wing of patient rooms.

"This way!" Charlotte cried suddenly, yanking Marcus sharply down another hall that twisted away like a serpent beneath their feet.

Only then did they see how close behind their pursuers truly were: hideous shapes bounding after them through swarming masses of frantic inmates. And leading them—an incongruous beacon amid pandemonium—the red and blue flash of a police light.

"It's working," Marcus gasped as they fled headlong into more tunnels.

But for how long?

——

The deputies stood around Jake as he gave them their orders, the headlights of their cars giving them some slight visibility as the skies darkened and the rain fell harder. "I want those graves dug up, you have your assignments and your partners, now get to it. And watch each other's backs. Call me if you find anything."

The sheriff turned to Bru and motioned for him to follow as Jake walked to his truck.

"Yeah, boss," the large man asked faithfully.

Jake cut his wary eyes across the cemetery. "Bru, take two guys that you absolutely trust, that you believe haven't been compromised, and walk the perimeter of this fucking place."

"What am I looking for, boss?"

"Anything out of the ordinary, things that don't belong…"

"Like fucking monsters," Bru deadpanned without humor.

"Like fucking monsters," Jake reaffirmed in the same manner.

"You got it."

"Wait a second," Jake said suddenly, "take this, it may help." He handed the large deputy and iron tire tool. Bru looked at it skeptically and Jake wondered briefly if he had been wrong about his long-time deputy. But Bru just shrugged and took it.

"Smash and bash?"

"Just like at the school."

Bru shook his head slightly and walked way mumbling, "fucking monsters."

The sheriff then turned his attention to the man sitting in his passenger's seat. Jason looked like a squirrel, ready to bolt in a second. "Look, I've got to get this done. You good here?"

Jason gulped and nodded; not altogether sure he WAS good there in the sheriff's truck by himself.

"Call me if anything, anything happens," Jake said, reaching over and handing Jason a flashlight. "And don't wander off."

Jason clutched the light as if it were a life preserver. "Got it."

Jake hesitated for only a moment before slamming the door and striding toward the other deputies, already drowned in rain.

The digging had begun, muddy earth turning in uneven clumps beneath their shovels. Jason watched from the truck, his heart pounding with every shadow that leapt across the window.

Bru moved out of sight quickly, two other men following him with wary eyes. Soon, it was just Jason alone with shallow breaths fogging up the glass.

Jason sat there, his heart pounding as he watched the deputies' flashlights flicker through the fog. The heater ran noisily, filling the cab with a false sense of comfort while droplets drummed on the roof like a thousand tiny fists. Every shadow seemed to shift and stretch of its own accord; every sound was a portent of doom.

He wiped a sleeve across the window and squinted into the storm. The headstones stood in neat lines like sentinels—silent, watching. He could hear the muffled thud-thud of shovels against wet earth and then—

Nothing.

A sudden thud against the truck window made him jump. He turned wildly, but it was just Jake's radio sliding off the dash. He scooped it up, clutching it like a lifeline as he scanned for any sign of movement outside.

The graveyard loomed beyond the fogged glass: rows of headstones jutting from the earth like crooked teeth in an open maw. As he stared, Jason's mind twisted them into new shapes— hunched figures, waiting and watching. He tore his gaze away in panic.

Bzzzt. The radio crackled to life in his hands.

"J-Jake?" It was Bru's voice, nearly swallowed by static. "You hear me?"

Jason fumbled with the controls. "I'll get him! Hold on!"

"No time—tell him—something big out here—"

The transmission cut off abruptly, leaving only white noise hissing through the speaker. Jason's pulse thundered in his ears as he struggled with what to do next.

He opened the door and slid out into the stormy night, rain biting at his skin as he ran towards Jake's last known position. It was chaos around him: flashlights bobbing frantically, deputies shouting half-heard warnings to one another across the dark expanse.

"Sheriff!" Jason yelled into the wind that whipped across the cemetery. "They need backup!"

The sheriff appeared suddenly through sheets of rain; his face set with grim determination.

"Where?" he barked over a crack of thunder.

"South side! He said it was big!" Jason shouted back.

Jake nodded tersely and grabbed Jason by the arm before hauling him towards the cover under a nearby shed awning.

"You stay here," he ordered. "We'll handle this."

Jason nodded wordlessly as Jake sprinted away to rally his men. Alone under gray skies and relentless rain, he sank down against the flimsy wall and tried not to feel like dead weight.

Then came another sound—a low growl that sent ice racing up his spine—and Jason knew that staying put might not be enough to save him.

Jake sprinted to his deputies in distress. He knew Bru could handle himself under normal conditions, but conditions were anything but normal. And that sound in Bru's voice would stay with him until the day he died. It wasn't just the sound of fear but the sound of fear from a man who had never known any fear in his life until that moment.

But what was it that could instill that fear in Bru? It wasn't the changelings. Bru had said it was big. Jake slipped around a giant mausoleum and that's when he saw it.

A hulking mass loomed in the flickering light, a grotesque silhouette against the rain-swept sky. Four legs like ancient tree trunks slammed into the earth with each step, and Jake could just make out Bru and the others circling like mosquitoes around an angry bull.

The thing let out another growl, deep and resonant, vibrating through the ground and up into Jake's chest. It wasn't a sound that came from any animal he knew, but something primal—like the earth itself was roaring at them.

"Draw it away!" Jake shouted as he ran to join Bru. "Don't let it back you into a corner!"

Bru nodded without looking; too focused on swinging his tire iron at the thing's massive flank. They had no choice but to harry it, keep it from charging them down one by one.

Flashlights bounced wildly, their beams illuminating glimpses of muck-caked fur and gnashing teeth. The rain lashed down harder, turning the graveyard into a mire beneath their feet. The creature moved with terrifying speed despite its size, whirling around with a speed that sent two deputies sprawling backwards into mud-soaked graves.

Jason watched in horror from his makeshift refuge, every instinct screaming at him to run but knowing there was nowhere to go. He clutched the flashlight like Jake had told him, though it felt as useless now as he did.

The monstrous shape turned sharply, setting its sights on Bru and Jake. With a deafening bellow, it charged—a tidal wave of flesh and fury—and Jason understood suddenly that no amount of smashing or bashing would stop this thing.

Then an explosion of light: flares shooting upward from behind the beast where one of the deputies had fallen. They burst brilliantly against low-hanging clouds before hitting the ground behind it in sputtering arcs.

The creature halted mid-stride, confused by the sudden brightness. Bru took his chance and hurled his tire iron with all his strength—it crashed against one of its legs with a sickening crack that sent shudders through bone and sinew.

Staggering sideways in pain or panic or both, the monster released an ear-splitting wail that left everyone momentarily stunned. But then it turned—eyes full of rage and hunger. Jake knew this was it, the monster seemed damn near unstoppable, and there was nothing he could do about it. He shot a look at Bru, who simply nodded.

Jake squinted his eyes and took a breath, "okay."

——

A bright red light lit up the surrounding trees. Dean and Pappy paused. In the distance they could hear shouting and the clanging of a battle of some kind.

Pappy looked at Dean with purpose, "there's no going back after this. You ready?"

Dean nodded briskly, "Yeah, let's go."

They hurried toward the chaos, slipping through the wet underbrush as shadows and flares lit the sky. All around them, the storm howled with fury. Dean felt adrenaline pushing him forward, and a sensation of fear mixed with excitement twisted in his gut.

Another roar echoed through the night, so loud that it seemed to tear through the rain itself. Dean and Pappy exchanged a glance—whatever was out there was something big, and they needed to get to it before it got to them.

"Straight ahead!" Pappy shouted over the din, pointing past a row of skeletal trees. "Sounds like they're on top of it!"

Dean nodded, picking up speed as he dodged low branches and leapt over muddy patches. He could hear his heart pounding in his ears, an erratic drumbeat urging him onward, primal and familiar.

They burst out of the tree line and into the open chaos of the graveyard.

Figures scrambled in near-panic across the field, but there was coordination in their movement—a desperate urgency as they heaved away mounds of wet earth from old gravesites. If they were afraid, they didn't have time for it. And that's when Dean spotted Jake among them.

He looked like he'd aged ten years since Dean had last seen him; every line on his face etched deep with worry. Of course, it HAD been a few years but still, this battle had gotten to him.

Jake saw them too and froze for half a heartbeat, not really believing what he was seeing, then he broke into a wide grin that didn't reach his eyes.

"Dean! Pappy!" Jake called out as they ran towards him. The relief in his voice was palpable; it washed over them all like a warm current against biting cold.

"That thing is huge," Dean gasped when they reached him. "What the hell are we dealing with?"

"Don't know," Jake admitted grimly. "And I don't want to find out—not up close."

Pappy spoke up in obvious recognition, "Fomori, and a right ugly one."

"It looks like a cyclops and a goat had a baby, and it ain't real happy about it," Jake quipped.

Dean and Pappy stared at Jake briefly then Pappy burst out with a huge guffaw, "you ain't wrong!"

"But why does it ooze like that, like it's unstable," Jake yelled as the dodged another wild blow from the creature that was assessing these new arrivals.

Dean looked at his old friend, "because it's half in and half out of this world."

Jake shook his head, "not you too."

Dean cracked a smile, "it's a long story."

The fomori burst through the other deputies, sending two flying against the headstones, knowing it was outnumbered, in a mad dash deeper into the cemetery.

"We're losing it!" Bru's voice rang out, desperate against the hammering rain.

"No," Pappy growled, setting his jaw. "Not if I have anything to say about it."

He pulled a bundle from his coat—a long cylindrical object wrapped in oilcloth—and tore it open to reveal a sleek hunting rifle. Dropping to one knee, he took aim at shapes barely visible through the downpour.

"Wait!" Dean shouted over another boom of thunder. "It's too far!"

Pappy didn't flinch. He squinted down the sights, steady as stone. "One shot's all I need."

The crack of the rifle split the air, louder than any thunderclap. For a heartbeat there was nothing—just rain and breathless anticipation—and then came a cry so raw and agonized that even the storm seemed to recoil from it.

Everyone froze where they stood as hope crashed against disbelief. The massive darkness on the horizon shuddered violently before collapsing into itself with a final mournful bellow.

Bru looked at the group, harried but regrouped. "It evaporated like those other things. Does that mean it's dead?"

"Not getting up after that," Pappy said with grim satisfaction.

"What did you shoot it with? Our guns had no effect on it," Jake asked, perplexed.

"Iron bullets," Pappy said as though it was obvious. He looked at their handheld weapons, shovels, tire irons, and what not in appreciation. "You fellas had the right idea, but that fomori's skin as as tough as a rhino, gotta pierce it to have any real effect."

Jake looked at his old friend appreciatively, "We're gonna need some of those."

A gleam sparkled in Pappy's eyes, "I thought ye might. We need to swing by the shop, I've got some equalizers for ya."

It was then that Jason ran up, eyes wide in disbelief. *"Sheriff!! You gotta come quick, you won't believe what we found."* A strange sense of recognition came over Dean at the sight of the man but he couldn't quite put it together. It was Jake's words that shook him from his revelry.

"Where?"

"The little chapel at the far end of the cemetery."

"All right," Jake barked as they rain began falling harder, "You heard 'em! Haul ass! We're not done here yet!" Jake looked at Dean, who was running beside him, "you may have been better off wherever you were, shit around here has gone off the rails."

Dean's face was twisted in confusion and understanding and in his mind he could hear a feint voice, *"The real monsters are coming, daddy. They are coming for your friend."*

———

Lord Bres was deep into his meditation as Geoffrey interrupted him, everything had to be perfect, the ley lines energy was surging, the path between worlds was at its thinnest. Syphoning his home worlds energy was a must for his plan to remotely succeed.

"What is it?" Bres asked, without moving a muscle, his voice a molten river of irritation.

Geoffrey shifted uneasily, not daring to meet his master's gaze. "The deputies—they're closing in on the chapel. They took the bait, but..."

"But?"

"They're more resourceful than we assumed." Geoffrey flinched as Bres opened his eyes, cold as obsidian and twice as hard.

"Incompetence is a luxury we cannot afford." Bres rose smoothly, every movement precise and deliberate. "Have you located the professor?"

"Not yet," Geoffrey replied, barely audible above the sound of crackling energy. "But I have agents—"

"Double them," Bres commanded sharply. "And what of the fomori?"

"It was neutralized," Geoffrey said, his face a mask of shame. "Humans," Geoffrey said, his words tumbling over each other. "They have weapons—old ones. They're more resourceful than expected."

Bres was silent for a moment. When he finally spoke, it was with a slow, terrible amusement. "Did you think they would cower like rabbits? Oh, Geoffrey. You disappoint me."

Geoffrey's voice quivered with nerves and anticipation combined, "The dearg-due, the sluagh, everything you seeded has risen and is stretched to the boundaries of the county."

Bres's eyes flared with something dark and dangerous. "Then unleash more. If they're drawn to the fear these humans possess, let us drown them in numbers."

"Yes, my lord." Geoffrey bowed low, eager to escape the suffocating presence of his master, but did not want to tell him of this next bit of business. "I'm afraid there's more. The interloper has improbably returned to himself. I thought that was impossible, lord."

"As did I," Lord Bres hissed calmly. "No matter."

"But Lord, the asylum is under siege," Geoffery protested.

"I would hardly call it a siege, more of an inconvenience. For they know not what they face in those wretched halls," he smiled sardonically. "And what of that imbecile Malone?"

"Absorbed and replaced. All city police are now at the asylum and on the hunt for the intruders."

"That leaves only one small, crucial piece, the girl. Everything is going as ordained," Bres said, pointedly looking deep into Geoffery's eyes.

"You shall have her soon, my lord, I have it on excellent authority," the wily butler finally smiled, confident, at least, in this last bit of new.

Bres turned back to the center of the chamber where symbols glowed with an eerie light. The air thrummed with power and anticipation. *Soon*, he thought. *Very soon.*

CHAPTER 22

The loud wrap on Kara's door jilted her from her thoughts. The endless rain and worry and lulled her into an almost comatose state. She hadn't heard back from Jake but the whole town seemed anxious as rumors swirled about the school and Halloween Trick-or-Treating being cancelled. On top of that there was no explanation as to why, only that it was in everyone's best interest to stay at home, which only served to have the opposite effect.

The knock was louder this time. Kara peeked through the curtains and let out a breath she hadn't realized she was holding. It was the pizza delivery driver, standing in the rain getting soaked. She quickly opened the door and apologized. "Sorry, Mark, I was in the back. Just set the pizzas on the table, I'll get your money."

Kara shuffled off to her room, rummaged through her purse and proceeded back to the kitchen when she heard Haley's voice, "We made some delicious cookies. You should try them; my mom makes the best."

She could hear Mark laughing as she rounded the corner, money outstretched, "Here you go," Kara said, handing him two twenty-dollar bills.

Mark looked surprised, "Umm, Miss Bennett, I think you gave me way too much. The pizza was only eighteen dollars."

Kara smiled, "you hauled them all the way out here, in this monsoon, and had to stand in it while I took my time answering. You more than earned it. Haley, give Mark some cookies to take with him."

Haley quickly crammed a handful into a little sandwich baggie and gave them to Mark. "Happy Halloween," she said gleefully.

He smiled, "Happy Halloween!"

"Tell your mother to call me sometime so we can get together."

"Yes ma'am, I will. And thank you!"

"You're welcome," Kara said kindly as Mark proceeded back out into the rain. "Be careful out there," she shouted toward his retreating form. He waved goodbye as he hopped back into his vehicle and Kara closed and locked the door behind her.

"That was fun, mommy," Haley smiled broadly, "our first Trick-or-Treater!"

Kara marveled at her daughter. All their Halloween plans had been ruined yet her she was, taking it all in stride and making the best of it. Most adults couldn't do that. It was then that she noticed Kaia, sitting on the couch staring after Mark's car as it disappeared into the distance, the dog's ears erect, posture rigid, and on high alert. She hadn't let out a peep when Mark was in the house. *What on earth is she seeing out there*, Kara wondered.

A chill ran through her, and she shook it off. Maybe Kaia sensed Kara's own unease about everything that had happened the past few days. She tried Jake's number again. Voicemail. Where was he? Knowing him, probably out with his camera trying to prove the town's weirdness was newsworthy.

"Are we going to eat?" Haley asked, already examining a pizza. "I'm starving!"

Kara smiled at her enthusiasm. "Sure thing, bug."

They set up a picnic on the living room floor, each grabbing a slice as Kara flipped on the TV. Static filled the screen, and she groaned, flipping through channels that had all become snowstorms. "Must be this weather," she muttered.

"Let's tell ghost stories!" Haley suggested, her eyes gleaming with excitement.

Kara hesitated. The thought of more ghosts made her skin crawl. But seeing Haley so happy eased her worry for a moment. "Alright," she relented, wrapping an arm around her daughter. "Once upon a time..."

Before she could start, Kaia let out a low growl and Kara felt another knot form in her stomach.

"What is it, girl?" Haley patted the anxious dog.

The phone rang suddenly, its shrill tone making them both jump. Kara scrambled for it, hoping it was Jake at last. A familiar voice crackled through the line, muffled by a terrible static.

"Kara, are you and Haley okay?" an almost desperate voice blurted out.

She sighed in relief as Jake's voice eased her tension, "Hey, I was starting to get worried. We're fine here." Kara stepped out of the room for a little privacy, "Jake, are you okay? What's happening out there?"

There was a pause, as if he was deciding how to approach this. "It's bad, Kara. The shit that is going on, I don't even begin to know how to explain it. All I can say for sure is to keep yourselves bottled up in that house until I get to you. Can you do that for me?"

Kara knew this was serious, she knew Jake, far better than she wanted to admit most of the time and he wasn't prone to fits of overprotectiveness or hysteria. If he said it was serious, then that meant it was worse. "We will, I promise." She paused, taking a steadying breath, "Jake..."

"Yeah…"

"…please watch yourself. We have a daughter to raise," she added, for the first time giving that truth the weight it deserved.

"I will, you too."

The phone went dead, leaving Kara with a million emotions all at once. Hopefully there would be time to sort those out later. Right now, there was only her daughter to protect and no matter what they had to face, no one was taking her baby away from her.

———

"Marcus?" Dan shouted again into the radio over its dead channel. "Marcus?"

Static hissed back at him like mocking laughter.

"They'll make it," Laurel offered quietly but without conviction from where she led them onward past hallway one. Her fingers tightened around the marble until she felt its pulse more clearly— a drumbeat growing faster again by the second—and changed direction once more: left where instinct said right then up instead of out because nothing here followed rules except for its own terrible logic. The marble wanted her to go down hallway two.

"We're getting closer," Jim insisted—but to what? He refused to let himself think too much about it when suddenly the overhead speakers announced the opening of the inmate's cells. "Oh no."

"That's not good," Evan agreed, sharing a look with Jim.

Judge Hawthorne looked around frantically, "what's not good?"

"All of the inmates have been released from their cells," Jim told him.

"That was an emergency release which means it opened every cell...even the experimental patients down there," Evan added darkly.

"Experimental," Laurel asked seriously. "What do you mean?"

They each exchanged grim looks. "They're not the same as the rest," Evan admitted.

"That's why only select people could go down there," Jim realized.

Evan nodded affirmatively.

"And y'all let that idiot Derek down there?" Jim retorted.

Laurel felt her stomach twist. As if on cue, a distant scream echoed through the halls, followed by the thundering of feet and voices.

"We need to find Marcus, destroy that altar, and get out of here!" Dan urged, as they picked up their pace.

"He's moving too," Laurel said with a certainty she couldn't explain. She let the marble guide them through an impossible path, her mind racing. Whatever was going on wasn't just madness—it was planned. And they were running out of time.

Another scream cut through the air, closer this time.

Dan turned a corner and skidded to a stop, almost crashing into Marcus who was tearing toward them, a wild look in his eyes, Charlotte right behind him. "Move!" Marcus yelled, not even pausing as he passed by.

"Marcus! Wait!" Dan shouted after him as a flurry of orange jumpsuits swarmed into view behind Marcus, chasing him at full speed. He turned back to the others to say something when his eyes widened at what he saw at the rear of the group: hulking figures loping along like animals, their malformed bodies grotesque against the red strobe lights flashing overhead.

"RUN!" Dan screamed.

Panic shot through them all as they bolted back the way they had come, Hallway Two was a bust. Laurel let instinct take over completely, leading them deeper into the asylum with nothing but adrenaline and terror fueling their legs.

She felt it before she saw it—a shift in energy—then suddenly Marcus again, this time standing still, waiting desperately by an elevator at the end of one corridor. "This way!" he waved frantically.

They piled in just as shouts and snarls reached fever pitch down the hall; Jim hammered the button for close like his life depended on it and maybe it did. The doors slid shut with a whisper and everyone sucked in breathless lung-fulls of relief.

Jake's voice echoed in Laurel's mind—you're one of the few people I trust—and she wondered how long they could hold off whatever storm had been unleashed...and how far its reach would be.

——

Haley snuggled against Kara with Kaia nestled close beside them both. Only a storm from outside made any noise now as rain rattled against windows like skeletal fingers.

"Is the storm ever going to end?" Haley asked sleepily.

"Soon," Kara promised softly, trying to keep every bit of fear out of her tone.

It seemed impossible but Haley had somehow fallen asleep amidst all this chaos—maybe feeling safer than Kara possibly could—but that was kids for you, she thought with some pride and awe for her girl: soldiers through anything so long as you kept smiling and pretending right alongside them until you couldn't anymore or until things changed for real again…even if that meant worse instead of better before it got there.

Her thoughts drifted to Jake, of how she had kept him out of their lives. They had fallen hard and fast for each other, so magnetically drawn together that only a sheer act of God could separate them. That act was Haley, and Kara's sudden realization that Jake's job and his propensity to walk where Angel's fear to tread would put her daughter at risk, or worse, take her daddy away from her. So Kara ended it suddenly, no explanation, without ever telling Jake about Haley. Of course, he would find out eventually and the fight they had that night was epic in proportions, but even Jake could see her side of it, he knew how badly Hale County was trending.

Now, she wished she could take it all back. She wished she could have told Jake from the beginning, gotten married, and raised her together. The thought of Jake and Haley, father and daughter, playing, laughing, dinner dates…she had robbed them of so much out of her fear. But, after what happened to Cutty and Jake's response to that, she knew she had made the right choice…at the time.

"Mommy?"

"Yes, bug," Kara answered as brightly as she could manage.

Haley beamed at her mother's reassurance then pulled another slice of pizza onto her paper plate. "Can you finish the ghost story? Please?"

Kara hesitated before sitting beside her daughter and picking up where they left off. "The lights began to flicker as the little boy entered the room…" she began, just as something heavy thudded against the front door.

Kaia barked furiously before bolting to the door, her fur standing on end, teeth bared.

Haley's eyes grew wide. "Was that a ghost?" she whispered excitedly.

Kara rose to her feet, wanting to say something comforting but unsure what that was but everything went silent again, except for the rain. She checked every window. Nothing. After several minutes she went back to the couch, Kaia once again cuddled up next to Haley.

"Must have been the wind," Kara said with a smile, though internally she felt the gnawing sensation that something was out of place. *Damn it, Jake, where are you?* she thought as the thunder rumble once more.

———

Shovels bit into sodden earth with renewed vigor as everyone scrambled back to their tasks. The temporary reprieve gave them speed—even Jason found himself helping on instinct alone, his heart pounding for reasons other than fear now.

Grave by grave they worked against time and weather both until finally came payoff: large wooden crate hauled up from deep in ground beneath cracked headstone; contents rattling ominously inside despite careful handling lifting it free soaked pit.

"Is that..." Bru eyed box warily; already reaching for crowbar with hand still bloody from earlier efforts.

"Changelings," Jake confirmed grimly; motioning deputies crack lid open under flashlights' unsteady beams.

"Aye," Pappy confirmed, "those are totems used to confer the changeling to the victim."

Inside were rows upon rows of crude clay figurines—all carved in likeness of people of Hale—all cracked and chipped where real people had been cursed to swap places with the creatures.

Dean looked at Jake, "there are hundreds of these things in just this one box."

The sheriff nodded, "they could be anyone. Yeah, I keep having this conversation, but this is on a scale I hadn't considered. But where are the people who were taken?"

"Where the fomori was running," Pappy said. "It was guarding them."

A grim silence took hold as they looked out toward the far end of the cemetery, where mists gathered like ghosts over the wet ground.

Dean's expression was pure steel. "We've got to move. Now."

With a nod from Jake, they charged into the night, rain driving against them in needling sheets. Each deputy had a box hoisted on their shoulder, shovels clattering to their sides as they ran. The floodlights dwindled behind them, but determination burned bright; this time fear had no claim on them.

They crossed old graves and twisted headstones, boots pounding in sync with the beat of anxious hearts. Dean glanced at Jake as they ran together and saw something new in his friend—an edge sharper than worry alone, honed by urgency and hope.

"You're not going to disappear on me again are you?" Jake called out between breaths.

"Not if I can help it," Dean shot back, a grin breaking through despite everything.

Ahead, the mist thickened into a dense wall. They slowed, scanning for any sign of movement—any hint of another ambush—but all was eerily still except for the eternal patter of rain.

A frantic call came out from a deputy over the radio, *"Sir, you're gonna want to see this…"*

Jake, Dean, Pappy, and Jason rushed to the deputy who was standing over a freshly dug grave, a look of confusion and fear on his face.

"Anderson, what…" the sheriff stopped in mid-sentence, not believing what he was seeing. The group looked at one another as Jake grabbed his radio. "Bru, I need you with me. You and you alone. Tell the others to keep digging."

Jason had gone pale. "Is that…"

Jake couldn't answer, simply nodding slowly, mind a whirl of emotions.

Everyone seemed to be looking at the other for answers, for some kind of sense to what they were seeing. Bru came hustling up to them, "Boss, you're gonna have to see…"

The large man stopped talking as the group eyed him warily. "What?"

The sheriff pointed to the grave the deputy had just dug up. Lying there, large frame a shell of the person it had been, was Bru. He was fully emaciated to the point of mummification, but it WAS Bru. There was no mistaking it. The big man stood there, dumbfounded. "I…I don't understand…"

Jake was waiting on the thing that was his deputy to suddenly grin that oversized changeling grin and attack them but all the would-be man could do is stare, shaken to his core by what he was seeing. "I…I don't…that's not…I'm me, boss, I swear I'm me…look,

I'm even holding iron…" he stammered, eyes full of desperation and something else, honesty.

Pappy looked upon the large deputy with sincerity and sadness. "He's been fully absorbed, drained of all his essence. The changeling has completely taken over. His skin is forming a natural barrier against the iron. Fascinatin'!"

"No!," Bru roared suddenly, "that's not true. I don't even have them big-ass teeth! I am Archibald Brubaker. I'm a person. A deputy. I…I…I've been a deputy for three years now. Loyal. Always doing what I've been asked!"

Dean watched as his old friend Jake struggled with what to do next. He knew Jake wanted to believe Bru with every part of his being. Even he himself almost believed Bru and he had just met the man. And he had a point, the very iron that was supposed to injure the creature was being held by a man who almost died fighting that Fomori a few minutes earlier.

"Bru…" Jake said quietly, locking eyes with his deputy.

Bru held the weapon out to his boss and slumped to his knees, tears welling in his eyes, "you gotta kill me boss. If I'm a monster ya gotta do it. I don't wanna be a monster."

Jake was frozen, jaw clenched tight. The sight of Bru lying there— the skeletal remains—was a haunting accusation, but the look in that man's eyes, the sadness, the fear, the hopelessness…

Dean put a hand on the sheriff's shoulder. "We need to keep moving, Jake."

"Boss?" Bru's voice cracked like the sky above them.

Jake inhaled sharply. "Get up, Deputy," he said finally, resolve hardening his face. "We have a job to do."

The confusion on Bru's face slowly melted into a look of relief and determination. "Yes sir," he said, rising to his feet.

Dean kept his eyes on Jake as they regrouped, unsure if this new urgency came from purpose or desperation or simply his affection for the younger man.

"We need to get that ammunition, Jake. Any chance we can get a ride into town?" Pappy asked, some urgency creeping in to his voice.

"Absolutely, I'll send some people with you and I'll keep a couple to help me finish up here. Meet me at the asylum when you're done." Jake watched as the color faded swiftly from Dean's face. "You okay, man?"

Dean stood there motionless for what seemed forever before shaking himself out of it. *The asylum, it always leads to the asylum*, his mind screamed. "Yeah, I'm good."

"They can take my car, boss," Bru spoke up, tossing the keys to Pappy, "I'll ride with Anderson."

"Nonsense, big fella, we'll ride with you," Pappy cackled, tossing back the keys, "If Jake trusts you, so do I. Not sure how all this is possible, but we'll get to the bottom of it, don't worry."

"Yes sir," Bru replied thankfully, marching toward his vehicle and rounding up other officers along the way.

"It does put up a big ole question though..." Pappy said as the large deputy sauntered away to round the others up.

Jake nodded in understanding, following Pappy's line of thinking, "how many are monsters, and how many are like Bru?"

"Take Professor Locke here with you, he can explain the situation we're in. I'll meet you guys there shortly." Jake looked at his long-lost friends, then to the cemetery where the other deputies were still working, "watch yourselves. If this is just beginning, then who knows what the hell we are truly up against."

———

Ashlyn pleaded to the thing that looked like JC to set her free as he moved her into a weird chamber of exotic plants and trees, an ethereal glimmer in the air.

Ashlyn lay surrounded by shimmering foliage, vines creeping around her limbs as if trying to pull her under. Her mind was a whirlwind of thoughts that weren't entirely her own: memories both distant and near; fragments of lives lived long ago or maybe just yesterday; pieces of herself she couldn't have recognized if she tried but felt woven into nonetheless; everything tinged with an urgency that felt too big for her mind to grasp.

She struggled against the binds that held her and screamed in frustration, "JC, let me go!"

The changeling turned to her with an all-too-familiar smirk. "It's easier not to fight, Ash. You'll see."

"No! I'm getting out of here!"

He gave her a pitying look and left her among the bizarre vegetation. The glow around her seemed to pulse, an almost soothing rhythm that was anything but comforting.

Ashlyn thrashed against the restraints, desperate to escape before the strange aura seeped into her. The plants rustled like they were whispering secrets she couldn't hear. She thought of mom, her determination, and she knew she had to hold on.

"JC!" she screamed again, voice choked with anger and fear.

The air shimmered more brightly in Ashlyn's chamber now, and she felt her mind slipping away bit by bit. Her thoughts were becoming disjointed—a wave here, a burst there—each one harder to focus on than the last.

She remembered JC's face for a moment, her JC—his smile—and then it flickered out like a dying ember as a new presence entered the room.

JC walked back in, a cruel softness in his eyes that made him almost look human. "You okay?"

"Go to hell," Ashlyn spat weakly.

He sighed with an exaggerated patience and crouched down next to her like he cared even one bit about who she was or how she felt. "You'll be happier once you stop resisting."

"I won't let you do this," she growled between clenched teeth.

His expression shifted ever so slightly as he reached out a hand and placed it on her forehead. A cold pain surged through her skull before everything went blindingly white.

——

Sheriff Jake Hooks stood silhouetted in the night against the backdrop of lightning and flashlights, rain falling steady and consistent. His scar was burning but all he could think of in that moment was how he could save his county. His whole world had been upended. Nothing made sense. Fantasy was now reality. How do you fight things that were always just fairytales until a few hours ago?

He heard the loud thud of a shovel hitting something solid, bringing him out of his train of thought. As he turned his gaze to the noise, a beam of light blinded his vision then was quickly removed. The Sheriff gazed into the face of the trepid deputy holding the offending flashlight. Jake didn't blink. "Well?" he asked irritated.

"Um, it looks like a coffin, sir."

Sure enough, just about three feet under the surface, Jake could make out something made of wood. The deputy seemed to shrink under the Sheriff's withering stare. "Get it out." *Why wouldn't there be a coffin you damn fool, you're in a cemetery.* Yet that was the point. There shouldn't be any new coffins here.

Jake motioned for the other deputy to come over and help. The steady rainfall made the object hard to grasp and even harder to lift. Finally, the deputies managed to hoist a six-foot-long makeshift wooden casket out of the hole. It was covered in mud, grass, and rain. The newness of the casket was obvious as the wood still had its light sheen as opposed to the grayish aged wood one would expect to find in an old cemetery.

There was something else, carvings, signs and sigils.

The thunder and lightning increased in intensity as the rain pounded the earth harder almost in outrage of the casket being removed from its place of rest. The skinny deputy with the offensive light looked up at the Sheriff in hesitation. They were fidgety, more-so than usual, and Jake knew why. Ulterior motives, everyone in Hale County had them and his deputies were no different and with what's going on, anyone could be playing for the other side.

Jake stared steadily back, unflinching. "Open it."

The deputy with the flashlight climbed his way out of the gravesite, leaving the other deputy to remain in the freshly excavated hole. "Y-y-yessir," the flashlight deputy said as he kneeled over the wooden casket.

Uncertain, but doing as they were told, the deputies used crowbars to pry off the lid of the fairly new looking casket. The deputies flinched back as a putrid odor rushed over them. Almost as fast as the lightning that was raging in the skies around them, Jake whipped his .44 Magnum from his holster.

The muzzle of the gun flashed in the storm, quickly followed by a deafening report that was almost masked by the thunder. The bullet slammed into the face of the larger deputy that was still in the hole, exploding from the back of his head and spraying the simple marker and mud with his brains, or that black goo that resembled brains.

The flashlight deputy had the temerity to actually look surprised before his face became a blank mask, all timidity gone. Jake didn't hesitate. His finger expertly squeezed the trigger of the massive handgun. The deputy made no expression as the bullet tore into his chest. The force was so great it lifted him slightly off his feet and flung him into the grave where he landed atop the corpse of the other deputy.

Jake knelt down by the casket to get a better look, his knees sinking into the rain-soaked mud. He pointed his flashlight inside, ignoring the odor. The only emotion on his face was the set of his jaw and the tightening around his eyes. "I'll be damned."

The woman, while covered in a weird glimmering oily black slime, was striking in her beauty. There was something familiar about her. *I've seen her, but where?* Suddenly it clicked. The woman from the picture in Doctor Michaels office...this was his wife! *But he said she was dead*, Jake thought, *he believes she's dead.*

Jake worked fast, knowing what would happen if he didn't. He holstered his gun and hoisted the slick-haired woman out of the casket. She was as stiff as a board, her skin pale and clammy. Carrying her to the truck, Jake laid her gently in the bed, not caring that he was now covered in the black ooze himself.

He took a deep breath and looked around. His scar throbbed, each pulse a reminder of all the things he had yet to understand. The rain showed no signs of letting up but Jake was used to storms; he'd been living in one his whole life.

He took one last look at the bodies of his deputies. How long had they been like that? How many more were like them? Why was Bru different? Ulterior motives… He got into his truck and slammed the door shut with grim determination.

The engine roared to life as Jake thought about Doctor Michaels. They had argued fiercely, but Jake knew Michaels was a good man, if a desperate one. He thinks she's dead…

The windshield wipers clawed at the glass as he sped down the empty roads toward the asylum. Normally he would take her to the hospital, but this was pretty fucking far from normal. Evan was at the asylum. He would be the only one who could help her now. Lightning split the sky over the distant foothills, illuminating the desolate landscape in white hot flashes that were so bright they made him squint.

The night was getting angry, a living, breathing sentient anger that hungered for chaos and Jake Hooks found himself directly in the eye of the storm.

——

The shop loomed in oppressive darkness as they pulled up—no stuttering streetlamps, no pulsing neon glow, only the relentless hiss of the wind and the pounding assault of rain against the cold tin awning. The expansive windows of Roundtree Outfitters— Pappy's dilapidated old supply depot—were smeared with years of grime, while the battered "Closed" sign swung ominously in the wind like a warning.

Dean stepped out of Bru's truck; shotgun slung heavily across his back. Bru and the other two deputies flanked him, weapons raised and eyes scouring the deserted street. Pappy advanced toward the door as if he'd braved it a thousand times before, but even he paused, one hand lingering near the iron rounds at his belt.

"This place looks abandoned," whispered one of the younger deputies, his voice tight with nervous tension.

"Abandoned, sure," Pappy snapped, his tone fierce, "but I locked this door before I left last time. Damn it."

With that, he reached forward and shoved the door. It groaned on rust-eaten hinges, its creak slicing through the silence—Unlocked.

Time seemed to freeze.

Dean gave a curt nod, and they surged forward as one unit. They swept through the front room—a jumble of dusty shelves laden with outdated hunting gear, battered lanterns, field knives, and camping supplies that held the stale promise of bygone days. Everything appeared undisturbed...until a shift in the wind carried a foul stench.

Rot. Faint. Sickeningly sweet. All wrong.

"Pappy," Bru said, his voice clenching with dread, "you got a back room?"

"Yeah," Pappy muttered, already moving with urgency toward the back. "Storage and loading dock."

Gun raised, Dean trailed, his finger tensed on the trigger like a coiled spring.

As Pappy rounded the corner and stepped into the back, he unleashed a low, furious curse. "They've been here."

The storage room was a scene of devastation—shelves upended, ammo boxes splintered, and wooden crates shattered on the floor as though clawed apart from within by unseen hands.

But that wasn't the worst of it.

Near the far exit, barely illuminated by a flickering emergency floodlight, two figures lurked. Tall, unnervingly rigid silhouettes that defied human nature.

Dean leveled his shotgun. "Don't move."

The figures turned in unison. One wore a butcher's apron, drenched in inky black ichor, a grotesque smile carved into a face that was too long, too distorted. The other bore the disheveled uniform of a bus driver, collar askew, eyes vacant and soulless.

The bus driver-like figure tilted its head unnaturally and stepped forward. "Your bullets won't help you," it intoned, its voice layering human and something far more alien.

Without hesitation, Dean fired. The impact sent the creature's head snapping violently backward, yet it refused to collapse.

Bru and the deputies unleashed their own hailstorm of iron slugs, pummeling the two aberrations. The butcher shrieked as a stray shot rent its side, splattering dark, gory ichor against the wall. The bus driver staggered, growling something in guttural Gaelic, before lunging forward like a predator in heat.

Pappy acted with lethal precision. He dove to a half-broken crate, yanked free a sawed-off shotgun wrapped in oilcloth, and squeezed both triggers in unison. The blast's force hurled the bus driver crashing back into metal shelving with a sickening, bone-crunching clatter.

Seizing the moment, Dean stepped forward and fired another round directly into the butcher's center mass. With a ghastly, wet collapse, it crumpled like soggy paper.

An eerie silence descended, broken only by the incessant hiss of rain and a ringing echo burning in their ears.

"Jesus Christ," the younger deputy whispered, voice trembling, "what the hell are they?"

"Leftovers," Pappy growled, reloading with deliberate calm. "Scouts. Testing the waters."

Dean turned toward Bru, whose chest heaved with heavy, panicked breaths as he gripped an imposing iron crowbar.

"You held it together," Dean murmured, eyes never leaving his companion.

"I'm still me," Bru replied quietly, defiance tempered by exhaustion. "No matter what that grave says."

Dean gave a slow, grim nod. "Then let's finish what we came here for."

Pappy tossed a weighty duffel bag toward Dean. "Iron rounds. Blades. Lanterns. Holy water. It isn't much, but it's old and it's true."

Eyeing the remaining shelves with a hardened gaze, he added, "We grab what we can, and we get out. We don't want to be here when the night swallows everything whole."

Dean shot a wary glance through the grimy window.

It was already too late for any escape from the darkness.

CHAPTER 23

Fear gripped the small group as they crept inexorably toward Hallway Five. As they rounded the corner, the group skidded to an abrupt halt. The walls and floor had transformed before their very eyes; the tired old tiles had been swallowed by a sinister, glimmering black onyx that pulsed with an unearthly glow. Evan's blood ran cold as he realized the stone had not been laid down—it had erupted, overtaking the walls and floors like a creeping mold.

"What is this damned place?" Judge Hawthorne demanded, his voice trembling with awe at the alien majesty that assaulted his mundane senses.

Dan reached out, his fingers brushing against a cold onyx crystal. He closed his eyes to shut out every distraction, a half-forgotten tale from his grandmother pricking at the edge of his memory. Finally, in a low tone laced with forewarning, he declared, "This is the fringes of the ethereal plane—the thin, perilous border that connects this world to the next. Ancient magics both tether and separate these realms. Only at special times—like the solstices when the veils thin—do the planes grow strong enough to merge. The fae scud along these ley lines, converging at these nexus points."

Marcus's eyes widened in disbelief as he stared at Dan. "They've been crossing over here for years?"

"Millennia," Dan corrected, his voice deep with ancient sorrow. "There was a time when they roamed our realm unchallenged before being exiled to Tir Na Nog. Yet even now, they cross over—to celebrate, to remember a lost age. In their world, magic and beauty entwine with peace and harmony. The Sidhe visit this nexus as one would a sacred memorial, to honor a cherished past."

Evan's voice cracked with panic, "This was an ordinary hallway this morning!"

Laurel's skepticism cut sharply through the mounting dread. "Then what in hell are we dealing with? This isn't just a tribute to the past—there's something malevolent at work here."

But Dan wasn't angered by her words, merely understanding her terror. "You're right—it's drastically different now. Somewhere within this crossing, darkness has seeped in... sinister, corrupt evil."

Char ground out her frustration, "This is all well and good, but what are we supposed to do now? Those horrors are right behind us and our only exit is... where?! I'm not signing up for a trip to Oz!"

A chilling thought struck Laurel. "What happened to the people in those rooms?"

Evan met her gaze, bile rising in his throat. The weight of his guilt pressed down on him as a low, ominous rumble of chaos steadily advanced from the distance.

Every escape route was closing in.

Jim clutched his weapon, his eyes frantically scanning for salvation. "Over there!" he bellowed, his trembling finger pointing to a winding stairway at the hallway's end. "That's our escape!"

Laurel's mind raced as she surveyed both the transformed corridor behind them and the precarious route ahead. Grabbing Evan's hand with fierce urgency, she commanded, "We must keep moving!"

Evan nodded, his eyes darting up the spiraling staircase. "We can get out—we just have to stay ahead of them."

Dan led the group down the eerie hallway, while Judge Hawthorne lingered, mesmerized by the shimmering, hypnotic expanse. The otherworldly beauty overwhelmed him—a blinding assault on his senses. Finally, he tore himself away and hastily caught up with the stricken band.

They surged forward in a desperate, frantic line, the cacophonous noise from below spurring them onward. Their shadows danced violently against the cavernous walls, leaping with every flash of lightning that smashed through the ghostly windows of the transformed rooms.

But as they neared the end of the hallway, dark, wispy figures began to materialize from the void and the twisting staircase.

Char glanced back in terror. "They're already here!" she screamed.

"They're at our backs too!" Laurel shouted over the clash of fear and chaos, her voice trembling with dread.

Trapped in a nightmare with no escape, the Judge's ragged breaths hurled into the oppressive silence; he stumbled, barely catching himself before plunging again into the nightmarish sprint ahead.

———

Dean stared up at the ominous form of Hale County Mental Institute. Abandoned police cruisers with lights still flashing were parked haphazardly. His mind was roiling with memories and emotions, raw and aching. He still didn't quite remember how he ended up there, but the torment he went through was very fresh, like a strobe light of memories, pain, and rage. A huge hand landed on his shoulder and Dean snapped his head toward the offensive person. Bru stood there staring at him, expression full of guilt.

"I'm sorry bout what they did to you in there. Sorry, what I was part of. I ain't got no real excuse," Bru said quietly, removing his hand and looking away in shame.

But Dean, to his credit, seemingly understood the man's plight. The whole damn county was sick and twisted. Besides, the large deputy just found out he was part monster, if not fully so. "It's alright, big fella, this place owes all of us."

Bru nodded brusquely, "yes sir."

Pappy and Jason walked up to stand beside Dean as Bru gave the other deputies their orders. The plan of attack was simple, straight in, put down anything that attacks and make it to the others. They had lost radio contact suddenly so there was no telling just what was going on in there, but they prepared for the worst. "Well, kid," Pappy said with a smirk, "you ready for the rat killin' to commence?"

"Yeah, guess it's time to get to it," Dean replied.

"My wife will never believe this," Jason said simply.

"You gotta wife," Pappy guffawed, "huh, I wouldn'ta figured."

Jason laughed lightly, "she's been outta town. I should've gone with her."

They moved forward, a patchwork army fueled by revenge and desperation. Bru fell in step beside Dean, his tall frame hunched under the weight of guilt and uncertainty.

The Institute loomed, a grotesque silhouette against the storm-clad sky. Shadows flickered in the broken windows, and Dean's mind flashed with images of confinement and fury. Each memory was an electric jolt, spurring him forward.

"We'll cover you!" Bru barked to the others as they approached the crumbling entrance. "Whatever happens, we stick together."

Inside, chaos ruled. The walls echoed with distant screams and shuddered under the force of unseen impacts. Darkness crouched in every corner, waiting to pounce. The site was inexplicably wild to behold, inmates and monsters clashing wildly in the hallways.

Pappy led them down a main corridor, his eyes sharp despite their age. "This way!" he called out, gesturing towards an intersection where debris lay scattered like forgotten corpses. The iron door leading to the dungeon loomed large to their left as they were passing through the fighting.

Dean stopped suddenly. He recognized this spot; it was where they dragged him when he first arrived. A guttural growl escaped his throat, feral and raw.

"We'll find them," Bru said firmly, misunderstanding Dean's focus as concern for his friends.

With new determination, Dean charged ahead. They turned a corner and came face to face with two orderlies—or what had been orderlies. The men were twisted into monstrous versions of themselves: eyes wild, mouths stretched into unnatural snarls.

"Get back!" Jason shouted as one lunged at him with alarming speed.

Pappy raised his shotgun and fired without hesitation. The creature shrieked—a horrible mix of human agony and beastly rage—before crumpling to the floor.

The second monster roared in defiance but froze when it saw who it faced.

Dean stepped forward, a cruel smile playing on his lips. "Remember me?"

The beast hesitated for a fraction too long. Bru shot it down with grim finality.

"Let's keep movin', they'll be trying to get to the top of this bloody nightmare," Pappy urged them on as more wails drifted from deeper within the building.

They pushed further inside, each man silently wrestling with his own demons while confronting those that roamed freely in the flesh around them.

Suddenly, Dean stopped again—this time not from memory but from intuition. There was something else here with them on this floor... something powerful... and angry.

He spun towards a set of double doors just as they burst open to reveal—standing in odd defiance, Ronald, his dark blue jumpsuit grimy with blood, mood, and sweat.

"Dean?" Pappy exclaimed in concern seeing the look of disbelief mixed with unbridled hatred on the face of his newly recovered friend.

"Impossible," Dean growled back as he watched the giant form of Psycho push across the fighting, striking monster and man alike. The large man came to stop at the steel doors leading down to the dungeon and methodically opened them before turning back to stare at Dean, the hate reciprocated on the dead man's face.

A cruel, cold smirk and the crazed man was gone.

Dean took a step to follow him but a dirty hand gently tugged on his shoulder. "That's the past, my friend. Others need our help now."

The war within Dean was agonizing, his other half, Wraith, only wanted to hurt the psycho. Yet Dean knew that Pappy was right. Taking a deep breath he followed Pappy down the hallway to the people who needed them all the while the mad man inside raged in fury.

—

Laurel broke away from the others as the first line of monsters attacked—an invisible thread drawing her deeper into one of the transformed rooms. She had no choice but to follow, trusting that wherever it led, it would bring her closer to answers.

The veil thickened, coiling around her like a living entity. It was more potent here, unleashed and undiluted—a force of nature that threatened to swallow everything whole.

She stumbled around the room littered with overturned furniture and shredded memories. The marble pulsed insistently, urging her across the debris-strewn floor toward a derelict stairwell descending into darkness.

A voice stopped her cold. It was faint, almost lost beneath the wailing chaos above—but unmistakably human. "Laurel…"

It was Amanda's voice.

Shock surged through her veins. "Amanda?" she called out desperately.

No response came except for another whisper of her name, fainter this time.

Laurel hesitated only a moment before plunging down the stairs two at a time. Her mind raced as fast as her feet: it couldn't be, her sister was dead. Still, what if it was…

The thought was both terrifying and hopeful. Her sister, alive—or so she hoped—or was she just another changeling from this cursed place?

But now nothing felt certain except what she felt in her gut: she was somewhere close, caught in the same nightmare that plagued Hale County like an incurable disease. The fearless reporter bolted from the room, the stairwell was her only goal.

As she reached the bottom step, movement flickered at the edges of her vision. She spun around just as several shadowy forms emerged from the gloom—patients warped by their own fear and despair into grotesque parodies of life.

"Stay back!" Laurel shouted, but they advanced with jerky, unnatural motions.

She drew a revolver from her waistband—a parting gift from Jake—and fired at the nearest creature. It staggered back with a shriek before dissolving into mist-like tendrils.

The others hesitated, then swarmed forward with renewed frenzy.

Laurel gritted her teeth and fought through them, firing steadily while she pushed deeper into the sub-levels. She could see her allies all in battles of their own. Each shot echoed like thunder in the claustrophobic confines but did little to stem their relentless advance.

Suddenly she was free of them again, bursting through another set of doors into what must have once been a treatment ward.

It lay abandoned now except for rusting equipment and scattered files—paper ghosts cataloguing the horrors conducted within these walls—but Laurel barely noticed anything except what was at its center:

A child's drawing pinned to an empty bedframe—its corners fluttering in an unseen breeze. It was crudely drawn but unmistakable: stick figures labeled with familiar names scrawled in bright crayon beneath them:

Mommy

Haley

And one more word that sent ice crawling up Laurel's spine:

Daddy

With trembling hands, she snatched it up just as something dark and ominous rose up behind her. There was no mistaking the figure with the hat, Jake. Jake was the little girl's daddy. Laurel heard the blow before she actually felt it.

She dropped to her knees, blood pounding in her ears. The black tendrils wrapped around her like snakes, squeezing tighter with each passing second. She clutched the drawing to her chest, refusing to let go.

"Amanda!" she cried, the word raw and desperate.

The shadows swirled hungrily, but the marble's cold pulse fought against their encroaching darkness. Laurel felt herself being dragged under, into unconsciousness—or something worse.

Something shifted then. A searing burst of white light shattered the grip of the shadows. The presence recoiled, retreating into the crevices of the ward as Laurel gasped for air.

She staggered to her feet, vision blurred and mind reeling from the onslaught. There was no time to rest. She had to move, had to find Amanda before—

A series of crashes echoed from the floor above, followed by shouting—human voices that filled her with a strange mix of hope and dread. She barely registered them, driven instead by an urgency that pulled her toward a heavy steel door at the other end of the room.

Laurel stumbled forward, each step a monumental effort against the Veil's oppressive weight. Her body screamed in protest, but she pushed on until she reached it.

The door was ajar.

Beyond lay another stairwell, this one spiraling impossible further upwards.

The marble pulsed fiercely now; it knew its purpose, even if Laurel did not. She forced herself onward, down into silence so thick it felt like a physical thing pressing against her skin.

Every instinct told her she was crossing a threshold—a point of no return—but doubt had long since ceased to matter. Her senses were coming undone, reality seemed flip its natural state, causing her to stumble.

At last, she emerged into a vast chamber unlike anything else in the crumbling Institute. There should have been a simple hallway there, instead the walls arched overhead like those of a cathedral built by madmen: twisting metal beams entwined with veins of black mist that pulsed rhythmically as though alive.

In its center stood a glass-walled room bathed in sickly green light.

Laurel approached with mounting apprehension—then stopped dead as she saw what was inside:

Amanda.

Her sister was strapped to an upright gurney, wires and tubes snaking from her slight frame to machines that hummed ominously in the confined space. Her eyes were closed; she looked more fragile than Laurel remembered—more like a ghost than ever before.

"Amanda!" The cry tore from Laurel's throat as she slammed against the glass wall separating them.

Amanda stirred slightly but did not wake. Panic surged through Laurel as she searched desperately for a way inside—a keypad next to the only visible entrance offered some hope but also confirmed her worst fears: this was no accident or twist of fate.

Someone put Amanda here deliberately—someone with access and knowledge far beyond what any changeling could possess alone.

Laurel's mind raced even faster than before: Who? Why? Was it Michaels? Did Jake know? Was he part of this? Paranoia began to take rood in the recesses of her mind.

Her hands shook as she keyed in numbers almost at random—the drawing still clutched tightly in one fist—until finally something clicked and hissed within the panel beside her:

The door unlocked itself with an eerie slowness that set Laurel's teeth on edge. *Why did that work,* something asked deep within. Laurel didn't have time to ponder her fortune. She rushed inside just as Amanda opened her eyes—a flicker of recognition crossing her sister's pale features.

"Laurel?" Amanda's voice was faint, barely more than a whisper.

Laurel's heart leapt with relief, but there was no time for reunion. The machines around them pulsed with increasing urgency, as if aware of the intrusion. "I'm getting you out," Laurel promised, frantically unstrapping the restraints that held her sister captive.

Amanda winced as she pulled free. "It's controlling them all," she said. "Everyone." Her words were cut off by a violent shudder. "We have to—"

The chamber trembled, and alarms blared from every corner. Laurel pulled Amanda toward the exit just as the glass walls began to crack under the strain of some unseen force. The Veil was coming for them, and it would not be denied this time.

They stumbled back into the cavernous hall, the black mist swirling in furious patterns above their heads.

"Stay with me!" Laurel urged, half-carrying her sister as they fled back toward the stairwell.

Amanda's breath came in ragged gasps, but she managed a determined nod. "Wait...you have to know," she warned, her eyes darting to shadowy figures emerging from the far side of the room: changelings and more familiar faces—

Chief Eddie Malone leading the charge, his expression one of grim resolve.

He shouted something Laurel couldn't hear over the din as they raced up the stairs, but his intent was clear: he was not here to save them, he was here to stop them at any cost.

Amanda forced Laurel to look at her, eyes pleading for understanding, "Laurel, I'm not your sister, not wholly."

Laurel was frantic, trying to find a way through or around, "what do you mean, of course you are. We just have to find a way out of here and..."

"No," Amanda said sadly, pulling away from her sister, "I died that night on the highway. At least, who I was died. They transferred my essence into this monster. And I'm not the only one."

Everything seemed to stop as Laurel locked eyes with Amanda, her investigative intuition knowing what she was saying was true but her heart, well... "But you recognize me, you KNOW me. Some of you is still here."

"I'm a shadow of her, a fractured reflection. I have some of her memories and mannerisms, but I am not her. I don't know what I am," the clone spoke softly before raising her head and looking fiercely at Laurel. "But I know that who I was loved you very much, and I will not let them have you." Amanda took Laurel by the wrist and raced up the stairs.

"It's just more stairs," Laurel protested, exasperated. She had found Amanda and all she wanted was to hold her, to save her.

But the Amanda clone would have none of it. She placed both of her hands upon Laurels cheeks, pulling her close and staring deep into her mind. "Don't believe anything you see. Focus, Laurel. I know you've missed me but there will be time for that later. Now, we have to end this."

Laurel took a deep sluggish breath and gave a nod. She knew this Amanda was right. Letting herself be led by the clone, they sprinted up the stairs.

They reached the last step just as another explosion rocked the floor beneath them. Laurel's heart pounded wildly as she pushed Amanda through the doors ahead of her—a final burst of adrenaline propelling them into an industrial corridor lined with massive pipes and flickering lights.

There was no time to think or plan; they could only run deeper into uncertainty, driven by equal parts fear and defiance.

Behind them came pursuit: footsteps echoing like gunshots in an impossible rhythm.

Ahead lay a nightmare built on madness—but somehow, they kept going. Each turn brought new dangers; each moment felt like it might be their last. Inexplicable rooms and passageways where they shouldn't logically be, all shimmering with a strange purple twinkle.

The presence loomed larger now than ever before: an immense consciousness that filled every atom of space around them, bending reality itself to its will.

Laurel clutched Amanda's hand tightly as they sprinted down what seemed like another endless hallway, the marble burning against her skin with a cold fire she could almost understand.

Then suddenly—

An exit!

A rusted service door stood ajar at its far end; daylight filtered through from beyond in wan gray shafts that seemed impossibly distant yet tantalizingly real.

Laurel pulled Amanda toward it with renewed desperation when—the world shimmered around them, phasing in and out of existence. It was a strange cul de sac, alien in appearance and in the center sat an pulsating alter. The marble in her hand glowed and hummed uncontrollably, it was home.

———

The tires of Jake Hooks' truck wailed in protest as he navigated a hairpin bend onto the small backroad leading to the Kara's house. Headlights fought valiantly against sheets of relentless rain and a thick, ghostly fog that clung to the rolling hills like spectral memories refusing to be exorcised. Black ooze, dark and viscous, smeared across his arms and chest, slowly hardening into a crust that burned with an itch reminiscent of a sinister curse burrowing beneath his skin. Yet Jake felt nothing but resolute indifference.

In the truck's back cab, shrouded beneath a tattered rain tarp, lay a woman in unsettling repose—unconscious, yet still tethered to life by soft, rhythmic breaths. She was Evan's wife, or at least a haunting mirror image of her; in this blurred moment of uncertainty, nothing was clear, save for one burning imperative— he had to deliver her to Evan before the sands of time slipped away.

Ahead, the trees loomed like the deranged spires of a cathedral, the jagged silhouettes carved against a storm-dark sky as distant lightning illuminated its grotesque spires. Without hesitation, Jake snatched his radio and pounded the button with urgency.

"Pappy—Dean, do you copy? This is Hooks."

A crackle of static burst before a voice responded, steady yet laced with tension: "Loud and clear, Jake. We're inside. But by the short and curlies do we have a problem!"

"More so than we already have," Jake growled through clenched teeth.

"I'd say so, that fellar that gave you that nasty scar is back, in living fucking color," Pappy said, dread in his voice.

"That's impossible…" Jake knew he had excavated that man's brains into the next timezone.

"And yet here that fucker stands…"

"Dean…"

"That's the other problem."

"Dammit, I've got something. Someone. I don't know what the hell she is, but Evan needs to see her. Meet me in the main foyer. I repeat—get everyone to the damn foyer, now. We don't have time for a reunion tour."

"Dr. Michaels isn't with us, none of the others are," Pappy replied matter-of-factly. "We've gotta find that altar, Jake, we're missing people. We are cut off from half the asylum. The more monsters we put down the more take their place. The only way to go is up. The source has to be there."

"Dammit! Just carve a path if you can, and if anyone looks like an enemy, take them down. We're running out of time. I'll find you." With no further hesitation, Jake flung the radio aside and slammed his foot on the accelerator.

But before he could join them he had a quick stop he had to make. If his instincts were correct, then he didn't know what to expect when he showed up at Kara's. He knew one thing for sure, there was nowhere in Hale County that was safe. He may have been an absent father without a choice but there was no force on the planet that was going to keep Jake from protecting his daughter.

The rain howled around the truck, the winds whipping against the sides in rage as if feeding off the sheriff's bad mood. It could rage away as far as Jake was concerned there was no one more stubborn than himself, a trait he was counting on if they were going to survive the night.

As if in answer, lightning lit up the night, thunder rumbling in protest.

CHAPTER 24

The cul de sac twisted around them like a ravenous beast—pulsing, writhing, repelling their very existence. Laurel's boots hammered into the shattered rock and the eerily glowing grass as she dragged Amanda forward, the sickly green light of the chamber behind them fading into a vast, hungry void.

"Amanda, don't you dare fall behind!" Laurel roared, her voice ragged and cracking like brittle ice.

Amanda stumbled, her eyes fluttering in weak protest. "He's coming," she whispered, terror bleeding through each word. "He knows we've escaped."

Laurel didn't need to ask who "he" was. The answer lived in the relentless pulse of the Veil behind them—swelling like an ominous tide that gnawed at the edges of her mind with the ferocity of worms devouring ancient wood.

"You're not supposed to be here, Laurel. This world is no sanctuary for your kind."

The air thickened with overwhelming pressure as something stirred in the corridor ahead—a ripple through the darkness, a figure unfurling grotesquely from the very wall.

Laurel skidded to a halt, yanking Amanda behind her for protection. At first, she thought it was a man—a towering, broad-shouldered silhouette in the tattered remains of an asylum orderly uniform. But as it stepped into the wan light, Laurel's breath caught in sheer terror.

Its face was a maddening smear of abject wrongness. Instead of eyes, hollow sockets oozed dark ichor, and its mouth stretched unnaturally wide, its cracked lips bleeding as it muttered gibberish in a voice laced with insectile chittering.

Laurel raised her revolver, her hand trembling but determined. "Move," she commanded.

The creature tilted its head in a jerky, almost childish gesture—and then it lunged.

She fired.

The scalding bullet slammed into its shoulder, ripping through to the other side, yet the monstrosity surged forward with a ferocity that hit her like a runaway freight train, smashing her against the wall as her weapon skittered over the cold floor.

Amanda screamed in pure dread as the creature advanced, its arms extending like grasping tendrils of death.

Desperate, Laurel scrambled to her knees, blood streaming from her nose as she cried out, "NO!"

In that agonizing moment, the marble—warm and alive in her pocket—erupted in a searing white blaze. A shockwave of blistering pressure burst outward as Laurel hurled herself between Amanda and the advancing horror.

The abomination recoiled with a piercing shriek of shattered mirrors, clawing at the air in futile terror.

Clutching the incandescent marble, Laurel felt its ferocious burn sear into her palm, the heat blistering her skin—but she clung to it without hesitation.

"BACK!" she bellowed, her voice echoing with an ancient, otherworldly command not wholly her own.

The creature convulsed violently, smoke and decay pouring from its open wounds. With one final, tortured scream, it turned and fled, dissolving into the wall as if the stone itself had liquefied into oblivion.

Silence claimed the space once more, shattered only by Amanda's shallow, ragged breaths and the distant, ominous groan of the building overhead.

Exhausted, Laurel collapsed beside her sister, her chest heaving while tears mingled with the fresh blood streaming down her cheeks.

Amanda stirred and whispered, "You... you used the marble."

"I didn't know I could," Laurel gasped, barely believing her own words.

"Now it binds you to it," Amanda murmured. "And to me. We're tethered to something ancient... something that watches. The Gatekeeper."

Swallowing hard, Laurel wiped her blood-smeared face. "Then we must keep moving before its gaze wavers—or intensifies."

With unsteady legs, she pulled Amanda to her feet and retrieved her revolver.

Behind them, the corridor quaked—not with pursuing footsteps, but with deep, labored breathing.

Something darker was approaching.

Something far worse.

As they prepared to retreat from the twisting path, the very air shimmered and convulsed anew. When the incessant buzzing finally subsided, the two women found themselves standing atop the asylum's parapet, where torrential rain and furious wind whipped around them—and there, looming in the midst of the storm, stood the dreadful altar.

The hallway pulsed with a sick rhythm, alive with distant screams and hushed, inhuman murmurs—sounds not born of the living, but of things that once wore human skin. The changelings were close. Their claws clicked against the tile in a staccato beat, like bent metronomes keeping time to a dirge only monsters could follow.

Evan Michaels and Jim Holt sprinted down the hallway, boots slamming through murky water pooled across the cracked floor. Overhead, a few remaining lights flickered in agony, casting epileptic flashes of shadow along the stained walls. Rusted pipes hissed and groaned, breathing like the last dying lungs of the asylum.

"They're gaining!" Evan yelled, heart hammering, lungs scraping for breath.

Jim didn't answer. He skidded to a stop mid-sprint, raised his flare gun, and fired.

The flare streaked down the corridor in a sizzling arc before exploding with a deafening *BANG*. A white-hot bloom of magnesium fire engulfed the end of the hallway. For a moment, the world lit up—sharp, blinding, violent. The changelings shrieked as the blast lit their pale, twisted bodies like mannequins of blistered wax. Skin peeled. Eyes burst. But others pushed forward, undeterred, crawling over the corpses of their own.

"MOVE!" Jim barked, grabbing Evan by the collar and dragging him toward the stairwell at the end of the hall.

The ceiling trembled. Tiles fell. Behind them, the chorus of clicks and snarls resumed, faster now—coordinated.

Jim reached a half-collapsed support beam and ducked under it, hauling Evan along as they stumbled forward. On either side, storage closets gaped open like open mouths—filled with rusted restraints, mildewed blankets, and moldering patient files. One door swung on a squealing hinge as if beckoning them to enter and die.

"This whole hallway's a tomb," Evan gasped.

"Then we don't die in it," Jim snapped, pressing forward.

Ahead, the hallway narrowed to a bottleneck staircase—one jagged metal rail barely intact, leading upward. The lights here were dimmer, the air tighter. The changelings had stopped screeching. That made it worse.

Then came the *skrrrraaaak*—wet, scraping, close.

Evan looked back.

A hunched figure crawled from the dark, not walking, but *sliding*—limbs crooked at wrong angles, face half-torn. It scuttled like a spider, claws raking the walls, lips smeared with blood.

"Don't look," Jim hissed.

But Evan did, and his scream nearly drowned the thundering of his heart.

Jim turned and fired. The shot echoed like a shotgun blast in the close hall. The creature screamed—a high, shrill cry—and vanished into smoke.

No time to confirm.

They bolted the last twenty feet, reaching the stairwell as more shadows slid into the light behind them. More changelings— hungry and crawling, not on two legs but many.

Jim grabbed the railing and pulled himself up the crumbling steps. "We're not making it unless someone hears us!"

"Help!" Evan shouted, voice ragged, reaching for the top step. "Someone!"

Then: voices. Echoing faintly from above.

"Dr. Michaels?! Holt?!"

Evan's heart surged. "Here! Down here!"

At the landing above, shadows shifted—and Marcus appeared, flanked by Dean, Char, Judge and Pappy, weapons drawn, faces bloodied but alive. Behind them, Jason Locke stood silent and still, eyes distant.

"Jesus," Dean muttered. "You two look like hammered hell."

Jim collapsed onto the landing, dragging Evan behind him. "We feel worse."

"Did you—?" Marcus began.

"They're right behind us," Jim rasped. "Too many. They're working together."

Char looked down the stairwell, jaw clenched. "No time. We hold or we move."

Jason turned suddenly. "We move. She's calling."

"Who is?" Char asked.

Jason didn't answer. He just started walking.

"Wait!" Marcus grabbed his arm. "Jason—who's calling?"

Jason's glassy eyes didn't blink. "Laurel."

Evan pulled himself upright. "What the hell are you talking about?"

"She's at the altar," Jason said, voice barely audible. "She's waiting."

"We follow him," Dean said. "If there's a chance this ends up there, that's where we go."

Pappy nodded, tossing a flask to Jim. "We stick together."

The group moved as one up the final flight, weapons clenched, breath tight. The sounds behind them grew louder—snarls, footsteps, metal dragging across stone. The changelings were closing in.

As they crested the top stair, the hallway split again—into flickering tunnels and smoke-veiled nightmares. And from far ahead, they all felt it: a pulse in the air. A low, slow thrum like a heartbeat built into the foundation itself.

The altar was awake.

Jason turned back one last time.

"She's waiting," he said again, voice barely more than wind.

And as they moved deeper into the asylum, the growls behind them fell silent. The hallway behind them emptied into darkness.

But it wasn't retreat.

It was preparation.

The hunt wasn't over.

It was only now beginning.

———

The emergency lights convulsed along the hallway, splashing violent bursts of blood-red and stark white over every exposed surface. Overhead, the pipes groaned in agony. The group crouched by the doorway, their breaths ragged and hearts pounding after barely surviving the brutal onslaught of the changelings. Outside, the relentless storm pelting the cracked tile floor created a metronomic, mocking countdown with every drop.

Pappy methodically reloaded his iron-slug shotgun with a deliberate, almost ritualistic precision. Dean, ever vigilant, backed himself against the wall, his eyes slicing through the darkness in search of hidden threats. Bru scanned the corridor they'd just fled, his jaw set tight, every muscle bristling with raw tension.

"Everyone okay?" Jim Holt barked as he strode beside Evan. "We hold here, catch our breath, and wait for the sheriff."

Evan managed a nod, though his gaze darted uneasily toward Jason—standing slightly apart, his hands twitching nervously, his face drained of color.

Pappy guffawed, his face full of joy and weariness from the fight, "My friend, the sheriff alone can't help us. We gotta work together. You got to have each other's backs once the fighting commences again, and it's a comin'!" The overweight man reached into his backpack and started passing out rations.

Dan looked at it happily, "Is this that beef jerky I hear so much about?"

Pappy cuffed him on the shoulder with a grin, "and there ain't a close second!"

Then the atmosphere shattered.

A sudden, heavy drop in pressure snaked through the air.

Char tensed; her voice razor-sharp: "Something's coming."

Instinctively, Dean's hand slid to the iron blade at his hip. "Where?" he hissed.

Before a word could be uttered, the floor convulsed violently beneath them.

Moments later, Chief Malone stepped out of the shadowed terminus of the hall.

But he was no longer Malone.

The once-familiar man had transformed into a towering monstrosity—his body unnaturally broad, skin straining over a contorted, malformed skeleton. Jagged, armor-like bone shards erupted from beneath his tattered uniform, and his face had melted into a hideous, lupine mask. His eyes, void-like and glistening black, burned into the soul like punishing voids.

"Found you," the abomination cooed, its voice a nightmarish blend of Malone's drawl and a cold, insectile cadence.

The group stiffened as he advanced, every movement measured and lethal. The temperature plummeted, and the lights buzzed in panic, beginning to sputter and fade.

"Oh hell," muttered Pappy, eyeing his shotgun as if it were a lifeline. "Malone's really gone full demon."

A grotesque grin spread across Malone's face, his teeth elongating into razor-like points. "Foolish old men playing with toys. You think this is war? No, this is a harvest. You're nothing but cattle destined for slaughter in a pen built from your own sins."

With a guttural roar, he lunged, and pandemonium erupted in the claustrophobic corridor.

Pappy discharged his shotgun first—an iron slug hammered into Malone's shoulder, sending him half-spinning—but the creature barely faltered. Dean surged forward, his blade carving out wide, desperate arcs. Malone deflected with a savage backhand, sending Dean crashing against a row of lockers with a resounding metallic crack.

In the ensuing bedlam, the Judge's anguished scream blended with chaos as Evan yanked him back through a side door into the adjoining chamber. Bru and Jim clashed intensely, their voices screaming over one another as they refused to yield ground.

Amid the uproar, no one tracked the silent departure of Jason.

He didn't bolt or skulk; he simply walked.

His eyes glazed over in an abyssal stare as his head tilted, as if attuned to a maddening whisper only he could decipher. Beyond the melee, the corridor lay in eerie silence. The garish red emergency lights dwindled out of existence as he moved deeper into uncharted darkness. The very air seemed to yield to him—opening a path, pulling him toward a destiny unknown.

Muttering broken, cryptic phrases under his breath—"The root… the root is underneath. It bends, not breaks. We were always inside the dream…"—one hand trailed along the cold wall while the other hung listless at his side. With each step, the stagger of his daze transformed into a deliberate, resolute stride, as though his soul had finally reclaimed a long-forgotten purpose.

Evan spotted him too late. Grabbing Jim, he cried, "He's there, we have to go after him!"

But Jason no longer heard their calls. He had already ascended the back stairwell—drawn inexorably by a pulsating force, by the seductive whisper of an unseen altar, by an ineffable summons that beckoned him home.

Jim exchanged a grim nod with Evan, and together they bolted across the corridor, sprinting up the stairs in pursuit of Jason Locke.

In the blood-soaked corridor, Bru bellowed with primal fury as Malone hurled Dan against the wall, his taloned fingers tearing savagely into Dan 's vest. Judge Hawthorne's frantic calls for help collided with the deafening clang of his iron bar, desperately wielded against the unyielding onslaught. The air was thick with chaos, each scream and metallic clash merging into a tempest of raw terror and merciless brutality. Out of the chaos, Dean lunged at Malone, propelling the hulking figure away from Bru with a forceful tackle.

"Mr. Roundtree…run!" the large deputy called out as he quickly got to his feet. Dan didn't have to be told twice, he knew what his role was and sprinted after Evan and Jim, cutting down a few changelings that crossed his path in stride.

Bru seized a changeling, driving his iron knife deep into its eye socket with a brutal thrust. As he rose, another creature loomed behind him, its gaping jaws poised to tear his throat apart. Bru spun just in time to witness the creature's deadly advance, but far too late to evade. Suddenly, an iron tip erupted through the creature's throat, silencing its hiss with a sizzle as it disintegrated into nothingness. Judge Hawthorne stood, a triumphant grin on his face, weapon poised for the next threat.

The judge stepped toward Bru, only to freeze as a blur sliced through his vision, and a warm river cascaded down his chest. Bewildered, he blinked rapidly, his gaze dropping to the crimson flood soaking his front. His eyes met Bru's for a fleeting, gut-wrenching moment before his head toppled from his shoulders.

Time seemed to halt in a chilling suspension. Bru and the others stood aghast, horror-stricken. It was then they saw the true danger that had entered the fray.

The redcaps had joined the battle.

———

"Fucking fairies." Jake scowled at himself as pushed his truck to its limit. It had been right there, in his face the entire time. All those attacks, all the deaths, everything. The supernatural, the paranormal, all the strange oddities and unexplained phenomenon, all of it adding up to something so sinister and unbelievable that the entire county sat on the precipice of unprecedented disaster. And if what he suspected was true, everything was about to change. He had been so focused on the doctor being the villain that he couldn't see that the troubled physician was just another piece on the board. The Queen had been sacrificed to protect the King. Every bread crumb lead neatly to the doctor's doorstep.

Citizens were seeing things, crazy, unexplained things. Families were turning on each other, murdering each other with no explanation. One minute they were normal and the next they were trying to bury a knife in your gut. "Miranda..." he scowled as the rain bounced recklessly off his windshield, the body in the back cab moaning restlessly. Everything had spun preposterously out of control. Why hadn't he listened to Laurel? To Marcus? They all tried to tell him. Why was he so hell bent on remaining closed-minded to the possibilities of what was happening that he couldn't at least entertain the idea of what was manifesting all around him?

Angels? Demons? Monsters? Fae? Ley Lines? Just what the fuck? He slammed a fist on the steering wheel, letting out a primal roar of anger. But he should have seen it. If he hadn't been so overrun with his own self-pity and cocky assuredness he would have put it together long ago. *The supernatural was real, and a gateway existed in my own fucking county.* All it lead to was death.

Jake *had* to get to his family, to Kara...to his daughter, Haley.

The truck skidded to an angry stop, the high-beams ripping through the rain to illuminate the house before him. Jake took a ragged breath and stepped out of the vehicle, walking with purpose and anger to the front porch. His knuckles banged on the wooden door, echoing his inner turmoil.

He could hear steps treading softly across a hardwood floor. The door swung partially open, his eyes locked with the piercing green eyes he had fallen in love with all those years ago. But those same eyes were now framed with worry.

Kara cast a quick glance over her shoulder then peered back at Jake, her surprised voice lowered to a whisper, "Jake, you're okay? Are we safe? What are you doing here?"

The sheriff was caught off guard by how normal she seemed, how composed yet surprised by his presence. "You know why I'm here, Kara."

"Jake, I have no idea what you're talking about, other than the fact you said you'd keep me updated" she responded, her face giving nothing away as she glanced over her shoulder once again.

"Am I interrupting something…"

"Yes," she stated matter-of-factly, "you are. Trying to get a child to sleep with all this insanity thrust into her life isn't easy, Jake. The school thing, cancelling Halloween. Not that you would know about that."

Ouch. That hurt. But she wasn't wrong. Jake felt a rush of anger that was instantly crushed by guilt. He couldn't fault her for that. And Haley was safe, he certainly shouldn't be upset. Kara could see the bite of her words in his expression. "I'm sorry, Jake," her voice softened, "that was out of line. I haven't been to bed yet. I've been up all day and night, worried. You said you would call!"

"No, it wasn't out of line." He paused, took a breath, not ready to explain to Kara just what it was they were up against. "You know I wouldn't be here unless it was important. What I have to say affects you both. I couldn't chance anyone overhearing it."

Kara could see he was serious, so she opened the door and ushered him in. The long body of the muscled German Shephard lay curled up in a dog bed by the fireplace. The dog looked up briefly, stirred by the sheriff's unfamiliar footsteps in her owner's home. "Do you want some coffee? Pizza" Kara asked, tightening her gown around her as she stepped into the kitchen, gesturing to the half-eaten box of pizza on the table.

"Yes, coffee, please," Jake responded as he took in the living room décor. Vintage farmhouse design, not overly cramped, leather furniture, antique coffee table. The only modern-looking piece in the room was the large, flat screen television hanging on the wall. The sheriff took off his hat and jacket, setting the wet gear on a hanger by the door, then gently took a seat on the couch. There was a fresh smell to the house, clean and breezy, like a spring day in paradise. He could feel his body relax, all the tension and pain sort of flowing out of him. Jake's mind seemed to drift free from his constant state of alarm.

"Here you go," she said softly, putting the cup of coffee on the small table in front of him. The sheriff shook his head as if shaking away cobwebs. "Jake, are you sure you're okay? Is this about the school?"

The sound of her voice mixed with the aroma of the freshly brewed coffee stirred him from his revelry. "I'm sorry," he said once again, reaching for the warm cup, "I must be far more exhausted than I thought." A sip of the coffee sent a wave of pleasure through him, warming his body, and clearing his mind. He wanted to curl up within himself and just drift away, let go of his constant stress and let the universe have him.

"...Jake...", the soft mention of his named broke through the revelry. He gave a soft shake of his head as if trying to focus, his eyes landing on Kara's concerned gaze.

"What's that..." he said, groggily. The sheriff brought the coffee cup to his lips, noticing it was significantly cooler. Jake shot his eyes back to Kara. "Was I..."

She smiled, finishing his question, "...for about 15 minutes."

He sat the cup down and stood up abruptly, his usual demeanor shoving away the welcome warmth that threatened to overtake him. "Damn, what's wrong with me..."

Jake shook his head, trying to clear the fog. Something wasn't right. He had come here for a reason, an urgent reason, but it was slipping away from him.

"Nothing's wrong with you, Jake," Kara said soothingly. "You're just exhausted. Why don't you sit back down and relax? Please? Just for once in your stubborn life, listen to me," she rebuked him warmly, no malice in her voice.

A small smile played at the corner of his mouth, her voice was hypnotic, lulling him back towards that blissful warmth. For a moment, he almost gave in. Then a flash of memory hit him - Laurel's broken body, Pappy's words to him, all those people.

Jake's eyes snapped fully open, clarity returning. He looked at Kara with new wariness. "No, something is very wrong here. Where's Haley?"

A flicker of...something...passed across Kara's face. "She's asleep upstairs, like I..."

Jake shook his head, trying to clear the fog that had settled over his mind, cutting her off mid-sentence. Something wasn't right. He felt off-balance, his thoughts sluggish and unfocused.

"Kara, I need to tell you..." he started, but his words trailed off as he caught movement out of the corner of his eye.

A small figure stood in the doorway leading to the bedrooms. Haley. The little girl's eyes were wide, fixed on Jake with an unnerving intensity.

"Sweetie, what are you doing up?" Kara asked, her voice gentle but with an undercurrent of tension. "You should be in bed."

Haley didn't respond, didn't even acknowledge her mother. She just kept staring at Jake.

An icy chill ran down the sheriff's spine. The hairs on the back of his neck stood up. Every instinct screamed that something was terribly wrong.

"Haley, honey, why don't you go back to bed?" Jake said gently, trying to keep his voice calm despite his growing unease.

The little girl's gaze never wavered. When she finally spoke, her voice was flat and emotionless. "You shouldn't have come here, Sheriff."

Jake's hand instinctively moved toward his holster. "Kara, get behind me," he ordered, his eyes still locked on Haley.

But Kara didn't move.

Jake felt a chill run down his spine as he looked at Haley. There was something unnatural about the little girl's intense stare. His police instincts were screaming at him that something was very wrong.

"Haley, honey, go back to bed," Kara said, her voice strained.

The girl didn't move or respond. Jake's hand unconsciously moved towards his holster.

"Kara, get behind me," he repeated quietly, not taking his eyes off Haley.

"Jake, what are you doing?" Kara asked, alarm in her voice. "That's my daughter!"

"I don't think it is," Jake replied grimly. "Not anymore."

Kaia awakened from her bed in front of the fireplace, fur bristling as she growled towards the little girl standing motionless between the door frame leading down the hall.

Kara looked at her beloved guardian in shock. "Kaia, what is wrong with you!?" she screamed at the angry German Shephard.

Jake kept his eyes locked on the little girl, half whispering, half growling towards Kara but never losing sight of the child standing before him, "she knows what I know...that isn't Haley." As if on cue, the thing that was pretending to be Haley twisted its neck in an unnatural way to stare at the growling animal, a similar responsive growl forming from the child-like lips.

Kara's eyes narrowed, her mother wolf protectiveness overriding her fear. "Where's my daughter?!" she screamed at the thing that stood before them.

Jake felt a surge of adrenaline as the situation rapidly escalated. The thing wearing Haley's face turned its unnatural gaze back to him, a sinister smile spreading across its features.

"Your daughter is gone," it said in a voice that was decidedly not Haley's - deep and guttural. "She was chosen for a greater purpose."

In a blur of motion, the creature lunged at Jake with blurring speed. The sheriff barely had time to react, throwing himself to the side as razor-sharp claws slashed through the air where he had just been standing.

Kaia sprang into action, leaping at the creature with a ferocious snarl. But the thing that looked like Haley moved with preternatural quickness, grabbing the dog in mid-air and hurling her across the room. Kaia yelped in pain as she crashed against the far wall, but the loyal dog would not be slowed. She shook her head as if to regain her bearings, setting her haunches beneath her, muscles tensed and coiled like a spring.

"No!" Kara cried out, lunging forward. Jake barely managed to grab her arm and pull her back as the creature that was not Haley twisted to face them once more, his weapon still pointed at the oddly disturbing likeness of their daughter. The sheriff sensed the dog's stance and knew what needed to be done. He lowered his weapon. "Okay, you can have me. Just tell me, where's my daughter?" he pleaded in a heartbroken voice.

The creature stared at the sheriff. "Weak and stupid humans," it hissed. A vile, evil smirk spread abnormally wide across its face. As it leaped for the sheriff, the powerful jaws of the German Shephard closed with a deep snap around the things neck, crushing bone and tissue, cutting off the creatures nervous system. It looked at the sheriff in shock. The thing no longer looked like Haley at all, just a lump of flesh with eyes and limbs. Jake was no longer pleading, he just raised his gun coldly, the barrel coming to rest atop the things forehead.

"Where is she?"

The light was fading from the creatures eyes as they fixed on nothingness, its body limp in the jaws of the massive dog. "bastille…" it half-hissed, half-whispered, unaware of its surroundings as death descended upon it, clouding every sense.

"Kaia," Jake spoke hollowly, "drop".

The obedient dog dropped the creature and went back to the fireplace, eyes never leaving the unmoving intruder. Jake raised his gun but Kara's hand on his prevented him from going any higher. He looked at her without question and gave her the pistol. She raised the heavy iron without so much as a strain, aimed it at the things face and pulled the trigger. The creatures head exploded with a loud finality.

Kara handed the pistol back to Jake and matched his stare. "Now what?" There was no emotion, no anxiety, no fear behind the question, only resolution.

"Now we go find our baby girl, and kill anyone, or anything, that stands in the way."

The race to Hale County Mental Institute was on.

The truck hurtled up the shattered driveway, bouncing uncontrollably over fractured concrete and scattered debris, each jolt echoing in the cacophony of the storm. The ominous asylum loomed large as they approached, a barely seen shadow in the raging curtains of rain. In the passenger seat, Kara's steely gaze was trying to pierce the chaotic weather, Jake's well-worn .44 magnum lay ready, gleaming coldly under intermittent flashes of lightning. The back of the truck held the unconscious woman, her still form a stark counterpoint to the tempest around them.

As they approached the foreboding front steps of the asylum, Jake abruptly killed the truck's headlights and yanked the steering wheel sharply, sending the vehicle into a dramatic skid that splashed a mixing of mud and gravel in every direction. The tires hissed in protest, their screeches melding with the growl of an engine sounding like a subdued, warning beast.

There would be no heed for warnings tonight.

Jake and Kara shared a look. With fierce determination, Jake seized his weapon, flung open the door, and burst forth into the pelting downpour towards the towering double doors. His scar pulsed with the heat of impending battle, each beat of his heart echoing like a relentless war drum announcing his arrival.

He pressed a small .38 into Kara's hands then slid a machete into her belt loop.

"No matter what happens in here, you keep going. Haley is your only goal. The rest of us are expendable. Understand?" He was staring intently into Kara's eyes.

"Jake…" she tried to say, her mind awash with so many thoughts.

But Jake knew only one thing mattered. Haley. "Do you understand?"

Kara nodded and opened the door.

Above him, the storm roared with unbridled fury, yet Jake Hooks pressed on, each step imbued with a raw intensity. Not a moment to falter now—

Hell had come to Hale County.

It was unending bedlam.

The hope they all had at the beginning of the fight, sparked by their ignorance of the enormous enemy they were facing, was all but gone. The judge's head was kicked around between the flailing of legs. Each time an enemy was vanquished, two more would appear. Now the redcaps were among them, vicious little goblin-like squatty creatures, with sharp iron teeth and yellow eyes whose skull caps were dipped in blood. The iron weapons gave the group no extra benefit.

Marcus turned to find himself face to face with the creature who was Eddie Malone, a look of unearthly disdain in the police chief's eyes as he sneered at the former mayor. "Oh, Marcus," Eddie growled lowly, "this has been a long time coming."

Dean casually slid up next to Marcus, glaring at Malone, "you're right about that, it's been a long time coming...for you."

The chief merely smirked, "the ghost, the lost man, mind torn asunder because of your failings. You think you're healed? An old friend might have something to say about that." Eddie jerked his head to the side, never taking his eyes off either man. Dean followed the motion, his eyes landing on the impossible, causing the world to sway beneath him.

There, across the room, stood the psycho, Ronald. Every impulse pulled at Dean, revenge overriding his common sense. The Psycho just glared back, evil bleeding eyes locked upon his mortal enemy. Malone smiled a wicked grin, seeing the war within Dean.

Marcus seized the moment of Eddie's pause, raising his revolver at Malone. His shot went wide as the changeling chief lunged, claws ripping through Marcus's shoulder. Dean watched in a stupor as Ronald smiled a wicked grin, time slowing around him—a long-forgotten horror now all too real.

Then Marcus's scream snapped him back into action. He charged at Eddie, hacking with his machete in a frenzy of desperation that left the air thick with screams and searing flashes of iron. The blade bit into Malone's shoulder, causing him to recoil but not retreat. Instead, Eddie laughed—a cold, soulless sound that echoed like a death knell—and swung wildly at Dean. "You'll all die here," he spat. "Just like before."

Dean staggered under the blow but stayed on his feet. The words cut deeper than any wound; they scraped raw against old scars he thought had finally begun to heal. Memories of the experiments, the dungeon, his other identity that was created in that hell hole. He felt Wraith's pull in his mind. He knew they couldn't hold out much longer unless they found some edge—some way to turn this overwhelming tide. It was then he noticed Marcus' body flying across the room and landing against the far wall with a sickening crunch. Malone stalked his prey, sensing his opponents last moments. Dean understood he was too far away to help.

Ronald's wicked gaze lingered on Dean, recognizing the familiar challenge like an old wound reopened. The world slowed, their eyes met in inevitable understanding. The space between them seemed to fold inward, charged with past hatred and present fury. Two wild animals racing headlong towards the other, bad intentions fueling every thudding step.

The tangle of the two rage-fueled bodies took them crashing wildly down a stairwell and out of sight.

In their absence lingered only echoes: iron against bone, laughs against screams—a symphony composed by madness itself—as Hale County Asylum swallowed them whole.

——

The altar entranced Laurel, its marble searing through her skin like a white-hot burn. Every hypnotic glance at its sleek, impossibly iridescent oily surface drove her deeper into a wild communion. Time slipped away, had she even been standing there, or was she lost in the altar's vortex? An incessant buzzing roared in her ears, swelling into a maddening clamor. In that moment, all Laurel craved was to banish that maddening noise and tenderly caress the enchanted altar like a devoted servant to its dark majesty.

A tug, subtle at first, then insistent.

She jerked her head and saw Amanda tugging at her sleeve.

Amanda? But wasn't she dead? What cruel twist of fate was unfolding? Amanda's eyes pleaded to speak—a surreal vision as if watching a dilapidated TV screen where every actor slogged in agonizing slow motion.

The buzzing mutated into urgent words, frantic and piercing: "LAUREL! SNAP OUT OF IT!" Her sister's cry sliced through the clamor like a razor, and in an explosive moment, Laurel's foggy stupor shattered, replaced by a brutal, assaulting surge of reality.

Amanda yanked at Laurel's arm, wrenching her away from the altar's hypnotic grip. Laurel staggered, severing a mystical connection with a whisper of regret echoing in her mind. Yet Amanda's desperation overpowered it. The searing heat that once burned within her began to fade, supplanted by a frigid, electrifying clarity that jolted her into full, raw awareness.

"Where do you think you're going?" A voice, cold and slithering, whispered through the room as a writhing mass of shadowy figures surged into view. More grotesque beings emerged from the mist, amorphous and oppressive, their presence pressing against her lungs like a crushing nightmare. Laurel's eyes narrowed in dangerous recognition.

"Jason?" she rasped in disbelief.

"Oh, I'm afraid Jason is indisposed—he's with his precious Rachel," the man declared with a wicked smile, tapping the side of his temple as his eyes sank into despairing depths. "It's only William, as it should have always been."

In a furious burst of defiance, Laurel seized a fallen pipe and swung it with reckless wrath. The pipe's iron edge slashed through the mist and flesh with savage precision as every sound exploded into a thunderous roar, every movement blurring into violent chaos.

"I'll be needing what you stole," William declared coolly, his voice a silken venom dripping with menace. It was as if he had forgotten his true station until now, freed from the constraints of conscience to complete his twisted mission. "Are you sure you're ready for this journey?" His taunting words slithered through the silence, omnipresent as smoke invading desperate lungs.

Amanda reappeared at his side, her glare seething with defiance. "You will not have her."

William laughed low and dark, his head shaking with a deliberate slowness as he advanced. "You lecherous experiments, failures of mad science. I warned Bres this would happen. He promised me it'd be worth corrupting your fragile minds." He fixed his gaze on Laurel with chilling certainty. "You DO know she isn't your sister, correct?"

A shiver of terror and rage coursed through Laurel. Of course she knew—yet seeing Amanda alive again rekindled the purpose she had nearly forgotten in this forsaken county. The asylum was a tomb of secrets and sorrow, each passing second dragging them further toward a suffocating end.

Amanda's voice then cut through the tumult, laden with conviction, "Of course she knows. Just like she knows I'm here to help her—regardless. I may not be her sister by blood, but part of her spirit lives in me. And we're gonna kick your sorry ass." With that, she charged, a bizarre spiral dagger interlaced with gold and onyx forming in her hand. William raised his hand, his eyes igniting with a violent purple glow, halting Amanda mere inches from his face, her breath coming in desperate, gasping struggles.

Evan, Jim, and Dan burst onto the parapet, eyes wide at the unfolding carnage. Laurel stood rooted in shock as the nightmarish scene unfolded: her sister—the mirror of her own defiant essence—desperately needing her help. Without missing a beat, Jim hurled his scythe into William's leg, eliciting a pained howl that, however, did nothing to free Amanda from his grip.

"Go on," William taunted Laurel, his eyes blazing with feverish malice, "leave her again like you always have!"

A conflagration of fury and guilt ignited inside Laurel. How did he know the raw torment she felt? The altar beckoned with the seductive promise of corrupt power and completion, yet Amanda's violent struggle demanded her attention even more forcefully. It was the first time Laurel had seen true fear mingled with determination in Amanda's eyes. Pulled by an overwhelming resolve, Laurel lunged through the choking fog of doubt.

"Take it back," she murmured fiercely, slamming the altar against her wavering resolve like a battering ram. Gripping a dagger snatched from Dan's pack, she leaped toward William, knocking him off balance long enough for Amanda to wriggle free from his vice-like hold.

Amanda grasped Laurel's hand, her eyes momentarily transforming into a prism of shifting, crystalline realities. In a nearly inaudible whisper, she said, "Thank you."

Their reunion was brutally fleeting as William's face contorted into a mask of unbridled fury and desperation. The shadows around him writhed like living serpents as he forced himself upright and renewed his savage assault, draining Amanda's life force with ravenous intensity.

"We can't keep this up!" Evan bellowed to Dan amid the chaos.

Dan, holding a scrap of paper scrawled with mysterious runes, glanced at the doctor with grim determination. "I know how to close the portal, but I can't say what price we'll pay when I do."

Jim's voice cut through as he glared at the two men, "We don't have a choice. There are more lives at stake than just ours. Keep him occupied at all costs."

The native man clutched his medicine bag, muttering protective incantations as he sprinted toward the altar, darting around William while Jim and Evan plunged back into the fray.

William's body convulsed and twisted grotesquely, bones snapping and flesh tearing in abhorrent angles. His screams were not cries of pain but the guttural roar of war. Shadows flooded the chamber, crawling like sentient blood over every surface.

In a heartbeat, a spear of pure darkness pierced Dan's side. He gasped, and the paper with the closing ritual slipped from his trembling fingers as he crumpled to the cold stone floor. Jim howled in rage and charged forward only to be flung back with a monstrous crash against the wall, the sound of snapping bone echoing ominously.

Evan scrambled desperately to Dan's side, trying to staunch the horror, but Dan's eyes already glimmered with distant resignation, his breaths shallow and fading. "The altar..." he rasped weakly. "Close...it..."

Amanda turned, her visage drained to ghostly pallor, and screamed as a sinister dark tendril ensnared her ankle and jerked her violently into the air. Laurel lunged after her, their fingers locking in a desperate hold, but the pull was overwhelmingly uncontrollable.

"I won't let go!" Laurel screamed as if her very soul depended on it.

Amanda's eyes glistened with tears yet burned with fierce resolve, "You have to."

In an instant, the tendril tightened with brutal force. Amanda was wrenched free, her anguished scream vanishing into the swirling, impenetrable black.

"No!!" Laurel's cry tore from her throat like a raw, shattered wound. She crumbled back, clutching the glowing marble with trembling hands as the world around her erupted into chaos.

Now, towering above her, William emerged from the writhing shadows, monstrous and all-consuming. "This world was never yours," he hissed venomously. "It has always belonged to the forgotten."

Surrounded by devastation—Dan dying, Jim rendered unconscious, Evan bleeding out—Laurel rose slowly, eyes ablaze with unyielding fury, the marble in her hand pulsing like a miniature sun.

And as the wind howled a dirge and the encroaching darkness threatened to swallow everything whole, she stepped forward.

With a final, defiant surge, Laurel advanced toward the altar, slamming the marble into an indention in its head rest, and in that blinding moment, everything turned white.

CHAPTER 25

The asylum trembled as if possessed by a malevolent force, its crumbling innards protesting with every shudder. Dust cascaded from the shattered rafters like a suffocating storm of ash, while fractures splintered through the warped, broken tiles like skeletal fingers. In the distance, sirens howled their relentless agony—a cacophonous blend of machine-like wails, terrified screams, and the mournful shriek of wind violently ripping through shattered windows.

Char knelt beside Marcus amidst the chaos, her hands slick with his crimson blood as she fiercely pressed a battered jacket against the jagged, bleeding gash in his shoulder. "Stay with me," she hissed through grit, her voice wavering with desperate resolve. "You're too damn stubborn to just die out here."

Marcus groaned, a pained smirk twisting his lips. "Just... tell me I don't look as bad as I feel."

With a derisive crack that cut the tension like broken glass, Char spat, "You look like shit."

Marcus managed a shaky laugh in return. "That checks."

Then a low, guttural growl reverberated down the hall, a promise of impending carnage.

In an instant, their grim reality sharpened— they weren't alone.

Out of the oppressive darkness, Chief Eddie Malone materialized—a grotesque mockery of humanity. His face was a macabre canvas, twisted into a monstrous snarl with an impossibly wide mouth bristling with jagged, obsidian teeth. Razor-sharp bones jutted from his forearms like serrated blades, and his tattered uniform was merged with patches of unnatural gray hide. His eyes, dark voids pulsating with sadistic hunger, fixed on Marcus with the predatory focus of a beast stalking its prey.

"I've been waiting for this," Malone rasped, his voice echoing with an unnatural duet—as if his words were accompanied by an ancient, malevolent force.

Without a moment's hesitation, Char unleashed her wrath—drawing her iron-forged pistol and letting the bullet fly. It slammed into Malone's chest with a deafening impact, yet the creature merely smirked and lunged forward.

A brutal, thunderous crack split the air.

In one fluid, violent motion, Malone was intercepted mid-leap by the whirlwind that was Jake Hooks. The sheriff's shoulder slammed into Malone's gut with bone-crushing force, sending the beast crashing into a wall. Plaster exploded like shattered dreams, and pipes burst as the corridor became a chaotic haze of steam and debris.

Jake pushed himself up, panting, a deep gash streaming blood down his temple. "Get Marcus out of here!" he bellowed, his voice raw and commanding.

Char's eyes widened in shock. "Jake—?"

"MOVE!" he roared, leaving no room for debate.

Without pause, she hoisted Marcus onto her shoulders and dragged him toward the service stairwell, their desperate escape punctuated by the building's tortured groans and violent collapse.

Malone reassembled himself from the swirling dust and charged anew with a roar of pure malice—only to be met by the crushing blow of Jake's revolver butt slamming into his deformed jaw.

Jake raised his gun and fired point-blank; the shot ripped through Malone's shoulder with a spray of visceral gore, yet still, the creature pressed on.

"You always were one hell of a stubborn bastard," Jake snarled, evading a vicious slash from Malone's clawed arm. "Human or monster, you're just a dick."

With furious determination, Jake unleashed a relentless assault—each blow landing with bone-shattering impact on the twisted form of Eddie Malone.

Then, as if summoned by the abyss, a redcap emerged from the shadows, its grotesque fingers clenching Jake's leg. In a heartbeat, the sheriff drew his .44 and slammed the barrel against the creature's head. The redcap's eyes ballooned in terror and its mouth contorted in a silent, panicked gasp. "Ohhhhhh," it croaked.

Jake met its frightened stare and pulled the trigger. "Yeah," he confirmed coldly, the explosion blasting the redcap's head in a spray of gore.

The momentary distraction, however, allowed Malone to strike—a savage backhand that staggered Jake, sending him sprawling against the wall. With brutal, inhuman strength, Malone hurled Jake into the hard surface; his revolver clattered to the ground as pain and blood mingled around his fractured ribs. Yet, even in agony, Jake spat a mouthful of blood into Malone's face and growled, "Still ugly."

Malone recoiled, readying a final, merciless blow—but Jake's response was a twisted, bloody smile. "Good thing you're not the real Eddie. Maddy would be so disappointed. That little dicked bastard couldn't satisfy his wife if his life depended on it."

At the mere utterance of the name, something in Malone shuddered—a surge of raw, begrudging fury at the reminder of the real Eddie's legacy.

But Jake wasn't finished. "Or maybe she'd be just as disappointed," he rasped, his breath a struggle, "because if you're a carbon copy, then you know exactly what that means..." he trailed off, winking in maddening defiance.

With a thundering impact, Malone sent Jake crashing across the room, slamming him into the opposite wall with a bone-jarring thud before letting him collapse in excruciating pain. Yet Jake fought against oblivion—taunting the creature to throw it off its murderous focus.

Then, the deafening roar of a shotgun blast shattered the macabre standoff. The slug tore through Malone's side, ejecting him into a spasmodic spin before he crumpled to the ground in a disheveled heap.

At the corridor's end, Kara stood like an avenging angel, her iron-loaded .38 still smoking, her eyes burning with unapologetic fury. "Nobody lays a hand on my sheriff," she declared, throwing a defiant glance at Jake before adding, "A gift from Pappy."

Behind them, Bru appeared—a hulking figure smeared with blood and wielding a brutal iron axe. "We gotta move, boss."

Jake dropped to one knee, retrieving his revolver with grim determination. "Let's finish this," he growled.

As Malone reared up once more, his breath ragged and form distorting under a mantle of ravenous shadow, Jake advanced slowly, every step laced with lethal intent. "For Cutty," he said, and in that final moment, his shot from the revolver ended the chief's reign of cruelty forever.

Down the stairs erupted the thunderous clamor of an all-out battle—redcaps shrieking in terror, their cries blending with ecstatic, deranged laughter. Pappy's voice echoed in the chaos.

Jake exchanged a brief nod with Bru and Char. "Get everyone out. Bru, I need you to help Kara bring me a package from just outside that far door. Where's Evan?"

Char's reply came with grim clarity. "He and the others went upstairs...to where that explosion tore through everything."

With that, Jake gave a curt nod to Kara, grabbed her hand, and bolted up the crumbling stairwell and into the collapsing asylum, every agonizing stride fueled by an unyielding desire to survive, to fight on, to save the daughter he never got to know.

———

The lower levels of Hale County Asylum were a crypt.

The air was thick with mildew and old blood. Water dripped in steady, mocking rhythm from corroded pipes, echoing through the black halls. Lights flickered overhead, casting sickly green glows across cracked concrete and rusted metal. The ground trembled— just slightly—as if the building was breathing its last through a mouth full of rotted teeth.

After their brutal plunge down the stairs onto the first level, amid a whirlwind of chaos, Ronald retreated into the depths—the dungeon. Home. But this was no desperate escape; it was an intentional march into darkness, fueled by grim purpose and dread.

Dean moved carefully, iron machete in hand. The others were fighting their way toward the exit, but he had been drawn downward—drawn here.

To the place where Wraith was born.

The doors here were heavy steel slabs, each one etched with patient numbers and red warning symbols faded to rust. One of them still bore his old designation: SUBJECT 22-A: WRAITH

He paused, heart pounding.

That was when the door at the far end creaked open.

Ronald—Psycho—stepped forward into the flickering, hellish light. His face was eerily unchanged, grinning as though in madness. A scalpel glistened in his hand, dripping a substance darker than despair itself.

"Welcome back, roomie," Ronald crooned, voice low and intimate.

Dean's jaw clenched. "This is where it ends."

"No," Ronald said, stepping forward with a twitchy grace. "This is where it began. This hall... these rooms... this is where *we* were born. You, me. Wraith. Psycho. Our mothers were science and cruelty. Why not die in their arms?"

Dean didn't wait for more. He surged forward, iron blade flashing.

Ronald countered, parrying the strike with a jagged, bone-like shiv, sparks exploding as metal clashed against metal. Their collision boomed like an explosion of flesh and iron, rattling ancient surgical trays and gurneys in a frenzied cacophony. Dean twisted sharply and drove his shoulder into Ronald's ribs, hurling him through cracked double doors into a derelict experimental surgery suite.

The stench of noxious chemicals and decay was overpowering. Restraint chairs with broken leather straps lined the walls, and a wall smeared with ghostly, faded handprints—some colossal, others disturbingly tiny—stood as grim witnesses.

They fought savagely across it. Dean's machete tore through wires and flesh alike, but Ronald moved like a thing that had never been human—ducking, twisting, laughing as he slashed low and fast, cutting into Dean's thigh.

"Still bleeding for them?" Ronald hissed, eyes wide. "Still thinking you're the hero?"

Dean grunted and slammed his elbow into Ronald's temple. "No heroes left. Just us monsters."

"I liked it better when you didn't say words," Dean gritted back at him. He drove Ronald back, blade biting into the madman's shoulder. The smell of burnt flesh filled the air as the iron blade hissed in his wound. Ronald shrieked, backhanding Dean into a steel examination table.

Dean hit hard but came up swinging—only to find Ronald gone.

The lights flickered.

Then Ronald dropped from the ceiling like a spider, driving Dean to the floor, pinning him. "They opened you up in here," he whispered. "Cut your soul in half. I remember the screaming."

Dean slammed his head back, skull cracking into Ronald's nose. Blood sprayed. Dean rolled free, rising with a roar as Wraith surged forward inside him—memories of pain, of needles, of sobbing in the dark becoming fuel for a final fury.

They tore through a door into the next chamber, the deranged observation room.

Fractured two-way mirrors lined the walls, now one-way remnants of their former selves, shattered by time. In those distorted reflections, Dean caught brief, horrific images of himself intertwined with Ronald—a maelstrom of gore and insanity wrestling like wild beasts in a confined cell of tortured memories.

"Look around!" Ronald howled. "This was our nursery, Wraith! This was where we were baptized in pain!"

"I liked it better when you didn't talk," Dean spat, avoiding another wild, clubbing blow from Ronald.

The psychotic man roared in rage, making a sudden, maddening leap at Dean.

Dean ducked under a slash, rolled, came up behind him—and drove the machete deep into Ronald's lower back. The blade struck spine. Ronald screamed, spinning wildly, blood pouring down his leg.

"You're not him," Dean spat, "just a cheap copy. You have memories that aren't yours. A thing created out of goo from a world that doesn't want you."

Psycho gripped the wall for balance, sneering. "You think this ends with me? There's something worse coming, Wraith. I've seen it. The rift... it's waking the *others*."

Dean's eyes were flat, cold. "Then I'll be waiting."

He tore his blade free and kicked Ronald through a shattered glass wall.

The dying man tumbled into the final chamber—the containment lab. A pit of twisted steel and cryptic sigils, a room designed for unspeakable restraint and dissection. Dean was now the hunter, the apex predator ready to put an end to the psycho's suffering.

Now, the room itself quaked violently. Stone shattered and trembled; pipes exploded; fire burst forth from a widening rift in the earth, bathing everything in a hellish, molten red.

Ronald lay twisted amid broken equipment, coughing blood. "You can't leave it behind, Wraith... you can't leave me behind."

"Daddy..."

Dean froze, looking at the rift forming at the far end of the room—a jagged tear in space, glowing bright white at the edges. The Veil torn open. And through that veil he could see a little girl.

"Daddy, please…help me."

"It's no…it's not possible," Dean saw the image of his little girl start to solidify and then phase out again. "Katie…"

Ronald saw his opportunity and lunged one last time.

Dean caught him, held him, and thrust a knife through Psycho's ear. The creature screamed horrifically twisting and melting in on itself until it was just a puddle of blackish purple ooze.

"Daddy…"

Dean glanced back at the shimmering tear. The asylum was coming down around him.

"Sorry, Pappy," he whispered and suddenly leapt into the light.

The tear slammed shut behind him.

A moment later, the chamber exploded, taking the hallway with it as the asylum began to collapse floor by floor, screaming like a dying god.

And Dean Cutler was gone.

——

The pain was blinding, a white-hot agony that surged through every nerve. Laurel's screams were lost in the deafening roar of collapsing stone and metal as the asylum continued to implode. She felt herself slipping, consciousness fading against the overwhelming torment. Her vision dimmed, narrowing to a pinpoint of light where the marble pulsed against her palm, resonating with the ancient magic Dan had unleashed.

Then—silence.

Laurel's eyes shot open. The world was colorless, soundless, an empty expanse where time felt suspended. Her senses returned slowly, dragging her back from the brink. The tremors had stopped. The air was still, charged with an eerie calm that prickled her skin.

The others...

She struggled to focus, lifting her head with great effort. Evan was stirring, grimacing through swollen eyes as he attempted to move his broken arm. Jim Holt groaned again, but this time it was stronger—a sound of defiance rather than despair. Jason remained still and silent; Laurel's heart twisted for him even as she forced herself to look away.

"Dan," she rasped, turning her gaze to the elder beside her. His breathing was shallow, but his eyes flickered with awareness—cloudy yet determined, refusing to give in.

Suddenly, Kara was by their side, giving aid the Cherokee elder. "I've got you. It's going to hurt; I have to keep pressure on it."

"It's... enough," he breathed, voice barely audible over the ringing in her ears. "Held it... for now..."

Laurel squeezed his hand with what little strength she had left, feeling his warmth and knowing it would not last. "We have to get him out," she said to Kara, more urgently than before. Laurel didn't know where she came from or how she had gotten there but she quickly understood that Kara was Dan's only chance to live through this.

A rumble echoed above them—distant but menacing—a reminder that they had only moments before this place swallowed them whole. She forced herself upright, gritting her teeth against the pain that lanced through her leg.

"Dr Michaels!" she called hoarsely. "Jim!" Her voice came out stronger this time, cutting through the choking dust and despair. "We need to move!"

Evan nodded weakly, dragging himself toward Jim with sheer determination etched into every grimace. He pulled Holt up with his good hand and together they staggered toward Laurel, Dan and Kara.

"Where is Jake," Laurel shouted to Kara over the roaring winds.

"I don't know, he was right behind me!"

"We have to close it," Dan panted, though his face suggested even he was doubtful. "We have to try."

"Dan, you can't take much more, you're going to go into shock!" Kara told him urgently.

Suddenly, the familiar feeling of a vacuum opening up rippled through the air, twisted by shimmering smoke. They tried to cover their eyes as a figure stepped through a portal. The Mayor of Hale County, Lord Bres, body no longer old and fragile looking. His greyish skin shone glossily over sleek, thin muscles, his yellowish eyes glinting like the sun. Escorting him, flanked on either side, were JC and Ashlyn, their eyes fierce, jawlines stretched to contain the rows of razor sharp teeth. "*I am the voice of the end.* I am the *harbinger.* You should be honored to witness my return. The Slúagh na Marbh are home."

"Son," Evan gasped, knowing at once this thing was no longer his beloved child.

"Father." JC's voice was taut with controlled rage. Bres let it resonate and echo, savoring the helplessness mingling in the air.

"You're too late," Bres said, his voice a sickly mockery of sympathy. "But take heart. You'll soon join him."

Laurel felt Dan tense beside her, gathering what little strength the dying man had. She clutched the marble fiercely, its pulse like a second heartbeat in her hand.

"But it won't be me, not my mind, not really," Evan spat out.

Bres looked at him with something resembling pity. "Such a fool. Brilliant, but foolish. Do you think these are mere copies? You never realized what your work truly was. A brilliant mind so easily lead astray, bent slowly, molded gently by your grief. Humans. Your very egos are your greatest weakness. This plan has been in play for centuries, long before your pathetic existence was even realized. Since the day of our banishment, since my fall as King, banished to the nether reaches of Tír na nÓg. But thanks to your work the essence of those humans are merged with the primordial goo of the changelings."

Evan's face fell with realization, "Clones, you created actual clones."

"No," Bres leaned in, a sardonic smile spreading across his face, "I perfected them. My race can now fully form in this world, be enhanced by it."

"Not all of them are behaving the way you expected," Evan declared, "some of their personalities have overridden the monsters within."

"Nine out of ten," Bres laughed smoothly, "that's close enough to perfect for me."

Evan stared at his son, hopelessness eroding his senses, "son..."

JC spat at him. "This one has hated you for years. Ever since you sent your beloved to die."

"You mean this beloved?"

Everyone's head turned to the sound of the new voice. The sheriff, gun in hand, stood in the doorway, flanked on one side by Bru. It was what was in Bru's arms though that caused everyone to gasp, especially Evan.

Miranda Michaels, still mostly covered in that strange catatonic inducing slime, lay against Bru's chest, frail and thin, her dark her plastered around her shoulders. Evan, weary as he was, quickly stumbled to his wife as Bru lay her on the trembling ground with care.

"It's impossible," Evan sobbed, clutching her near.

"This is a surprise indeed, it is good to know such a thing is still possible" Bres mused, eyes narrowing with bemusement. "The good Sheriff, here to save the day." He scanned their weary faces, reveling in their exhaustion, their desperation.

"Let's see you laugh when I blow that smug face off," Jake retorted, determination steeling his voice.

"Sheriff Hooks," JC said with obvious disdain, "still clinging to your lead bullets and false hope." His eyes flicked to Ashlyn who nodded knowingly. "Pathetic."

Two shots rang out. The whole night became still for a moment. Then, just as quickly, a quarter sized hole opened up in both their heads, sending them flying backwards and twisting in on themselves. "Iron," Jake said without emotion, quickly turning his revolver to Bres. "Your turn."

A roar built in the distance—ominous and alive—the mist returning for its prize. Everyone felt it; the pull toward oblivion growing stronger by the second.

"We need to close it, and then we need to get out!" Laurel shouted over the chaos. She looked down at Dan, seeing his resolve matched by her own fearlessness.

Dan's voice wavered as he chanted. The sigils on the walls glowed white hot, searing through smoke and shadow. The unnatural air began to vibrate violently.

Bres snarled, taken aback by their defiance. He gestured, and another changeling erupted from the void, massive and angry, moved with terrifying speed, reaching them before Laurel could react. Rodney, the huge deputy that had gone missing, attacked Laurel as she tried to protect Dan, who himself was deep into the spell.

"Jim, get them out!" the sheriff shouted over the noise.

The injured man nodded, beaten up, but not broken. He would do what his son did, give his life to help others. He helped Evan lift Miranda and the two men bolted from the parapet down into the asylum.

Bru saw his former partner and bolted straight at him, two trains head-to-head on the same track.

"You have to hang on to the marble," Dan Roundtree shouted through the pain, he life energy starting to fade. He knew he had to finish the spell, silently praying to his ancestors for strength.

Pain exploded again in Laurel's mind—a blinding light that rivaled even the collapse of the asylum—but she did not let go of the marble. She screamed through gritted teeth, still defiant. "Not... enough!"

Jake and Lord Bres were in full fight mode.

The sheriff ducked to the side as Bres hurled a mass of shadow towards him, the darkness singing the air. He fired a shot that blew through Bres's shoulder, but the Fae Lord only laughed, a vicious grin splitting his face as the wound sealed itself. The mist surged around him like a living thing, feeding on his power.

"You cannot win," Bres taunted, "I am the dawn. I am your dreams and nightmares." Shadows erupted from every corner of the yard: monstrous hounds with impossibly long limbs and twisted faces barreled toward them with vicious speed.

Jake slumped his shoulders in disbelief, "what the actual fuck…"

Laurel saw them as well. "Oh my god…"

Dan caught sight of them from the corner of his eye. "Laignech Faelad," Dan gasped out between breaths. "Hounds of old." Then went right back to his deep Cherokee chant.

Kara's eyes went wide in disbelief as she sprinted towards Jake, "are you serious right now?!"

Evan and Jim, carrying Miranda, had barely cleared the doorway when Samantha stepped in their path, eyes gleaming with hate and jealousy. "Going somewhere, lover," she hissed at the doctor. Evan passed Miranda over to Jim, standing up to face the replica of his most loyal nurse. He walked straight to her without breaking stride. "Yeah," he said cooly, "I'm going home with my wife." Samantha barely had time to register the dagger he buried into her eye before she swirled and sputtered into oblivion.

Jim shouted to him, "come on! We have to go!"

More changelings erupted from behind Jake and Kara—menacing forms with one purpose: destroy. They moved toward Jake as he shot again and again, taking them out with precision and grit. He handed Kara his other pistol and she immediately loaded the weapon and began firing. But Jake knew it was only a matter of time.

Laurel dropped to one knee under Rodney's assault. He loomed over her, fist raised for a killing blow when Bru slammed into him, the impact shaking the ground beneath them. He wrestled Rodney away from her, shouting for Laurel to run.

She didn't. Her hands wrapped tight around the marble, she reached for Dan, who was fading fast. "I'm not going without you!" Laurel could feel Dan weakening beside her; every breath he took seemed harder than the last. She wished she could promise him salvation but knew better than to lie—especially now.

Rodney roared in anger and turned on Bru with renewed fury. The two giants tangled in a death struggle as Laurel crawled toward Dan, shadows creeping closer to them both.

The fae hounds surrounded Jake and Kara, whose guns were empty, machete in one hand, knife in the other. Jake knew this was it, the heaviness of his failure to his friends, his daughter, to Kara, almost suffocating him. "I'm sorry, Kara," I thought…

"It's okay, Jake…it's okay," she smiled at him briefly, face full of regret.

Lord Bres took in the moment, relishing in his long-term scheme. This important first phase was complete. "*Across the moor, into the night, the Sidhe take march, to take what's right…*" He met Jake's eyes, resolute, and stubborn. "Sheriff! You're only postponing—"

A roar built in the distance—ominous and alive—the mist returning for its prize. Everyone felt it; the pull toward oblivion growing stronger by the second.

"We need to close it, and then we need to get out!" Laurel shouted over the chaos. She looked down at Dan, seeing his resolve matched by her own fearlessness.

Laurel stumbled forward with renewed urgency, each breath thick with dust and desperation. She caught a glimpse of Dan's face— shining with strange grace amid ruin—and felt a surge of terrible clarity: This was his choice; this was his peace. And if he could make the sacrifice, so could she. Laurel smiled softly at him as he finished the chant and with complete calmness and clarity, she smashed the marble upon the altar, fragmenting the ancient stone.

"Go!" Dan choked out, his voice barely audible over the cacophony. "It's going to—"

The world convulsed violently. The sigils blazed with light—the spell completing itself with terrible finality. Laurel felt herself pulled away by an invisible force as the fractured marble burned hotter than ever in her hands.

Bres screamed in rage as the tear between worlds collapsed upon itself. An explosion of light and shadow obliterated everything in its path—the changeling King and his minions swallowed by their own ambition. The whole of the asylum collapsed in on itself, enveloping everyone in darkness and rain.

————

Rain fell in soft, unrelenting sheets over the blackened remains of the Hale County Asylum, each drop a mournful whisper against forgotten stone. The storm, having finally calmed into a delicate, sorrowful drizzle, seemed to echo the grief of a sky lamenting the terrible events that had unfolded.

The altar burst into a searing, blinding pulse of light that overwhelmed every sense. Energy arced skyward like celestial lightning, its dazzling tendrils caressing the heavens with raw, unpredictable power. In the midst of the chaos, Laurel's desperate shout rang out—a garbled, unintelligible cry—while the very fabric of reality seemed to rupture. An explosive collision of luminescence, thunderous sound, and unbridled supernatural force shattered the calm of the night.

Jakes watched in dismay as the world splintered before his eyes— his friends' bodies flung apart like ragdolls by the violent blast. Clawing at the air, he strained to hold Kara within his grip, his arms tightening in a desperate, vice-like embrace. Yet with a wrenching inevitability, he felt her being wrenched away, as though the force of the explosion were systematically erasing all connections.

As the asylum itself groaned and shuddered from its very foundations, deep cracks snaked their way along the walls, resembling intricate spiderwebs etched by fate. The once-solid marble beneath the altar was reduced to a cascade of shattered fragments, and the anguished shrieks of redcaps filled the air as they were ferociously sucked into the collapsing void. The roaring of flames ignited a chaotic symphony in the tunnels as dust and stones tumbled down like a macabre rain.

In that moment, Jake's voice was stifled, stuck in his throat— rendered mute, with no power left to scream, curse, or plead. Everything around him descended into oblivion. The world as he knew it crumbled away. A dreadful, final silence swallowed all sound.

Then—a sharp gasp punctured the nothingness.

Jake jolted upright; his body drenched with cold sweat as his lungs heaved for air. His trembling fingers scraped against the cold, unyielding tile beneath him. In a disorienting shift, he realized he was no longer within the asylum's confining walls. The altar had vanished. Pappy, Dean, Bres, Laurel, the changelings, even the monstrous shapes—they had all disappeared. In their place was an overwhelming silence interrupted only by the persistent drip of water in the dark.

The chamber was small and windowless, the oppressive darkness breaking only where a solitary bulb hung overhead, its feeble light buzzing with an eerie regularity. In one shadowed corner, unmistakable even as a dim silhouette, stood Dr. Daniel Lane. Alive, undeniable—his presence as striking as ever.

Jake's voice cracked, choked with disbelief: "You're dead…" The words trailed off as Lane stepped forward into the faint light, his figure calm and oddly composed in a blood-spattered lab coat. His eyes, glassy and oversized with an unsettling joy, shone with an intensity that bordered on madness.

"I was never dead, Sheriff," Lane replied, his tone light but laced with a disturbing undercurrent. "Not in the real world, anyway."

Jake staggered backward, his heart hammering in his chest as confusion and dread warred within him. "What… what the hell is going on?"

A low chuckle escaped Dr. Lane as he drifted past Jake, his fingers delicately brushing dust from an old console that flickered intermittently with ghostly lights. "You've all been so very busy, haven't you? Battling phantoms, creatures lurking in the shadows, chasing elusive apparitions through forgotten forests, even delving into ancient, forbidden rituals. It's all very theatrical—quite amusing even."

He paused, his words hanging heavy in the stale air. "None of it was real," he declared softly, as though revealing a well-kept secret.

Jake's mouth felt parched, his confusion deepening. "What?"

With a slow, deliberate turn, Lane continued, nearly whispering as each word sent tremors through the atmosphere: "The asylum crumbled. The town erupted in riots. You saw your so-called monsters. You witnessed the demise of souls. You waged war alongside your comrades, fought with a valor you believed was true. You even managed to reclaim what belonged to Evan." His tone softened, almost conspiratorial.

The sheriff collapsed to one knee, nausea roiling in his gut. "No… we fought… Dean… Laurel…I found Miranda…"

Jake flinched at the recollection. "You rescued her from that cemetery… you shot the evil deputies, loaded her into your truck and raced against time for Evan…" Lane's voice dropped to a conspiratorial murmur. "But the woman you clutched in that cemetery, whom you carried with a hope so bright, was not Miranda. Well, not the living Miranda."

Raising a dumpy pale hand, Lane allowed the flickering light to reveal a slumped figure seated in a battered chair behind Jake. It was her—the very Miranda he thought he had saved. Yet now, she was transformed into nothing more than a withered, mummified corpse. Decay and death had gripped her form; tattered clothing hung loosely around her emaciated frame. Her teeth, set in a macabre grin, were frozen in a perpetual rictus, her matted hair pooling in clumps, her lips a ghost of what they once were.

Unable to bear the horrifying sight, Jake sank to his knees, nausea and despair overwhelming him. "No… no, that's not possible…" he gasped, his voice a fragile whisper lost in the void.

"Oh, it's very possible," Lane replied, his voice now quivering with a hint of manic glee. "You've been inhaling my work for months— the gas, those 'shadow creatures' if you will. It pervades every crevice: riding on the wind, seeping into the groundwater, expelled from the ancient steam vents buried under the county. Reality and delusion mixed to perfection." He inched closer, crouching beside Jake with the menacing calm of a coiled serpent.

"You were never truly in the real world. None of you were," he hissed. "You've been mentally confined in my world—all along. More to the point, the world I have created. My grief, painted across your minds like a twisted masterpiece. But your bodies, well, you have some 'splaining to do…"

Jake's head pounded as memories began to blur into one another: Dan's selfless sacrifice, the hospital, Jason, Laurel…Kara, the eerie presence of the changelings, Pappy's final, defiant stand. Was any of it real? His thoughts swirled with doubt and disarray.

"Oh yes, fragments of it were real," Lane continued as though unveiling an exquisite work of art. "That's the elegance of it—my craftsmanship. Madness claimed my family, took my children, my wife, stole Miranda, my naughty little crush. Evan was so steadfast in his pursuit of a cure, so focused that he couldn't perceive the missing puzzle piece. My research into psychotropic healing was the true answer—a radical fusion of methods that only needed a simple delivery system. That machine was sheer perfection."

"But you…" Jake sputtered, his voice mingling disbelief with horror.

"Ah, good old friendly Doctor Lane," he sneered, every syllable dripping with twisted amusement. "I wear many hats here—the town doctor, psychologist, pharmacist. Everyone in this cursed town has sought me out at one time or another. The right dose, the right word—this fragile human mind is the most delicate yet deadly resource there is, requiring only a gentle push for people to unravel. The more you interacted with one another the more seeds were planted until you were all woven into this glorious tapestry. It was far more Shakespearean than I could have dreamed. I was the storm, Jake. And now, Hale County burns, not in the fiery heat of protest or plague, but deep inside the minds of those who breathe its tainted air." His laugh, distorted and eerie, echoed in the confined space. "It's truly marvelous," he finished, a statement so normal in his tone that it sent shivers down Jake's spine.

As the unsettling symphony of moaning and anguished screaming began to ripple off the stone walls, Lane mused, almost absentmindedly, "Hmm… the others are awakening—the survivors, at least. That means our little experiment is nearing its conclusion. You were a good man, Sheriff. But this experiment of mine will change the world in ways even Freud could scarcely imagine. The world is cruel—it demanded transformation. And I am that change."

The chamber itself shuddered, the ancient pipes hissing like specters in the dark, as Jake's eyes locked once more onto Miranda's corpse. Her skull leaned forward, as though mocking him with a macabre bow. "I would love to give you all my villainous reasons but we are out of time."

"Don't be sad, my friend. You vanquished the monster in the end. I'll have to rebuild the machine," he said without menace. "The human mind is truly an incredible thing," Daniel marveled aloud.

Standing with a calm finality, Lane extended his arms toward Jake, his silhouette framed by the flickering light. "Do you understand now? It was never about monsters or deities. It was all about me."

And as the room began to fade into an overwhelming, all-consuming darkness, Jake's last tether to sanity was the sound of Lane's laughter—a sinister, relentless sound that echoed into the void.

The world lay wrapped in an oppressive darkness—not the gentle shade of night or sleep, but a cold, suffocating void that smothered every hope. Jake Hooks lay still amid shattered splinters of stone and twisted rebar, half-buried in debris. The bitter taste of dust filled his mouth while coppery blood clung to his tongue, a stark reminder of his pain. Each breath came in short, ragged gulps; his lungs fluttered weakly, like torn sails buffeted by a dying, turbulent wind.

Somewhere beyond the suffocating black, amidst the silence that blanketed the ruined world, he heard it—a fragile sound cutting through the void. A whisper. A child's voice.

"Daddy…"

Jake blinked against the onslaught of darkness as that tender sound rekindled a spark of familiarity.

"Daddy… help…"

The voice was high and delicate, carrying the soft lilt of a half-remembered lullaby from another life. It mingled with a bittersweet melody of longing, echoing in the hollows of his battered mind. Desperation clawed at him as he tried to move, but searing pain surged through his body in relentless, punishing waves. Above him, the rubble groaned mournfully, while specks of dust drifted down like forlorn flakes of snowfall.

"Daddy, please…"

He recognized that pleading tone—all too intimately familiar, stirring deep-rooted memories and aching love. Overwhelmed by raw instinct and old, unhealed grief, Jake rallied what strength he had left and shoved against the debris. A heavy beam shifted ominously above his chest. With a desperate roll, he stifled the scream clawing its way up from deep within him.

"Daddy!"

Then, as if by divine intervention, a shaft of pale morning light burst through the gloom. It sliced through the darkness like a celestial hand reaching into a tomb, illuminating the desolation around him. Amid swirling dust and ruin, he spotted a solitary silhouette, frantically digging through the wreckage with trembling urgency. Hands scraped desperately at the cold stone, and soon another figure emerged, pulling aside the debris while calling his name in a voice laced with desperation:

"Jake!"

Kara's voice trembled with panic and fierce love. Her dirt-smeared face, etched with determination, shone with hope against the backdrop of devastation. Behind her, a pair of small, determined hands clawed at the wreckage— a young girl's small hands, chiseled with courage despite her evident fear.

"Daddy!" Haley cried once more. Though her tiny face was streaked with tears and grime, it broke into a radiant smile of relief as she proclaimed, "I found him, Mama, I found Daddy!"

Jake's sight blurred with a mixture of pain and disbelief. "Haley...?"

In a heartbeat, the fragile bundle of life was lifted into his arms, his daughter's small form a lifeline anchoring his fractured soul back to the realm of hope. Kara, ever determined, worked to clear the final barrier of debris, her urgency woven into every movement as she called his name. Jake looked at the woman who drove him mad, "she knows?"

Kara wrapped him in a massive hug, tears streaming down her face. "Of course she knows, you idiot," she half laughed, half sobbed.

Haley looked up at him, eyes shining, a warm smile filling her whole face. "Mommy said we had to keep it a secret to protect you," she said conspiratorially.

Jake laughed and kissed her chubby little cheeks. "But how did you...who found you..."

She pointed a little finger towards Pappy, "the funny fat man."

Nearby, Pappy sat with bruises and streaks of ash marring his face, a weary grin playing on his lips as he dabbed a cut on his forehead with a frayed rag. He offered Jake a salute steeped in both exhaustion and defiant pride.

For a long, lingering moment, time itself seemed to pause. They clung to one another in silent communion amid the ruins. No words disturbed their embrace; only the others' heavy, uncertain breathing merged with the distant, melancholic whisper of the wind through shattered stone.

When Jake finally raised his gaze, the sky above had shifted its bruise-like gray into a tender cascade of golden hues. Morning had finally stretched its arms over the devastation.

They were not alone.

Across the broken landscape, survivors gathered in the weak, smoking daylight. Dan Roundtree, supported by a twisted, makeshift walking stick, stood resilient despite his torn coat and the swollen darkness over one eye—alive and determined. His resonant chant had, somehow, sealed the breach, sparing him in its wake.

Marcus leaned heavily on a haphazard crutch, blood staining the side of his worn shirt. His injured arm was cradled in a sling as his distant, glassy gaze betrayed the toll of the struggle he had endured. Yet, in a silent exchange, he nodded—an unspoken affirmation of survival—when Jake met his eyes.

And then there was Bru—oh, Bru. The towering deputy lay slumped against a crumpled wall, his broad body marked by deep lacerations and his left leg twisted grotesquely. Yet, with each ragged breath, he defied the oblivion. His eyes flickered open when Jake approached, and with a rasp that was equal parts pain and resolve, he murmured, "Bout time you woke up, Sheriff."

Jake's rough hand squeezed Bru's in a moment of shared triumph. "You did good, Bru. You did damn good."

But not every soul had weathered the storm.

Covered in a tattered sheet torn from a fallen banner, Evan Michaels lay next to Miranda's cold, lifeless form. Even in death, his arm remained protectively wrapped around her. The crushing weight of his guilt had trailed him to the bitter end, and perhaps, in those final moments, he had found a measure of peace. JC, the last remaining Michaels, huddled next to their bodies, in tears as Ashlyn tried to comfort him.

Char lay near broken, twisted metal from the collapsed stairwell, her weapon still clutched in hand, her face a frozen mask of defiant resignation, streaked in blood. Jake knelt beside her, carefully brushing the dust from her brow as if trying to restore a small fragment of dignity amid the devastation.

"She saved my life, Jake," Marcus said through tears, "threw her body over mine without even hesitating."

Jim Holt was little more than a ghost of his former self, half-buried under a fallen iron beam. He had died as he had lived—fighting, his principles as unyielding as the sword he had wielded until the very end, like his son before him. Jake would be sure he was honored just as nobly.

And Judge Hawthorne... At first, Jake scarcely recognized him. His melted crucifix, fused to his vest, told the tale of an ordeal beyond measure, but it was the nearby gavel—bent yet unbroken—that revealed his identity.

With a heavy heart, Jake bowed his head. "Rest easy, boys."

There was no sign of Dean. No body marked by a trail of blood or a final, anguished scream. Only the lingering aroma of scorched iron and the whisper of shadow remained, a testament to the gaping void where the rift had once yawned wide before collapsing into a convoluted tapestry of stone and burnt earth.

Gone. Just… gone.

It would take weeks, even months, to fully recover all the bodies and identify the remains; months before the families of the mayor, Chief Malone, and the rest of the inmates, employees, deputies, and policemen could finally be laid to rest and have some closure. There would be questions, inquiries, depositions. The once quiet and forgotten county would make headlines around the world.

Jake watched as the wind stirred a melancholy dance of ashes over the cracked, desolate floor. An absence loomed in his heart— an emptiness deeper than any wound inflicted upon his body.

Kara enfolded him in an embrace, one arm wrapping securely around his waist, while her other gently held Haley close. Together, they watched the sun climb higher over Hale County, bathing the remnants of their shattered world in golden light. The monsters had been vanquished, the asylum reduced to ruins, and forces both real and elusive—figments of the mind and true evil— had been dragged back into the consuming dark.

Yet the scars of this surreal battle would remain, etched into the very soul of the county for generations.

Somewhere, hidden beneath the surface or lingering beyond the veil of what is known, something still waited. The echo of its presence was a somber reminder of mysteries yet unresolved. Or perhaps that was all in Sheriff Jake Hooks' mind, an unaccounted for remnant of Dr Lane's insane experiment.

But for now, the war was over, and in that fragile light of dawn, they were together, alive and bonded by the unbreakable ties of love and survival.

EPILOGUE

Six months later.

Washington, D.C. An unmarked building buried three floors underground. The camera flickered to life with a scarlet blink.

"Begin recording," commanded a voice from behind reinforced glass.

Inside, the room was a cold, sterile void—steel walls encasing a bolted table, no windows to offer escape. Only a single fluorescent strip overhead cast a sickly glow and hummed in the silence. Dr. Daniel Lane sat unruffled; his hands neatly folded before him. Shackled wrists did nothing to disturb his composed demeanor. Gone was his worn lab coat, replaced now by a pristine white jumpsuit that perfectly suited his transformation.

Opposite him sat a woman in a sharply pressed gray suit, youthful yet unnervingly composed. Her badge read: Dr. Evelyn Glass – DARPA Behavioral Sciences Division.

"Dr. Lane," she intoned evenly, her voice a flat current of curious formality, "you know why you're here."

A faint, enigmatic smile spread across Lane's face. "Of course. I've been expecting your people for some time."

Dr. Glass's eyebrow arched with measured skepticism. "Then you understand this facility isn't on any books. No trials, no sentencing. You're here because we believe what you created in Hale County holds... merit."

Lane's eyes sparked with a disturbing enthusiasm. "Merit? My dear, what I delivered was nothing short of genius. The town, the gas, the behavioral triggers—pure neural cartography. I shaped trauma itself. I turned grief into a weapon. And you're only now beginning to see the larger picture."

Unmoved, Glass slid a tablet across the table. On its screen, blurred video fragments played: Jake Hooks dragging himself through rubble; Miranda's lifeless form; Bru writhing in agony; Evan's scream echoing in the void.

"You turned an entire town into a living hallucination—a meticulously orchestrated massacre," she stated, her tone a mix of awe and disquiet. "You convinced a senile old man he was some Lord of ancient Irish mythology, another believed he was a creature itself. It was sociopathic and maniacal. And yet... it was brilliant."

Lane's smile widened, a chilling display of dark satisfaction. "But won't there be investigations. The whole world..."

"...will believe exactly what we tell them to believe," Dr. Glass finished for him.

Leaning in, her voice lowered to a conspiratorial murmur, she proposed, "We want to recreate the experiment—legally. In controlled environments with volunteers, veterans, war criminals. We have drafted a proposal for long-term neural conditioning and perceptual modification based on your formulas."

Lane tilted his head, intrigued. "So... you want me to rebuild the system."

"Not merely rebuild," she corrected, her tone steely, "but refine it. Imagine reprogrammed memories, confessions extracted without a touch, resistance broken without violence. Picture sending men into warzones convinced they are gods—or monsters. Transform civilians into soldiers... or convert enemies into haunting apparitions."

In a near-whisper, Lane added, "And all it costs is a little truth."

A heavy silence fell before Glass delivered the ultimate condition. "There's one catch."

Lane's eyes narrowed for a heartbeat. "And what might that be?"

"You will never leave this facility again. You will live confined, monitored in a perpetual box—stripped of your name, your family, your legacy. Only your work will remain, eternally."

A slow, predatory smile curled on Lane's lips as he replied, "That's all I've ever wanted."

Elsewhere, two floors above, military officials peered through tinted observation glass. A general, hands unsteady as he lit a cigar, muttered, "He's not just a madman; he's a fucking oracle."

One by one, the observers nodded silently. "Hale County was merely a pilot program. Let's see what he can do with real funding."

Below, in the concrete cell, Lane tapped his fingers in time with the flickering, oppressive light.

In the deep recesses of the facility, behind sealed vault doors, a machine stirred—something metallic awakening from its dormancy. Not magic. Not myth. But the cold precision of mind control.

Later that night, a lone security guard watched the monitor from Sub-Level 3. Dr. Lane's cell cast a dim glow on the screen—quiet, motionless.

Then, without warning, the feed flickered briefly. When it resumed, Lane was slumped forward in his chair.

The guard leaned in, frowning, and tapped the intercom. "Dr. Lane? You alright in there?"

There was no response.

Switching his view, the guard detected only stillness—Lane's body inert and his hands perfectly folded.

Then, in a moment barely perceptible, a shift of shadow stirred just behind Lane. So slight it might have been imagined.

The guard squinted at the playback, rewinding frame by frame. On the screen, Lane exhaled a final, measured breath. His lips moved—not in terror or desperation—but in quiet confusion, his eyes widening as they fixed on something unseen, something beyond the camera's grasp.

And then he simply stopped. No alarms blared, no violence erupted, only a final twitch of his hand, a solitary blink—and suddenly, complete stillness.

Rubbing his eyes, the guard rewound and replayed the footage. The mysterious shadow had vanished, leaving only Lane's unmoving form. The cell was locked; no one had intruded. And yet, something had departed.

In the control room above, Dr. Glass scrutinized the footage frame by frame. In one fleeting instant, a dark blur had flashed in the upper corner, a movement too swift, too unnatural.

She said nothing, but she closed the file and locked it under clearance code SABLE-IV. Then, she picked up her phone with deliberate precision.

"I need Sub-Level 3 quarantined."

A suspended pause, then she continued, "No autopsy. Just burn it all. No remains"

In the cold, oppressive darkness of Sub-Level 3, where once genius had grinned behind glass and steel, the air turned unnervingly still. Yet it was far from empty.

Something had walked out of that room.

And it wasn't natural.

Jake stood on the front porch of Kara's house, the wooden planks creaking gently beneath his feet. Beside him, Kaia sat like a vigilant sentinel, her eyes fixed on the shadows as if sensing an unseen presence lurking in the night. Above them, the stars glittered brilliantly in the vast expanse, the first clear, breathtaking night Hale County had experienced in weeks. The serene atmosphere was interrupted by the sharp hiss of a bottle cap being twisted off, drawing Jake's attention.

Kara emerged onto the porch, the cool night air wrapping around her. She carried a chilled bottle of beer and set down a box of steaming pizza on the banister, the aroma mingling with the crisp night breeze.

"Thank you," Jake murmured, his voice barely above a whisper, as he took a long, satisfying sip of the beer and bit into a slice of pizza. The flavors spread through his mouth, and his stomach welcomed the nourishment with gratitude.

"You're welcome," Kara replied with a gentle smile, her eyes lingering on the man standing before her, taking in every detail of his presence.

"How is Haley?" Jake asked, the words heavy with concern, as he avoided meeting Kara's gaze directly.

"She's a trooper," Kara said, her voice steady but warm. "Worn out, but tough, like her daddy."

Jake turned to her then, his eyes locking onto hers, a tumult of emotions swirling within him. "Kara, I'm…"

She placed a hand softly on his, the warmth of her touch mirroring the regret reflected in her eyes. "No, Jake, I'm sorry. I should never have kept you two apart. I was blinded by the hurt and pain, and I never truly gave you a chance. I was wrong. We've been given a second chance, and I don't want things to revert to how they were. You are her father. She needs you. We both do."

The space between them closed, an invisible warmth enveloping them both.

"You were right…" Jake started.

"Yeah?" she questioned with a curious smile.

"It is cold…" he said with a playful wink, lifting the pizza in mock emphasis.

"You asshole…" she laughed, her laughter ringing through the night as she chased him back inside, both of them laughing like carefree teenagers, finding a moment of joy in a world that had tried to shatter them.

Outside, Kaia's ears pricked up, her alert eyes peering into the dense, darkened forest, her teeth baring in a silent warning to whatever lay hidden beyond the trees.

About the Author

I had dreamed of being a writer ever since I was a little boy growing up in Northeast Texas. My imagination has always been wild and carefree. My first typewriter was a little plastic blue toy typewriter when I was 10 years old. I wore that thing out writing stories and screenplays, even though I didn't know the first thing how to do so. When I was in high school, I told myself and my friends that I would write a novel one day, and then life happened. All these years later most of those friends are gone, even a friend or two who inspired characters within these pages. It took me 14 years to write this book, the only thing in my life I never truly compromised. So, to that young me sitting on the hardwood floor those many decades ago, typing away, letting that imagination soar, I just want to say, "we did it."

There are many more stories to tell.